Praise for Archer Mayor's Joe Gunther Series!

"I have a soft spot for quiet writers like Archer Mayor, ... suming voice and down to earth style stamp his regional crime novels with a sense of integrity. The strength of these narratives has always come from the author's profound understanding of his region and from his hero's intuitive ability to relate to the people who live there."

— *Marilyn Stasio,*
The New York Times

"Superb"

—*Publisher's Weekly*
(starred review)

"It is our good fortune that Mr. Mayor's skills are equal to the vigor of his imagination."

—*The New Yorker*

"Mayor's elegiac tone and his insights into the human condition make [each book] a fine addition to one of the most consistently satisfying mystery series going."

—*Thomas Gaughan,*
Booklist

"Archer Mayor is producing what is consistently the best police procedural series being written in America."

—*The Chicago Tribune*

"As a stylist, Mayor is one of those meticulous construction workers who are fascinated by the way things function. He's the boss man on procedures."

—*The New York Times*

"Mayor is not given to gimmicks and manipulation. There are flashier writers, but few deliver such well-rounded novels of such consistent high quality."

—*Arizona Daily Star*

"A fine thriller"

—*Wall Street Journal*

"First rate . . . Mayor has a way with white-knuckle final scenes, and he does it again in this atmospheric story."
—*Los Angeles Times*

"A powerful series, and this is only book two."
—*Kirkus Reviews*

"Lots of cat-and-mouse suspense . . . enough twists and turns to keep the reader on the chair's edge."
—*Publisher's Weekly*

"All the Joe Gunther books are terrific . . . As they say in New England, wicked good writing."
—*Washington Post Book World*

"Lead a cheer for Archer Mayor and his ability not only to understand human relationships, but to convey them to his readers."
—*Washington Sunday Times*

"Excellent . . . a dazzling tale that combines detection, compassion, small-town sociology, local politics, and personal priorities . . . How much better can Mayor get? This combination of detection and non-stop action is his best yet."
—*Toronto Saturday Star*

Open Season

Open Season

Archer Mayor

AMPress
Newfane, Vermont

PO Box 456
Newfane, Vermont 05435
www.archermayor.com

pyright © 2007 Archer Mayor
rights reserved. This book, or parts thereof, may not be
roduced in any form without permission.

rary of Congress Cataloging-in-Publication Data

Mayor, Archer.

Open Season / Archer Mayor.

p.   cm.

I. Title

PS3563.a96506 1988   88-803 CIP

813´.54—dc19

ISBN 978-0-9798122-0-0

ISBN 978-0-9798122-0-0

To Annie and Brantz
for their relentless optimism.

1

"So what did she use?"

"A shotgun."

The snow lay before our headlights like a freshly placed sheet, draped from curb to curb without a wrinkle and pinned in place by white-capped parking meters. The snowstorm had passed quickly, leaving a star-packed sky and a freezing clarity that made me feel we were driving into a black-and-white photograph.

We were on Main Street, inching our way downhill to where Main becomes Canal before climbing the opposite slope.

"Slippery?"

The patrolman driving the car gave an embarrassed smile. "Well, I think so. You wouldn't. I haven't really gotten used to this stuff yet.

This was his first New England winter—he'd only been here for six months or so. Marshall Smith had been a deputy sheriff in Florida before coming here and he was getting a lot of ribbing for his fumbling in the snow. During the first light dusting of the season, he'd rear-ended a truck and had half a cord of wood dumped on his cruiser. That obviously wasn't going to happen again—not if he kept driving at fifteen miles an hour.

"Floor it a little at the foot of the hill—it'll give you more traction." Flooring it brought us up to twenty. It didn't matter. The car had snow tires and we were in no rush. From what I'd heard, everyone was dead who was going to die, at least for tonight.

You don't get many killings in a town the size of Brattleboro. In ten years, we'd had four, and for some reason they'd all been clumped together. The last of them had been about three years ago.

I placed both hands against the roof behind my head and arched my back in a stretch. The car's heater was making me drowsy. I rolled the window down a crack and watched the run-down buildings slide by. In the reflection off the glass, I noticed Smith turn his head to glance at me. Lit only by the car's green panel lights, his face had a ghostly, dreamlike translucence, as if he, like the pajamas I wore under my clothes, had been part of my sleep only ten minutes earlier.

"Did you have a nice Christmas, Lieutenant?"

"Not bad."

"Me too. I went back home. Expensive, but the wife and I thought it would feel strange having Christmas here."

I couldn't think of anything stranger than Christmas in Florida.

We drove beyond the hospital and turned left onto Clark Avenue. Ahead, halfway down the block, two cruisers and an ambulance blocked the road, their sparkling colored lights imitating some cock-eyed Christmas scene. I noticed discreet lights on in several neighboring houses. It was 3:48 A.M.

I slid out of the car's warm cocoon and stood in the snow for a moment, watching Smith return to Canal Street. His rear lights glowed fiercely just before he got to the corner and cautiously swung right. The day, despite the darkness, had begun.

I looked over to the house. By New England standards, it was not old—maybe built in the forties—but it looked ancient. Its skin was peeling and blotched with rot. The roof line, mercifully covered with snow, sagged in the middle like a swayback horse. Where boards had once met squarely with precision, time and neglect had instilled a blurry vagueness. I doubted the entire building contained a single intended ninety-degree angle.

A shadow detached itself from a tree near the street. "Hi, Joe."

"Stan, Stan, the newspaper man. Hot on the trail?"

"I heard about it on the band. What happened?"

"You tell me. I just woke up."

"Can I tag along?"

"Nope." I walked across the sidewalk and up the uneven porch steps, nodding to the patrolman guarding the door. Once inside, I was standing in a hallway running the length of the house. At the far end were the shattered remains of the back door, its top half looking like an artillery target. In the middle of the floor halfway down the hall, lay a toppled hardback chair. Next to it was a shotgun.

A bull-shaped patrol sergeant stepped out from one of the side doors. "Hi, Joe. Sorry to get you out of bed."

"That's okay. What happened?"

"Old lady got a bunch of obscene phone calls over the last few days. The guy finally said he'd visit tonight and do to her what he did to

2

the cat. She waited for him in that chair and blew him away when he opened the back door."

"What he did to the cat?"

The sergeant, George Capullo, approached the fallen chair and motioned at a doorway. I stepped over the chair and looked around the corner. It was a bedroom, cluttered but neat, lit from a single bare bulb on the wall.

"On the bed," said George. He stayed where he was.

I approached the bed, a ramshackle iron spider's web held together with crisscrossed wires. Covering it was an old quilt, not especially pretty but carefully made, and under the quilt was a small lump. I flipped back the corner.

The cat lay on its back, spread-eagled, its dry eyes wide in arrested agony. It had been slit open from neck to crotch and its innards pulled out for display: lumpish, red, and still slightly wet. I swallowed hard and dropped the quilt back.

"Christ, George. You could have told me."

"Gross, huh?"

"More like weird. Did somebody call the State's Attorney?"

"Do unto him like I did unto you?"

"Spare me. And spare him too. He doesn't have my sense of humor. Is J.P. here?"

"Yeah, and I already called the SA. He should have been here by now. J.P.'s out back taking pictures."

I returned to the hallway. "Did you respond first?"

"About two-thirty. She called it in herself. The neighbors claim they didn't hear a thing. That's bullshit, of course. She let loose with both barrels at once. Must have made the whole block jump."

"Who's the body?"

"Don't know. We haven't searched him yet." George hesitated. "To be honest, I didn't get too close. He makes the cat look good."

I glanced at the shattered door. "Where's the woman?"

He jerked his head down the hall. "In the kitchen. A Rescue guy's with her."

"She all right?"

"Yeah. A little shaky."

"Okay. I'll see her last."

George nodded and led the way to the back. He pulled open the splintered remains of the door and ushered me through.

J.P. Tyler, the department's only detective with any forensic training,

3

was standing in the yard with his back to us. He was taking a photograph. "Look at the shoe," he said without turning around.

On the top step, lying on its side, was a loafer. I leaned down and picked it up. It was expensive—glove leather, designer label, more of a moccasin really. Real terrorist apparel.

About six feet from the foot of the steps, surrounded by a dazzling white circle of flood lamps, lay the body. Like the cat, it was flat on its back, arms and legs outstretched. For a second I thought of when I used to lie like that in the snow, as a kid, making snow angels. But here the gentle arc formed by the arms was uninterrupted by a head. A tall man in a pea jacket rose from his crouch by the body—Alfred Gould, the regional medical examiner.

Gould walked over to us. "Morning, Joe."

I nodded to him. "Hi, Al. Anything to add to the obvious?"

Gould half smiled and shook his head. "I would like to talk to the old lady, if that's all right."

"Sure, be my guest." I stepped out of the way and let him pass. The snow all around the body had been trampled by a small army. "Were there any prints before all this happened?"

"Nope, just his. I got shots of it all." J.P. put his camera down, a pleased look on his face—a man in love with his work. "I'm wrapping up out here. I still have to check out the gun. Hit the lights when you're through, okay?"

I nodded and he squeezed between us, heading inside.

"The head's over here." George pointed to a dark hole in the snow not three feet from where I was standing. I instinctively looked down and saw a half-shadowed face staring at me, its eyes enormously wide. My stomach turned over.

"You're getting a kick out of this, aren't you?" George smiled and shrugged. "You're a tough guy."

I took the flashlight he had hanging from his belt and shone it on the head. The shock over, it looked like a plastic fake.

"Al said the blast 'atomized' the guy's neck—his word, not mine. He said it was kind of like pulling a tablecloth out from under a bunch of plates—it just sort of fell off when the body went sailing into the wild blue yonder."

I handed the flashlight back and went down the steps to check out the body.

There wasn't much blood visible. The ragged chunk between the man's shoulders lay at the edge of a small black hole of melted snow.

The whole thing had an almost tidy air about it. I realized then I was probably standing over an aquifer of blood spread out between the snow and the earth below. I dropped a nearby blanket over the stump and hole. Then I crouched by the body's side and began to search.

Whoever this had been, he was no pauper. The blood-spattered scarf was cashmere, the long coat camel hair, the pants fine wool. Layer by layer, his clothes never dropped below $50 per item, including the tailored pale blue shirt with the monogram "J.P." Inside his jacket, I found a leather wallet with, among the usual documents, ten new $100 notes.

A shadow fell across the body and I looked up to see State's Attorney James—never Jim—Dunn. Vermont state's attorneys, elsewhere called district attorneys, have to be at the scene of any "unattended death." James Dunn had two assistants with whom he rotated being on call, but he hardly missed showing up personally at the dramatic ones, regardless of time or weather. He wasn't married, which must have helped, and he was good at his job, so we didn't complain. He never said much, certainly never touched anything, and generally stayed out of the way. In a few instances, he had even been a help, pointing out the occasional legal pothole. Still, I didn't like him. He was a cold and snotty man.

I nodded to him, he returned the silent greeting, and I read aloud from the dead man's driver's license. "James Phillips—Orchard Heights. Ring any bells with anybody?"

"From the address, I'd say we didn't travel in the same circles," George answered from the steps.

Another pocket yielded a long, thin metal chain. "Interesting tool for a break-in."

George's curiosity wore him down. He walked over and crouched next to me. "What is it?"

"A dog leash. Here's something else." It was a miniature leather photo album, about the size of a checkbook. Inside were ten pictures— seven of a prissy toy poodle standing alone; two of the poodle and a smiling man, who was on all fours next to the dog; and one of the man, the poodle, and a woman standing in front of a house. In the last shot, the woman was holding the dog. She looked like she'd rather have been elsewhere.

George tilted his hat back on his head. "Weird. You ever have a picture book of your pet?"

I pushed myself up off my knees and grunted to a standing position.

Dunn was still standing there, silently watching. I continued to ignore him, as he once had asked me to. "I wonder what our Mr. Phillips was up to? What's the old lady's name?"

"Thelma Reitz."

She was sitting in the kitchen, thin, frail, and beaten, her white head bowed and shimmering under the harsh fluorescent glare. The attendant from Rescue, Inc. was making notes at the table. I took a chair like the one lying in the hallway and sat facing her, elbows on knees, my legs slightly apart. Out of the corner of my eye, I noticed Dunn enter the room and lean against the wall.

She stared at her lap, where her hands were slowly destroying a damp and wadded Kleenex. I noticed the thin gold band on her left ring finger had almost vanished into the flesh around it, as over the years something nailed to a tree becomes absorbed by the bark.

"Mrs. Reitz?" I let the fingertips of my hand brush hers. She looked up. Her face was so pale it blended imperceptibly with her hair.

"My name is Gunther. I'm another policeman. I know you've explained what happened, and I know you must be tired, but I was wondering if you could go over it again—just for me." I paused a moment "Do you have somewhere you can stay, by the way? A son or daughter, maybe?"

She shook her head. "My daughter doesn't like me." Her voice was high and thin—a piano string stretched as tight as it could go.

I called George in from the hallway. "Call Susan Henderson at the Retreat and ask her if Mrs. Reitz can spend a few days there until she gets her feet back on the ground." I glanced at the Rescue guy. "Okay with you?"

He shrugged.

George nodded and left. Thelma Reitz watched him leave and gave me a wan smile. "Thank you."

"No problem. I'm sorry about your daughter." She shook her head. "I lost her a long time ago. I don't know why. I called her when all this started—I was so frightened—but she told me phone calls like that happen all the time. She said I should be flattered."

"What were the calls like?"

That brought some color to her face. "I couldn't repeat them. They were dirty. Very dirty." She opened her mouth to say more but changed her mind. She was obviously deciding something and finally rose pain-fully to her feet and crossed the room. She handed me some index cards from a drawer. "He left these too. On my pillow, in

6

my bathroom, in here—he came into my house any time he wanted. I found them every time I got home."

The notes were short, brutal, and graphic ditties; a rhyming hodge-podge of sexual threats offensive enough to embarrass an Elks meeting. I wrapped them in my handkerchief and put them in my pocket. "Why didn't you call us?"

I held her elbow as she sat back down. She smiled again and sighed. "I did."

It was my turn to be embarrassed. "Did you tell them the notes were found in the house?"

"They weren't. They were phone calls." She closed her eyes and put her hand to her forehead. "I'm not making sense."

I took her hand in mine. "My fault. You mean the notes didn't start until after you called us?"

She nodded.

"And when you told us about the calls, you were told there was nothing much we could do about them."

"Yes."

"I'm sorry about that." I let a few seconds go by. "So then he attacked your cat?"

Her eyes filled with tears. "Yes. Poor Albert…What had he done? What had I done? Poor kitty. He was all I had."

"When did you find him?"

"Tonight. I'd stayed out all day. I knew the notes would be there… I couldn't stay inside—I was so scared. I went to the library, I went to the movies, to the store. I tried to stay out as long as I could, but it was cold, and places kept closing and then it snowed. I had to come home. I had nowhere else to go. That's when I found Albert. And that's when he called—right at the same time—as if he were standing there seeing everything I did. He said I wasn't home when he'd visited, and that's why Albert died. And then he said he'd come back later—tonight—to do the same thing to me. And when I didn't say anything, he said, 'What's wrong, Thelma—the cat got your tongue?'"

She stared hard at me suddenly, the tears finally pouring down her face in earnest. The piano wire was broken, and her voice was ragged and full of pain. "It made me mad—so mad. I told him, 'You come. I'll be here,' and I got my husband's shotgun out of its box and I waited—a long, long time. And then I killed him—that…bastard."

Her hand flew to her mouth and she folded in on herself, sobbing. The ambulance attendant glared at me. A little self-consciously, I

7

reached over and patted her back. After she'd calmed down a bit, I placed one of the pictures we'd found of Phillips and his dog in her lap. "Do you recognize this man?"

She didn't touch the photographs. She became utterly motionless. My hand on her back could feel the distant thump of her heartbeat—her only sign of life.

Still without moving, she asked. "Is this the man outside?"

"We think so."

"Mr. Phillips."

I sat opposite her again. She wouldn't look at me. "You knew him?"

"Yes."

"From where?"

"Jury duty. We served together. He used to pass that very picture around. He loved that dog like I loved Albert...I don't understand... He was nice. He was the last one to vote guilty. He said he couldn't condemn another man, no matter how horrible what he did."

"It's not your fault; you know that, don't you?" She thought a while before answering. "No."

She wasn't the only one.

2

Orchard Heights is an exclusive developer's dream come true. Once a farmer's rolling field off Orchard Street west of downtown, it sits high enough to both "afford" a view and to overlook but not actually see Interstate 91, which separates it from Brattleboro. The field consists of five low hills, each crowned with a $200,000 ranch-style house that looks down on a narrow, winding street, fed like a stream by one slim driveway per house. Token trees have been planted tastefully here and there, hitting a medium between privacy and the view. In all, the effect is so carefully manicured that even the mountains, the snow, and the distant woods look totally artificial, as if some low-key, expensive Hollywood set were awaiting the arrival of the camera crew.

The sun's first predawn pallor was just staining the far horizon as I turned off Orchard Street into the Heights in George's borrowed squad car. I didn't need to check for the house number—I recognized it from the photo in Phillips's puppy album. It would have been hard to miss in any event. Of the several homes I could see, it was the only one lit up like a bonfire, complete with strings of Christmas lights. It was a tan brick, one-story affair with columns in front and a carport on the side—as unique to Vermont as to Pasadena, California.

One half of the paneled double front door jerked open as my finger approached the bell. A wreath hanging on the door's knocker fell to the ground and rolled into the snow. The woman I'd seen holding the poodle stood before me, fully dressed and made up, her face drawn and anxious.

Her eyes flicked from me to the police car and back again. "Oh shit," she muttered and turned and walked away. I followed her in and closed the door behind me.

Through the hallway, I saw her sit down on a living room couch. She crossed her arms tightly over her stomach and stared furiously at the floor—a curious mix of sorrow and rage. As I entered the room, its festiveness struck an incongruous note: the fire was burning, the tree lit up, poinsettias and evergreen boughs abounded, and strings of cranberries and popcorn laced back and forth in front of the man-tel-piece. Christmas had been over a week ago, yet all this looked like a permanent display, as in a museum of American culture or an adver-tisement for Smirnoff vodka.

"He's dead, isn't he?"

"I'm afraid he is."

"That stupid dog."

Her tone was so flat I couldn't tell if she meant her husband or the poodle in the pictures, and I wasn't exactly sure how to ask; her re-actions were odd enough already. I waited hopefully for more, but she was silent, so I sat on the end of the armchair opposite her and kept quiet, watching her rocking back and forth in her seat. I don't get much practice telling people their companions have had their necks atomized by little old ladies with shotguns.

"Mrs. Phillips?" I finally asked.

"What?" She didn't look up, but she didn't explode either.

"What was your husband doing out there?"

"Getting the dog."

That seemed a decent enough opener for something more compre-hensible, but she obviously didn't think so. As if having explained all there was to explain, she lapsed back to her silent rocking. I got up and took off my coat. "Could I have a glass of milk?"

That seemed to do it. She looked up at me as if I'd just walked in. "Milk? Of course. I should have offered."

She got to her feet and efficiently marched through a set of swinging double doors to the dining room and the kitchen beyond—the perfect hostess skating on ice. I followed her.

The kitchen was enormous, white and dazzling. No appliance was below industrial quality, no pot or pan lacked either a copper bot-tom or a French-made high-gloss paint job. Knives worthy of a Swift packing plant gleamed along magnetic wall strips, yards of thick un-scratched cutting-board counter space stretched in all directions. Just as the front room was pure *Family Circle,* the kitchen was high-tech *Gourmet* magazine.

I sat down at an island separating production from consumption. Be-hind me was the eating area—table, chairs, a sofa, two Laz-Z-Boys and a TV set; in front, where Mrs. Phillips had set to work, were the makings of the cleanest, most expensive, futuristic greasy spoon I'd ever seen.

She didn't talk nor did I. By chance, I'd hit on the best possible therapy for her, and I wasn't about to screw up what dumb luck had handed me. But I was starting to regret I hadn't ordered breakfast.

She made a pot of tea for herself, and as I watched, her distress surfaced through her automated gestures. She put water on to boil but not enough for a single cup, much less the pot, and had to start over. She took a bag of lemons from the steel-faced fridge, ignoring several pre-cut slices, and carved up a new one with a dull butter knife, butchering the lemon in the process. She grabbed a glass the size of a tankard and poured my milk into it until it overflowed. It was not a comfortable performance to watch.

Finally, her Christmas-bright dress splotched with the debris from her efforts, she loaded up a tray, moved it from her counter to mine, and unloaded it.

"Sugar?" she asked.

"No, thank you. I'll just take the milk."

Her perfect, brittle smile twitched just slightly. "Of course. How silly, I forgot."

I reached gingerly for the milk and slid it toward me without spilling too much. Mrs. Phillips perched on a stool and began poking at the tea bag inside the pot with the butter knife—she'd forgotten a spoon.

"Do you feel you can talk a little?" I asked.

She didn't answer at first but just kept jabbing away. Finally the bag punctured, releasing a flurry of tea leaves, and she stopped.

She bit her lower lip and put both her hands to her cheeks. Her eyes were dry and terribly, terribly sad.

"Yes, I'm sorry about all this."

I smiled at her. "Don't worry. You should see where I usually go for breakfast." I paused, and she placed her hands flat on the white counter. Her wedding band, unlike Thelma Reitz's, rested around her finger—an attractive and impermanent piece of jewelry. "Why was your husband out there tonight?"

"He went to pay the ransom for our dog, Junior. Jamie was very attached to him. He even carried around pictures of him."

I refrained from blurting out that I had seen them. "How long had the dog been missing?"

"Several days—long enough to make Jamie really frantic." She shook her head slightly. "It was my fault, I guess. He didn't say that, but it wouldn't have happened with him."

"What wouldn't?"

"Junior wouldn't have been stolen. Jamie always took him for walks, you know? On a leash? It always seemed so stupid to me—I mean we're almost out in the country. I used to just let him out when Jamie wasn't around and call for him after he'd done his business. He'd always come back. When he didn't that last time, I had to tell Jamie what I'd been doing."

"Was he upset?"

"He was stunned. Not angry with me though. He never was." She stopped speaking for a few seconds. "That dog was like his child. We don't have any children; and Jamie didn't have any by his first wife." She held up her ring finger. "We haven't been married very long—just four years."

"And the kidnapper called?"

"Yes—yesterday. He told Jamie to deliver a thousand dollars to a certain address or he'd kill Junior."

"Was there anything more specific about those instructions? A time or a certain door to be used, or some special clothing that your husband was supposed to wear?"

"I don't remember the address, but he had to go to the back door of the house at two this morning and just walk in. He wasn't supposed to knock. There was no mention of clothing."

"The thousand dollars didn't have to be in mixed bills, or old currency, or something like that?"

"No." She passed a hand across her forehead, picked up the unused pot of tea and poured it into the sink. With her back still to me, she asked. "How did he die?"

"He was shot. The house he went to belonged to an old lady who'd been terrorized by threatening phone calls. She fired before she even saw him."

Her head drooped forward onto her chest, and she leaned on the sink. "Don't tell me he went to the wrong house."

"No, I'm afraid he didn't."

She turned and stared at me with a look of disbelief. "Then what are you saying? What happened?"

This was more than I wanted to admit at the moment, but I couldn't turn her away now. "My guess is that the old lady was used to kill your husband." I held up both hands to stop her from responding. "Mrs. Phillips, like I said, it's a guess. This thing just happened. I'll need more time to nail it down, but you asked, so I told you. But I'd like you to not tell anyone else, okay?"

She nodded.

"Did Jamie ever mention the name Thelma Reitz?"

"Is that the woman who shot him?"

"Yes."

She thought for a moment. "He may have—I don't remember it."

"They served on a jury together."

Again, the hand went to her face. "Oh, no." She crossed over, grabbed the glass of milk I hadn't touched yet, and poured it into the sink, leaving a trail of white droplets across the counter and floor. "That was the worst experience of his life. He couldn't sleep, he almost stopped eating, he had to be treated for stomach troubles. I thought he was getting an ulcer. That trial nearly did him in."

I was thinking maybe it had. "What trial was it?"

She whirled around from washing my glass. "You don't know? It was the Kimberly Harris murder. My God. I heard about that case until I was blue in the face. Every single thing he heard in that courtroom he brought home to me. He went over it again and again, as if he were judge and jury wrapped up into one. I remember Thelma—he never told me her last name. I never thought I'd forget any of them. She was the one he accused of going with the crowd—of not having a mind of her own. First he'd persuaded her to vote his way, then when the majority voted against him, she switched without a second thought. For months after the trial, it was all he could talk of."

"You mean Thelma?"

"No. All of it. Thelma was just a piece of the whole thing. He didn't have it in for her—he pitied her. He said she'd been following men's orders for so many years she was totally incapable of original thought. It was just the whole thing. And the guilt."

"Guilt?"

She was still holding the wet glass. "Well, he voted with the majority too. He did the same thing Thelma did in the end. After all that anguish, he caved in. He hated himself for it. He said he should have stuck by his guns and caused a mistrial, or whatever it's called—you know, when the jury can't make up its mind."

"Was this trial still an obsession with him?" For the first time, her expression changed gradually. Her face lost its tension and became softer and more reflective. Her eyes slid off me and focused somewhere beyond the walls around us, and she smiled in sad remembrance. In the last five minutes, at some point I hadn't recognized, she'd accepted his death. It occurred to me then that she was built of sterner stuff than I'd imagined.

"You obviously didn't know Jamie. I suppose the trial had become an obsession. But that word isn't right—it's too negative for him. I mean, the trial was a negative thing, but that was the exception. Jamie went from enthusiasm to enthusiasm—even the trial was kind of like that. He got totally involved in things—to where you'd think he was becoming a little nutty—and then he'd focus on something else. Most of the time, they were harmless enough—the dog, this kitchen, Christmases were big. I think even I was one of them. All of them—or I should say all of us—were possessions. We weren't discarded after our time—he treated me at least as well as he treated Junior, and that's saying a lot—but we just weren't the latest acquisition."

She finally put down the glass and dried her hands. "Jamie gave his love to me, and to Junior, and to building projects, and even to that dumb trial. If things had turned out the way he'd wanted, he'd have turned the hearts of every person on that jury, just like Henry Fonda did in *Twelve Angry Men*. The fact that he couldn't do it really bothered him a lot, but he didn't carry it around with him for too long. Maybe longer than usual, but it passed eventually."

"But he ended up betraying his own convictions. Why didn't he force a mistrial?"

She got a normal-sized glass out from a cupboard, poured a moderate amount of milk into it, and handed it to me before answering. "He was a social creature. If he couldn't change someone's mind after a good argument, he'd quit, and he wouldn't bear a grudge."

I resisted saying how big I thought that was of him and merely muttered, "A man's future hung on that good argument," and drank my milk.

But she took it in stride—better, in fact. "Was the man innocent?"

I handed her back the glass. "Good point. I suppose not."

She was silent for a moment, looking at me. When she spoke, her voice was hesitant, even a little scared. "Where is he, now?"

"He's been taken to Burlington for an autopsy. They have to do that by law. They'll bring him back, probably by the end of the day, or tomorrow at the latest."

"Will I be able to see him?"

"Yes. In fact, someone will want you to, just to make sure." This last part didn't make me feel too good, so I tried to skate around it a little. She had settled down amazingly from when I'd walked into her house, but I didn't want to presume too much, especially just as I was leaving. "Mrs. Phillips, he was pretty badly hit. His face is okay, but I think you should realize that you won't be seeing someone who just looks asleep. It's not like the movies."

I got to my feet and she let me get away with simply that much. "Thank you...Did you tell me your name? I probably forgot."

"Lieutenant Gunther—Joe Gunther."

She escorted me to the living room and my coat and held the front door open for me. I noticed she was still holding the glass. "Mrs. Phillips, is there someone I can contact to come stay with you? Even someone from the police force, just for a while—to help you drive or whatever? I mean, you'll have your car returned to you today sometime, but still, you might want somebody to talk to, even if it's about the weather."

She reached out and patted my shoulder, as if I were the one in need of comfort. "Thank you, Lieutenant, I'll be fine. There are people I can call if I need them."

Not your run-of-the-mill human being. As I drove back home to get the pajamas out from under the rest of my clothing, I thought Jamie Phillips had been wise making her one of his enthusiasms.

15

3

The Brattleboro Police Department is located in a hundred-year-old converted high-school building perched on a slope overlooking the junction of Main Street, Linden Street, and the Putney Road—a notorious traffic quagmire that the Board of Selectmen has never been able to straighten out, despite an inordinate number of expensive and ludicrous studies on the subject.

From the vantage point of the usual five o'clock traffic jam, the Municipal Building, as it's officially known, looks a little like Norman Bates's gothic pile in *Psycho*, looming overhead—dark, ugly, and prickly with spires. It's one of the few examples of architecture I know of without the slightest redeeming value. Added to that, its heating is satanic, its parking facilities a bedlam, its toilets a throw-back to primitive times, and its lighting a credit to Dickens. It is, however, cheap. So that's where we live, occupying several rear offices on the ground floor, with five cage-like holding cells in the basement. I kind of like the old dump.

I parked on the icy snowbank bordering the back lot and walked through the double doors leading to the building's overlarge central hallway. To the left are the offices of Support Services, our name for the detective division, and to the right are the rest of them: Dispatch, Traf-fic, Parking, Patrol, the secretarial pool, and the chief's office. Before the state police moved out to new quarters in West Brattleboro, they occupied the left, and we were all on the right. That arrangement lent itself to a lot of frayed nerves.

In fact, stepping through the door this morning brought back memories of those days. There was a tension in the air quite beyond the usual grousing about the overeager furnace. I stuck my head through Dispatch's open door to check in and was greeted with a "Where the hell have you been?"

Dispatch from 7:00 A.M. to 3:00 P.M. was Maxine Paroddy, a thin

16

chain-smoking, middle-aged ax handle of a woman with the telephone voice of a teenage girl. She was usually a lot more genial.

"I've been up half the night with that shotgun killing. What's wrong with you?"

"Nothing. Forget it. Murphy wants you."

"Come on, Max. What's cooking?"

She turned in her chair, ripped the phone headset off her ear, and chucked it onto the counter. "I just don't need everybody else's grief, is all. I'm a glorified receptionist. It's not my fault when the shit hits the fan. If somebody is pissed off at somebody else, they ought to have the decency to wait until that person gets on the line. They don't have to fill my ear with crap. There's nothing I can do about it."

"About what?"

"John Woll got mugged last night. Somebody handcuffed him to a telephone pole and stole his patrol car. Now everybody and his uncle is all over me on the damn phone because either the chief hasn't come in yet, or he has come in and he won't call 'em back." The switchboard let out an electronic burp, and Maxine cursed and reached for the headset. "Go see Murphy—he's one of the yellers."

I crossed the corridor to my own bailiwick—a short, straight hallway with doors on both sides opening onto five tiny, high-ceilinged offices—and leaned against the door frame of Frank Murphy's; his had one window, mine had the other. He was on the phone, his feet on his desk, his eyes fixed on some invisible object on the opposite wall. Frank was one of the police force's two captains, and the head of Support Services.

He covered the phone with a thick, freckled hand and said, "Go to your office. John Woll's hiding out there. You hear about him?" I nodded and he waved me off. My office was directly opposite.

It was a cubicle really, eight feet by eight, with a ten-foot ceiling that always made me want to tip the room over so I'd have more room and more heat. As it was—and Murphy himself once tested this out with a thermometer and a ladder—when it was sixty degrees at my ankles, it was ninety degrees just beyond my reach. The only workable solution to this problem anyone had come up with—since fixing the heating system was out of the question—was to pile up several desks and to set up shop at the top. Instead, when I had a lot of paperwork and had to stay put, I settled for wrapping my legs in a blanket.

John Woll stood up when I entered and mumbled a greeting. I motioned to him to sit back down and parked myself on a corner of my desk. "So, rumor has it you got intimate with a telephone pole."

He shook his head. He was a young man, maybe twenty-four with the obligatory mustache of the nervously assertive male. He'd been with us for three years and hadn't quite been able to make his personality match his upper lip. "This is really embarrassing."

"It sounds it. What happened?"

"I was making my patrol, like always, and I saw something weird on Estabrook. I knew it was a man, because I could make out the shape, but I couldn't see his face and I couldn't figure out what he was doing. He was all sort of bunched up and leaning on a garbage can, like he was really hurting, you know? He waved me down—"

"Without showing his face?"

"Yeah. He just sort of lifted an arm, but most of his back was turned so I couldn't see much. I stopped and got out and walked over to him. I was a little twitchy, you know, because of the neighborhood, but I was mostly worried he'd be a drunk and throw up all over me. That's happened before. Anyhow, I walked up to him and poked him a little and asked him if he was all right, and he straightened up, pulled out a sawed-off from under his coat, and shoved it under my nose."

"You must have seen his face then."

He shook his head. "He was wearing a ski mask. He told me to turn around—"

"What was his voice like?"

"It was a whisper. I couldn't make it out. Didn't sound like an accent or anything, though."

That's a breakthrough, I thought. "So he turned you around…"

"Yeah, and then he shoved me over to the pole, took my cuffs, told me to hug the pole, and locked me up. And that was it. He got into my car and drove off."

Frank Murphy appeared at the door and waited for Woll to finish.

"We may have something on this. Go ahead." I turned back to Woll. "So who found you?"

If I ever thought an adult couldn't squirm in his chair, I was wrong. "That's the embarrassing part. It was a reporter from the *Reformer*. She drove up about ten minutes later and started asking me questions. I felt like a real jerk."

"Pretty girl, too," added Murphy. "Alice Sims. She called us after she found him."

"And presumably Ski Mask called her to tell her about Woll." Frank beamed. "Top of the class."

"John, is there anything you might have missed? Something about his hands maybe, or his eyes, or the way he walked? His clothes?"

Woll shook his head. "It was too dark and he wore gloves. I've thought about this a lot. I can see him in my mind, but it's like seeing a storefront dummy—there's just nothing about him that stood out, except that shotgun."

"What about that? What make was it?"

"Nothing I recognized. It looked like an old single-shot. It was a handmade job, though, because I could see the burning around the barrel where he'd cut if off with a hacksaw. That looked new; it was still shiny."

I got up and hung my coat on the back of the door. Murphy was still standing there. "So what did you dig up?" I asked him.

"The sheriff just called and said one of his men found the car in some guy's backyard, not far from Williamsville. They're bringing him in now." Murphy tapped Woll on the shoulder. "You can go now. If you can stand it, try to resist talking any more to pretty little Miss Sims, okay?"

"Yes, sir," Woll muttered as he slipped out the door.

Murphy took his place in the guest chair. I sat behind my desk. "What was that all about?"

"Alice Sims didn't just ask him a lot of questions—he answered them."

"While he was handcuffed to the pole?"

"Yup."

"Jesus, she's meaner than I thought. That's pretty heartless."

"Pretty obnoxious too. The morning edition already has the story on page one and every asshole in town has been calling up with one tune or another."

"So that's why Max is so pissed off."

Murphy chuckled. "Yeah. She bawled me out too. Still, it's no joke. This could become a great local gag, right up there with pet rocks. At least that's the way the selectmen seem to see it, or the ones who called the Chief, who then had the good graces to sic them onto me."

"Well, I guess we'll find out soon enough."

"Yeah." Frank pulled at his lower lip, which was a form of "period-paragraph" body language he'd developed for changing the subject. "What about last night's shooting?"

I shrugged. "You seen George's report yet?"

Murphy nodded.

"Then you know what we found. Tyler and some uniforms are going over the house today, dusting for prints and all...I doubt they'll find much more than we got. They're going to re-interview Reitz once she gets back on keel.

"I visited Jamie Phillips's house and talked to his wife. She had this wild story about their dog being kidnapped and held for ransom—a thousand dollars to be paid at Thelma Reitz's back door. The message was: 'Don't knock—walk right in.' Unless it was a setup to have him blasted by Reitz, that's a pretty unlikely deal."

"So you believe her?"

"No reason not to yet. I have someone looking into the Phillipses as an item: whether they got along, if they had any money problems, possible insurance angles, stuff like that. He was a little strange, I guess— had a real thing for the dog. And she was the one who let it out of the house the day it got snatched. There might be something there, but again I doubt it. We'll talk to everybody a few more times just to nail it down, but if gut instincts are worth anything, I'd say what we see there is what we got. There is one interesting little tidbit: both Phillips and Reitz served on the Kimberly Harris jury."

Murphy sat up straight, suddenly agitated. "Are you kidding?"

"Nope. I was about to pull the jury list when you hit me with Woll."

"Oh, Christ, not that again. Once was bad enough." He stood up, no longer jocular. "Do what you will, but keep it under your hat, okay? No mention of it in the daily reports, no chitchat with anyone but me. After the Woll thing, people are going to have us under a microscope for a while and I don't want them catching sight of you digging up Kimberly Harris. You got that?"

I snapped a salute. *"Oui, mon capitaine."*

He gave me a deadly look and left. Murphy would never have been described as a laid-back, laconic type, but his reaction surprised me. The Harris killing had been sensational in itself, but its solution had been quick and easy and the legal rigamarole hadn't hit any snags from start to finish.

I shook it off and left my office, heading for the central corridor and the stairs leading up.

A familiar voice stopped me as I put my hand on the handrail. It was Stan Katz, the reporter I'd seen at the Reitz house. "Hi, Joe. Running for cover?"

I didn't care for Katz—he had too much ambition and too little tact. "Meaning?"

20

"No offense. Just a little joke. What with Woll's car being hijacked, I thought you guys might be a little shy of the press."

"Stanley, I'm always shy of the press, you know that."

He smiled. "That's true. You could never be accused of being one of my prime sources."

"So why do you keep trying?"

"It's the job. So what about Woll?"

"Nothing. We're working on it. We'll let you know. Why are you on this anyhow? I thought it belonged to Alice Sims."

"She answered the phone, that's why she went. This is my beat."

"So you hip-checked her, huh?"

"I'm the police reporter." His tone regained the familiar competitive edge I was used to—no more chitchat, as Murphy put it. I began to climb the stairs. "Joe, what about the shooting last night?"

"What about it?"

"Who was the stiff?"

"We'll let you know soon, Stan, along with everybody else."

"What was a guy like Phillips doing on Clark Avenue in the middle of the night? It's sort of off his beaten track, isn't it?"

I came back down the stairs. "Stanley, just because you're so brilliant and I'm so dumb, stupid games like that aren't going to make me spill my guts. So back off. Do what you've got to do, but save the Woodward–Bernstein imitation for the other guys, okay?"

He gave me a look as if I'd just grounded him for a week, but he had the courtesy to keep his mouth shut.

If the average waist-level temperature downstairs was seventy degrees, as it probably was today, the second floor was about eighty-five. I walked slowly down the corridor to avoid working up a sweat and went through the door marked clerk of court.

A young woman in an appropriately summery blouse looked up and smiled. "Hi, Lieutenant. We haven't seen you up here in quite a while."

I let out an exaggerated puff of air and patted the top of my gray hair. "People my age have to watch what they do. The stairs you dance up without a thought could kill me."

She laughed. "From what I've seen, they'd have to be loaded with dynamite to do it." She suddenly leaned over the counter and poked me in the belly and then shook her hand as if she'd hurt her wrist. "Look at that—hard as a rock, see? And cute, too." She was laughing now. "And I'm not the only one who thinks so."

I felt my cheeks warm up. "All right, enough. Could you do me a big favor?"

"Shoot."

"Get me the jury list for *The State of Vermont versus Davis?*" She furrowed her brow. "When was that?"

"About three years ago, maybe a little more. It was that big murder thing."

"Oh—the black guy. God, I remember that." She looked around, glancing through a half-opened back door. She lowered her voice to a near whisper. "And you want that right now, of course—an emergency."

I shrugged, but she quickly laid her hand on my arm. "It simply can't wait, right? I mean, you don't have time to go through normal channels." She drew out the word "normal."

I smiled—a little slow this morning. "Absolutely not. It's an emergency."

"Boy—you guys, so pushy," she said in a louder voice, walked over to the door, and spoke to someone out of sight. "I've got to go upstairs for some files—police priority request."

"Get it in writing," was the only response.

The young woman gave me a thumbs-up and went to a large filing cabinet to look up the file number. She scribbled it on a small pad and then handed me a form from her desk. "You can fill out the request while I'm looking. Follow me—you're in for some more exercise."

We climbed to the top floor and an environment of Saharan hostility. The air was breathlessly hot, forcing both of us to pause on the landing. With sweat already prickling my forehead, I peeled off my jacket and draped it over the banister.

"My husband says they ought to sink an insulated shaft down the middle of the building and put a fan in it to suck some of this heat downstairs. It wouldn't be much to look at, but it would be cheaper than anything else they've come up with."

"Nothing's cheaper than doing nothing." She laughed and set out on her search. We wandered from room to room, turning on overhead lights and checking the labels on stacks of brown boxes and dented filing cabinets. I remembered reading *My Brother's Keeper* when I was younger. It was a story of two brothers who never leave their family home, and who slowly fill it with newspapers, magazines, and assorted junk until they're reduced to crawling through tunnels of the stuff just to get around. A cave-in ends the story and the brothers. I wondered how many more days it would take to reach that state here.

My guide finally let out a little cheer in the doorway of a long-abandoned bathroom. "Here we are—the whole kit and caboodle. My Lord, it's got the entire room to itself." She paused, still looking, and finally pointed to a stack balanced high on the porcelain sink in the corner. "We're in luck; the one you want is right on top."

I volunteered to do the climbing while she supported my legs, and managed to lug the box down with a minimum of destruction and a sweat-soaked shirt. She rummaged through its contents while I filled out her request form in the half-gloom of the dim overhead bulb.

"Just the jury list, right?"

"That's it."

We exchanged single sheets of paper, both smiling at the absurdity. "Always happy to help in a police emergency," she added.

Back downstairs in the temperate zone, I found a note on my desk to go to Interrogation—a fancy name given to a room with a table and some vending machines between the squad room and the patrol captain's office. There I found Murphy, Dennis DeFlorio, a Windham County deputy sheriff I didn't know, and a scared-looking young man who was built like a gas pump. DeFlorio was one of the five corporals in Support Services under Murphy and me.

Murphy caught my arm and steered me back outside. He kept his voice low. "What have you been up to? You're sweating like a pig."

"Been upstairs. Is that the guy who stole Woll's car?"

"Let's say he's the one in whose driveway we found the car. He claims he doesn't know a thing about it. The deputy in there says he dragged himself out of bed to answer the door—hardly guilt-riddled."

"Any prints on the car?"

"J.P.'s doing that now, or will be soon. We do have the shotgun—found it in the car. The guy admits it's his but doesn't know how it got there."

"What's his name?"

"Wodiska."

I looked down at the jury list I was still carrying. "Henry A. Wodiska?"

"The one and only. What have you got?"

"Something you're not going to like. Wodiska was on the same jury as Reitz and Phillips."

Frank closed his eyes. "Shit. You're right; I don't like it. You want to talk to him?"

"If you're finished."

"I'll ask Dennis. I've assigned him to it. Remember, keep the Davis–Harris thing under your hat." Murphy went back into the room briefly and reappeared leading all but Wodiska out behind him.

DeFlorio stopped me as I headed in, understandably curious. "What's up?"

I decided to do unto Murphy as he'd done unto me. "It's something Frank's got cooking. I'll let you know if this guy says anything new."

"All right." DeFlorio wasn't thrilled, but there wasn't much he could say. He'd only just gotten the case, and on paper we all worked for the same masters. Still, this was as close to palace politics as I ever cared to get.

Henry Wodiska looked up at me with wide, childlike eyes as I entered. "I swear I didn't steal no police car. I'd have to be stupid."

"From what I've been told, you're claiming to be deaf."

"Huh?"

"Does your driveway slope up or down to the house?"

"Up." His voice had a bewildered lilt to it.

"So someone drove the squad car up the driveway, parked it, cut the engine, and wandered off, and you never heard a thing?"

"The bedroom's on the other side of the house. I never hear stuff like that."

"What about the shotgun? How do you suppose it got in the car?"

"I don't know, man. I came home and I went to bed, like always. I don't know anything about any of this shit. I swear to God."

"Why were you asleep when the sheriff's department came calling?"

"I work nights. I didn't get home till six this morning."

"Where do you keep the shotgun?"

"In my pickup."

"And you didn't notice it was gone?"

"I wasn't in the pickup. I drove with a friend. We switch off like that—it saves gas."

"A car pool."

"Yeah."

"And it was his turn last night—or this morning, I mean?"

"Yeah. I haven't touched that pickup since yesterday, or the shotgun."

"You didn't cut the barrel down?"

His tone picked up a little heat. "Shit no. That thing was like a collector's piece. It was my father's, a real nice gun. I wouldn't fuck it up like that."

I nodded and sat opposite him. "No. That makes sense. So you figure someone stole the gun, maybe last night after you'd gone to work, sawed it off, did his number on our patrolman, and then planted both the gun and the car at your house after you'd gone to sleep. Is that it?"

"I guess so."

"How close is the next house? Can you see it from your place?" He shook his head. "It's not far, but there's trees in the way." He suddenly leaned forward, pleading again. "I swear to God I didn't do any of this."

I held up my hand. "Hey, I'm a believer. I don't think you did either. We're going to have to check it out some more, but I think you're telling the truth. Like you said, you're not stupid, right?"

He nodded hopefully. "Right. I mean this is all too crazy."

"Right," I agreed. I pretended the sheet of paper I had in my hand related to his case. "Wodiska...That really rings a bell."

"I never done anything."

"No, no. I don't mean that. It's something else. It's like I read your name in the paper or something. Did you win a trophy or something a few years back?"

He sat back in his chair, the anxiety cleared from his face. "The only time I been in the paper was for that trial."

"What trial?"

"The one with the nigger. You know, the murder case. Real steamy stuff. I got interviewed 'cause I was on the jury."

I slapped my forehead. A little hammy there. "Right, that's it. The Harris case."

He grinned. "Yeah, that's it."

"Sure. I remember now. You guys didn't waste any time there, did you?"

His voice became slightly defensive. "He was guilty, wasn't he?" I spread my hands. "Hey, we thought so. In fact, I remember a few of the guys complaining you took as much time as you did." I got up and put some money in the soda machine. "You want something? I'm buying."

Whatever apprehension he had left disappeared. "Sure. Pepsi?"

I pushed the button and passed the can to him.

"We took so long 'cause of that little fruitcake with the puppy pictures. He made a big deal about making up his mind, but he didn't fight for long. No one else believed him. Real pain in the butt."

"Did you ever keep in touch with any of the jury members after the trial?"

"No. There was one good-looking girl, but I never did anything about it."

"Hey. You shouldn't waste your opportunities." He grinned—an amazingly unappealing hunk of humanity. "Yeah, well. . ."

I got up and hesitated. "You never got hassled after that trial, did you? I heard one of the jurors got some crank calls."

"Crank calls?"

"Yes, like from people who were mad you convicted Davis."

"Mad? Hell, nobody was mad. They were mad at him—a nigger flat-lander up here, pretending it was New York or something. He got what he should of got. Everybody knows that."

I shrugged and half-turned to leave. "Right…By the way, I have a feeling somebody from the press is likely to ask you about all this. We've been made to look pretty silly, and the news guys always love that. Come to think of it, whoever did this made you look pretty stupid too. Good headline stuff—give people a laugh."

"Yeah. Well, the press can go fuck itself. I'm gonna give them squat."

Music to my ears.

4

Martha Murphy opened the door and looked at me from top to bottom, shaking her head. "If you'd have come an hour earlier, I could have put a healthy dinner in you."

I slid past her. "Good to see you too. I'll have you know some twenty-two-year-old all but propositioned me today, stimulated entirely by my fabulous physique."

"Twenty-two? Joe, she was looking for a father figure—probably wanted to feed you some proper food."

I hung my coat up in the hallway, something I did in this house almost as frequently as I did in my own. "You still worked up over that dinner I served Frank a few weeks ago?"

"Mayonnaise, pickle and Velveeta sandwiches…I mean, really." I kissed her on the cheek. "Don't you ever walk on the wild side?"

"Sure, but I try not to kill myself. You should have seen what that meal did to his system."

"Hell, that was probably all the scotch he poured on top of it." That hit a nerve, and I was sorry I'd said it. I patted her shoulder. "Okay, you win. Beans and sprouts from now on."

She shook her head and sighed. I worked my way back to Frank's den beyond the kitchen. He was lying on a brown vinyl couch in front of the television watching the news. There was a tall glass of scotch on the floor by his hand.

"Hi, Joe. You want a drink?"

I shook my head. I'd given up drinking several years ago. Frank knew that, but there's something inside a hard-drinking man that can only see abstinence as a passing and regrettable phase. And Frank was a hard-drinking man; I'd seen him absorb five stiff scotch-and-sodas and not show a hair out of place. The only visible evidence of his daily drowning was an ever-expanding soft gut and a growing inability to move quickly—physically and mentally. I'd thought about going the same route after my wife Ellen had died many years back, but watching Frank even then had kept me straight. Unfortunately, either despite or because of Martha's concern, Frank had kept right on going.

"You have any tonic water?"

He lugged himself out of the couch and ambled over to a free-standing bar set up near the wall. "Still on the wagon, huh? I don't see how you can drink tonic water without something to kill the taste."

He filled my order, handed me a glass and motioned to the couch. "Take a load off. I'm finding out who was asshole of the day—at least according to the TV. I've got my own opinion, of course."

"John Woll?"

Murphy grunted. "That's not a bad place to start."

"It was hardly his fault."

"Oh, hell. I said 'of the day,' and the day's almost up. I'll find someone else tomorrow. Besides, what I think doesn't matter much anyway."

I cupped my ear. "What's this? Violin music time?"

He glanced at me and shook his head. "Yeah. Sorry. I'm getting sick and tired of being the resident lame duck."

"No one listening anymore?"

"Oh, they listen. They just don't pay much attention. I know what's going through their minds: if we just stall him long enough, he'll be gone and we can forget about it. I can't say I blame them. It's just a lousy way to wrap things up. I've given those bastards a lot of good time."

He leaned forward and turned up the volume a bit. The sports report was beginning—Frank's idea of heaven.

As slow as he had become, his insight hadn't suffered any. He was right about what people were thinking. He was retiring in four months, after thirty-five years on the force; it was the last chance a lot of folks had to subtly let him know they weren't heartbroken.

I thought that stank. He was a good cop and a better friend. When I came out of Korea, I was twenty years old and scarred by something nobody wanted to hear about. Korea was the "action" between the Good War—World War II—and the Living Room War—Vietnam. We had racked up almost as many casualties in three years as they had during ten years in Vietnam. The Vietvets complained that people spat at them when they got back home; most of us didn't stimulate even that much attention.

Also, warfare had revealed sides of humanity I'd never dreamed of, growing up in the hills of Thetford, Vermont. I'd witnessed extremes of boredom and action, of cowardice and foolhardy bravery, of viciousness and grace. I'd been touched by an experience so concentrated and searing that my former life, beckoning from my father's farm, no lon-ger seemed possible.

I floated for a while, utterly at sea. I was decommissioned in California, so I stayed there and spent a few years going to college in Berkeley. That was when the Beat movement was just beginning to stir, a phenomenon that filled my suitcase with some pretty strange books and all but finished the metamorphosis of one erstwhile farm boy, but it still hadn't settled my mind one bit. So I quit and came back home, hoping something might switch me back on track.

But I'd become rootless, frustrated and alienated, and Vermont's green hills did little to soothe. That's when Murphy rounded me up. He was older by nine years, a veteran not only of Korea, but of World War II. I'd known him earlier; he'd been reared nearby in Ely, an older brother of sorts to a lot of kids my age—or if not a brother, then a cousin maybe—the only teenager in the area to have fought overseas and killed people and won medals. He listened to boys my age, and some girls too, I imagine, with a wisdom and sympathy we couldn't find in the adult world. And he managed to track me down after California, although by that time he lived in Brattleboro, some seventy-five miles to the south. To this day, I'm not sure how or why he did that. I have the sneaky suspicion that my mother may have called him.

In any case, he got me interested in the police force he'd been on for several years already. It mimicked some of the more pleasant aspects of military life—that combination of specialness and fraternity—and it replaced the muddiness of my life with the welcomed rigidity of rank, paperwork and assigned tasks. It also meant carrying a gun–the ulti-mate symbol of the simple answer to a complex world—and it gave me a chance, every once in a while, to do something which by that time in my life was becoming an elusive quality. Korea and California had fouled the clear moral waters of my upbringing and had left me nostalgic for the innocent idealism of my younger years.

During my first weeks as a Brattleboro cop, I thought I'd finally found the solution. I was to walk the line between the good guys and the bad, keeping one from being done in by the other. Real Lone Ranger stuff, complete with silver bullets, or at least close enough. The fact that I started out directing traffic and ticketing cars didn't matter. I was a Lawman—the armed instrument of Might and Right.

Not that Murphy instilled that simple-minded notion in my brain. That was my own doing, and I was quickly disabused. The younger, probably wiser Murphy showed me that most bad guys were usually regular joes with a screw loose—barring a few exceptions. But even while I was reluctantly conceding that the world was more gray than black and white, its complexities and contradictions stopped bothering me as much. The gun lost its appeal as I began to rely more on my instincts than on its authority. I came to see it finally as the unreal thing it is: the admission of your brain's collapse under panic and impotent rage. For that personal growth—even rebirth—I had Frank Murphy to thank.

The wide-eyed awe I had for him during those early years died the same peaceful death as my polarized view of human nature. But it, like the latter, was replaced by something more realistic and worthy. I came to love Frank as a fellow flawed human being, with whom I could disagree and argue and yet always respect. It rankled me to see him being kicked around by those who only saw his crusty armor.

"There's no reason not to leave now, you know. The benefits aren't going to change any."

He pushed his lips out in a pout. "I wouldn't give them the satisfaction. I said I'd leave May first, I'll leave May first."

I wasn't going to argue with that. It was damned near the only thing he had left.

"When are you going to call it quits?" he asked, his eyes still on the screen.

"I still have almost ten years to go before full benefits."

"You don't really need them, do you?"

I wasn't sure where he was headed. "It wouldn't hurt. Seems a small price to pay after all this time. I might as well do it right and get what's coming, even if it is a mouse fart."

He didn't say anything for a couple of minutes. His total concentration seemed focused on whether Pepsi or Coke would win the taste test. "You want to make captain."

It wasn't an accusation, nor was it a question. It just floated there, and given my druthers, I might have let it drift away. Instead, I gave it some serious thought for the first time. Another ad passed and the weather girl appeared. She'd changed her hair—made her look like a poodle. "I don't know. Maybe. You don't get out much; I'd miss that. I don't want to end up playing footsy with the selectmen and the chief, and figuring out everyone's schedule. I hate that stuff."

"It has its compensations . . . I can't think of them, but they're there. They told me so." He got up and fixed himself another drink. "There's something to be said for going as high as you can go. It feels pretty good. And you can get out if you don't like it."

"Well, hell, I might as well shoot for chief then." Frank chuckled and settled back on the couch. The report was more snow tomorrow. I'd never aired my ambitions before, probably because they weren't much to talk about—the Brattleboro Police Department was hardly over-loaded with roads to the top. But with Frank's impending departure, that would change. I was next in line, the docs all said I had a body ten years younger than my age—despite the penchant for Velveeta and pickle sandwiches—and I was in no trouble with the powers that be. I wouldn't have admit-ted it to anyone, but the thought of new respon-sibilities was very attractive.

Frank's voice cut in on my musings, in more ways than one. "How about coming down to Florida with Martha and me? We might could set up a business or something."

That caught me by surprise. In the past, during the bad times we'd shared, we'd both thought of leaving the force and doing something else. But that had been pure escapism, a safe way to let off steam. This was different. Despite the fact that his eyes were still glued to the tube, he was making a serious proposal—or at least sending up a trial bal-loon—and that put me in a jam. Not only was I still happy doing what I was doing, I also knew in my gut I couldn't work with Frank in any other circumstance. Time, age, and self-abuse were catching up to him, widening the nine-year gap between us and making it a chasm. In many ways, he had evolved from a near brother to a near father, at least in the way he had aged. Of all the things I wanted least to do in my life, watching Frank Murphy disintegrate in retirement was the most repellent.

That pissed me off. He had helped me out when I was on the ropes, both after Korea and California and after Ellen's death. The least I could do was keep him company for a few years in Florida. But I wasn't going to do it, even to put a new wind in his sails. The irony of our relation-ship was that he had taught me to stand on my own two feet—to look to myself before seeking the guidance of others. It was that education that was making me turn my back now.

"Why Florida?"

"Martha. It turns out that our entire married life, she's hated the winters here."

"But she was born in Vermont."

He shrugged. "What can I say? She has the heart of a beach bunny. Going to live in Florida after I retire is the eleventh of her Ten Commandments. I can't say no; she's put up with me through a lot. I told her it was her call, no arguments."

"Do you know where you'll go?"

"Yeah." He glanced over at me and smiled. "Surprised, huh? You thought you knew everything." The smile faded and he took a long swallow from his glass. "Maybe I was hoping that if I didn't mention it, it might go away. It's not too far from St. Petersburg—a trailer park, but fancy. You'd never guess to look at it. It's near the water, has a bunch of tennis courts, a pool, stuff like that. It's okay."

His voice was as flat as a board. If I'd had any doubts before, they were gone now. "I couldn't do it, Frank. Florida's not my style."

He leaned forward and punched the television off with a hard stab of his thumb. "Well, hell, I'm not surprised. Just thought I'd offer. You might have been nuts enough to say yes."

"What are you going to do down there? Do you know anybody?"

"Naw. I suppose I'll fish. There's a lot of that down there. And suntans. I might work on one of those. There's stuff to do—I just have to go down and find out about it." He got up and freshened his drink and brought another bottle of tonic water over to me. "So what do you got on your mind? You didn't come over here to shoot the shit."

I was more inclined to shoot the shit than he thought, but I respected his wish to change the subject. "I want to dig into the Harris case."

I sensed a palpable stiffening, fully expected. "Why?"

"Because somebody else already has. It's pretty evident Reitz, Phillips, and Wodiska were set up; I want to find out why."

His face darkened and he opened his mouth to say something but then closed it again. "Got any theories?" His voice was forcefully neutral, if that's possible. I sensed he was doling out just enough rope for me to hang myself.

"Not really. Maybe it's revenge against the jury by some friend of Davis's, or maybe one of the jury is after all the others. Or one is the target and the rest are a smoke screen. For damn sure the one man who stood out during the trial, and who dragged his feet when it came to convicting, is the only one dead so far."

"And what's that tell you?"

"Not a thing."

Murphy had been standing through all this, and he now settled in to his favorite position on the couch. "You weren't here when we busted Davis, were you?"

I shook my head. "I was on vacation, but I was here for all the rest."

"Seems to me a man who has to be held in solitary confinement for his own protection would have a rough time rounding up friends to settle his scores for him."

"Why's he in solitary?"

"Because in this state, he's on the far side of the moon. There's not a guy in that jail who doesn't want to take a poke at him just for the novelty of it. I mean, let's face it, where else are they going to be able to mess with a black guy? Last I heard, they'd left turds on his pillow, torn his mattress, destroyed his property, and given him as much trouble as they could get away with. Compared to that, solitary's probably like vacation."

I was impressed with Frank's knowledge. A man in prison was no concern of ours, and to find out about him, you had to go out of your way. Frank obviously had done just that, and I was curious to know why. "What's he still doing in Vermont? Shouldn't he be in some federal can by now?"

"Red tape. Maybe it's crowding or something. I do know the locals would love to get rid of him."

"Where's he being held?"

"Woodstock."

"How do you know all this?"

He looked over at me. "Captain's prerogative." He paused, I was hoping to say more, but instead he turned to the television and punched it on again. A Muppet was being shot through a cannon.

"You gotten any word on the insurance angle yet—for Phillips's grieving widow?"

"Yeah. He had life—a hundred thousand dollars. That's not much considering his assets."

"Which were?"

"Almost a million. I don't think there's anything there, like I said before."

"What about Reitz's neighbors? Anyone see anything?"

"They don't even admit to hearing the shotgun blast."

"And Reitz's daughter. What about her?"

"I don't know. What about her?"

"The report said they didn't get along. Did you interview her?"

"Not yet."

"How about everyone living on and around Estabrook? Did any-one see Woll get mugged?"

"Not that they admit."

"How about the guy with the mask?"

"Nope."

"Did you ask Woll if he'd pissed anyone off recently?"

"No. I will, though."

The television was turned off again, and Murphy looked at me. "So you think the guy who rousted Woll is the same guy who arranged for Reitz to kill Phillips, and that he did all that because he wanted to draw attention to the Kimberly Harris case. Is that right?"

"It's a possibility—the jury connection goes beyond coincidence; at least I think so." I could feel my palms begin to sweat. Murphy's questions were making me angry, as was his implication that I wasn't doing the job properly.

"It's also a possibility that Reitz's daughter hates her guts, that Mrs. Phillips has had enough of the dog-lover, or that Woll rubbed some guy the wrong way, maybe even Henry Wodiska. Do we have any-thing besides his word that he spent the night where he said he did?"

"Of course. We checked where he works. We have done this kind of thing before, Frank."

"Well, we better start showing it. Did you see tonight's news? At six o'clock?"

I shook my head.

"They carried the Reitz shooting. Not much, but the ball's beginning to roll. If we don't do something fast, we're going to get buried. The way I see it, we've got enough on our hands finding the guy who made Reitz pull that trigger without digging up old news."

"Is that a subtle way of telling me not to touch the Harris thing?" His eyes narrowed. "Where'd you get that bullshit? I'm just being helpful. Isn't that why you came over?"

I didn't answer, much as I was tempted. Slowly he turned away and took another swig from his glass. He looked suddenly deflated. "It's been a long day. Do what you have to do, Joe, but keep it under your hat and make damn sure you keep your priorities in order. A lot of people in the department were happy to see Davis go down. If they find out you're digging into that stuff, you're going to start feeling the heat, even if you can tie it together with what's on our plate now. And if the press gets the slightest whiff of it, we'll never hear the end of it. Have you told everyone to keep their mouths shut?"

34

"I think I convinced Wodiska. Woll's the only one I can order. Will you back me up on Harris?"

He paused before answering. "I'm not here for long; they know that. My backing isn't going to be worth diddly."

"Will you do it anyway?"

"You haven't convinced me yet. As far as I'm concerned, the guy who set up the Reitz-Phillips thing and Woll's mugger are two separate people, and neither one has anything to do with Harris."

I rose and returned my half-empty glass to the bar. "All right." I put my coat back on and headed for the hallway. "See you tomorrow, Frank."

"Hey."

I turned around, and he hoisted his glass at me. "I'll be thinking about you in Florida."

"Sure." I hated to admit it, but right now part of me wished he was already there.

5

The weathergirl with the poodle hair was wrong: it was already snowing as I left the Murphy house. From where they lived high on Hillcrest Terrace—an area my friend Gail Zigman, who was a Realtor, described as "middle-class, non-intellectual"—I could see the light below on Western Avenue, Brattleboro's main artery to West Brattleboro, and the glistening snake of Interstate 91, twisting its way north along the Connecticut Valley floor. The scene looked safely Christmas-like, all twinkling lights and snowy motes. Most of the other houses on the block added to the mood with lingering holi-day mementos: wreaths on doors, snowmen, colored lights, even an illuminated Santa on a roof, complete with blinking ho-ho-ho.

I don't know what made me notice the dark green Plymouth Duster parked across and down the street. Maybe it was that I had once owned a Duster and had considered it the best car I'd ever had; maybe it was that the snow hitting its hood melted instantly. I couldn't see through the windshield. In any case, at the time I didn't give it much thought.

I drove down to Western, caught the interstate to the exit below, and bought some groceries at the Finast nearby, not far from Thelma Reitz's house. I then retraced the route I'd traveled a very long day ago.

Brattleboro is an appealing town, at least to me. Modernization and the trendy urban remodelers have all but passed it by, settling for the outlying areas like the Putney Road north of town to set up their shopping plazas and fake colonial restaurants. The city itself, whose heart is the T intersection of Main and High, hasn't changed much from its industrial nineteenth-century heyday, when two organ companies, one sewing-machine company, and a factory turning out baby carriages guaranteed a healthy income for most of the town.

There's a pretty good reason developers stay away from downtown—apart from the challenge of tearing down the massive red-brick buildings that line the major streets—and that's the hills. Brattleboro has a hard time gathering together a single flat acre. For reasons I've never figured out, the original settlers passed up the more spread-out regions to the north and south and planted their town on a crazy quilt of slopes and ravines tumbling precipitously down the banks of three rivers—the Connecticut to the east, the West River to the north, and Whetstone Brook, which neatly slices the town in two.

Homes and businesses, large and small, brick and wooden, hang on to the hills for dear life, like a haphazard collection of Matchbox toys left scattered across a rumpled blanket. The streets conform to the topography, plunging straight down or twisting back and forth, sometimes barely gripping the sharp inclines. It is not unusual to have a wall of trees, rocks, and grass on one side of a house, a view of the neighbor's rooftop on the other.

All this is covered with a thin layer of generations-old city grit. A Dunkin' Donuts has incongruously appeared smack in the middle of downtown—with all the architectural finesse of a broken-down spaceship—and a few other buildings have been built with more sensitivity to their older neighbors, but generally the place is pretty static. The rich live in old rich homes of Victorian excess, the poor live in old poor homes that look like small-town slums all over New England—wooden, peeling, ramshackle, and depressing on a sunny day. Vaguely speaking, Whetstone Brook marks the DMZ below which the handful of "haves" rarely wander, but above which the more numerous "have-nots" have established a few minor toeholds. Gluing the two together, as always, is a majority middle class, which more than anything else has given Brattleboro its identity. It's a regular-people kind of town.

My apartment represented this smorgasbord rather well. Located on Oak Street—an area Gail labeled "intellectual—young rich"—it was

on the top floor of an ineptly remodeled Victorian townhouse on the corner of High Street, a short stroll from both the Municipal Building and downtown. There were two other tenants, both as young and as rich as I, and all three of us had been living there for years. Trying to explain this anomaly, Gail figured we could afford it either because the High Street traffic noise had kept the rent low, or because our benevolent octogenarian landlady, Miss Brooks, had never seen fit to raise it. Personally, I never much noticed the traffic.

I did, however, notice the Plymouth again. As I put down the groceries to open my mailbox, it passed quietly down the street. The snow was falling harder now, and I couldn't make out the plates.

I'd never been tailed before, so I had to wonder if it wasn't coincidence. Neither Hillcrest Terrace nor Oak Street are exactly off the beaten path, and it was early enough that a good many cars were still on the roads. Conceivably, it could even have been a different car.

But I didn't believe any of that. As I climbed the creaking, carpeted steps up to my door on the third floor, I knew in my bones someone was watching me.

The apartment was, of course, quite empty. There was no reason it shouldn't have been. I dumped the mail on the living room coffee table and the groceries in the kitchen and went into the bedroom to change into a pair of comfortable furry slippers.

I then fixed dinner—diced, fried Spam stirred into scrambled eggs and peas, a glass of milk, and a half can of fruit cocktail for dessert—and settled down in a large, slightly bedraggled armchair to read the mail. I tend to do this every night and rather thoroughly at that. Catalogues, mailers, the free *Town Crier,* all of them get the same attention as the occasional letter and the morning *Reformer.* I even fill out the sweepstakes, idly wondering what I'll say to Ed MacMahon when he hands me my million-dollar check. Habits, now old, born of comfortable isolation. I hadn't dropped by the Murphys' after their dinner hour to avoid Martha's cooking, which was indeed better than my own, but only because I wanted the evening to myself, as usual.

My wife Ellen died of cancer about eighteen years ago. We'd been married eight years—she'd been a teller at the bank I use to this day. She couldn't have children, and for some reason we never thought of adoption, so we paid a good deal of attention to each other, going to movies a lot, planning picnics and day hikes for the weekends, reading books aloud while she sewed or I built plastic airplanes for Murphy's kids.

We had our run-ins, of course. Days when all we did was get in each other's way. I would long for the bachelor life then, sensing how within reach it was. A divorce for us, after all, would have been a simple parting of the ways—no children, little property, still young. But we never did; it never got that bad, and it never lasted long.

The doctors said she died quickly. The whole thing took about four months from diagnosis to burial. But that was a long time for me, watching her die in slow motion, piece by piece. This was, after all, the woman I had undressed many times, scattering her clothes around the house. We'd made love with real enthusiasm, often on the spur of the moment. She'd been an extremely sensual woman.

So her death had been a catharsis of sorts, her slow and steady

38

deterioration had been draining something vital from my core until at last, mercifully, by dying she released us both. For a long time afterward, I was alone—I needed no more companionship, no more emotional ups and downs. I was free to work, to read, to go to the movies utterly alone. I had come to realize that my home life, even with some-one as accommodating as Ellen, had begun to echo the complexities of my job. Day in and day out, each twenty-four-hour cycle was a constant struggle, swimming against dozens of competing currents in an effort merely to tread water. Perhaps I'm a man whose ambitions are too slight, or maybe I lack the basic toughness most have to deal with a crowded life without respite. I could be just selfish. Whatever it is, by the time I snapped out of mourning Ellen's loss and renewed my interest in the opposite sex, I was a confirmed bachelor, devoted to keeping at least one small part of my soul entirely to myself.

Which brings me back to my Realtor friend, Gail, the only reason I might have interrupted my monk-like solitude and scrambled Spam. One of Brattleboro's peculiarities is that it has become a retirement village for sixties flower children—"trust-fund hippies" and "granola-heads," as we used to call them. Initially flocking to locally resented communes, attracted no doubt by the quaint woodsiness of the state, this vanguard of "creeping vegetarianism"—to quote one alarmed member of the Holstein Association—gradually grew older, cut its hair and, with values mostly intact, joined the homegrown establishment. The result was a leavening of the town, setting it apart from other has-been industrial centers. Mixed in with the beer dives and neo-cowboy bars were health food stores and vegetarian restaurants. Kids named Sheela, Alayna, and Charity ran up and down the streets, while their parents became business leaders and declared Brattleboro a nuclear-free zone. My fondness for this crowd wasn't based on any Berkeley-born nostalgia, however. It was firmly attached instead to one of its leading citizens.

Gall Zigman had followed the above recipe word for word, arriving in Marlboro, near Brattleboro, in the mid-sixties to join a commune. Long-haired, free-loving, pot-smoking, and more involved in the lives around her than I'd ever been at her age, she eventually tired of communal life, moved into town and went through the gentle and predictable transformation from anti-establishment outsider to successful Realtor and selectman. She was also on every committee possible, from daycare to arts council to Ban-the-Bomb. She and I had been lovers for the past several years.

For two people supposedly committed to their community, we showed remarkable restraint regarding each other. Ours was a balancing act with both of us keeping the seesaw level. When one pushed for closer involvement, usually because of outside troubles, the other counter-pushed. The irony was that life's traumas, so routinely counted on to bring people together, forced us apart. We cared for one another and showed it as much as we dared, but our separate independencies had, over the years, become too valuable to give up. We were a perfect match, both too old and too self-centered to change our ways. Frank called us roommates without a room.

I threw out the junk mail, piled the bills on my desk, and picked up the phone.

"Hello, Joe," she answered before I'd said a word.

"How did you know it was me?"

"You're the only one I told when I'd be back." I liked that. "How was New York?"

"As usual; awful and lovely."

"And your parents?"

"Awful and lovely. Dad gave me a "how-to" book about finding a way out of mid-life crisis, and Mother and I had our annual boy-talk. You'd never have guessed I turned forty two months ago. How was your Christmas? And what's Leo up to?" Leo was my brother, and an endless source of fascination for Gail.

"He's dating a wild woman who dyes her hair green and drives a Corvette. She runs a Sunoco station she picked up in a divorce. According to Leo, she doubled the business the first summer because all she wore were grease-covered hot-pants and a halter top. Trade falls off in winter. I like her."

"What's her name?"

"Ginny. She's a tough thirty-five, which makes her Leo's junior by a mile."

"I'm your junior by a few years."

"Yeah, but you don't drive a Corvette or wipe a dipstick on your butt. This woman could be the death of him."

"What's your mother think of her?"

"She's amused, but she won't admit it."

"Is this serious with Leo?"

"Good Lord, no. He's more serious about her car. She's just part of the package, and a rather athletic one at that, according to him. But you know Leo. He's happy the way he is."

"Seems to run in the family. What are you doing tomorrow night?"

"Same as tonight—nothing."

"You want to come over?"

"Now?"

"No, I'm sorry," and I could tell from her voice that she was. "I meant tomorrow. I have homework to do tonight. But I do want to give you a squeeze."

"You got a date."

I hung up the phone and sat there for a while, my feet on my father's old rolltop desk. If ever there was loneliness, this is when it hit. Sexually, our arrangement was perfection—once we'd built up a hunger, we could always take care of it. But times of friendly noninvolvement, of watching television in one room while she read peacefully in the other, didn't happen. Those belonged with memories of Ellen. Of course, that hadn't been perfection either, any more than this was, but the rationalization didn't comfort. It truly was a world in which every up side had a down.

I got up and turned on the television, filling the darkened room with a shimmering fluorescence. A cop show. Perfect. I went over to the window and looked down at the street. The Plymouth was parked near the corner.

6

Murphy met me at the door when I walked into the Municipal Building at 7:00 the next morning. "You got that jury list on you?"

"It's in my office." I poked my head into Maxine's cubbyhole. She waved and handed me a sheet from the dailies box—a record of the night's activities.

I came to a dead stop in the middle of the corridor. "Is this what's on your mind?" I pointed at the lead item: the sexual assault on one Wendy Stiller.

"Is she on it?"

I smiled at his downcast expression. "Afraid so, Frank."

"Shit. Let's go to my office." He led the way, ushered me in, and closed the door. "You may have a bit of a problem."

"Why?"

"Kunkle was on call last night, so Capullo brought him in on this."

"And?"

"Kunkle quote-unquote headed the Harris investigation. He got a citation, a letter of commendation and a bonus from the town manager. Considering his personality, he's not going to be thrilled with this jury thing. He's going to think you're out to get him."

"I'm not the one going after the jury."

"I know that, for Christ's sake. But you're going to want to talk to this girl, aren't you?"

"Yes."

"So what are you going to tell Kunkle? And don't give me what you gave DeFlorio yesterday. He pestered the hell out of me trying to find out why I supposedly told you to interview Wodinsky."

"Wodiska."

"Whatever. Give me a break this time, will you?"

"Jesus, Frank, even a paranoid like Kunkle ought—" He held up both hands to stop me. "You know that. I know that. I'm the den mother

42

here, all right? I'm trying to keep everybody happy. Just tiptoe a little. Kunkle's screwier than ever right now—home problems— and I don't want to hear him complaining that you've got doubts about his handling of the Harris case."

I gave up. "Okay. Mum's the word."

"Thank you. Now I've arranged for you to have first crack at her this morning, but Kunkle won't be far behind."

"I thought he had his little chat last night."

"She had to be sedated. He didn't get much out of her—nothing really, so get in and get out, and keep me up to date. She's at Memorial Hospital, room three-twelve."

Memorial was a typical small-city hospital. A little threadbare, a few patches, not staffed by the best or the brightest, but it made up in heart what it lacked in glitzy technology. Ellen had died there, admittedly a long time ago, but if caring alone could have cured cancer, she would have pulled through.

I found Wendy Stiller sitting in a green plastic chair by the window in a four-bed room. She was the only occupant. She was dressed in a long pink terry robe and had her feet tucked under her. Her blond hair hung in a tangled mess about her shoulders. Her face was pale and hollow-looking. It occurred to me that this was the third victimized woman I'd approached in just twenty-four hours. I wondered if that meant anything.

"Hi." She smiled wanly. "Hello."

"Do you feel well enough to talk a little?" I avoided introductions. The less she knew of me, the less she'd tell Kunkle when he Joe Fridayed her later.

She nodded. "I guess so." Her voice was light and dreamy. I sat down on the bed near her chair. She was quite pretty, in her late twenties, not slim in a high fashion sense but not fat either—the kind of woman they choose to advertise laundry soap. "Can you tell me what happened?"

She turned away to look out the window at the snow-covered trees. She didn't answer for a few seconds. When she did, the softness of her voice was almost lost to the building's own gentle murmurs.

"There was a man inside my apartment when I got home last night."

"What time was that?"

The answers came slowly, as if each one had to be gingerly coaxed to shore. "About midnight. I'd been out on a date. The door was locked. I don't know how he got in."

"Did your date come in with you?"

"No."

"What did you do after saying good night?"

"I went straight to the bedroom.

"And he grabbed you?" She nodded, just perceptibly.

"He was hiding?"

"Behind the door."

She hunched her shoulders a bit and paused. I didn't interrupt. This wasn't the first conversation I'd had like this, and I knew it might take time, Kunkle or no Kunkle. She took a deep breath. "He told me to get down on my knees and then he covered my mouth with some tape. I could see him in the mirror on the bathroom door. He was all in black—pants, shirt, ski mask, everything."

Again she stopped, sighed, and shifted in her chair. The last long sentence seemed to have tired her.

"What happened then?" I tried to make my whisper match hers.

"He told me to get in the shower…Tied my hands to the shower head …"

A half minute passed. "Did he turn on the water?"

"He asked me if the temperature was all right."

"Did he touch you other than to tie you up?"

"No…He turned the water off and looked at me…Then he took my clothes off." Again she stopped. I could hear the traffic outside. In the window's reflection, I saw the glistening of tears on her translucent cheek.

"Would you like to take a break?"

She shook her head, but she didn't speak again for a full minute. When she did, she faltered but kept on, a runner committed to finishing. "He took my clothes off and rubbed soap all over me. He left it on."

Another pause, another deep breath. "Then he played with my nipple. With his finger. That's how I knew who he was."

That took me by surprise. "You knew him?"

"Yes. His name is Manny Rodriguez."

"How do you know?"

"We served on a jury together once. He had a tattoo on the back of his hand. An American eagle."

"What did he do then?"

For the first time, she turned and looked at me, her face grief-stricken and baffled, the tears now dripping off her chin. "Nothing. He left.

44

Why did he do that?"

I patted her shoulder. "I don't know. I'll try to find out. Did you get along with him when you were on the jury together?"

"I talked to Mr. Phillips most—he was nice."

"And you never saw Rodriguez after the trial?"

"Once. He works at a glass shop on Canal. I saw him there."

"Had he offered you a deal or something?"

"I didn't even know he worked there. We just talked."

"How long ago was this?"

"I don't know; a year maybe."

"And the conversation was okay?"

"We didn't have much to say." She wiped at her eyes with her sleeve, and I got up and handed her a box of Kleenex from the bedside table.

"Are you going to be all right, Miss Stiller?" She blew her nose and nodded.

"There'll be a policeman who will come to visit you soon, and he'll probably ask you many of the same questions I just have. His name is Willy Kunkle."

"I met him last night, but they gave me something that made me too sleepy." Her voice was stronger.

"Well, he'll be back. Is that all right?"

"Yes. I feel better now. Thank you." I rose and headed for the door. "There is one last thing."

"Yes?"

"We are going to pick up Manny Rodriguez, but until we get his side of the story, none of us is absolutely positive he was the man who assaulted you."

"It was his tattoo." She said this in the same flat voice.

I returned to her and crouched by her chair. "I realize that, but it may not have been his hand. I know that sounds crazy, but just lately we've had a couple of things like this, where someone pretends to be someone else. All I'm saying is that Rodriguez may be innocent."

She looked confused. "All right."

"The reason I bring it up is that the newspaper is always hot to follow up a story like this one. They'll try to find out and interview you. So if you mention Rodriguez's name and he turns out to be innocent, he'll have a tough time with it. You will, too, of course. We'll do our damnedest to keep what happened to you private, but secrets are hard to keep unless everyone cooperates." She nodded. "I understand."

I squeezed her hand. "Thank you."

45

I sent a nurse in to check on her and called Murphy from a pay phone. I told him Wendy Stiller's story. "I know Willy's got his problems, but there's no way I'm going to sit around waiting for him to waltz in and do what I've just done before rounding up Rodriguez. The guy might have one foot on the bus right now, if he's still in town."

Murphy spared me the problem. "I called Kunkle and told him that she'd asked to make a statement and you were hanging around

with nothing to do. He didn't like it, but he swallowed it. I'll send him to pick up Rodriguez and you file a report to back me up. Once we've got the guy downstairs, I'll make sure you get a crack at him."

"Tell Kunkle to be quiet about it, okay? I think I got Stiller to clam up with the news boys. The less they get, the better."

"Amen."

I hung up. A friend of mine—a former cop—once told me I'd get a lot more money and a lot less grief if I went into the security business as he had done. I'd answered I could live without the corporate politics. He'd laughed.

Rodriguez hadn't left town. Kunkle found him at work, contentedly etching frost curlicues on a custom mirror. On first mention of Wendy Stiller's name, he didn't even know who she was. He'd been reminded dramatically by the time I got to see him in one of the basement holding cells.

That part of the building isn't designed to boost morale anyway. The cells line one wall of a low-ceilinged beige room lit with bare bulbs and spotlights. They're fancy kennels, really, with one steel fold-away cot and a porcelain toilet per cell. Surveillance cameras are mounted on the opposite wall.

Rodriguez was our only tenant. He was sitting on the cot with his hands between his knees when I walked in. He sprang to his feet as soon as he saw me. "You've got to get me out of here. This is a mistake. I haven't done anything." His voice was high-pitched and tinged with hysteria.

"Relax. It feels worse than it is."

"But I'm in jail." He grabbed the bars and shook them to demonstrate his point.

"Not for long. Sit down and calm yourself. Come on. Sit." He sat reluctantly. He was about thirty years old, good-looking, with a full head of dark hair and a neatly trimmed beard. He was wearing denim work clothes, also neat and clean. "Good. Now hold out your hands, palms down." He looked at me as if I'd lost my marbles, but he did it. There was a wicked triple scratch running across the center of the eagle tattoo on his right hand. It looked infected and painful.

"How did you get the scratch?"

He looked at it as if for the first time, thrown further off balance. His words came out more slowly now. "My cat. I threw him out of the house a couple of days ago and he clawed me. We don't like each other—he belongs to my kids."

"Does it hurt?"

"Yeah."

"I'll send someone down to look at it." I turned to go.

He leaped to his feet, revved up again. "Wait. Don't leave me. I don't want a Band-Aid. I want to get out of here. I don't belong here. I'm innocent. I didn't rape anybody."

"The police report says you got a call last night that sent you on a wild goose chase. Is that right?"

"Yes, I swear. I had some tools stolen a few days ago. The man on the phone said he'd found them; that his brother had stolen them, and that he felt bad about it and wanted to return them. I know it sounds crazy, but it's true."

I paused at the bottom of the steps. "Mr. Rodriguez, I'm sure it is true. We picked you up on the available evidence, that's all. I've just got to make a couple of calls to clear this up, and I'm pretty sure we can get you out within the hour. By the way, what color are your eyes?"

"Brown. What about a police record?"

"No record. We'll clear it up with your boss, too. If it all works out, the only thing you'll have to worry about is keeping your mouth shut. If you go to the press, or talk to them if they come to you, you're the one who's going to get the bad publicity. Fair or not, that's how it works. Ask any celebrity."

I went upstairs and knocked on Murphy's door. I was sorry to see Kunkle sitting in his guest chair. "I'll talk to you later, Frank."

Kunkle got up before I could leave. "Did you see Rodriguez?" As usual, he was abrupt and hostile—a man on perpetual simmer.

"Yeah. I just talked to him."

"Why?"

"Maxine told me about the scratch on his hand."

"What about it?"

"Wendy Stiller didn't mention it."

"So?"

"So I thought I might ask her if she'd seen it." Kunkle gave me a hard stare. I decided I'd better not leave it there. I asked Murphy if I could use his phone. He pushed it across his desk to me, and I dialed the hospital and asked for Stiller's room.

"Hello?"

"Hi, Miss Stiller. This is the man who spoke to you this morning about the attack."

"Oh, hi."

"When you saw that tattoo, was there a scratch running across it? Maybe a Band-Aid or some makeup or something?"

"No, it looked like it did at the trial."

"You're sure?"

"Yes."

"Great. Thank you. One last thing: do you remember the man's eye color?"

"They were blue—pale blue." The answer was immediate. I didn't question how she could be so positive.

I thanked her again and hung up. "We've got the wrong man. The scratch wasn't on the attacker's hand, and his eyes were blue."

Kunkle snorted and looked at the ceiling. "Jesus, that's pretty slim. I mean, the man lathered her up and flicked her tit. You think she's going to take time out to catalogue his eye color and the odd scratch here or there? Give me a break."

I felt my face flush with anger. He brought back the image of every self-confident, stupid bully I'd ever known in grade school—the guys who made ignorance a martial art. The fact that he was actually a pretty smart guy who was drowning in his own troubles made no difference; he'd been on this kick for too long.

I spoke directly to Frank. "That scratch is a mess. It's infected and a couple of days old. No way either she could have missed it or he could have gotten it between midnight and now. Show her Rodriguez's hand, and his eyes. She'll tell you he's not the man."

Frank nodded and I turned to leave. Kunkle grabbed my arm. "Pretty sure of yourself."

I shook him off. "I'm also right."

I walked into my own office and slammed the door. Stan Katz was sitting on the edge of my desk. "Get out, Stan; you're trespassing."

"Testy, testy."

I grabbed him by the scruff of the neck and shoved him toward the door. Kunkle's style was catching.

Stan opened the door and paused. "I just wanted to get your side before I started writing."

"My side of what?"

"The events of last night, and the night before."

"What about them?"

He gave me a smile custom-made for a fist. I buried my hands in my pockets.

"You ought to know. You've been involved with all of them, according to the scuttlebutt. What's going on?"

That cooled me down a notch. He was fishing. "Investigations are going on, like they always are. This is a police department, Stan. We bust people. And Woll was just a screwup."

"Why are you the hot man, all of a sudden? You're popping up all over. I heard DeFlorio pulled the Woll case, but you've been poking around in it. I also heard Kunkle was pissed off that you were treading on his turf."

I put my hand on his shoulder and pushed him—gently—out into the hall. "We always get into each other's hair; it's standard. Besides, I'm their lieutenant; I'm supposed to keep an eye on 'em, you know that. Your problem is you don't have enough to keep you busy. That happens when things are slack. Don't take it out on me, okay? Go see a movie." I closed the door in his face.

I had just sat down when Murphy stepped in. He leaned against the wall and smiled. "Well, well, Mr. Diplomacy."

"Lay off, Frank. Kunkle's a jerk. If he's got problems, you can change his diapers."

"I won't have to. He just told me I might as well hand the Stiller case over to you since you stole it anyway. I must say, you two aren't very friendly."

"I'm tired of trying."

"By the way, I sent a unit over to fetch Stiller. We probably ought to dot the i's and so forth before we kick Rodriguez loose."

"Fine. I just threw Katz out, by the way. He's sniffing the air like a hyperactive pointer. You better make sure any paperwork he's liable to see doesn't have any names on it and that all this shit is on a need-to-know basis, or he's going to start making the same connections I have."

Frank sat down and shut the door with his foot. "Which are what so far?"

"Rodriguez makes it the fifth jury member in two days. Whoever's doing this really did his homework. He stole Phillips's dog, Rodriguez's

49

tools, spent days terrorizing Reitz, and cased both Wodiska's and presumably Stiller's daily habits. He's been working on this for a long time."

"Why?"

I shrugged. "The number-one question. I still think it's the Harris case."

Frank sighed.

"It's the common thread. Of course, maybe it's the moon or the alignment of the planets, or maybe the entire jury took LSD time capsules and simultaneously flipped out three years later."

"I'd take that over reopening Harris."

"I don't think we've got a choice. Even you have to admit a similarity in all these cases, and the likelihood that they were all orchestrated by the same man. Besides that, none of these set-ups was built to last—they were to get our attention, not to sidetrack us. Whatever it is Ski Mask wants, he obviously thinks it involves Harris."

Frank grunted. "And Phillips's death guarantees we can't just ignore him." He got up. "So I guess we won't." He paused at the opened door. "You can look into Harris, with my incredibly valuable backing, but still try keeping it under your hat, okay?"

7

Early on September 15, 1983, the police were called by the manager of the Huntington Arms on Putney Road. One of his tenants, Kimberly Harris, had made arrangements with a local cab company to be picked up and driven to the Keene airport, but she wasn't answering the repeated knocks on her door. From what the manager could see through the living room window, the apartment appeared ransacked. He said he didn't want to use his pass key until the police were with him.

Two patrol cars were dispatched to the scene, driven by Sergeant George Capullo and Patrolman John Woll respectively, each of whom was near the end of his shift. They entered the apartment with the manager and found the nude and strangled body of Kimberly Harris tied to her bed. Calls were put out to Support Services, the State's Attorney and the regional medical examiner. Detectives Willy Kunkle and J.P. Tyler arrived ten minutes later; Kunkle took charge of the investigation while Tyler went about gathering physical evidence.

A preliminary review of the site led officers to believe that a struggle had taken place, ending in Kimberly Harris being tied to her bed. The rope attaching her right hand to the bedpost had worked loose, and her fingernails were jagged and bloody, indicating she had scratched her assailant. A broken, blood-smeared lamp was found on the floor near that same hand, rousing suspicions that it may have been used for self-defense. Wet, viscous deposits in and around her mouth and pubic area led Tyler to assume she had been sexually assaulted.

The regional medical examiner, Alfred Gould, recommended that the state medical examiner take personal charge of the forensic investigation, and James Dunn, the State's Attorney, agreed. Dr. Beverly Hillstrom was therefore contacted and arrived on the scene from Burlington three hours later.

Meanwhile, based on the manager's statement that the leather belt found around the victim's neck belonged to the janitor, Kunkle quickly secured a warrant allowing a search of the janitor's quarters. During the search, the police found a woman's undergarments, a small quantity of heroin with the appropriate paraphernalia, and the janitor, a black man named William Davis. Davis was sitting on the edge of his bed under the influence of the drug, nursing both a bad head wound and several deep scratches on his left cheek. He was booked on a charge of felony-murder.

Several days later, Dr. Hillstrom reported her findings. They were compared with additional tests conducted by the state crime lab. According to both reports, the blood under Harris's nails matched Bill Davis's; his fingerprints were in various parts of her apartment and on the belt used to strangle her; the blood-smeared dent found on the lamp matched the cut on his head; the rope used to tie her down was cut from a coil found stored with the rest of his tools; and the semen found on her body was compatible with his blood type.

One additional detail surfaced but was deemed largely irrelevant: Kimberly Harris was five-and-a-half months pregnant at the time of her death. Davis's blood chemistry ruled him out as the father.

Davis's statement to the police, obtained after he'd been apprised of his rights, was a rambling, barely coherent denial of the accusations made against him. He claimed he'd been hit on the head from behind sometime the night before and had woken up in his bedroom shortly before the police had arrived. He also claimed he'd been injected with heroin while he was unconscious. He denied ever having an interest in Harris. When asked if he had a lawyer, he burst out laughing. The public defender was called in to take his case.

From that point on, the legal dance began, and the police all but vanished from the scene. Davis was arraigned, his counsel pleaded for release, the judge set a stiff bail, and Davis ended up as a target for the white pranksters in the Woodstock State Correctional Facility, all in short order.

All that was according to the official written report, tailored for public consumption and rendered in such obtuse pseudo-legalese that I had trouble translating it. There were three remaining sources of information I could use to dig into the case: the court records, located upstairs in the derelict, saunalike bathroom; the police case file, a bound logbook stuffed with additional odds and ends scribbled on napkins, paper placemats, and what have you; and the officers' notebooks, those small black jobs we all carry around to make personal notes and which don't belong to anyone but ourselves. The notebooks are usually the most telling, of course, assuming the owner has kept them and can still decipher his own handwriting, but they are sacrosanct—some of what's in them could get a cop into serious trouble. Had the head guy on the job been Murphy, I might have gotten some access to his notebook. Considering that man was actually my dear friend Kunkle, I wasn't going to waste time worrying about my chances.

The case file was the logical first step, but it too demanded some deciphering. Many of the items thrown into it were comprehensible only to the throwers, and since Frank wanted me to act invisible, I was in a bad position to ask for favors.

So, for the moment, the court records were the only road I could travel. I closed the written report before me, returned it discreetly to the filing cabinet in the main office, and lumbered my way back upstairs to the Clerk of Court.

The girl behind the counter was her usual summery self. "Two days in a row? I thought you didn't like the stairs."

"I'm working on a medical disability. I need your indulgence again."

As before, she glanced at the door behind her and lowered her voice. "Shoot."

"Are you the only person from this office who goes upstairs?"

She nodded. "You've obviously never seen my boss."

I had. It was a rhetorical question. "What would you do if you found someone going through those files without your clearance?"

She pursed her lips. "Other people have junk up there."

"This would be your junk—like, say, in a bathroom."

"If he was someone I knew," she smiled, "and he wasn't removing anything or making a mess out of the filing, I think I'd just say 'Hi' and maybe offer him a fan."

I smiled back. "Thank you."

The first thing I did was search the upper floor for a light with a stronger bulb than the one hanging from the middle of the bathroom ceiling. The best I could manage was seventy-five watts. I then stripped to the waist, shifted the boxes into a rough beginning-middle-end order, and settled as comfortably as I could on the toilet seat. I opened the first file from the first carton and began to read.

Gail lived on Meadowbrook Road, north of West Brattleboro, actually not far from Orchard Heights. But where the latter had appeared as if by the wave of a Realtor's wand, Gail's neighborhood had followed an unrushed evolution from countryside to farms, and from farms

53

to large family homes. Lately, the occasional one-and-a-half story modern ranch-style was starting to appear, but with discretion—even lending a certain democracy to the street.

Her house had been an apple barn once, a small part of a large area still referred to as Morrison's Farm. No one named Morrison lived on the road anymore, and perhaps predictably there wasn't a real farm anywhere in the vicinity. But the apple barn remained, high at the top of a field facing east, overlooking where the main house had once been and where a long uncared-for driveway now struggled up the slope to meet it.

That, of course, was unplowed. Every year I reminded her to set up a contract with someone to plow the drive regularly, and with equal consistency she forgot about it until she'd been snowed in several times. Her stubborn absent-mindedness had become an early winter rite for both of us, a demonstration of her reluctance to let the fall slip away without protest. Sentiment aside, I thought it was a pain in the butt.

I made as good a try as I could at the hill, fishtailing like crazy, bald tires whirring like dynamos, and ran out of steam about half way up, as usual. With a world-weary sigh—always good for the soul when no one else is around to lend sympathy—I got out into the early evening darkness and trudged the rest of the journey in my ancient, half-laced boots. I saw her watching me from behind the sliding-glass door of the porch, a mug of something hot cradled in both hands. She was wearing blue jeans and a work shirt, and they and the soft backlighting from within the house showed off her slim, almost skinny outline. She turned on a light as I reached the porch steps, and drew open the door.

"When are you going to put on snow tires?"

"Ha, ha." I got to the top and she carefully wrapped her arms around me and gave me a kiss. I lifted her slightly off her feet, swung her into the house, and closed the door.

"I think I just poured tea down your back," she whispered in my ear.

"Then it's probably on your rug, too."

We separated and looked at the small dark stain on her rug. She shrugged. "One of thousands. That's why I put it in front of the door. You want some?" She proffered her cup. I sniffed suspiciously. "What is it?"

"Sleepy Time."

I wrinkled my nose. "How about some nice, sweet, artery-clogging cocoa or something?"

"You got it." She headed for the kitchen, and I went for the huge, overstuffed couch in front of the fireplace. I settled in its buxom embrace, stuck my stockinged feet out on the coffee table, and laid my head back on the pillows. I loved this woman, if not for herself then for her truly unique sofa. High above me a shiny aluminum mobile turned slowly in the air currents near the cathedral ceiling. The house was a mishmash of open levels, bare beams, and narrow staircases; you couldn't walk ten feet without climbing up, stepping down, or fighting vertigo at some railing-free edge. Even then, it paid to watch your step. Dozens of little knickknacks—pots, wooden boxes, statuettes, rocks, sea shells, and God knows what else—lurked like frozen pets all over the house, hiding on the stairs and around corners as if waiting for dinner.

She came back in, handed me a mug, and wedged herself in the opposite corner of the couch, wriggling her toes under my thigh. She looked beautiful with her long hair spread out against the pillows.

"I'm glad you're back."

She took a sip of her tea and smiled. "Did you miss me?"

"Yes. A lot."

She was quiet for a while and I just lay there, trying to melt through the pillows to the floor. The crackling of the fire massaged my brain.

"Sounds like you've been busy." I rolled my head on the pillow to look at her. "Oh?"

"The shooting. It's all I've heard about since I got back."

"Yeah. It's still up in the air. We'll see."

"You want to talk about it?"

"The shooting?"

"That or whatever is causing that furrow on your brow. It always gets deeper when you're thinking about something."

Involuntarily I touched the permanent crease between my eyebrows. My father had sported one too. When he got mad it had given him the look of a wrathful Zeus—used to scare the hell out of me.

I smiled at the memory. "I guess it's time for a vacation."

"You just had one."

"Wasn't long enough."

She laughed and put her cup down. "Okay, let's hear it."

I was a little embarrassed. The urge to share my thoughts quarreled with the stiff-upper-lip image I had of myself. She'd also made me feel I was on a psychiatrist's couch, which was not some-where I ever yearned to be. "Do you charge for this?"

"Maybe—but not money." She gave me a friendly leer.

"Well, hell. Let's pay now and talk later." I stretched my hand up the inside of her thigh.

She caught my fingers with her own. "Seriously, what's up?"

I leaned back again and waved my hand. "I don't know; it's nothing specific. Feeling old, I guess."

"I used to do that when I was thirty-five."

I tapped the side of my head with a finger. "You and me both. No… Murphy asked me to quit and join him in some business in Florida. I turned him down."

"What kind of business?"

"No kind—he had no idea. He just wanted the company. I felt badly because I owe him a lot."

"You have your own life to lead."

That made me smile. "That's what they say."

"What happens to you once he leaves? Captain?"

"Probably. The chief and I get along; I'm next in line."

"Nervous?"

"Not from the command angle—I'm used to that. I just hope it doesn't change me."

"Like Frank?"

"You're pretty good at this. Yeah, like Frank. I'm digging into something right now, and I get the feeling he wishes he was already in Florida. It bugs the hell out of me."

"Does it tie into Phillips? A cover-up?"

I shook my head. "Nothing quite so glamorous, although Stan Katz will probably start along those lines soon. I think maybe it's what they used to call OTJR—On The Job Retirement. Frank doesn't want to get dirty this close to the end. He has a nice clean record and a clear conscience. I can't blame him, but it's sad to see. I just hope to hell it never happens to me."

"What is it?"

I hesitated to tell her. "Your selectman hat could get us all into some trouble here."

"I'm not wearing it."

"You might start." She looked at me silently.

"It *is* connected to Phillips. What have you heard so far?"

"Just what's been in the newspaper. Some of the screamers on the board have been making a few phone calls, trying to get information."

"Mrs. Morse?"

"She's convinced you tell me everything."

"Don't I?"

"You're not now."

It was silly to hedge with her. I didn't tell her everything, but what I did she always treated confidentially—always had and always would. That was the nature of the woman.

"I'm digging into the Kimberly Harris murder."

"Wow. We're not talking parking meters here, are we? No wonder Frank's nervous. You mean this shooting's tied in to the Harris case?"

I hesitated a moment. Maybe Frank had a good point. This whole thing was a can of worms just waiting to be opened. She shoved me with her toe. "My lips are sealed."

I took her at her word. "Someone in a ski mask has been setting up ex-members of that jury—five so far. I think to force us to reopen the investigation."

"Bill Davis's jury?"

"Right. Reitz and Phillips were on it. Since them, three others have been snared, none as permanently. Just last night a girl was molested by a masked man and led to believe he was someone who served with her on that jury."

"All in two days. He doesn't waste time."

"No, he doesn't. And he may have a valid point."

She raised her eyebrows.

"I spent almost the whole day reading the trial transcripts and all the rest—years' worth of legal back and forth. It was kind of weird. Perry Mason always got his man in half an hour. These guys took two years and didn't come up with anything more than what they started with. If I'd have been Bill Davis, I would have been a basket case by the end of it. I mean, they pulled stunts like taking eight months to process the paperwork before the defense could get an appeal heard—it dragged on forever."

"But wasn't Davis guilty?"

"He was found guilty. We had a full plate of evidence against him, and the prosecution fed it to the jury one spoonful at a time—blonde, beautiful, young, pregnant girl found tied down and raped on her bed. The stuff of Hollywood dreams. Dunn played with the fantasy, building it up, filling in all the details. The struggle, the ripped clothes, the rope around the wrists and ankles, one final burst of resistance with a lamp and fingernails, then the rape, the semen in the mouth, the strangulation. It was a real performance."

"But essentially true, or not?"

I couldn't answer that. The question wasn't relevant. What had occurred in that courtroom in the quaint county seat of Newfane hadn't happened in a vacuum. Outside, in the street, in the bars, in the chance encounters of friends, the murmurs had floated—of outrage, of revenge, of racism. The supposed violent meeting between one of their own and a black flatlander junkie had stirred up a long-denied Yankee prejudice that rose slowly like a bubble in a tar pit.

"I remember at the time hearing that racist jokes were being kicked around between some of the jurors and the bailiff. It was hardly the most impartial of surroundings."

I leaned forward and picked up my mug. The cocoa was cool now. "I'll give Davis this much. He took it on the chin. Without saying a word, he told us all to take a long walk off a short pier."

"So do you think he was guilty or not?" she asked again.

"As far as I know, he's as guilty as he's always been."

"Then why are you digging into all this? The publicity's already pretty hot without it."

I rubbed my eyes with the palms of my hands. Why indeed. "Because I think things are going to force me to change my mind."

8

I parked outside my home about ten that night. Gail wanted an early start the next morning. I spent the night with her every once in a while, usually on weekends or days when we didn't have to tear off to some job at the crack of dawn. We were both old enough now that we wanted our time together rounded out and comfortable, including a good night's sleep and a casual, stretched out breakfast. That hadn't stopped us from making love on the couch before dinner tonight, but we hadn't seen each other in a while.

Happier and whole again, I felt a little silly remembering the tape I'd placed across the apartment door that morning. It was something I'd seen James Bond do some twenty years earlier in a movie—a way for him to detect intruders while he was away. Of course he had used a hair, but I didn't have enough left to start plastering them across doorways.

Why I had done it was another matter. The Plymouth Duster had definitely unsettled me, and the appearance of the masked avenger— or whatever he was—had hardly helped. Putting tape on the door had been an impulse but one that had made me feel a bit more in control, as if proving to the Plymouth's driver that he wasn't the only one taking notes.

But whatever confidence it had gained me quickly vanished. As I reached the top of the stairs, I could clearly see the tape was broken. I stood there for a moment, uncertain of what to do. Outside some stranger's apartment, a similar setup was easy to deal with. You pulled a gun, organized your troops, knocked politely, and, if necessary, had the door broken down. It was scary but routine—at least on paper. This was not routine.

I stepped out of the way of the door, slipped my key in as quietly as possible, pulled my gun, and turned the lock. The door opened with a loud click. I waited a bit, breathing hard through my mouth. I felt terribly hot. I pushed the door wide open, still from around the corner, and listened, cataloguing each sound—the clock, the heating pipes, the hum of the refrigerator—until I could hear no more. Only then did I step cautiously across the threshold and into the semidarkness.

It took me fifteen nervous minutes to find out the apartment was empty. I went through it twice, increasingly angry that my own house had become a place of menace on the strength of one half-seen Plymouth Duster and a torn piece of Scotch tape. I was angry that the place had been invaded and all my things picked over, and I was angry that I might be inventing the whole goddamned thing to begin with—torn tape notwithstanding.

Finally, and I suppose fundamentally, what bothered me most was that basic elements in my life were being disturbed, some by the simple pressures of time, like Murphy's retirement, and others by a more malevolent force. I didn't like it, and I didn't like how they were all mixing together, forcing everyday events to assume ominous proportions. Having to put tape on the door was bad enough; finding it broken and stalking through my own apartment with a gun was downright disturbing. I wanted to be tightly focused as I began this investigation, but it wasn't happening. Whether it was Murphy's timidity or something subliminal I'd gotten from reading those transcripts, I was beginning to feel out of sorts.

The telephone rang and I picked it up in the darkness. I listened without speaking.

"Joe?" The voice was unfamiliar.

"Yes."

The line went dead, but I paused with the receiver halfway back to the cradle. I remembered that when I'd answered, it had been wrong end around. That, for a man living alone, was a sign of things amiss.

I unscrewed the mouthpiece and poured its contents on the desk. A small silver disc rolled into a corner and shimmied to a stop. It glistened brightly in the glow of the streetlights outside. I turned on my desk lamp and slipped a piece of notepaper under the bug. On television these things were as common as lifesavers—even flat broke private eyes had them. But this was a first for me. The listening devices we used belonged to the state police and were far less fancy, with wires and battery packs. This, I thought as I poured it into an envelope, was in a whole different league.

Murphy looked up over his reading glasses. "What's up?"

"This." I crossed his office and dropped the bug on the report between his hands.

He didn't touch it but bent over carefully and peered at it. "That's pretty neat. Where'd you get it?"

"You can pick it up. It's been dusted. I got it out of my phone."

He scowled and pinched it between his thumb and forefinger as if expecting it to sting. "When?"

"Last night. When I got home. I noticed some tape I'd put across the door was broken. That thing was all I found. I searched the rest of the apartment, but I'd need equipment to do a proper job."

He rolled it in his palm. "I saw something like this at that FBI course I took a few years ago. It had a range of about a city block." He let a few seconds pass before adding, "Do you always put tape across your door?"

"No."

He put down the bug and leaned back in his chair. "Why now?"

"I thought I was being followed."

He rubbed his eyes and refocused on a favorite spot on the wall near the ceiling. "Who by?"

"A green Plymouth Duster. No plate and no ID on the driver."

"And you're sure about this?"

"Nope."

That brought his eyes off the wall. "Nope?"

I shrugged and pointed my chin at the bug.

"What other case are you working on?"

"Small stuff. A burglary, a vandalism—nothing that would tie in. Do you have any friends at the FBI that could take a look at that thing? J.P. says it's way over his head."

"Yeah, I think I might. You sure it's worth it?"

"So far, we've got one killing, one sexual assault, one policeman mugged, and one maniac running around with a ski mask. You decide."

He allowed a half smile. "All right, I'll Express Mail the little bastard." He stopped and squinted at it again. "I wonder if it's still working?"

I raised my eyebrows and turned to go. He stopped me. "Hold it." He dropped the bug into his drawer and slammed it shut. "Where are you off to?"

"Woodstock. I thought I'd go have a chat with Davis."

"That's a hell of a distance for a chat."

"I'm hoping for a hell of a chat."

Bill Davis had changed a lot in three years. At the jail, he'd been a study in restrained frustration—a man whose consistent claims of innocence had been, in the public's eyes, undermined by icy self-control. At his sentencing, standing straight and silent, he had merely shaken his head, incredulous at the stupidity of all those around him.

Now, in the low-ceilinged visitors' room at Woodstock, the silence was still there, but it floated on bitterness and defeat. He sat opposite me, his arms crossed, staring at the table between us, as far away from this room as his mind could possibly take him. I imagined his years of isolation had made him an expert.

"My name is Gunther. I'm with the Brattleboro Police Department." He continued staring at the table. "I wanted to ask you some questions." Still nothing.

"I've been spending the last couple of days reading over your case, but I haven't been able to come up with much."

A small crease appeared between his eyes. He glanced up at me. "About what?"

"About why you are where you are."

He smiled gently and gave that familiar shake of the head—a glimpse from long ago. "You people."

"I'm thinking of reopening the case."

"You killing time?"

I wondered if I should tell him about Ski Mask but decided against it. "How much of the evidence found against you was planted?"

One eyebrow lifted. "What's your problem?"

"Like I said, I've been going over the case. It feels wrong. I thought you might help me."

"What for?"

"Right now? To kill time."

The smile again. "I know how to do that."

"I thought you might. So how much was planted?"

"All of it."

"What really happened?"

"Sweet Jesus. If you don't know that by now, you do need help."

"So you've got nothing to add? Nothing you've thought of since the trial?"

He shook his head.

"You were about to go into your apartment, heard someone call your name from around the corner, went to investigate, and got knocked on the back of the head, and that's all?"

62

"That's it."

"What had you been doing before coming home? It was late, wasn't it?"

"You know it was. I was out drinking."

"At Mort's B & G? Like every night?"

"Uh-huh."

"A couple of beers, a few hours of the bar TV, then home?"

"Right."

"No dope?"

"No dope."

"But you woke up with heroin in your veins."

"That's right."

"How did you know that?"

"I didn't. They told me. I just knew I was high."

"Had you ever taken heroin before?"

"Don't all us niggers?"

"Had you?"

"No."

"What about Kimberly Harris? Were you two friendly?"

This time he positively grinned. "That's the biggie, isn't it? Did you ever see a black chick you wanted to lay?"

"No."

"Well, I've never seen a white chick that interested me neither. Believe it or not, a black man's idea of dying and going to heaven has nothing to do with any white piece of ass."

"I just asked if you were friendly."

"Bullshit."

"Maybe. Did you talk at all?"

"Sure we talked. She spent damn near every day lying around that pool. Said she wanted a tan like mine. Real funny."

"No job?"

"Not that I could tell."

"Did she have any friends?"

"We talked, man. That means the weather, ball games, stuff like that—not her love life."

"I didn't mean that. Any comings or goings at all?"

"I barely knew her. Ask Boyers—he's the man with the eye for detail."

"Boyers?"

"The manager."

"He really watched the door, did he?"

Again Davis laughed. "Doors aren't his thing—more like windows. He is white, though; I guess he's allowed."

"You saw him doing that?"

"Sure. I tend to blend in at night."

"Did he do anything else?"

"Not that I saw."

"Could he have killed Harris?"

"You thought I did."

Good point. "Do you know where he was when you were knocked out?"

"No. His lights were on, but that might have been anything."

"What about someone who might have had it in for you? Had you crossed anyone?"

He leaned forward, his face transformed by anger. "I was fresh off the goddamned bus, man...the only black face in that whole honky town. I came up here to get away from all that shit—the ghetto, the Vietnam stuff. I swallowed all that Vermont, home of the Underground Railroad crap—hook, line, and sinker. But a cracker here's like a cracker anywhere else. You dudes know what a nigger is just like they do in Georgia or Alabama or anywhere else. Hell yes, I crossed someone. As soon as I hit town, I crossed every man, woman, and child what saw me."

He stood up, overturning his chair, and walked away.

I returned through the gates and locked doors, past the listless guards, and slowly traded the jail's gray embrace for the gentle blur of falling snow. I knew he'd overstated his case—he had good reason. But I couldn't shake the feeling that his basic argument was probably right on the mark.

The chief medical examiner's office for the state of Vermont is located in Burlington on the second floor of a renovated residential building on Colchester Avenue. The first floor is occupied by a local dentist. I arrived at the unmarked side door—a concession, no doubt, to the more pessimistic of the dentist's clients—near the middle of the afternoon, having spent the previous three hours on the interstate from Woodstock. The snow had continued to fall all day, and what little traffic there was had been gradually reduced to using the right lane only. The sole plow truck I'd seen was going in the other direction.

The ME was not in. This was her week on duty, and she pretty much hung her hat at the Medical Center all day. Her secretary suggested I speak with the assistant, who was also not in, having had an emergency call from home, but who might be back later. When I asked whether I could see the ME anyway, wherever she might be, I was informed that was impossible—her schedule indicated she was in the middle of an autopsy at the very moment. I thanked the secretary and left the building.

The drive to the Medical Center took five minutes; locating the morgue took fifteen. I finally found it in the basement, behind several signs warning against unauthorized personnel, on the other side of a door pasted with an oversized dancing Snoopy. I wondered who was responsible for the curious mix of messages.

The room I entered had two large gleaming steel tables surrounded by arcane and expensive-looking equipment on wheels, all lit by a single globe mounted in the center of the ceiling. A scene to warm Dr. Frankenstein's heart. A small man dressed in green and wearing a transparent rubber apron appeared at another door. I checked in vain for a hump.

"Looking for someone?"

"Dr. Hillstrom."

"She's in there. I'll be right back." Igor crossed the room and disappeared down a hallway, leaving me to pick my way carefully through a tangle of dimly lit cables and stray chairs to the door he had indicated. I pushed it open and walked in.

It was a smaller version of what I'd just left: one table, half the equipment. It was also well lit and occupied by one tall, angular blonde woman dressed in green and one enormously fat dead woman lying naked face up on the table. "Are you from the police?"

"Yes," I answered, surprised. I hadn't realized her secretary was that efficient.

"I'm Dr. Hillstrom." She reached over to a counter behind her and picked up a clipboard. "Could I have your name? State law requires I note everyone attending an autopsy."

"Joe Gunther."

"Rank?"

"Lieutenant."

"Rutland Police Department."

"No, Brattleboro."

She stopped writing and looked up. "What?"

"Brattleboro."

She glanced at the clipboard and then back to me. "Are you on some kind of exchange program or something?"

There was a sound behind me. A nervous young man with a wispy, struggling mustache slid into the room. "Who are you?" Hillstrom demanded.

"Sorry I'm late. I'm John Evans. I'm supposed to collect some stuff on the autopsy..." He reached into his coat pocket and pulled out a notebook. "A Mrs. Ricci?"

"Then you're from Rutland."

Evans nodded and repeated. "Sorry I'm late. I couldn't find a parking space.

Hillstrom stared at me. "Perhaps this gentleman took it."

I let out a small sigh and smiled. "I think we've started out on the wrong foot."

"If you leave right now, we haven't started out at all."

"I was hoping I could talk with you."

"About what?"

"The autopsy on Kimberly Harris. It was a case you handled . . ."

"I remember it—three years ago. Did we have a meeting scheduled that I've forgotten or something? This doesn't ring the slightest bell."

"I'm afraid it wouldn't; I drove into town unannounced. Your secretary mentioned you were here and your assistant wasn't at the office, so I took a chance."

Igor walked into the room with two shiny steel slats and stood by the table. Hillstrom nodded to him. "I'll be right with you, Harry. A chance at what, Mr. Gunther? That we could have a little chat over a lukewarm corpse? I don't just carve these people up like Thanksgiving turkeys."

I opened my mouth to speak, but she lifted her gloved hand to silence me. There was a moment of quiet in the room as she briefly closed her eyes. When she spoke again, eyes open, the edge was gone from her voice. "I apologize; that was short-tempered. I take it you are in a bit of a rush to have this conversation, is that right?"

Assuming that if Ski Mask didn't sense some action on our part soon, he'd feel obliged to stimulate us once again, and perhaps as fatally as he had with Jamie Phillips, I was hard put to argue. "I'm afraid time is a little tight. I didn't mean to be this much of a nuisance."

"You're not—so far. It's been a long day." She turned an icy gaze onto the young cop from Rutland. "Filled with delays."

"I'm sorry," he said for the third time.

She took a deep breath. "All right. Let's start over. I'm Hillstrom; this is Evans, Gunther, and this is Harry Bergen. Let's all hope I'm about to open up Mrs. Emma Ricci, sixty-three, the victim of a pedestrian-auto mishap having occurred in Rutland at 6:30 P.M. yesterday. Is that right, Mr. Evans? What's your rank, by the way?"

"Corporal, ma'am."

"All right, Corporal; now, you're here for a blood sample, some photographs, and cause of death, correct?"

"Yes, ma'am."

" 'Doctor' will do fine. Good. Well then, as I determine potential causes of death—and there will be several judging from her appearance—I'll let you know and you can take your photos. Harry will be doing some of that himself for our files. Lieutenant Gunther, I'll be happy to talk with you after this is over. If you'd like to attend, be my guest. Have either one of you attended an autopsy before?"

"No ma'am—Doctor."

I nodded. We didn't have to do it often, and when we did, it was usually a case just like this one, involving a car.

"Well, if you get dizzy or worse, let us know so we can help you out. There's nothing disgraceful about having normal human reactions to all this. Ready, everyone?"

We both nodded like schoolchildren and watched her and Harry Bergen get to work. Harry had the gentle touch of a caring mother—more than Dr. Hillstrom—smoothing Mrs. Ricci's hair and occasionally resting his hand on her lightly as if to lend some little comfort. I felt that if any of Mrs. Ricci's relatives had been here, their horror might have been blunted by his touch.

I had stood over quite a few dead bodies in my time, considering it covered both the Korean War and some thirty years as a cop. Most of them had been in context, from shell holes and blasted trees to twisted auto wrecks and smashed living rooms. Autopsies were different. The bodies were stripped, both of clothes and environment. They were laid out, cold, white, and flat on their backs, and they were dissected, just like frogs in a classroom. In many ways, an autopsy for me was the careful disassembling of a complex machine, piece by piece. I will admit, though, that I kept this side of me private. People tended to get twitchy around other people who enjoy autopsies.

Hillstrom and Bergen struggled to roll Mrs. Ricci onto her side so they could fit the two slats beneath her. That done, she lay somewhat suspended above the surface of the table, allowing a gentle stream of water to course under her, carrying away whatever fluid she might give up.

She was an enormous woman, gray-haired, lightly mustached, with heavy, unpleasant features. She reminded me of those discontented travelers I'd seen on buses or trains, their sleeping faces reflecting all the inert unhappiness of their lives. I also noticed, for no reason whatever, that she had incredibly unattractive toenails, yellow and gnarled in contrast to her pasty-white rubber-like skin.

Hillstrom picked up a scalpel and quickly made a long curved incision from shoulder to shoulder. She then intersected the slit just below the throat and cut a straight line between the breasts down to the groin, creating a slightly rounded T.

"Were you the officer at the scene, Corporal?" Hillstrom asked without looking up.

Evans, his eyes glued to the scalpel, swallowed hard. "Yes."

"Could you give us the circumstances?" She buried her hand into the cut near the breast and pulled the thick outer layer of skin away from the body, cutting the few small pieces of tissue that still connected the two as she went and revealing the lungs underneath. The large flap in her hand consisted of two to three solid inches of bright yellow, glistening fat. A cloying, nauseous odor filled the room.

I could hear Evans's breath coming in short and rapid gulps. "She was, ah, crossing the street...legally. You know, a crosswalk. Car should have stopped..."

"Why don't you have a seat? No point standing around getting sore feet."

"Okay." Evans gratefully took a seat and leaned forward, his elbows propped on his knees, the perfect image of studied casualness.

"You might also want to get your camera gear ready." She motioned to Harry, who picked up Evans's camera bag and placed it on the floor between his feet. Evans bent further forward to unzip it and rummaged among its contents.

"Was the driver intoxicated?"

"Yes, ma'am." His voice was distinctly clearer. "She became hysterical at the time of the accident, so we haven't been able to question her yet."

Having folded both breasts back under the body's arms, Hillstrom started examining and removing the organs, as carefully as she might have unpacked a duffel bag filled with china. The odor was absorbed by the ventilating system.

"You might want a shot of this."

Evans, steady once more, slowly approached the table, camera in hand.

"She's suffered a punctured aorta, in itself enough to cause death, although possibly not the primary cause here; and right behind you can see where her spine is broken. I can get you a clearer view of that later." Hillstrom placed her pale hand behind the aorta to give the picture more contrast. Evans focused and shot.

"You might want to add, by the way, that so far we also have a punctured lung, several broken ribs, a ripped diaphragm, and an entire pelvic area that looks shattered beyond belief. Also a perforated bowel. Did she go under the car, do you know?"

"I don't know. We found her with her head resting on the curb in front of the car."

"Yes, I noticed that." She moved to the body's right side and slipped her finger deep into a hole hidden in the hair above the ear. "Your primary cause may be lurking under here."

Evans sat down.

The autopsy continued for another hour and a half, during which Harry retrieved vitreous fluid from the body's eyeballs with a syringe, and Hillstrom cut around the back of Mrs. Ricci's head, peeled her forehead down over her nose like a rubber mask, and revealed the naked skull. She used a hand-held vibrator saw to remove the top half of the cranium and established that a broken brain stem had been the elusive primary cause of death. Both events sent Evans back to his chair.

Hillstrom's prowess at this was impressive. She cut, sawed, and sliced with absolute grace, never nicking a wrong part, never hesitating once she'd started. It made me realize that, had Mrs. Ricci been alive, she could have done a lot worse than to pull this doctor for an operation.

We ended up, the two of us, off by a side counter where Hillstrom did her organ dissections. She was cutting thin slices of lung and studying them under the bright light. She held up a large piece of tissue. "See how the furrows are ingrained with black? That's pollution. You don't find it in country people; you get a ton of it in New Yorkers and the like. I'd guess she lived around Rutland, or a similar-sized city, all her life." She looked up from her work at the others in the room, now out of earshot. "So, what about Kimberly Harris?"

"I just have some questions about your findings."

"Think I messed up, huh?" The question was put with perfect neutrality, but I decided I wouldn't run the risk. Things had started out badly enough.

"No, I think I came here at the wrong time, without an appointment, and said all the wrong things. Will you let me get my foot out of my mouth?"

She looked at me for a moment and smiled slightly, as if letting me halfway off the hook. "What would you like to know?"

"At the trial, you testified to the presence of sperm on the body..."

"Semen."

"Right. Is there anything else you can tell from that?"

"Like blood type? I did."

"No, I mean anything else—like race or if the man was taking medicine or had a cold."

"Are you asking if I did or if I could?"

"Both, I guess."

"I didn't and I might. I couldn't tell if he had a cold." She stood up and took off her gloves. Harry began gathering up the organs and placing them into a large plastic bag, which he packed in the body's empty cavity before sewing it up.

"But you didn't do any of that?" I followed her across the room where she filled out some forms stuck to her clipboard.

"No. It's usually not required in those cases, especially the quote-unquote open-and-shut ones like Harris, which I gather from your presence has undergone a change of status."

"No, no. It's still officially closed. I'm a bit of a Lone Ranger on this."

She stopped writing and genuinely smiled at me for the first time. "Really? You trying to reopen the case on your own?"

"Sort of. Things have happened that have made me curious."

She nodded. "I'm glad."

That got me. "You are?"

"Yes. You want to follow me back to my office? My records are there, and I'm finished for the day. I also have some very good hot cocoa on hand."

"That would be hard to turn down."

"Then don't."

9

She drove a dark blue Mercedes with license plates marked "QNCY."
As we drove along a snow-blurred, Christmas-card-pretty Colchester
Avenue in the darkening cold air, I had to admit that while I enjoyed
the occasional autopsy, I wouldn't make them a habit. For all their
incredibly vicious, stupid, venal and self-centered moments, I still pre-
ferred my fellow humans alive.

Her office was small, warm, and friendly, decorated with childish
drawings and family pictures taken at the beach and on a mountain
top. It was also cluttered with hundreds of books, magazines, and
mysterious black-bound volumes that were parked neatly on every
available surface. In many ways, it reminded me of movies I'd seen
featuring the favorite professor's hideaway study. Classical music
drifted from some hidden radio behind her desk.

She served the cocoa from a machine parked on the window ledge
and handed me a cup. In the midst of her own cozy environment,
immune from the swirling dark snow outside and all it hid, her earlier
tenseness slid away. She raised her cup in a toast. "Truce?"

I toasted back. "Gratefully."

"I'd like you to know that I am not an I-do-my-job-and-you-do-
yours bureaucrat. When a case reaches me, most of the emotion has
been drained from it; I see its background on a printed report, I usu-al-
ly never meet the principals involved, and in ninety-nine cases out of a
hundred, I've never even heard of the individual I'm working on.

I have to fall back on procedure: I do what is required by law and
what is additionally asked of me by the appropriate authorities. I am
a middleman who does her utmost to steer clear of other people's
squabbles. I followed that precept in the Kimberly Harris case, but I
will admit here and now that I wasn't fond of the way things turned
out."

"Why not?"

"Human beings are sloppy creatures—nothing about them is perfect, either inside or out-and it is most often their imperfections that help us see what makes them tick. Kimberly Harris's body fit that category just fine; the circumstances that put her body in my autopsy room did not—they were nice and clear and tidy."

"So you think Bill Davis was framed."

"If I did, I would have said so. What I think is that I'm happy someone is sniffing around this case again."

I had to smile. I had never felt so suddenly in the presence of a kindred spirit. "What kind of information can you get from a semen sample, given the chance and a blank check?"

"A lot, with time, money, and the proper training and equipment, none of which I have. Realistically, if you're as alone as you say you are, you're not going to get any more than what I already supplied."

She got up and left the room, returning a couple of minutes later with an open file. "The semen was spermatic, although the sperm count was a little low—nothing exceptional there. We were lucky we even got a blood type. If the depositor had been a nonsecretor, we would have been up a tree."

"A nonsecretor?"

"A secretor is somebody whose blood type appears in his or her body fluids as well as in the blood itself—handy if all you've got is a sweaty shirt or, as in this case, semen. A nonsecretor's blood type can only be ascertained through the blood."

I opened my mouth, but she cut me off. "Davis is also a secretor, if that's what you were going to ask, and he is group O, which you probably knew. That part is especially unfortunate for him."

"How so?"

"Let me give you a fast course in blood grouping. All secretors make a blood substance called 'H' in addition to whatever else they make. For example, type A secretors make A and H; type Bs make B and H; type ABs make AB and H. Type Os only make H. When we tested the semen, it came up H—period. What's unfortunate for Davis is that forty-three percent or more of the entire population is of that type. It makes him an easy target—kind of like saying, 'he's guilty because he's a man,' if you get my drift. That, needless to say, was a subtlety lost on the jury." She put the file on the desk and sat down.

"You said a lot more could be gotten out of this."

"Yes, but not by me. Staying with blood grouping for a while longer, they've been able to break down those broad categories through something called PGM typing, or enzyme typing, and even PGM subtyping, as well as other methods I don't even know about. Well, I've heard about them, but I don't know the details. In any case, the result is that each stage of typing makes the tested sample more specific to one individual. So, if you compare Davis's sample to the semen and go down the line, the first difference in typing lets your man off the hook. Of course, it's not going to give you the real depositor of the semen, but it might help an innocent person."

I caught the first glimmer of a chance to take control of this case. "What about the fetus?"

She shrugged. "There again, we did a blood grouping on it. It wasn't Davis's, but that didn't help him much. I had to admit in court that it's unfortunately not rare to find a young unmarried pregnant girl in our society. I might have added that it's also not unheard of to find a third person's semen involved in a two-person rape case—she may have had relations with someone prior to being raped by someone else."

"Are you suggesting that?"

"Not exactly, although there might have been several people involved—a depositor and a killer and even the father. Another possibility is that the semen was carried to the site and placed by hand, explaining why it wasn't found in the vagina but only the mouth and pubic hair."

She smiled, presumably at the crease in my forehead, which had to be there by now. "There's something else, too. While I was doing my investigation prior to the trial, I spoke with the hospital staff that treated Davis's head wound. They described it as a serious trauma, one likely to have rendered most men unconscious. Of course, he may have a hard head.

"But the lamp brings me back to the 'too-nice-and-neat' problem I mentioned earlier. Harris was found tied down with one hand free. From her torn nails and Davis's cheek, the assumption was that she got that hand loose, hit him with the lamp, scratched him—or vice versa—and then was strangled. Now I can theoretically swallow one or the other—the scratching or the lamp—but not both. Had she gotten away with one, her assailant surely wouldn't have let her do the other. It's almost as if somebody planted one piece of incriminating evidence too many. Makes you wonder, huh?"

"Makes me wonder why you're not doing what I do for a living."

"Well, I am, aren't I?" She laughed. "Actually, the truth is I see every homicide in this state, year after year. That only comes to about twenty or so on the average—about what New York racks up in a day—but it still makes me the resident expert. I've seen a lot more than you have—in that area at least."

"Okay. All this leaves one final question—a pretty big one. Do you still have the samples?"

She let out a conspiratorial laugh. "You're a lucky man. I always keep my own slides, but usually the samples get dumped after two years. This time I held on to them, including the fetus."

"Why?"

"I don't know—intuition."

"You're right—lucky me." I stood up. "This has been a big help, really. By the way, since you can't do those tests you told me about, who can?"

She quickly scribbled a name on a sheet of paper and handed it to me. "Bob Kees, University of West Haven—that's just outside New Haven. All this is his specialty. Whenever I get stumped, I call on him. So does everyone else, I might add, so any work out of there will take time—but it'll be worth it."

"How does he handle his fees?"

She looked at me quizzically. "Why?"

"My captain's the only one who knows I'm on this. If vouchers start appearing with Harris's name all over them, I'll be up the proverbial creek."

"Politics?"

"You got it."

"Don't worry about it. In situations like this, Bob usually waives his fee, and I'll make sure he does this time."

"How about getting the stuff to him?"

"No problem there either. It all fits into a small picnic cooler, and I can get the state police to act as couriers if time is a problem. They'll go from door to door, within the state at least, and you can take it from there. I can code it so no one knows what's inside. Your only problem should be letting me know when to start things rolling. In the meantime, I'll gather it all together in one spot so as not to slow things up when the time comes."

She got up and shook my hand. "Happy hunting."

"I have to admit, when we met I never dreamed it would end this way."

"You're a hard man to say no to."

This time, the tape on the door was intact. Still, I checked the rooms and closets—and phones—to see if I could sense anyone having come by. At the end of my search I gave an obligatory glance down into the street. The Plymouth was back, just visible by the street lamp's blurred light.

"You son of a bitch," I muttered, and headed for the door. It was still snowing, though just barely at last, and the ground was covered by a good ten to twelve inches. I stepped onto the unshoveled sidewalk and walked rapidly north, away from High Street and the Plymouth. I heard the muffled sound of a car door slamming—whoever this clown was, discretion wasn't his strength. At the first left, a narrow, cluttered back street that twisted steeply up to join Chestnut Hill, I climbed as quickly as I could, fighting to keep my footing. At the point where the street curves left, I stopped and ducked behind a parked van.

I waited a full minute and a half, hearing all the while my follower's labored progress up the slippery hill. Obviously he didn't have the proper footwear because several times he resorted to pulling himself along on parked cars, garbage bins, and the occasional spindly sapling. I began to wonder why he was even bothering; had I been anything short of an elephant riding a wheelchair, I would have been long gone. But he was nothing if not persistent; by the time he finally reached the van, he was breathing hard and quietly swearing nonstop.

I stood very still, resting against the back of the van, facing the street, where my pursuer had gone for firmer footing. As he came abreast of the rear bumper, I swung my leg out with full force and caught him across both shins. His feet flew out from under him and he landed face first in the street with a dull thump.

I stepped on the nape of his neck and pushed my gun barrel into his ear. "Put your hands behind your back."

Both snowy hands appeared. I snapped my handcuffs onto them. "Roll over."

He did as he was told. I looked at him in the dim light; his face was covered with soft powdery snow which he was trying to blink from his eyes. His nose was bleeding. "What's your name?"

"Robert Smith."

"Nice try."

"Really—I'm a private investigator. I have a license inside my coat. Top left."

I opened the coat, found a wallet with the license, along with a revolver clipped to his belt. Robert Smith came from Burlington. "You want to tell me what's going on?"

"I was hired to follow you." He was sniffing the blood up his nose and trying not to choke.

"I don't want to play question-and-answer here. Tell me what I want to know."

"Can I get up? It's cold."

"Of course it's cold—it's January. Talk to me."

"I was hired to follow you at night. Once you get to your office every morning, I'm supposed to let you go. I'm told by phone when and where to pick you up each night."

"How?"

"This guy rented an answering service—he leaves messages for me, I leave messages for him."

"How do you get paid?"

"By mail—cash."

"This guy has no name, of course."

"Mr. Jones."

"Cute—Smith and Jones. How did he contact you first?"

"He called my office in Burlington."

"What did he sound like?"

"Average. No accent. Not a high voice or a low one—nothing unusual."

"Did you bug my place?"

"No."

I rapped him on the forehead with my knuckles. He let out a cry of surprise and pain. "I didn't, goddamn it. I didn't even know it was bugged. I just followed you and gave my reports—that's all."

I jerked him to his feet by the collar. "All right. Come with me."

"Where are we going?"

"To make a phone call."

I dragged him down to the public phone booth outside Dunkin' Donuts and made him call the answering service. He left a message that he'd seen me put a suitcase in the trunk of my car, as if preparing for an early morning departure. Did Mr. Jones want him to follow me if I left town, or would somebody else take over? It wasn't much, I'll admit, but I felt I had to put Smith to some use before I let him go.

We stood by that phone for forty-five minutes, feeling the cold creep up our bodies like freezing water in a bathtub. I was better dressed for it than Smith, but even I was starting to hurt. I had decided on a public phone on the off chance that someone else might be watching the apartment, but I was beginning to think that frostbite might be too high a price for discretion.

When the phone finally rang, Smith could barely hold the receiver. "This is Bob Smith," he chattered. He listened for a moment and hung up. "I'll be damned."

"What did he say?"

"He left a message. I'm fired and we're both supposed to get out of the cold. Thanks a lot."

I handed him his gun and wallet and walked away without saying a word.

I was asleep in bed. That much I knew for sure—I remembered turning the electric blanket on high to thaw the chill out of my bones. But I was also having a dream unlike any I'd ever had before. It was a sound dream, with no pictures, and just one voice.

The voice was just as Bob Smith had described it: not high, not low—average. It didn't have a detectable accent, either, which made me think of somebody else's description of it—John Woll's. I'd been scornful then—as if all bad guys had accents—but now I thought maybe there was something to that. Maybe the man was a foreigner faking a non-accent, or an actor pretending to be a foreigner faking a non-accent. All of a sudden, I became convinced that the solution to this whole thing lay in the absence of the accent. Of course…that was it; it had been in front of my eyes all along. Or at least my ears.

My ears, in fact, were beginning to hurt. It was the voice, of course, yelling. I opened my eyes.

Black against black; it was hard to see, and it was all spinning slightly. I could make out a head, or something like a head, with pale holes where the eyes normally were. And there was an enormous white hand near the head, moving quickly back and forth, making slapping sounds to which I was keeping rhythm with my head. In fact, the head with the pale eyes wasn't moving—my head was. And the hand was slapping me. That was it; I was almost sure. But I didn't feel anything.

The voice stopped and things suddenly tilted. I felt my bed shift under me and slide away, leaving me to thump on the floor. The softly lit ceiling moved before my eyes. I saw the top of my bedroom door go past, then my living room ceiling. It was almost like being dragged along the floor, except I couldn't feel the floor.

Abruptly, it got colder. I saw the ceiling of the landing outside my apartment door. Somebody grabbed my collar and propped me up against a wall; there was that head again in front of my eyes, looking just like an animated ski mask.

"Can you hear me, Joe?"

I noticed the eye holes of the mask had pretty red stitching all around them—nice touch. "Nod if you hear me."

I could do that, if that's all he wanted. Things bobbed in front of me a couple of times, and I felt slightly nauseous. Had I nodded?

"Good." All right. I guess I had. "Look at me."

I've been doing that. I even complimented your mask.

"They tried to gas you, Joe. They tried to kill you. It would have looked like an accident or something. Do you understand?"

Sure, I guess. "Do you?"

He wanted another nod, but that hadn't felt too good. I grunted. "Is that a yes or a no?"

Oh, for Christ's sake. I nodded again and swallowed hard. "They want you dead, but they don't want it to look like murder. They don't want to draw attention to the Harris murder. The Harris murder is the key, Joe; you're right about that. Stop chasing down blind alleys. We've brought them out into the open, you and me, so keep the heat on."

He shook me violently—that felt just great. "But remember: they'll try to make something normal turn against you, like your stove or your car, to make it look accidental. Remember that. Do you understand?"

I tried to grunt again. This time he bought it. In fact, he disappeared. I went back to sleep.

I woke up at dawn, shivering in the cold, wondering if I'd just collapsed at the foot of the public phone. I was still on the landing, dressed only in my pajamas, bathed in the dim red, blue, and yellow hue from the stained glass window over the stairwell. My neck ached from being propped up against the wall, but when I tried to move, the pain brought tears to my eyes.

Slowly, a living monument to mind over matter, I got to my feet and opened the apartment door. A freezing draft of air made me gasp and lurch toward the open windows. I slammed them shut, cringing at the noise. Then I locked and chained the door, relit the stove's pilot lights, and got back in bed.

As the blanket brought some feeling back to my body, I went over what had happened, and for the first time since Korea, the taste of real fear rose in my throat.

10

As soon as I thawed out and could stand without falling on my face, I swallowed half a bottle of aspirin and dialed the office.

"You sound like death warmed over," was Murphy's cheery greeting. "Where the hell are you?"

"At home. Did you get any reaction to that bug?"

"Not yet. How was Woodstock?"

"I'll tell you later. You haven't sent anyone back to where Kimberly Harris was murdered, have you?"

"Why would I?"

"Talk to the manager again, whatever residents date back that far; you know, whatever."

"That's your hot potato. I've got people all over town digging into every nook and cranny on the Reitz-Phillips thing. I'm not about to touch Harris too."

"Okay. I'll be in in an hour or so."

I left the apartment and headed north on the Putney Road to the Huntington Arms. It was a medium-sized rental complex of twenty units, forming a U on three sides of a too short, too shallow, empty swimming pool. The open end of the U was blocked by a ten-foot-high brick privacy fence.

It looked like all its clones across America: two stories, an out-door balcony running around the inside of the U on the second floor, rhythmically intercepted by metal staircases leading down, a tunnel-like entrance from the parking lot to the inner court. It was flat-roofed, red-bricked and generally looked like a motel, albeit a fairly good one. I knocked on the manager's door, the first left off the entranceway, and showed him my badge. "Are you Mr. Boyers?" My voice rattled around my head like a billiard ball.

He was a short, skinny man with glasses—the high-school nerd grown old. "What's up?"

"Is your name Boyers?"

"Yes." He seemed embarrassed by the fact.

"So you were the manager when Kimberly Harris was killed."

His mouth opened and shut a couple of times in astonishment. Whatever subtlety I'd used on others when mentioning the Harris case had been literally beaten out of me by now. All I wanted from this bird was some answers.

"Kimberly Harris?"

"You do remember the name."

"My God…Of course."

"Tell me about it."

"But that was years ago. I mean, they caught the guy."

"I'm aware of that. I'm cleaning up some paperwork."

"Paperwork? I thought you people were all working on that shooting."

"Most of us are. I will be too once you've helped me out a little here."

"This really is a little crazy, you know? What's left to be said?"

"Humor me, okay?"

He looked at me oddly, bobbed his head, and disappeared for a moment. He came back out pulling on an overcoat. It was bitterly cold, about ten degrees. The sky was pale blue and utterly cloudless, giving the white world around us the look of a dazzling, gigantic wedding cake. The brilliance burned straight to the back of my skull and made me feel slightly woozy.

"I can't believe my story isn't already in your files ten times over."

I didn't answer, despite a long opportunity, so he finally gave up with an exaggerated sigh. "The cab driver knocked on my door and said he wasn't getting any answer from Miss Harris's apartment. That had happened to me before. Usually people call several cabs and take the first one that comes. That way, they're sure of not being late. You know, the cabs around here are not famous for being on time."

"Go on." We were standing in the entrance tunnel, our hands in our pockets, our mouths and nostrils spewing vapor like chimneys. I wondered why he hadn't invited me in.

"Well, anyway, I didn't think that's what she was doing because she'd never done it before, you know, and she used cabs a lot. So I knew it had to be something else, like maybe she had forgotten or had changed her plans, or maybe was even in the shower."

"So you went to her door."

"Right. And I knocked and got no answer. That's when I noticed through the window that the place was a mess. I called you people first thing. I never even went inside, not until they took the body away a long time later. Even then, it was horrible. I threw up the first time I went in to clean up."

"Show me the apartment."

"Oh, I can't do that. It's rented."

"Is anyone there now?"

"No. She's at work."

"Then there's no harm done."

He looked at me anxiously, torn between caving in and telling me to take a hike. The conflict made him grumpy. "I don't know if this is right. Anyway, it's ridiculous."

"There's nothing wrong with it. If I was a prospective renter, you'd show me one of your apartments in a flash, wouldn't you?"

"This isn't the same."

I officiously looked at my watch, hoping to hell he wouldn't ask for a warrant. "You want to get the key, please?"

He reluctantly stepped back through his door and reappeared with a large key ring. "You'd think you people had better things to do."

I let him grumble. He led the way, stepping awkwardly through the snow he hadn't yet shoveled. We ended up at the door nearest the brick wall on the first floor.

"I hope you aren't going to stir this whole thing up again. The publicity last time almost cost me my job, and it took me months to rent this unit out."

"Don't worry. I'm just clearing up some details—pure paperwork."

He paused at the door. "You want in?"

"That was the idea." I pressed both palms against my eyes for a moment's relief from the light.

While he pounded on the door to make sure the place was empty, I looked around the corner at a narrow alleyway between the back of the building and the high brick wall. It was more of a slit, really, just a bit wider than the breadth of my shoulders, and barred at the far end by a tall chained gate. A glance across the courtyard showed the same layout for the opposite wing of the building.

I walked down the alleyway, which was fairly free of snow, to a small rectangular window mounted head-high on the wall. The manager appeared at the corner. "No one's home. I'd appreciate it if we could get this over quickly. I've got shoveling to do."

I nodded to him and cupped my hands around my face to ward off the sunlight as I peered through the window. I was looking straight into the bedroom and the bathroom beyond—a perfect view of the glass-walled shower stall.

"What are you doing, anyway?" Boyers's voice had a whine to it I was finding increasingly unattractive. I didn't answer him and retraced my steps to the apartment door.

Lightly scented warm air billowed out as he opened the door and ushered me in. He called, "Hello? Is anyone here?" and then closed the door behind us. The darkness was a pure blessing.

We were standing in a small living room, boxy but pleasant. Nice wall-to-wall, nice furniture, good paint job. There was a short hallway beyond, kitchen on one side, closets on the other. The bed and bathroom I'd seen from the window were at the back. It wasn't imaginative, but it was clean, tidy, and well maintained.

"Do you rent this furnished?"

"Yes."

"Did you when Harris lived here?"

"Yes, that's right."

"What did you charge her?"

"Let's see. I think it was two seventy-five a month, heat included. It was close to that anyway."

"And now?"

"Three twenty-five. Why, you interested?"

I ignored that. "Who rents it now?"

"A young lady."

I looked around the bedroom and picked up a framed photograph on the bedside table. A good-looking blonde girl in her twenties, arm-in-arm with some hunk with football on the brain. "Is this her?"

Boyers sidled up and peered around my shoulder. "That's right."

"Pretty."

"Oh, yes. Friendly, too."

"Did Harris pay her rent on time?"

"Every month like clockwork."

"How?"

"With a check. Vermont National."

"How do you think she was set financially? Well off? Scraping by?"

"Well, she wasn't scraping by, I know that. There are cheaper places to rent than this, and for most of her stay here, she didn't seem to have a job."

"What did she do with her spare time?"

"I don't know everything, of course. In fact, all I can say is that every time the sun came out, she was tanning by the pool. She had beautiful skin."

"What kind of swimsuit did she wear?"

He glanced at me, quickly and nervously. "Oh, I don't know. I guess it was a bikini."

"You don't know if it was a bikini?"

"Well, I imagine it was, if that's still what they call it."

"In other words, she didn't wear much of anything."

His face reddened. "It was a small suit."

"Tell me about Davis."

He straightened his back—safer ground. "That was a mistake."

"What was?"

"My hiring him. I felt sorry for him—a Vietnam vet down on his luck. He said he'd come here to get away from the stink of the city. Instead, he brought it with him."

"Where did he live?"

"Across the courtyard. It's the match of this apartment, in fact, on the ground floor, but it's an efficiency to allow for the laundry and utility rooms."

"Did you ever notice Harris and Davis having anything to do with one another?"

"No. They'd be out by the pool together on sunny days, but only when he was working out there. And of course there were usually other people too—you know, other tenants. I never saw them even speaking to each other."

"Did Davis mix with anyone here that you know?"

"No, never. He came and went and minded his own business, so it seemed. Of course, God only knows what he was doing during his time off in other parts of town."

"Did you ever see him drunk or doped up?"

"Oh, no. I would have fired him if I had."

"No friends ever dropped by to see him?"

"Not that I ever saw."

"How about Harris? Any friends there?"

"You know, I never did see anyone. That's strange, but I guess they both were loners. I'd never thought of that before."

I walked over to the bedroom window. The light was pretty dim because of the brick wall.

"Isn't that a shame? There used to be a pretty view out that window years ago. But they built that mess out there—that storage rental place.

That's when people started trespassing to use the pool late at night; there were some ugly incidents, as I'm sure some of your people would remember. That's why they built the wall. The view was ruined anyway, so I suppose it doesn't matter."

I drew the curtains. Something blocked them from closing all the way, leaving a two-inch gap. I tugged at the curtain cord several times without success.

"What are you doing?" The nervousness was back in his voice.

"The curtains don't close all the way," I pulled at them with my hands and finally reached up to feel for the mechanism along the top, searching for what was blocking it.

"I'll be a little angry if you break that, you know. You're only here because I was nice enough to let you in. I'll get someone in to fix that later."

I found what I was looking for and worked it loose. It was a paper clip, bent over to form a bumper between the two ends of the curtain mechanism. I pulled the cord again and the gap disappeared.

"I've got work to do. Are you finished here?"

I leaned against the wall, twirling the paper clip between my fingers. He couldn't take his eyes off it. "Not quite. Do you have a proprietary interest in this?" I stopped the twirling and held it up before him.

"What do you mean?"

"Is this yours?"

He let out a short laugh. "What do you mean? You just found it there. It can't be mine."

"Unless you put it there to keep the curtains apart." He didn't answer.

"Is that what you did?"

"Of course not."

"It's a simple thing to verify if the tenants of this particular apartment have always been attractive young single women, at least while you've been here."

"That's not true."

"You want me to find out?"

He backtracked. "Even if it was—so what?"

"You're a peeper, Mr. Boyers."

"That's a lie. You can't prove that." His face was no picture of righteous indignation. He looked more like an actor mouthing lines without meaning.

"Your bosses won't ask for proof if I give them a call about you. Nor will your wife, for that matter. I am a cop, after all."

He stared at me; I watched him. I thought I'd let him stew a little just for the hell of it. He finally sat down on the edge of the bed. "What are you going to do?"

"Do you admit to being a peeper?"

He nodded.

"Answer me."

"Yes." The voice was a whisper.

"For how long?"

"A long time."

"Are there other apartments, or is this one it?"

"This is it. It's the only one with a window like that."

"So what's your preference? When they're taking showers? Going to bed? Making love? What is it?"

He covered his face with his hands. His glasses fell off and bounced on the rug.

"Come on, Mr. Boyers, let's not drag this out."

"I watched whenever I could. If they kept to a routine, it made it easier."

"Did you watch Kimberly Harris?"

"Yes. I watched them all."

"On the night she was killed?"

"No. My wife wasn't well that week, so I didn't go out."

"What can you tell me about her?"

He took his hands away and looked up at me, confused. "What do you mean?"

"You spent hours studying a woman dress and undress, bathe herself, go to the bathroom, put on a nightgown. Surely you formed an opinion about her. What kind of woman do you think she was?"

He picked his glasses back up and slowly put them on, meditatively. "She was the most beautiful. She knew it, too. The one who's in here now, she's just a grown up high-school girl—pretty, but normal. Kimberly was special. Watching her was like watching a dirty movie almost. She caressed herself—when she showered, when she put on baby powder. She wore dainty things underneath that no one else could appreciate, lace panties, sheer nightgowns. When she went to bed, it was as if she was expecting someone, she was so sexy, but no one ever came—they weren't supposed to. She did all those things for herself. She was the only one I ever watched who masturbated. Lying on the bed…it was something she prepared for, sometimes oiling herself. Sex was like some kind of special thing with her, something private she did for herself. She was the most beautiful thing I ever saw."

"But always alone."

He turned his head toward me as if I'd just stepped into the room. "Yes. I never saw her with anyone." He sighed deeply and closed his eyes for a moment. "So what happens now?"

"Do you have any vacancies?"

"A couple."

"Tell what's-her-name here that you need to work on the apartment —something major enough that she has to move to another unit permanently. Then have this window bricked up or have frosted blocks put in. It also wouldn't hurt if you got a little counseling. What you do for a pastime isn't only sick, it could get you into some real trouble."

He stood up. I noticed he was shaking slightly. "And that's it? You're not going to tell anyone?"

"Not this time. But you better not give me any reason to regret it. If you ever get caught, I'll make damn sure you end up in very hot water. You're in my debt. Don't forget it."

I left him with a look of stunned disbelief on his face.

11

I drove into the Dunkin' Donuts parking lot before showing up at the office. Dunkin' Donuts is not my usual breakfast fare, but I was feeling flattened enough that a high-voltage sugar fix seemed the only way to go. It never works, of course—it just makes your system do back flips, especially on top of an aspirin appetizer. But at this point the mere act of chewing was the only way I had of showing the world I was still awake, or alive. I bought three cream-filled twists and a coffee. Back flips or not, they tasted great going down.

As things turned out, I shouldn't have worried about staying awake. As soon as I walked in, Max handed me a note from Murphy. It said, "Right now." She'd read it too, of course, so instead of waving as usual, she blew me a kiss. Small comfort.

Murphy was typing when I showed up at his door. It was not something he did with any skill or grace and was guaranteed to make a bad mood worse. "Sit down."

I sat. He picked up the phone, dialed an interoffice number, said, "He's here," and threw a newspaper across the room into my lap. "Have a read."

The front page headline had the wholesome flavor of a big city tabloid: masked man on rampage. Maybe some of the old rural values were indeed going by the wayside. Police baffled by series of attacks. The byline, no surprise, was Stanley Katz.

> The *Reformer* has uncovered a link between several recent but seemingly unconnected crimes in Brattleboro, beginning with the shotgun killing of Mr. James Phillips by Mrs. Thelma Reitz, both of Brattleboro, reported in this paper two days ago. Over the last 48 hours, several crimes have been committed involving the same un-identified man wearing a ski mask.
>
> According to the *Reformer*'s anonymous sources, one case each of animal theft, obscene telephoning, assault on a police officer, car theft,

and sexual assault have been connected to the same masked man who arranged the fatal meeting between Phillips and Reitz at Reitz's home. At this point, the police are at a loss to explain the motives of the mysterious man.

These first two breathless paragraphs were followed by a more or less accurate account of each crime. The names of Reitz and Phillips were spread all over, as was the now-miserable John Woll, but Wodiska was missing and the Stiller-and-Rodriguez episode was alluded to only vaguely, culled no doubt from secondary sources. It seemed my efforts to tiptoe around Harris had worked so far—the jury connection was not mentioned.

I tossed the paper back onto Murphy's desk. "I can't believe he dragged in dog theft. That's tacky."

Frank's eyes narrowed, but whatever he had to say was interrupted by Chief Brandt walking in. Not that Brandt said anything at first. He merely parked himself on a two-drawer filing cabinet and pulled out his pipe. We kept quiet.

Tony Brandt was a dead ringer for an Ivy League dean. He was thin, bespectacled, and tweedy, with a long nose, soft gray eyes, and thinning hair. He wore elbow patches on his jackets, maintained a shine on the seat of his slightly wrinkled wool slacks, and had a fondness for conservatively colored argyle socks.

That, lucky for us, was where the similarity stopped. For this, despite his looks, was no high-thinking theoretician. He was a lifelong cop, trained in the streets of Keene, New Hampshire, and Boston and a member of our force for the past eighteen years. He'd been chief for eight. Married and with three kids, he could still be found wandering the streets late at night, picking up tips, keeping in touch with informants, compulsively being a cop.

Despite this, he was not one of the boys, and his austerity was the single biggest reason he held the position he did among his men. In the constant struggle between labor and management, no different on a police force than in a car factory, he'd maintained his balance between gaining their respect and winning their support. Whenever he slapped you down, you knew you were to blame.

He finished loading his pipe, lit it and said in a pleasant voice, "So, what the hell is going on?"

Murphy's face reddened. This was not what he wanted to hear a few months shy of retirement. "We did what we could to keep a lid on all this."

Brandt shook his head. "Most of what's in there," he pointed at the newspaper, "is either public-record stuff or the byproduct of bull sessions. Stan has a lot of friends around here. What I want to know is what's not in the article—and what hasn't been in the daily reports. I also want to know how it ties in with this." He pulled a piece of computer printout from his pocket and handed it to Murphy.

Murphy looked at it and scowled. "That was supposed to go to me."

"I thought so. That's why I called this little meeting."

"Could you guys bring me in on this?" I asked.

Murphy waved the printout. "This is the FBI report on your bug. They say, to quote them, 'it's highly sophisticated but slightly out-of-date military ordnance.' Judging from the speed of their response, I'd say they'd love to know where we got it. It sounds like it's hot."

Brandt blew out a large cloud of smoke. "Frank and I attended the same FBI course a few years back. It seems we made the same friend in Philip Danvers, who heads one of their research branches. I guess we both figured he'd be a handy man to know. Anyway, obviously he confused the goose with the gander and sent me the results of Frank's request. So, what's up? Between the local paper and the FBI, I smell a rat, and I sure as hell know you two are sitting on it."

Frank sighed. "Joe's tied the ski mask attacks to the Kimberly Harris murder. All the cases Stan mentioned involve ex-jury members."

Brandt's eyebrows rose. I took over. "At first, I thought it might be a vengeance thing, maybe coordinated by Bill Davis or done by a buddy of his without his knowledge. Or maybe someone going after one juror and tying in the others to screw us up. Or even an insurance scam or a huge coincidence. On the face of it, the vengeance angle's the best of the bunch, except that besides Phillips, none of the jurors has been seriously nailed; even the attack on Stiller was mostly theatrical, as if to bring attention. So that made me think of something else, which is that Ski Mask wants us to reopen the Harris investigation and find out that Davis didn't kill her. Whatever it is, Frank and I figured we better keep the cork on any Harris angle until we could prove something."

Murphy rubbed his eyes with his palms, but Brandt just sat there, as impassive as before. "So maybe Davis didn't kill her?"

"He might have, but there's room for doubt. We may have jumped a little fast."

"Run it down."

"I don't have much right now, except for a gut feeling that procedure was a bit rushed on this one."

"What's that mean?" Murphy demanded.

"I interviewed the Huntington Arms manager this morning. I found out he's a peeper whose biggest kick so far was Kimberly Harris. Apparently, she performed the daily duties common to us all with unusual flair."

"Did we ever question him?" Brandt asked Murphy.

Frank pulled a poker face. I knew this was chewing at him, and I didn't enjoy seeing it. "I don't remember. Maybe Kunkle did and ruled him out on the spot. It would be in the case file."

That was a lateral pass to me, which I deigned to accept. "It might be, but again, for discretion's sake, we decided not to open the file just yet."

Brandt nodded.

"I might add, though, that the confession I got from the manager sounded brand-new to me. It was not something he'd already told another cop."

The chief relit his pipe. "What else?"

"I also visited Dr. Hillstrom yesterday afternoon in Burlington." I noticed Frank's surprised look. "She's tickled pink someone is digging into this again. She also feels things were pushed a little too hard and were a little too easy."

"She was part of it." Frank said.

"She admits that, and she's not saying Davis is innocent. She just feels that when circumstances stood against him, they were taken at face value instead of being analyzed more carefully. His blood type, for example, is incredibly common, and yet that's what the prosecution used to connect him to the semen. Her point is that if we really chased down that comparison, the semen and the blood type might no longer match."

"Why didn't we do that?" Again, the question was to Murphy.

"We never do, you know that. You were there, front and center. We follow standard guidelines. The ME does her routine, the State's Attorney does his, and we do ours. That's what happened. If there was a screwup, it's the system's fault, not ours. I mean, hell, what do we know about homicide anyhow? We all felt great about nailing Davis, and there was nobody kicking sand in our faces then. This is all Monday-morning quarterbacking."

There was silence in the room. Things had become personal, and we all knew it. We also knew Frank was right. I hadn't been involved in the investigation, but I had been a cheerleader all the way. At the time, the case had seemed miraculously clean and straight, and we had all shared in a lot of self-congratulatory backslapping.

Brandt cleared his throat. "So what have you done? Is Hillstrom doing the tests?"

"She can't. She doesn't know how. She did recommend a guy outside New Haven who does this stuff all the time."

"All right. Aside from the blood tests and the manager, what else have you got?"

"An interesting comment Hillstrom made about the location of the semen. It seems it was found in Harris's mouth and pubic hair, but not in the vagina, indicating that it could have been placed on the body artificially."

"Or that Davis jacked off on her. We're not talking about two people making love, you know," Frank muttered.

Brandt nodded. "I agree that one's thin. Besides, even if it was placed, Davis could have done the placing. Anything else?"

"Yes. She thinks the scratching and the lamp together make for evidence overkill—she doubts Harris could have done both. Also, she said that while she never got a chance to examine Davis physically herself, she did call Memorial to talk to the emergency staff that treated him. Apparently that's a routine part of her own investigation. The impression she got was that the blow he received was a humdinger— definitely enough to knock him out. If that's true, it runs in the face of the theory that Harris clubbed him with the lamp just before he strangled her."

"But presumably that's an educated guess—different heads having different tolerances for abuse, right?"

I conceded the point.

Brandt rubbed the side of his nose with his finger and thought a bit. "Is that it?"

"We have a very motivated man in a ski mask."

"Jesus," Murphy exploded, too loud in a too-small room. "You say that son of a bitch is turning this department upside down just because he wants the case reopened. Where the fuck did you get that, Joe? I mean, who is this guy? What's his angle? This whole thing might have nothing to do with Kimberly Harris, did you ever think of that? We have every plainclothes we've got digging on this, plus a few uniforms; there's all sorts of stuff they might come up with. Why are you obsessed with some cockamamie rigamarole that'll only end up making us look like a bunch of grade-A morons?"

"Because I'm getting some help from the outside. Last night, somebody tried to kill me, and Ski Mask pulled my fat from the fire."

It was a little over-dramatic, but it made a nice point. It also stopped Murphy in his tracks.

His whole demeanor changed. "What the hell happened? Why didn't you report it?"

"Nothing to report. Somebody turned on the gas in my apartment after I went to bed, and Ski Mask dragged me out just in time. I spent the rest of the night sleeping it off on the landing—almost froze my butt off. But that was it. I have no better description of Ski Mask than what we've already got and I have no idea who tried to bump me off. Ski Mask might know, because he said they would keep at it, and that they would probably rig it to look like an accident."

Brandt shook his head. "I doubt that. They have to assume you've reported the attempt. If you died accidentally now, we'd be suspicious anyhow, so they no longer have any real reason to be discreet."

"That's a big comfort. He also said the key to this thing was Harris; that they were trying to cover it up and that Ski Mask and we had flushed them out enough that they were getting desperate."

Murphy slapped his hand on the table like a gavel. "Hold on here. You don't actually swallow that, do you? Ski Mask saves boy wonder here from the bad guys in the nick of time so he can continue the investigation? Give me a break. How was Ski Mask in the right place at the right time? And if he was, why didn't he tail the people who gassed your place and get his own answers? None of that makes sense. I think he gassed you and then saved your hide. That way, he looks good and we get more interested."

Brandt gave up fiddling with his pipe and put it in his pocket. "That does make sense, Joe."

I swallowed a surge of anger. They were right, and I'd been made a fool of again. "Maybe. The only thing I have against it is that I came pretty close to croaking. It was too fine a line for Ski Mask to rely on."

Murphy let out a groan, as I might have in his place. "I think you're being snookered. He doesn't need you alive. If you had died last night, that really would have gotten us going and he could have played on that. Either way, it was a no-lose play for him." He shook the page of computer printout Brandt had received in the mail. "And even though he talked about Harris and you found this fancy bug, it doesn't mean he was positive we'd even thought about the Harris case. For all we know, his only source of information is the newspaper and the whole purpose of his theatrics was to get the name Harris front and center in our minds."

That was a depressingly good point. I knew Ski Mask had used us to start the ball rolling, but I had flattered myself into thinking he needed me personally, and that I might have some control over him as a result. But Frank was right; as far as Ski Mask was concerned, any cop would do.

The revelation made me doubt everything I'd come up with so far. Maybe he was a disgruntled former juror, or the Huntington Arms manager, or someone hired by Mrs. Reitz's daughter, or even a crony of Davis's. The whole thing was as clear as mud, and I was beginning to feel I was drowning in it. I sure as hell wasn't going to mention the private eye from Burlington now.

Curiously, it was Brandt who came to the rescue. "Of all our options, one does seem to stand out. If you took those blood samples or whatever down to the guy Hillstrom recommended and had them analyzed, that would at least give us something concrete to work with." He looked directly at me. "Has anything else surfaced at this point? Anything about the Phillips shooting or the other stuff?"

"Nothing. Dead ends all around."

"Frank?"

Murphy angrily shifted his weight in his chair. "This whole damn thing only started a couple of days ago. We've barely scratched the surface."

"But we have interviewed everyone involved that we know of, right?"

"So far."

"And we have eliminated the obvious? Insurance, revenge, robbery, jealousy, whatever."

"It may be there. We just don't see it yet." Brandt looked at the floor for a few seconds. "I agree with Frank about letting Harris out of the bag too soon. We would look like morons if you came back from testing Hillstrom's samples with positive proof that we have the right man behind bars. Find out what you can as quickly as possible—and I'm talking a couple of days at most here—and then we'll see where to go next."

He slid off the filing cabinet and walked over to the door. "By the way, Frank, don't feel like a sitting duck here. Technically, I headed the Harris investigation. I was given all the facts and had all the options. If there has been a screw-up, nobody's going after you. I can promise you that."

Murphy nodded and watched him go. He waited a few seconds until we both heard the hallway door close, and then he let out a snort. "He can't promise anything if they fire him first."

I stood up. "I wouldn't worry, Frank."

He gave me a deadpan look. "It's not your problem, is it?"

12

I left Frank brooding and called up Dr. Hillstrom from my office. She said she would have all samples and slides on their way within the next few hours via state police courier. She also said she would call Bob Kees and tell him to expect me some time tomorrow. I mentioned that the chief had given me only a couple of days and she burst out laughing. The best she could do, she said, was to pass that along and hope Kees had an abundance of Christmas spirit left over. I was almost out the door when the phone rang.

"Joe?" It was Gail.

"Hi. What's up?"

"I just saw Katz's screaming headlines. I was wondering how you were doing."

"I'm okay. He didn't do too much damage. It would have gotten out anyway and he missed the jury connection. I would guess he's just talking to his buddies and sewing that together with what we release anyhow. His real trick is the hysterical undertone—you know, stuff like, 'police don't deny' and 'informed sources speculate' and 'there are possible connections.'"

"Speaking of hysteria, have you heard from the town fathers?"

I hesitated. Her tone was suspiciously neutral. "Am I hearing from them now?"

She chuckled, which was a relief. It was a little early to start getting heat from the politicians, at least at my level. "You might. I wanted to let you know they're getting pretty worked up—they feel they're being left in the dark on purpose. Some of us got together a half hour ago, and I had the distinct impression that if I'd mentioned the words 'Kimberly Harris,' it would have been like dropping a match into a swimming pool full of gasoline. It gave me quite a sense of power."

"Yeah, over my job. Try to control yourself, okay?"

"Seriously, Joe, Mrs. Morse especially is really on the warpath. She wants Brandt called before a special session, and Cutts and Pearly are starting to think about it. If Katz does make the jury connection, that'll be the match. How are things going?"

"We're digging. It'll all hinge on getting some more forensic stuff out of Connecticut. There's an expert down there that might help us out, but it'll take a few days."

She was quiet for a few moments. "God, I hate these things. I wish they'd leave you alone—*we* would leave you alone, I should say. I really feel like telling them off sometimes, and I'd do it if you and I weren't… well, you know. It kind of ties my hands; I can't be too partial."

"I know. I'm sorry."

Her voice was suddenly stronger. "Well, hell. I'm probably just being too sensitive anyway. Mrs. Morse is always stirring them up; now's no different. She's not going to get them to do anything for a few days at least, unless your friend in the mask pops up again. Then you will be in trouble, or at least Brandt will be."

"I'll let him know he's walking on egg shells."

"Oh, he knows that—that's what phones are for. I shouldn't even have bothered you about all this."

"Hey, I appreciate it. Makes me feel good to have a spy on the board."

"A lot of good I am."

"Don't let it get to you, Gail. That's not why you're there. We're all big boys and girls."

"I know that. There's just something about all this that makes me nervous for some reason. A man in a mask, that whole Kimberly Harris thing cropping up again…It's creepy. I had nightmares last night."

I hoped to hell she wouldn't find out what I'd almost had last night. "We'll get to the bottom of it soon—not to worry."

My first stop of the day was the bank where Kimberly Harris had kept her account, at least according to the apartment manager. If true, I was in luck; it was the same bank Ellen had worked in when we'd met and where I'd maintained ties with people who were now high in the ranks. The head of Records, Peg Wilson, had been a bridesmaid at our wedding.

I found her in her office, standing on a chair watering a plant. She looked up when I knocked and spilled some water on her desk. "Joe, look what you've made me do. There're some Kleenexes in the top drawer."

I mopped up the puddle and helped her off her perch. She put down the can and gave me a hug. "Gosh, it's been a long time. I haven't seen you in months. No...more; it's been a year. It was last Christmas. You ought to be ashamed of yourself—a whole year. It's enough to make a girl feel neglected."

"What about Tom?"

She waved her hand. "He's just a husband. I need a handsome bachelor on the side."

"Well, I hope you find him."

She held my face between her hands, as a mother might a child's. "You look pretty good to me, big boy." The smile faded slowly. "Actually, you look like death warmed over. What's wrong?"

I kissed her and sat on the edge of her desk. "I just missed a night's sleep. I can't pull it off like I used to."

She settled back in her chair. "Ugh. Tell me about it. I have to spend half an hour every morning in front of the mirror just to look alive."

"You do a great job."

She patted my knee. "Flatterer. What do you want?"

"Did Kimberly Harris bank here?"

She looked at me for a full count of three. I could almost hear the files turning over in her head. "Yes."

That I found refreshing. No comments about the murder, digging up dead bodies, or why-do-you-want-to-knows. Just a straightforward answer. Peg was one of my favorite bureaucrats. She also had a machine-like memory. "Are her records still available?"

"No court order, right?"

"Right."

She got up. "You're a bad boy, Joe Gunther. Grab a magazine." She left the room and I picked up an issue of something called *Banker's Quarterly*. I had just gotten to the biography of *BQ*'s Banker of the Year when Peg walked back in. She put a folder on her desk and said, "I have to go to the bathroom. I should be about ten minutes, so please do not touch anything on my desk, okay?"

"Got you."

She left, closing the door behind her. I picked up the file. It was a computer printout, naturally, several sheets long. Kimberly Harris had banked here for a little over a year. She hadn't made great use of her checkbook, opting instead to write checks for large sums of cash and then presumably working from a kitty. That was unfortunate, in that I couldn't trace her daily activities, but it did show me someone who was in a good position to leave at the drop of a hat. Most people I know who are settled in a community don't walk around with rolls of hundred-dollar bills in their pockets.

97

I was also able to identify four stages of her financial life. The first was brief and pretty skinny. It made me wonder why she'd bothered to open an account in the first place. Within a couple of months, however, regular income started pumping in—a biweekly transfer of funds from another account at the bank owned by Charlie's Pharmacy—presumably a paycheck. The third period was a transition. Charlie's paycheck was augmented by cash deposits of four thousand dollars a month for several months. Lastly, Charlie dropped out of the picture, leaving only the mysterious, and hefty, monthly allotments. These lasted until her death.

That was all. I closed the folder and sat back. What the hell was going on? I now knew for sure that Willy Kunkle's sensitivities, not to mention Frank Murphy's, James Dunn's, the Board of Selectmen's, and everyone else's, were going to have to be abused, to Stan Katz's delight. I was going to have to sneak a peek under the lid of this one and run the risk of blowing it off.

Peg walked back in. "Are you satisfied now?"

I surreptitiously slid the folder onto her desk. "I'm more informed; I can't say I'm satisfied."

She sat down and picked up the file, idly leafing through it.

"Do you remember if any cops came by for that after she died?"

She looked up, surprised. "Oh, yes. It was what's-his-name—the rude one."

"Kunkle?"

"That's right."

That was something. But it made me all the more anxious to find out what the official conclusions had been about the four-thousand-dollar payments.

I thanked Peg and left the bank. The day was as brilliant as it had started out—cold and sharp and brittle. The snow creaked underfoot. People marched about, laden with rejected Christmas presents, peeking out between scarves and wooly hats. Most of the pre-holiday tension had been replaced by the return of everyday life.

Charlie's Pharmacy was around the corner on Elliot Street, only a hundred feet from the bank. It had a long, thin railroad car layout that made me wonder if somebody hadn't just put a roof and two doors on an alleyway. It was pleasant and cheery, however, its first few feet cluttered with magazines and card racks, the rest given over to the usual hodgepodge that makes drug stores the next best thing to the old five-and-dimes. Muted classical music hovered overhead, a distinctive if trendy touch that reminded me of Hillstrom's office.

The man behind the prescription counter, the only other person in the place, looked up. "Can I help you find something?"

"That might take the fun out of it."

The pharmacist grinned. "I know what you mean. I bought this place for the same reason: I've always loved drug stores. Of course, they were a little different when I was a boy."

I walked up to the counter. He was an older man, probably in his seventies, with more hair than I had and a pair of unnaturally clean gold-rimmed glasses. They sparkled in the overhead light. He seemed as custom-fitted to his job as an elf to a toy shop.

"Are you Charlie?" I knew he wasn't, but it didn't make sense to me to come on like Big Brother.

"Oh, no. That's kind of an inside joke. Before she died, my wife used to kid me that my only ambition in life was to own a store on Main Street and call it Charlie's."

"You almost made it."

The other man laughed. "Just a few yards to the corner. Oh, well, that'll keep me dreaming. My name's Floyd Rubin, by the way." He stuck out a clean, pink hand.

"Joe Gunther."

"Glad to meet you. Is this the first time you've been in?"

"No. I've come here once or twice before. You've done a nice job—very cozy."

"Thank you; that means a lot. I'm not too sure of myself as an interior decorator. Of course, I had a lot of help."

"Well, it's nice," I repeated. "Actually, to tell the truth, I'm kind of here on business."

"Oh?"

"Yes, I'm with the police department. I wanted to ask you about a girl who used to work for you named Kimberly Harris."

Rubin's face turned in on itself in sorrow. He lowered his head. "Oh, dear."

I was surprised at the strength of his reaction. The loss was obviously still quite fresh, as it might be with a sibling or a parent, or a lover. "When did she work here?"

"She quit three Aprils ago, at the beginning of the same summer she died. She said she planned to spend the whole season outside, just to prove you could get as good a tan in Brattleboro as you could in the Bahamas. She said she'd be like a billboard for the suntan lotions I sell here." His voice died with a murmur and he sat tiredly on the stool behind him.

"It sounds like you were very close."

He looked up and smiled, but he took a long time answering. "I think we were friends. That's rare for someone my age." I remembered from Peg's file that Kimberly was raking in cash by the time she left Charlie's. "She must have saved a bundle to take the whole summer off."

Again, he hesitated, but this time he merely seemed pensive.

"I never thought of that."

"How long did she work here?"

"Just under a year. She came in for some lotion. I think if she had a vain spot, it was her skin—of course, it was quite beautiful. Anyway, I had a sign in the window asking for help and she took the job, right on the spot. She worked out very well."

"Why did she leave?"

"I don't know." Again the long pause. "She never told me."

"Do you think she was happy working here?"

"I thought so. She always said that. I believed her."

I felt like I was eavesdropping on a man talking to himself. "Did she ever come back to visit after she'd left?"

"No. I saw her once, on the street, but she didn't see me. She was very much her own person."

"What do you mean?"

He was sitting slumped on the stool, his eyes on a far corner of the room, his hands on his knees like two carefully placed artifacts. I felt I had a gold mine of information here—the first person who could tell me what Kimberly Harris had been like in life—and yet I sensed I would end up with little to show for it. He was staring, self-absorbed, into a private pool of grief. The facts of his relationship with Kimberly Harris, what I most wanted to hear, were as immaterial to him as the dawn of the next century.

"What did you say?" he asked.

"You said she was very much her own person. What did you mean by that?"

"She was very private, very much in control. She seemed to have a great deal of purpose in life."

"Did she ever talk about her past?"

"Not once. I'm afraid I cornered the market there, like most old men."

"Did she have any friends? People who would come in and visit, or maybe people she'd see after hours?"

He shook his head. "No. I don't know what she did with her spare time. Weekends were special, but I don't know why."

"How do you mean, 'special'?"

"Towards the end of her stay here, she began asking for three-day weekends. I was happy to oblige because she always made up for the lost time immediately. To be honest, I put that sign in the window for temporary help; I don't do enough business to justify a full-time employee. So her weekends were no burden to me."

"She never said what she did during those times?"

"I never asked. I wanted to be her friend, not her guardian. She sensed that—at least I think she did."

"Would you be able to pinpoint those weekends?"

He hovered closer to earth—the lure of a physical reality. "Of course. I have time sheets for all my employees—even for myself. It would take a little time to dig them up, though. I could do it tonight after closing, if that's all right."

"That's fine. I'd appreciate it. By the way, did the police interview you at the time of her death?"

"Yes. I'm not sure I was much help then, either."

"You've been a help. It's difficult talking about someone you loved who's died."

It was a long shot and it missed. He focused on me very carefully, a man on the alert. "I didn't say I loved her. I was fond of her. Her death was a waste."

"Of course. I'm sorry—I misunderstood. I might be gone for the next couple of days, but I'll be back to pick up those time sheets, okay?"

He smiled, but there was less friendliness in his eyes. "I'll have them ready."

I left the store and began walking back up Main Street to the Municipal Building, swathed in the gloomy pre-evening winter light. I was not happy. It might have been last night catching up with me, or the frustration of tiptoeing through my own department with a major case, but Rubin's coolness at the end made me feel I was increasingly surrounded by a bunch of people who'd just as soon see me disappear. That was starting to wear thin.

It was also about to change. Every rock I'd looked under had concealed more old, unanswered questions. So far, I'd found a dubious medical examiner, a career peeper, a clue-cluttered crime scenario, anonymous cash payments, mysterious three-day weekends; and now I'd just left a squeaky-clean septuagenarian with a did-he-or-didn't he passion for the victim. None of these had been brought up before that I had ever heard, and I was beginning to think that if I couldn't get at least one of them to lay me a nice fat egg, I was in the wrong line of work.

Of course, the largest question remained: if I did end up proving I was in the right line of work, who in the end was going to benefit? Ski Mask had set an elaborate plan into action, but what was his motivation? It was difficult to believe he'd put so many people through hell—not to mention causing the death of one of them—just to get Bill Davis off the hook. I had to assume that his interest was more in who he thought should be in Davis's place. But that still didn't give me much.

I spent the waning hours of the day doodling in my office, going over what I'd found, making charts on a large yellow pad. I made everyone I could think of Kimberly Harris's killer and then tied him to what I knew. Of course, I ended up with mostly question marks. But the process was comforting and it helped kill the time. Tomorrow, with the trip to Connecticut, I felt things were going to change. I would stop turning over old earth and start digging in a patch of my own.

Most bachelors have their quirks, I suppose. Mine—at least one of mine—is to shop for food almost every day on the way home. The logic is that the larder rarely ends up holding unopened passing fancies that slowly graduate to botulism growth farms. But in fact I think I do it just to spend a few minutes of each day among the normal people of this world. Some men have their six o'clock martinis: I have my fifteen minutes in the crowded aisles of Finast.

I had parked my car after returning from this ritual and was crossing the street to my apartment, grocery sack in one hand, keys in the other, when I heard my named called. Frank Murphy was standing in the shadows under a tree.

"You don't look too good."

"It's been a couple of action-packed days."

"I won't argue with that." He climbed the steps to the front door with me, glancing at the bag. "You had dinner yet?"

"No."

He put his hand on my shoulder. "Come home with me. Martha's fixing lasagna—right up your alley."

"No. I'm bushed. I don't think I'll bother with dinner."

"Sleep on an empty stomach? You'd never wake up. Come on, you don't have to be sociable. I won't even mind if you fall asleep at the table, but you got to eat."

I shook my head again, but he tightened his grip. I looked up at him. "Please. As a favor."

He had more than dinner on his mind. "All right."

I walked back down the steps with him, crossed over to his car and deposited my groceries in the back seat. That's one advantage of Vermont winters—all the world is a refrigerator, especially if your car heater works like Murphy's.

We'd been driving for five minutes before he spoke again. "So, any ideas?"

"Why the sudden interest?"

It came out sharper than I'd intended, and Frank lapsed back into silence. I didn't want to be doing this. I needed rest and some time alone to think things out.

"Maybe there *are* some bad guys out there." I closed my eyes for a second. "What?"

"Maybe Ski Mask did save your skin. I mean, it's not impossible. We never did find out much about Kimberly Harris. Could be all this is out of her past—a Mafia thing or witness protection or something like that."

I couldn't believe it. "Spare me."

Murphy shrugged.

"Look, maybe he did sucker me with the gas thing, but that doesn't mean he shouldn't be our main line of business. It's like we're standing knee-deep in shit and wondering where the smell's coming from."

Murphy groaned.

The predictability of it got under my skin. "Well, Christ, Frank. Wouldn't you like to know what the hell is going on? I mean, we know goddamned well the Harris thing and Ski Mask are connected, and that we don't have any other line on who the hell Ski Mask is. So why don't we just face that and get on with it?"

"We are. That's why you're going to Connecticut." His voice was gloomy. "I was just hoping we could do it quietly."

I clamped my teeth and stared at the traffic ahead. This was stupid.

I was right; he was right. There was a momentum building in this case; Ski Mask was our main line of business; Harris was the obvious avenue to pursue. I wasn't all by myself. I was just feeling as frustrated as I'd ever felt.

When Murphy spoke again, his voice was quiet and slow—confessional. "I owe you an apology."

"What for?"

"I've been acting like a jerk on all this."

I couldn't disagree, so I kept quiet.

"I remember the morning it all started—black rapist strangles white girl—I couldn't believe it, complete with bondage, drugs, and stolen underwear. It was straight out of a horror movie. I remember thinking we'd never hear the end of it. The networks would grab it, and some headline lawyer from New York would show up. I'd end up looking like some Alabama redneck nigger-stomper, fat gut and all."

"Jesus, Frank, where did you get that?"

He shook his head. "I don't know. It was just suddenly there. It was like Korea: when your tour was nearly up, you just knew something dumb was going to get you killed. You lost perspective—you got paranoid. Didn't that happen to you?"

"Yeah, I felt it."

"But not as bad, I know. Some guys really flipped out, probably wound up getting killed just because of it. I guess I was somewhere in-between. Anyway, it was the same feeling with this Harris thing. I felt like an ant trying to get out from under a giant foot in time. I felt its shadow right over me."

He paused.

"Pre-retirement crazies?"

He gave a short laugh. "I guess. It's not getting any better, in case you haven't noticed. That trial...Well, not the trial, but the whole process lasted a full two years. All along, I kept expecting something to foul up, something that would turn on the spotlights. I did everything I could to speed it up—Christ, I've never been so efficient. That paperwork didn't sit ten minutes on my desk. And when it was finally over, I couldn't believe our luck. We'd actually pulled it off—nice and neat and legal as hell."

Again, he paused and then sighed. "And up she pops again, like a cork to the top, three months shy of the exit door."

I wasn't sure what to say, or even if saying something might break the spell and deprive him of whatever comfort he was getting from all this.

"The real joke is I don't even want to leave. If I could, I'd happily die at my desk. Florida to me is like one big cemetery, waiting to swallow me up."

"Then don't go."

He looked over at me and smiled. "I envy you that. There was a time I'd have said the same thing. But things change. Martha or no Martha,

I'd probably have found some hole to die in. Might as well be Florida."

I looked out the window. We were getting close to his house. I'd have said Frank Murphy was the one man in this world to whom self-pity was foreign. I guess he was right: things change.

The car pulled into Hillcrest Terrace. "That didn't sound too good, did it?"

"Nope."

He parked and killed the engine. "I'm not even sure I meant it. It's kind of like standing belly-deep in the pool and wondering if you're half dry or half wet."

Somehow, for no reason—or for all sorts of reasons—I started giggling. "You are losing your mind, you know that?"

He laughed with me but briefly. "I wonder sometimes. Five years ago—maybe more—you couldn't have caught my coat tails. Now...I don't know. I seem to have run out of spit."

I rubbed my eyes, took a deep breath and stretched. "Oh, hell, Frank, it happens. Don't beat yourself up. Dive in...or get out." I started laughing again.

He smiled and started up the car. "Where're we going?"

"I'm taking you home. You do need the sleep."

13

A long-standing maxim holds that overly tired people don't sleep as well as they do normally. I didn't have that problem. I slept for twelve hours straight and woke up in the same position I started out in—on my stomach, fully clothed. I won't claim I felt refreshed, but at least I could function.

I washed, changed my clothes, and packed a bag. Assuming Beverly Hillstrom was as efficient as I thought she was, the Kimberly Harris samples had probably arrived in Brattleboro sometime during the night.

When I got to the office around 10:30, Murphy, as was now becoming his habit, found me in the hallway. "I took you home to go to bed, not take a vacation. What have you been doing?"

"Sleeping." I reached through Maxine's small sliding-glass window and pulled out a daily report. The night had been blessedly boring. "What's the rush?"

"Brandt thought it might be nice if you got on your way in the pre-dawn darkness, especially since you'll be carrying a cooler marked Caution–Human Remains."

"So they came?"

"Yeah; about three hours ago. It's in the fridge. I put it in a brown paper bag."

"They pack that stuff in dry ice, Frank. You could have just shoved it under my desk."

Murphy scowled. "It doesn't matter."

I shook my head, opened my office door, and turned on the light. Murphy turned it off. "You don't have time. You're leaving."

I closed the door with a sigh and retraced my steps to the hall. Murphy left me to get the cooler. He returned carrying a grocery bag. "See? It doesn't look weird."

I shook my head and relieved him of it. "I'll take your word for it."

He escorted me out the door and to my car, looking around as if Katz would swing by on some vine, camera in hand. The mother-hen routine was a far cry from yesterday. Not that I was complaining, but I was still a little wary. I could only imagine last night's conversation must have been a huge weight off his shoulders.

He put his hand on the car door as I was about to open it. "You think someone ought to go with you?"

"I don't see why. I might be gone several days."

"You and what's-his-name, you mean."

The thought had occurred to me. I looked at him closely. "Is this a complicated way of inviting yourself along?"

He beamed. "Yeah."

"What about Brandt?"

He walked over to his car and got a small overnight bag out of the passenger seat. "I already cleared it with him...and Martha."

The drive to West Haven takes about three hours, a straight drop south on the interstate. The weather was beautiful, cold and blue skied, and we shared a good mood. I was happy to have him along, and happy to see him out from under his self-imposed cloud. Comments about the end of the road and living on borrowed time go with the territory of old age, and Frank didn't hold a candle to my mother, who in her mid-eighties was complaining that God had just forgotten her.

But it was a sliding scale, and Frank had temporarily slid him-self too far down. I felt he was back now; still fearful of bad news but committed to finding the answer.

The University of West Haven is an unpretentious collection of ugly concrete buildings scattered across the top of a hill with no view. We got directions to the Business Administration Center, where the guard insisted we would find Dr. Kees, and parked in front of a gray and largely windowless five-story cube that was still very much under construction.

We got out and stared at it. There were other cars in the lot but not many. In fact, the entire campus had a forlorn, empty look to it.

"What do you think?" Murphy asked.

"Well, Hillstrom's office is over a dentist. Maybe this guy likes abandoned buildings."

He gestured to the back seat. "Should we take the stuff?"

"Might as well. I don't want to lose it now." The red-and-white cooler, free of its brown bag, did indeed have Caution–Human Remains taped on one side. On the other was a happy penguin and the words Chilly Willy.

We picked our way over the construction-site debris that lay scattered across the frozen mud and entered a doorless front lobby. The buttons for the elevator hadn't been installed yet. Nor, for all we knew, had the elevator. We began to climb the stairs, the clatter of our footsteps echoing off the bare concrete walls.

On the fifth floor, we found a door and behind it a wall of warm air. We walked down the unfinished, uncarpeted hallway, looking through doorways as we went, vaguely following the sound of a radio. We found it, and the young woman in cowboy boots listening to it, about halfway down. She was standing at an equipment-jammed counter, dropping blood from a pipette into a row of tiny saucers in perfect rhythm with the music.

She finished and smiled brightly at us. "Hi. Can I help you?" Murphy and I looked at each other. "Does Dr. Robert Kees work here?"

"Sure does."

She clomped out of the room and down the hall, leaving us surrounded by a truly impressive hodgepodge of gleaming, metallic, totally mysterious machines. The radio sounded tinny and cowed by its competition.

She returned in a couple of minutes, followed by an athletic middle-aged man with thick, swept-back black hair. He smiled broadly and stuck out his hand. "Hi. I'm Bob Kees."

We introduced ourselves and he looked at the cooler. "Is that your friend?"

"Both of them. Maybe all three of them. Actually, that's why we're here; we don't know how many are involved."

"Beverly tells me you want all your information in twenty minutes or so, is that right?"

Murphy's face brightened. "Is that all it takes?"

Kees laughed. "Not a chance. Assuming I was sitting around here dying for something to do, it might take me sixty to seventy-two hours, if I was lucky. The way things are, I could get to you in three weeks to a month."

"A month?" Murphy burst out.

"How much did Dr. Hillstrom tell you about this?"

"She said it had something to do with reopening a case—that you might have put the wrong guy in the slammer."

"This is going to sound a little corny, but we think an innocent man died because of what's in this cooler."

Kees pursed his lips and motioned us into the hallway. "Jeannie, let me know what you get from these as soon as you're finished, okay? And hold off on the Spiegelmann stuff until I tell you."

"Okay."

He led us down the corridor and through a maze of overstuffed offices bulging with furniture and strange machinery. "In case you didn't notice, we haven't quite moved in. The university, in its wisdom, contracted for the destruction of our old quarters before the new ones were built. Then the workers went on strike."

"What about the students?"

"You mean the lack of them? They went out on strike too—in sympathy with the workers and just in time to extend their Christmas leave. Protest isn't what it used to be."

We ended up in a pretty nice office, complete with rug on the floor and pictures on the walls. Half of it was piled high with junk too, but the other half looked neater and more pleasant than anything we had back home. Kees sat behind an old and unpretentious turn-of-the-century desk and locked his fingers behind his head. To his right, on a separate table, two glowing computers hummed softly to themselves.

"So, tell me your tale."

The stereotype of the self-proclaimed "busy" man is a guy who spends half his time telling you he's got none to spare. With one assistant and the rest out on strike, combined with what Beverly Hillstrom had told me about his popularity, Robert Kees struck me as having his life under control. He let us bumble through our story without one glance at his watch or a single sigh of impatience. When we finished, he got up, plucked the cooler from my lap, said, "Okay," and left the room.

Frank raised his eyebrows. "What did that mean?"

"I guess he's either doing it right now, or he just threw it out the window."

"Were we supposed to follow him?"

"Not unless you know how to work any of that stuff." We sat there for over an hour, staring out the window, staring at the floor, staring at each other, until he finally returned.

"That's quite the collection."

"How do you mean?"

He parked himself with his hands behind his head again. "It's filled with goodies. A standard batch of samples, even from Beverly, has a few slides, a few swabs, maybe some tissue, and that's about it. She threw in everything but the kitchen sink—she must have had some serious reservations when she did the autopsy."

"That's what she told me."

"Then why the hell didn't she tell us at the time?" Murphy muttered. "It sure would have saved us a lot of wear and tear, not to mention an extra body in the morgue."

Kees smiled. "Ah, but that's not the game, is it? You demand, we sup-ply. Nobody wants to ask us about our doubts—that's for the defense. If we find something odd, the prosecution doesn't want to know about it, not unless we can guarantee where it'll lead them. Besides, according to the paperwork she enclosed, you've got the right man in jail."

Frank passed his hand across his mouth. "Then what are we doing here?"

"I can dig deeper than she can. I think that's why she kept as much as she did—just in case. I don't know if you're aware of it, but you've got yourself a very good medical examiner up there."

"So what happens now?" I asked.

"You wait. I work. Most of the stuff is in an incubator right now. It'll stay there overnight. There are a couple of things I can do in the meantime but not much, except make a few phone calls and rearrange everyone else's schedule."

"We do appreciate this—a lot."

"It's okay. Why don't you come back in about three days? We'll see what we've got."

I got up, but Frank didn't move. "You wouldn't have a corner we could bunk in, would you?"

Kees's eyes widened. "You mean stay here?"

"Yup."

"Why?" I asked.

"Because we don't know for sure what's going on. We think Ski Mask is just pushing to reopen the case. We think he's bumped off some guy just to get our interest. We think he and us are the only people involved in this thing, and I'd lay bets he followed us here. But we don't know any of that for sure. There's an equally strong possibility that there's a separate bunch just as hell-bent on keeping a lid on this, to the point that they almost killed my partner here, and that they too are hot on our tail. That cooler is the only thing so far that isn't pure invention, and I'm not about to leave it behind in a half-demolished building and spend two days going to the movies. Is that all right with you guys?"

Kees shrugged. "We've got the room and the furniture…God knows we're not too crowded. Be my guests. Just don't get underfoot, okay?"

Murphy stood up and nodded. "You got it."

I followed him out the door, closing it behind me. "You really going to do this?"

"You bet your butt. You get a star witness that can bust a case wide open, what do you do with him? You sit on him until they need him. That cooler's our witness."

"It may not be, Frank."

He turned and poked me in the chest with his finger. "Maybe not. That was my tune until last night. Now I'm singing yours. So humor me."

I held up both palms in surrender. "Consider yourself humored."

We found a room with a few pieces of machinery, all of it unplugged, and a pile of tables, desks, filing cabinets, and armchairs. Several pillows on the floor made for serviceable if lumpy beds. Murphy borrowed my car keys, disappeared for a couple of hours, and returned with some magazines, a couple of pulp novels, enough junk food to hold us for a week, and a rented TV.

The next two-and-a-half days passed slowly. Frank and I watched, as the hours crawled by, morning news shows, midmorning talk shows, midday news shows, hours of soap opera, more hours of pre-dinner sitcom reruns, evening news shows, prime-time whiz-bangers, late night action shows, more now-stale news, and finally the twilight zone of Leno, Letterman, old movies and more reruns.

We stood around, we sat, we lay on our pillows, we read a little, we washed at the basin in the half-finished bathroom. We waited.

Every once in a while, we caught a glimpse of Kees or his cowgirl in the hallway. They politely bade us good night on their way out every evening and gave us a cheery good morning hours later, but we kept out of their hair and they didn't seek us out. On the morning of the third day, the sound of heavy equipment starting up outside told us the strike had been settled.

But it wasn't until the fourth day that Kees appeared in our doorway and asked us to follow him to his office.

After that amount of time, and the bored tension that went with it, my druthers were to come face-to-face with tangible results—like a reconstructed body or at least a steamer trunk filled with evidence. But aside from a few sheets of paper lying in the middle of his desk, Kees's office looked unchanged from before.

We sat down like two rumpled old men awaiting counseling and watched Kees assume his by now traditional pose. "What do you know about blood typing?"

Murphy opened his mouth, but I beat him to it. "Hillstrom told me something about Hs and secretors and PG-something-or-other sub-typing that gets the blood more and more specific to a single person."

"Okay. That gives me an idea of how to approach this. Let's back up, though, and look at what we've got. From what you told me and from Beverly's samples, I figure we've got two categories: the physical evidence —things like the underwear, the rope, the broken lamp, the general signs of a struggle, stuff like that. And the tissue samples, taken from a variety of sources—the fetus, the semen, the stains on the sheet, etc."

"Now on the first, you guys are the experts. Your living is going around matching evidence with unwitnessed action. What I do isn't that different. What I'm going to tell you is part scientific fact, and part educated conjecture. When you leave here, in other words, you'll have more than you had, but you're still going to have to put the pieces together on your own. Okay?"

We both nodded.

"All right. Now you nailed the suspect...What's his name?"

"Davis."

"You nailed Davis as a group O secretor—the same as both semen samples. We tested both as separate entities because as far as we know, they might have been placed by different men."

Murphy shook his head. "Lovely thought."

"But unfortunately realistic, although not necessarily in the way you think. She may have been attacked simultaneously by two men, but she might also have had intercourse with one man, come home, and been attacked by a second. Here's an instance where conjecture takes over, in fact. I seriously doubt that a woman would receive semen in either one of these two areas, and then put her clothes back on and walk home. It is only reasonable to assume it all happened at once. Had one of the deposits been inside her vagina, I wouldn't necessarily take that position.

"In any case, the whole thing is a little ephemeral because the mouth sample pretty much stops there—at O secretor. It's far too contaminated by the victim's saliva to be analyzed any further. That, luckily, is not the case with the pubic sample.

"The typing and subtyping Beverly told you about is called Phos-pho-Gluco-Mutations typing, or PGM for short. Basically, it's an enzyme that is polymorphic, meaning different people have different types. At this point, we've determined ten subtypes in the population. With time, we'll probably get more, but in your case, this was enough."

"So you did get something," Murphy asked.

"Oh yes. Here, look at this." Kees took the top sheet of paper off his little pile and slid it across the desk. In neat, penciled handwriting, there was a single column of figures:

> Suspect:
> Group O secretor
> PGM type 2 – 1 subtype 2 + 1 + ESD 1
> GLO 2-1
> ACP BA

"That's Mr. Davis. Here's the semen." He slid the second sheet over:

> Semen:
> Group O secretor
> PGM type 1 subtype 1 + 1 + ESD 1
> GLO 1
> ACP BA

I couldn't resist a smile. "So they don't match."

"Nope."

"How about the fetus?"

"Okay, now on the fetus…Well, to back up a little, you know that a fetus is a product of its parents."

Murphy sighed.

"Meaning that if you have one parent and the fetus, you can get a vague notion of the missing parent's makeup. You can also therefore exclude people who do not fit that vague makeup. Which leads me to this." And he slid the third sheet toward us:

Mother	Fetus	Father
Group A	Group B	Group B or AB
PGM 2	PGM 2 – 1	PGM 1 – 1, 1 + 1 –, 2 + 1– or 2 – 1 –
subtype 2 + 2 +	subtype 2 + 1 –	-------
ESD 1	ESD 1	ESD 1 or 2 – 1
GLO 1	GLO 2 – 1	GLO 2 or 2 – 1
ACP B	ACP B	ACP B, BA or CB

We both stared at it; Kees saved us from asking any idiotic questions. "To summarize that in English, Davis is neither the semen depositor nor the father of the fetus. But neither is the real semen depositor the father, so now you've got three men."

"Davis, the man who attacked her, and the father." Kees made a steeple of his fingers. "No. Davis, the depositor, and the father. If Beverly's guess is right—that the semen was brought to the site and deposited artificially—then Davis could have been the one who attacked her. After all, you still have all that physical evidence against him."

"Oh, come on," Murphy said. "I don't buy that crap about the semen being poured all over her like salad dressing. People don't do that."

"Perhaps not, but other possibilities exist. There might have been two attackers—Davis and the depositor—and you only got Davis."

Murphy rubbed his forehead.

"Or even, to humor Beverly once again, the father and Davis might have been in cahoots and the semen secured from some innocent third party and, once again, artificially placed."

"Come on."

Kees laughed, enjoying his devil's advocacy. "If push came to shove and I were placed on the witness stand and a very sharp lawyer asked me, 'Dr. Kees, since all you could get from the sample in the mouth was Group O secretor, doesn't that mean it could have been Davis's semen, even though the other sample was not?' I would have to answer yes. I would also have to concede that in cases of gang assault such evidence is not rare."

"Meaning that Davis might have deposited one of the semen samples?"

"It's possible. I told you I couldn't give you answers—just information. Now I have to admit I tend to agree with Captain Murphy. People usually do the simplest thing in these situations. They are rarely operating at their highest mental capacity. Chances are Davis was framed by a man who sexually assaulted the young woman and then killed her, or the other way around. But I'm afraid what I've given you doesn't prove that—it merely suggests it."

There was a long silence in the room. I have to admit, the joy I'd felt at hearing the semen wasn't Davis's had vanished. I'd seen enough lawyers at work to know that the information we'd just received didn't even warrant a reopening of the case, much less a retrial. My only consolation was that Frank looked as down as I was. Several days ago, he would have been grinning from ear to ear.

Kees, on the other hand, was still smiling. "I feel I ought to add at this point that *that*," and he pointed at the three sheets of paper, "is not the only thing I found."

We both looked at him, Murphy obviously peeved.

"One of the reasons all this took a little longer than I planned was that I ran the semen by a couple of extra tests. One of them came up with the fact that the depositor was taking a drug called prednisone at the time he ejaculated.

"It's a common prescription drug, a glucocorticoid, to be exact. Pharmacists sell it for its anti-inflammatory properties to treat everything from asthma to arthritis to poison ivy. Now there is a large family of glucocorticoid drugs. Prednisone is cheaper than most of the others, but it is more potent and far likelier to cause side effects. As such, I would doubt it was administered for something minor like poison ivy; I'd guess it was more like arthritis or asthma."

"It sounds like you're saying the depositor was an old man in a wheelchair."

"For the arthritis, you may be right. That is mostly found among the elderly. But asthma is something else. A lot of young and otherwise healthy people suffer from it."

He got up from his chair and stood by the window, looking out. "I'm also inclined to think it was either one or the other of those because they're long-term ailments, and indications are that the depositor had been taking this medicine for four weeks or more."

"What indications?"

He hesitated a moment. "Understand that all this gets into the speculative. I mean, I have certain scientific indices to go by, but my conclusions are really my own."

"All right."

"During the testing, I found both a slightly lower sperm count and a lower amount of the body's naturally produced hydrocortisone. Now the first is no real indication of anything—tight pants can knock off sperm—but the second, taken with the first and coupled to the presence of prednisone, is a red flag for Cushing's syndrome."

Neither Frank nor I moved or said a word. Both of us felt that in his understated way, Robert Kees was about to make us a gift.

"I almost hate to tell you this, because it's so thin, but I do feel I've let you down a little with the other stuff. But take it all with a giant grain of salt." He cleared his throat. "If you take prednisone for a month or more, chances are you'll start to bloat—retaining fluids you normally pass to the outside. Usually, that's where it stops, but every once in a while—and I'm talking rarely here—you develop Cushing's. You become weak and overweight, with a rounded, pinkish moon face; you bruise easily, suffer from occasional delirium and depression, and any psychological disorders can become exaggerated. But the most telling thing about Cushing's, at least physically, is the emergence of a kind of buffalo hump high on the back."

"You mean the guy's a hunchback?" Murphy asked.

I put my hand on his forearm to quiet him.

"Now, assuming that all this fell into place, which is highly unlikely though possible, there is no way to determine how long the depositor was on the medicine, why he took it in the first place, or whether he's still on it. Furthermore, just as the syndrome appears after a month or more, it disappears a month or less after treatment is terminated."

Kees sat back down. "What I'm giving you here is my educated guess. Because of the low hydrocortisone level in the sample, I'd say there's an outside chance your man did develop Cushing's—that would make him stand out in a crowd. Furthermore, for the hundreds of people who might be issued one of the prednisone family of drugs from any given urban pharmacy, only two to five will have prescriptions running for over a week to ten days."

I glanced over to Murphy's face. He looked back, smiled, and nodded. "Now that's a lead."

14

It was midafternoon before we picked our way through the scaffolding, the workmen, and the piles of construction material outside the doorless lobby of Kees's building. It was snowing again, as it had been almost all week. TV reports had broadcast travel advisories for that morning, and from what I could see, or couldn't see, things were not improving.

We found the car, the only white, furry-looking, rounded lump in the now-crowded parking lot, and put our bags and the cooler in the back seat. Glancing over my shoulder as I pulled out the ice scraper, I saw the building we'd just left as the vaguest of shadows on a whited-out television screen.

"Christ, it's really coming down," Murphy said as he wiped the snow from the windshield with his gloved hand.

I handed him the scraper after I'd done my side. "You want to pass on going home? We could spend the night at some motel."

He shook his head. "I'm sick of sleeping where I don't belong—we've been through worse than this." He finished clearing the windshield and opened the door, adding, "Besides, it wouldn't hurt to give Ski Mask a little run for his money. If he is on our trail, maybe we'll find out if he's a flatlander or not."

Boasts like that aside, drivers in New England handle heavy snow the same way everyone else does—they cling to the right lane and crawl. By the time I got to the interstate heading north, I knew we were in for a very long trip. Occasionally, in the straightaways, when the wind would briefly shift and open up visibility, I'd venture onto the white-crusted, slippery passing lane to overtake a couple of my more timid fellow travelers, but for the most part we were stuck in line. My eyes strained to see through the flurries to the blurry outline of the car just ahead.

"I wonder how many people go off the road because they follow the guy in front of them?"

Frank grunted. "You thinking of doing that?"

"I've heard of it happening."

He didn't respond. He was wearing a shapeless black coat and a fake-fur trooper hat with the flaps pulled down over his ears. His chin was buried in a brown scarf. He looked like a tired Russian commuter sitting on a bus.

"Why don't you turn up the heat?"

He shook his head. "Makes me sleepy."

"So sleep. You can take over at Hartford."

"Naw. So what are we going to do now?"

"I say we dig into Kimberly Harris. We know damned well she wasn't the innocent victim of a drug-crazed loner."

"Got any guesses?"

"A couple. Floyd Rubin, for instance."

"The pharmacist?"

"He could be the father."

"Are you kidding? I thought she just worked there."

"He said they were friends, but it may have been more. It's pure hunch right now, but she was five-and-a-half months pregnant when she died—and that was five months after she quit Charlie's."

"Does that make him Ski Mask too?"

"You've never seen the man. I think he's clear there, but he could easily be her four-thousand-dollar-a-month sugar daddy. Those payments also started near the time she quit and went up to the end. I'd love to be able to look at his bank records, but I doubt we could get a warrant."

"We could get around that, maybe."

"Wouldn't risk it. If it does give us something, we'd never be able to use it in court. We might wear him down—imply we've already got the records or something."

"What about Ski Mask? Why not bring in some outside help?"

"I doubt we have the choice anymore. We had one body when we left four days ago; that's more than we've had in the last three years. I'd be surprised if the selectmen haven't forced Brandt to bring in everybody but the Mounties by now. Gail said they'd soon be looking for someone to hang."

For once, Frank didn't even groan. Slim as it was, Kees's conjecture about Harris's killer had given him something to chew on besides his endangered reputation.

He muttered, "I bet he's a government man."

"A spook?"

"That, or a vet. Special Forces or something. He's got to be on his own, though. Sure as hell that bug was stolen."

"He might be the fetus's father."

"Sure, or even the real killer. It's not impossible that since we missed him the first time, he's renewing the invitation—the man's obviously bonkers."

I nodded. "I like that one."

"The only problem with it is he doesn't fit my image of the Hunchback of Notre Dame, and according to Kees that's who did her in. You ever notice Ski Mask having trouble breathing?"

"You mean asthma? No, from the little I've seen, he's in good shape. Of course, Kees didn't say it had to be asthma."

"I know, and I've heard of crippled kids becoming gymnasts. But I can't believe a guy who was so sick three years ago would be a jock today."

The car in front suddenly swerved out of control and started slowly spinning around and around, working its way toward the opposite guard rail like a gyroscope losing power. I down-shifted and pumped the brakes a couple of times, feeling the road slide out from under the wheels. I hit the accelerator gently and crabbed by the other car, which had come to a stop a few inches from the edge of the road. My tires finally caught and brought us back into line.

"Everyone okay?"

Murphy was looking back over his shoulder. "Yeah. No damage." He settled back and we both watched an abandoned eighteen-wheeler lying in a ditch loom up and disappear like a half-remembered thought. "Interesting trip."

I waited a couple of minutes for my heart to start beating normally. Maybe it was time to get some snow tires.

"Of course, no one says he even had a humpback. Kees did mention he might have just had poison ivy or something."

I shook my head. "Kees was just covering his tracks. I don't say the guy had the hump necessarily, but he was seriously into this prednisone stuff or Kees wouldn't have brought it up. I have the suspicion he thinks we have, or at least we had, a full-fledged Cushing's victim on our hands. In any case, hump or no hump, a run through the local prescriptions ought to give us something."

"Assuming he was local."

And so it went, hour after hour, traveling through white space with only the occasional slipping of the tires to let us know we were attached to the road. The conversation lapsed now and then, but only long enough for us to come up with a few more weird ideas.

It was a morale booster if nothing else. By the time Frank took over the wheel in Hartford, I knew for certain my old friend was back where he belonged. We had never worked together on a case as convoluted as this, but we had shared lots of long, winding conversations that had eventually set us on the right course. After all the uncertainty and frustration of the past few days, that simple process, even without final answers, was a big comfort.

Night had fallen halfway into the trip, narrowing our already limited view to a hypnotizing funnel of onrushing snow. Coming from the space-like void, it blazed briefly in the headlights before careening off the windshield, without sound or trace. It was like flying through densely packed stars while standing perfectly still. I was no longer sure if we were moving, or if the earth was slipping rapidly beneath us. And we were utterly alone. North of Springfield the traffic had ceased to exist and we hurtled along in total isolation.

The illusion was shaken first by the dark, deep rumbling of a diesel engine coming up from behind—an oddly menacing sound that enveloped the car. Murphy muttered, "Christ, the son of a bitch must be flying."

I looked around. The ice-caked rear window glowed with two shaking headlights from an eighteen-wheeler. The noise grew and became a vibration, tickling the soles of my feet and making my hands sweat.

"How fast are we going?"

Both of Frank's hands were tight on the steering wheel. "Forty-something."

The light was getting stronger, along with the noise. "He's got to be going fifty or better."

The truck was abreast of us now, a mechanical monster looming like a nightmare.

"What the fuck's he doing? He's going to kill us." Frank tugged at the window crank, fighting against the ice outside. The window suddenly came free. Blazing snow, wind, and the screaming of a diesel engine swept into the car, making us both shout in alarm. Across Murphy's chest I could see the trailer's side marker lights gleaming inches from his door; had he reached out his hand, he could have touched them. The wind blew the hat from his head, and in the demonic red glow his face was tight with fear.

120

"Let up on the gas," I shouted.

He was ahead of me. The truck's speed picked up as ours lessened, but too late. The riveted steel wall of the box veered closer and connected. There was a thump and a screech of metal. The car was lifted as by the wind. The smoothness beneath our wheels rippled loudly and then sent a punch that lifted us from our seats. Briefly, as in the flash from a camera, I saw the guard rail dead ahead, heard a sudden smashing and then all was quiet and darkness.

For a moment we were airborne, the headlights gone, the windshield a spidery web of cracked glass, the car filled with wind. The nose made contact first, throwing me against my seatbelt. The windshield blew out and we began to roll, slowly at first, then faster and faster. I felt my body float in harness amid an orchestra of noise. The end I don't remember. There was a flash of light from deep behind my eyes, and there was water. The lovely sound of rushing water.

15

I woke up in a hospital room, staring at a ceiling of pockmarked little tiles, complete with a brown water stain directly overhead. I can't remember ever seeing such a ceiling without a stain like that.

I was flat on my back and my head hurt. I knew it was a hospital because of the smell, the whiteness, the drip bag suspended from a coat-hanger contraption to my right, and the fact that I'd been woken up by a voice paging Dr. Winters.

I turned my head slightly to better examine the drip bag and instantly closed my eyes against the burst of pain. A scraping noise made me open them again. Gail's face came into view.

"Joe?"

"Guilty." My voice had a canned sound to it, as if it came from the outside.

"How are you?"

"Not good, I guess." My head pounded regularly now, in perfect time with my heart.

Her face came very close, and I felt her lips touch my own. They were soft and trembling. I had never felt so totally in love. I wanted the kiss to continue.

She touched my cheek with her hand. "You've been asleep a long time." Her eyes were brimming.

"How long?"

"Two days."

I lifted my right hand to rub my eyes and found an intravenous tube taped to my wrist. It was hard to concentrate. "Did we land in some water?"

"A river. You were half-frozen when they found you. You've had a concussion."

"Jesus. How's Frank?"

She pursed her lips and a tear ran down her cheek. "He's dead, Joe."

The pounding got worse and was joined by a humming sound. I looked at her for a long time, feeling increasingly detached, as though the inside part of me could just get up and leave the room. I closed my eyes and went back to sleep.

When I woke up, Brandt was looking down at me. "Welcome back." His face was serious, his eyes slightly narrowed, as if trying to guess what lay hidden just beneath my skin. I watched him silently from my hiding place. "How do you feel?"

"All right."

"How's the head?"

I thought a moment. "Fine, I guess." I moved it slightly and the bomb went off again. "Maybe not so fine."

"The doctor says it'll probably hurt for a few days. It's amazing you survived at all."

"Where's Frank?"

Brandt blinked and looked away. He nodded at someone I couldn't see—or didn't try to see. He then took off his glasses and scratched the side of his nose. "You know Frank's dead."

"Yes."

"We had the ceremony yesterday, Joe."

The pounding had faded to the background. It returned with a vengeance. "You could have waited."

"We waited three days. We couldn't any longer."

"Three days? Gail told me I'd been out two."

"You went under again."

A deep rage gushed up inside me, making my entire body hot. I tried getting onto my elbows, fighting against the nausea. Gail appeared at Brandt's side and put her hand on my chest. "What do you want, Joe?"

"I'm sick of staring up everyone's nostrils."

She placed a control box into my hand and pushed my thumb against a green button. The bed behind my pillow began to rise. The world slowly straightened. The pain in my head backed off a bit.

Brandt sat on the edge of the bed. "That better?"

I nodded to Gail. "Thank you."

"What happened out there, Joe?"

"A truck ran us off the road."

He frowned and reached into his pocket for his pipe. He sat there for a moment looking at it, turning it over in his hands. "What kind of truck?"

"An eighteen-wheeler. Wasn't there a report?"

He shook his head. "As far as the Massachusetts State Police are concerned, it was a single-vehicle accident."

"A single...Jesus Christ, didn't they check the side of the car for paint? The son of a bitch sideswiped us." I had to breathe deeply to keep the pain in check.

"There wasn't much left of the car. I saw it myself."

I stared at the opposite wall, trying to remember. Again, I saw Frank's face in that red light, the side of the truck coming nearer. I looked back at Brandt. "The truck box was unpainted—plain metal. Still, there ought to be something to go on."

"We'll give it another look."

"What about the road? Skid marks or debris?"

"Nothing besides yours. Of course, it wasn't bare road. It's hard to see skid marks on the ice, especially at night."

It was hopeless. I was four days away from the event. The evidence had been snowplowed by now, the truck long gone. Suspecting nothing, they'd let it all slip away.

"When can I get out of this dump?"

Gail spoke up from her chair. "Two or three days."

"Take it easy, Joe. There's no rush."

"The hell there isn't. What about Ski Mask?"

Brandt glanced quickly at Gail, who to him was first and foremost a selectman.

"She knows all about it. I told her. What about him? And what about the samples? What happened to them? Did you find them?"

"Slow down. Yes, we found them. The troopers were a little curious, to say the least, but we got them back. I returned them to Hillstrom. She told me the damage was slight—nothing crucial. And we haven't heard a peep from Ski Mask since the accident."

I slowly leaned forward and peeled the bed sheet back.

Gail rose from her seat. "What are you doing, Joe?"

"Don't get worked up. I just want to see if everything's still functioning." I swung my legs over the side of the bed. My head began to swim.

"I wouldn't do that. Not unless you're suicidal." A young doctor with glasses and a pocket stuffed with the obligatory implements moved in from the door and lifted my legs back. "A concussion means blood gets loose in your head. That builds up pressure and you conk out. Build up too much pressure and you croak. You start running around now, you'll start bleeding again and it's bye-bye. Get the picture?"

I lay back against the pillow, partly happy for the interference. "How come all the doctors on television don't talk like that?"

"They're actors. They don't think it's real." He pried back my eyelid and flashed a light in my eye.

"So how soon do I get out?"

"Two days at the soonest. You'll be able to get around before that, but I don't want you out of my sight until I know you're okay. I know your type—pure John Wayne."

"Give me a break."

"All right—pure Jane Fonda. Take your pick." He finished his examination and had a nurse take my vitals. He said he'd see me the following day and left.

Brandt took up his station by the bed. "Well, I guess I'll let you be."

"Tony, we got a lot of good stuff down there."

He patted my arm. "It'll keep, Joe. Just try to relax and shake this thing off."

"But what's been going on?"

Again, he glanced at Gail. She took the hint. "You want me to step outside?"

"For Christ's sake, Tony."

Gail squeezed my hand. "He's right, Joe—it's good politics. What he says isn't pillow talk, and that can be bad enough."

Brandt smiled at her as she picked up her purse. "Thanks. I'll vote for you next time."

"Well," she said, with exaggerated, tinny humor, "I should hope so."

I waited for the door to close behind her. "So?"

"Nothing new on the Phillips killing. I think we've dead-ended on all possibilities except Ski Mask, and there we're digging into Davis's past with a microscope. I have managed to get Tom Wilson to stand between us and the board concerning the links to the Harris case."

Wilson was the town manager and Brandt's direct boss. "He's lying to them?"

"Withholding information is more like it. I convinced him that if we let them know about the Harris connection, it'll wind up in the next day's paper; until we have something solid, it would be best to leave that hornet's nest alone."

"I can't believe he agreed to it."

"He's so scared we may have jailed the wrong man, he's damn near irrational."

I closed my eyes and lay back against the pillow for a moment.

"You ought to get some rest."

I opened my eyes again. "No, wait. So no state police?"

"Not yet. They've been informed—hell, they read the newspaper too—but so far they're out of it." He looked at me closely. "You look lousy. Get some sleep and I'll come back later, okay?"

"All right. Thanks."

I watched the door swing shut behind him. I felt a little like all this was happening to someone else; my concern with keeping the state police off our turf seemed incongruous now that I thought about it. Frank was dead, I damn near was, everything had gone to hell in a hand basket, and I was worried I'd lose the case.

My eyes were shut when Gail walked back in and resettled herself in the corner chair. I could hear her turning the pages of a book. "How was the ceremony?"

She put the book down and looked at me sadly. "There were a lot of people there. They had an honor guard—I think Frank would have been embarrassed."

"How's Martha?"

"Not well. She's staying with her daughter somewhere in Massachusetts."

"Wendy. I think she lives in Braintree." Gail nodded. "That's it. She seemed very nice."

"Where did they hold the ceremony?" I knew the ground was too hard for burial.

"At the cemetery—Martha insisted. They just put the casket on the snow. It was beautiful—cold, but sunny. When they played taps, it was like the sound would go on forever. You could hear it hit the mountain across the river."

I could visualize it. I knew the plot he had chosen; he'd shown it to me one summer afternoon years ago. It was on the eastern edge of Morningside Cemetery, right at the crest of a slope falling sharply to the railroad tracks and the Connecticut River far below. We'd stood there for a few minutes, taking in the view of Wantastiquet Mountain across the river in New Hampshire, looming a good thousand feet above us. In the middle of the river was a small wooded island that acted as midpoint to the bridge crossing there. At the turn of the century, it had been a permanent carnival area, the town's hot spot all summer long, complete with merry-go-round, Ferris wheel, the works. Now it was just an island—a lover's lane during the warmer months. Looking out over all that—the wash of green trees and the sparkling water—I had complimented him on his choice.

I could see it in my mind's eye, but none of it really sank in—I didn't actually feel anything. I knew he was dead, that I'd never see him again, that he now lay in a box in some refrigerator, awaiting the spring thaw. But I only felt bitter. "What killed him?"

"Tony said you'd ask." She wasn't smiling. She got up and sat on the edge of the bed.

"Professional habit."

"He drowned, Joe. He was unconscious when you hit the river. The autopsy said he wouldn't have survived anyway. You should have been underwater, too, but somehow you got tangled in your seat belt and it kept your head up."

"Who found us?"

"A motorist called it in. He saw the hole in the fence and the fresh tracks and used the call box by the side of the road."

The pain in my head stopped. Everything stopped. For a moment I flashed back to the last sensation I'd had that night: the rushing water and the cold—the sudden, numbing cold. "That caller didn't leave a name, did he." It wasn't a question.

"No."

"No—he wouldn't."

She took up my hand. "Wasn't this an accident?" Her voice was barely audible.

"I don't think so."

"But why?"

"I don't know. The other attempt kind of made sense—if you were a little nuts—but not this one. We thought he was trying to stimulate us—to get us interested in the case."

She stared at me in shocked silence for a moment. "What do you mean, 'the other attempt'? What does that mean?"

I took a deep breath. I didn't want to get into that. "A few days ago someone turned on the gas in my apartment after I went to sleep. Ski Mask pulled me out."

Her mouth opened and shut. "I didn't know that. Why didn't I know that?"

"I didn't tell you. Only Frank and Brandt knew about it. There was no harm done."

"Ski Mask saved your life?"

"Maybe. We don't know. I thought so at first. That's what he said; that someone was trying to derail the investigation into the Harris thing by killing me and making it look like an accident. Frank thought that was all baloney—that Ski Mask was just trying to stoke up our interest and keep us off balance. Makes sense."

"So you think Ski Mask ran you off the road."

"Who else?" I shut my eyes again. The effort of keeping them open was wearing me out.

"Isn't it possible he was telling the truth?"

"Why would anyone involved in the original murder stir every-thing up when the best thing would be to lay low? It's just too far-fetched. That's why we figured the attempt on me was just Ski Mask throwing out red herrings. There couldn't be anyone except him out there."

"That may have been true then; it's hardly true now. Why would Ski Mask kill the two people most helpful to him. And why would he try to destroy the very evidence that might reopen the case? It seems to me there probably is somebody else, trying to hush the whole thing up. And they almost succeeded."

I pushed against my temples with my fingers. This conversation wasn't helping things. "Frank was starting to think that Ski Mask killed Kimberly and was daring us to catch him. That he was play-ing a kind of help-us-here, hinder-us-there game. That might explain driving us off the road. He was convinced Ski Mask had followed us to Connecticut. Jesus, this thing is such a mess."

Gail wouldn't let it go. "I think Frank was right, at least partly. Ski Mask probably did follow you, saw the other people force you off the road, and anonymously called in the accident."

It was bad enough having one loony in a mask; now we were staring at a whole separate bunch of them. And nobody knew what the hell any of them wanted, or why this whole bloody mess had been started in the first place. "Jesus, Gail. I don't know." I put my head back on the pillow and looked up at the brown spot.

Gail put her cool hand on my forehead. "Why don't you take a nap?"

I didn't answer. She pushed the button on the control box and low-ered the bed. She bent over and kissed me again. "I love you, Joe. I know you miss Frank, but I'm happy you're alive."

I lifted my hand and touched her breast with the backs of my fingers. My head weighed a ton. "I love you too. I wish I could get you into this bed right now. How long have you been here?"

"From the start. The hospital's not too full, so I took the room next door."

That made me smile sleepily. "Must be costing you a fortune."

"It ain't cheap. I'll send you the bill when you're feeling better."

She stayed by my side, rubbing my forehead until I went back to sleep. I did stay two more days. In fact, it took me that long to feel halfway solid on my feet again. Gail would help me walk around the room and later down the hall, and then I'd pile back into bed as if I'd spent the entire day doing push-ups. Most of the time I just lay there, reading, talking with Gail, seeing visitors—mainly cops—and watching television. I never got to see it, but Gail told me that right after the accident I'd been a feature on the local news, complete with a file photo that made me look twenty years younger. Katz, of course, had gone wild, running a story each day on the goings-on at the police department; Gail showed me the back issues. He didn't have anything new, of course, but on his daily visits, Brandt let me know the publicity was making for some pretty frayed nerves among Tom Wilson and the selectmen. It was typical of Gail that she never commented on what was happening at the board meetings.

On the morning of the seventh day, Levin—the doctor with the hip dialogue—told me to "take a hike." The release was provisional, however. I had to spend at least two additional days away from the office and, as he put it, eyeing Gail, "any sexual temptations." In other words, home to Mother.

Gail had contacted her and my brother the same night I'd been brought in, and I had phoned them as soon as I was able. Leo had volunteered to drive them both down, but I'd told them to stay put. My mother's traveling days, whether she admitted it or not, were over, and I knew Leo would be nervous leaving her behind. Besides, I saw little point in disrupting their lives just so they could see me lying in bed.

I did, however, promise to visit as soon as I could, and by Levin's stern look, that time was apparently now. I went to my apartment, packed enough clothes for two days, and was driven north by Gail, again under doctor's orders. As it turned out, he knew his patient well. As soon as we were on the interstate, I went into hibernation for the duration of the trip.

The family farm is no more. The house remains by the side of a dirt road branching off from the main drag between Thetford Center and Thetford Hill, but a row of trees now stands between the home I knew as a kid and the fields Leo and I and my father used to till long ago. The land was sold after Father's death, clearing his few debts and setting Mother up with a nest egg that had served her adequately ever since. Romantic notions aside, I don't think any one of us ever missed those fields.

The degree of Mother's comfort, of course, wasn't guaranteed by the money. We had Leo to thank for that. For reasons none of us had ever discussed, and probably never would, Leo had decided to stay at home. He worked as a butcher at the grocery store in Thetford Center, tooled around in an ever-changing menagerie of exotic and impractical cars, chased as many women as he could simultaneously and took tender loving care of our mother. He was, as far as I had ever been able or willing to probe, as happy as he could possibly imagine.

Mother was not as easily read. Her life since early youth had been a series of roles imposed by circumstance and other people's needs. The only girl in a large family of boys, she had filled her mother's shoes at age nine when that exhausted woman had been done in by her eleventh childbirth. She cooked and cleaned and mended and nursed and virtually carried her small male army as far as she could take it, and on her eighteenth birthday she ran away with the only man she was ever to know in bed.

I'm sure it was her decision. My father was not a passionate man. Older than she by a good twenty years, he had walked behind his plow alone for as long as anyone could remember. When my mother's family discovered what she had done, it never crossed their collective mind to blame my father, and I don't doubt they were right.

As far as Leo or I could tell, marriage and fatherhood never had the slightest effect on the old man. He continued doing what he had done all along, and treated us with the same solid neutrality he handed out to the occasionally hired day laborers. I have often thought that it was in an effort to reflect his stolidity that Leo had never married and I had evolved the way I had. It hadn't worked for either of us, of course. Certainly, as I came to realize following Ellen's death, I had aimed for the image of a man untouched by events all around him and instead had ended up like a fish in a sea of complexities. I became so immersed in seeing at least some value in every viewpoint that I began to wonder if my father's aloofness hadn't perhaps been rooted in some less-than-human brain dysfunction.

I never saw my parents touch. I sensed a mutual respect, but I could never tell if that was based only partly on the fact that they both did their jobs to perfection. For even in the gloom of the Depression, life didn't vary at home. Our farm marched ahead at my father's steady pace, good times or bad, reflecting as much of reality as he did. Had Leo and I not left the house to go to school and grow up, I think the Depression, World War II, the atomic bomb, McCarthy, and all the rest would have passed us by without notice. And through it all, Mother did as she had done before, only now the children were her own and far fewer in number.

That, of course, was the crucial distinction, and one she had set out to create by choosing my father. Because despite his machinelike lack of emotion, ours was a happy home, made partially so by his stolid ability to make every new year as predictable as the last. Her role was to make those years pleasant and fulfilling, and as Leo's caring for her now testified, she'd made it a success. When the phrase "earth mother" cropped up in the sixties, my picture of Mother was forever titled.

Of course, the problem with earth mothers, I have since found out, is that they're so good at handing out goodwill, they all but stop being three-dimensional human beings. They don't volunteer what's in their hearts, and few people bother to find out. After my father's death and my departure from home, Mother buried herself for years in community activities until finally, one day, old and on walking sticks, she quit—totally.

She lived in a wheelchair now, her world restricted to the downstairs of the house. She was surrounded by books, magazines, crossword puzzles, a radio, a television set, and two cats. Outwardly, she remained pleasant and good-natured, but I always sensed a tiredness there, as if she'd been asked to smile for the camera just one shot beyond her tolerance. Leo always said I was full of it, and maybe I was. I had to believe, after all, that if anyone knew what really made her tick, he did—unless he was too close to see.

Gail stopped the car in front of the house but left the engine running. I stopped halfway out the door and looked back at her. "Not coming in?"

"I don't think so, Joe. Despite all the reassurances I gave her on the phone, your Mom knows how close you came to dying. I think she'd like to see you alone. Tell her I love her, though, okay?"

I leaned back inside and kissed her. "Okay."

"Give me a call when you want a ride back." I pulled my bag out of the backseat and waved goodbye, watching her car until it disappeared over the rise.

16

She was in the living room, surrounded by three small tables, her daily pastimes piled around her like the borders of a nest. But her hands were motionless in her lap. She was watching a soap opera, something I'd rarely seen happen before. She was an avid radio listener, but daytime TV was a sign of things amiss.

She caught my movement and turned suddenly toward me. For a split second, I saw the face of a woman with no reserves left—blank, hollow-eyed, sagging from the lack of life. It was gone so fast, it was more of an impression than a real image, but it left me shocked. In its place was an older version of what had welcomed me into this house as far back as I could recall.

She gathered me in for a hug. "What foolishness have you been up to?"

I kissed her warm wrinkled cheek. "I wish I knew."

She held my face out at arm's length. "And Frank?"

I could only shrug.

"Where's Gail?"

"She went back. I think she felt awkward."

"She's a good girl."

I straightened and glanced at the television. Mother hit the remote-control button by her side and killed the picture.

"Stories without end. Not like life at all."

I had to smile. "I can't argue with that."

She was watching me closely, her eyes bright and sharp. She had one of those faces in which every line followed her mood. She smiled, and hundreds of wrinkles smiled; she frowned, and they were all sad. "How do you feel, Joe?"

"A little detached." I walked over to the bay window and sat on the bench sill. This had been my favorite reading spot at night as a kid, surrounded by the cold wind on three sides, and yet warm and safe.

"It sounds like after Korea."

"I suppose so. I hadn't thought of that. God, you have a long memory."

"A mother's memory. For you, that was just a phase. For me, it was the death of my child—it robbed me of something special. It's not a time I will ever forget."

"I ended up going to college, at least for a while."

She shook her head. "The price was too high."

I smiled. She was right. I had been the one to break the cocoon holding this house and its inhabitants. That had changed things forever, and no achievement of mine would ever justify it.

"How long are you going to stay?"

"Just a couple of days—until I get my legs back."

"You were hit very hard, weren't you?" The softness in her voice made the answer superfluous, but I didn't want her to retreat to what I had seen when I'd entered.

"Not hard enough, I guess. I'll be okay in a couple of days. But I've got to go back to wrap this thing up. I can't leave it hanging."

"Did you stop by to see Leo on the way up?"

"No, I came straight here."

"Go down and see him. He'd like that."

"What about you?"

She gestured at her piled-up pastimes. "I've got my projects. Go."

I kissed her again and went outside. As I closed the door behind me, I heard the television start up. The stories without end had acquired a certain appeal, and I found that sad.

I crossed over the icy snow to the barn and swung back its big double doors. The blank, gray light fell on a semicircle of eight dusty, mummified cars, all looking like alien pods wrapped in canvas. This was Leo's pleasure palace—his other obsession besides women. Under each tarp was an automobile loved for its own special virtue, whether it was looks, engine, popular appeal, or merely that it had been around for so long. None of them were in mint condition. Leo kept them covered, but only because the barn was so dusty. Their paint jobs were dull, and they were dented here and there; on the street they attracted attention for their quaintness, not their gleam.

But while their shells were weather-beaten, their innards were immaculate. Each car ran with the smoothness of its first mile.

I uncovered the one nearest me, hoping it wasn't the pale green T-bird, and found the '49 Cadillac—the first car he'd ever collected. I knew there was a Mustang somewhere, probably the most practical choice given the time of year, but I didn't have the energy to dig it out. I got the key off the wall. The Cadillac would have to do.

It was only about three miles to Thetford Center and the grocery store where Leo worked—a nice walk if you were up to it. Not that the reasons for such a stroll were compelling. The town didn't boast of much beyond the grocery and, at fifty miles an hour, it could be missed entirely during a good sneeze.

Leo was actually part-owner of the store, having tacked a full-fledged butcher shop onto its back to save it from bankruptcy. He had been operating in Hanover, New Hampshire, about twelve miles south and across the river, catering to the blue-blood barnacles attached to Dartmouth College. There, over the years, as head of the meat department at the town's trendiest "food emporium," he'd become the Walter Cronkite of viands—the area's most trusted butcher. But he remained an employee. When he heard of the plight of the grocery store in Thetford Center, he took the chance that his clientele wouldn't begrudge him the extra fifteen-minute commute. Apparently, they hadn't—much to his, and the grocery store's, profit.

But the thing that struck me wasn't his uncanny marketing, but that he was now less than two minutes from our house. At this rate, in fifteen years he'd have his profession, his hobby, and his home all under one roof. I thought of our mother sitting in a single room surrounded by all her possessions. Maybe the two of them were more compatible than I'd thought.

He must have seen me from the window, because he came running out of the store in his blood-smeared apron and pounded me on the back, patting my chest with the other hand at the same time—a true meat lover. "Joey—Jesus, I'm glad to see you. You look lousy. How do you feel?" He looked over my shoulder. "The Caddy—good choice. How's Mom?"

I muttered something to his back as he trotted ahead to open the door and usher me in.

He gave me a fleeting, sorrowful look. "I was sorry to hear about Frank, Joey. A lot of people felt the loss up here. He was a real favorite."

He closed the door and the subject with an expansive wave of his arm. "Look at this. Dynamite, huh?"

I had been here less than a month ago—I was never allowed home without visiting the store—and the place had been so stuffed with Christmas greenery, it had looked like Sherwood Forest. Now, it was Danish modern: blond wooden chairs, white counters, butcher block everywhere. I could still smell the sawdust and new paint.

"Christ, Leo, it looks like a furniture store."

"Great, huh? I even have a play area for kids. Now the mothers can take their time." He laughed. "And spend more."

This last was addressed directly to several of those mothers, clustered in front of his meat display counter. They giggled like groupies. He dragged me around to the other side of the counter and shoved an apron at me. "This is my big brother, ladies. He comes to help me out sometimes for therapy—he's a cop, you understand."

He pointed me at the meat grinder and went to take care of his customers. Leo, in short doses, was good for the soul. How my mother put up with him, I could never guess.

We spent the afternoon back there, I making hamburger meat, cutting fat, or wrapping pieces in plastic for display, Leo hustling the trade, making the fancy cuts and keeping up a running patter of conversation. This had become a traditional part of my visits, both here and when he'd worked in Hanover. He was right. In a way, it was therapeutic. Our father had taught us to butcher, and to go through the memorized patterns of an earlier age was a relief from having to think.

Leo knew that. Beneath his marathon conversational style, he was a keen watcher and a champion depression squasher, acutely attuned to getting other people out of their slumps. I don't know how much else he had on the ball, but he was a hell of a friend. Over the hours, I noticed him glancing at me occasionally, making sure I was all right.

At closing time, he looped his arm over my shoulders. "So, do the docs say you can booze it up?"

"Nope."

"I was afraid of that. Girls?"

"That's why Gail isn't here."

"Bummer. Well, I guess it's home, then. Pizza tonight."

"You ordering out?"

"Hell, no. Mom does the slicing and dicing and I do the rolling—that part's rough on her wrists. It's a group effort."

He jogged off to his car—a '65 Corvair—and I followed him back to the farm. The afternoon had been well spent. My headache was finally gone. I was as tired as I ever remembered feeling, but not exhausted. It had all the omens of a good night's sleep.

Mother was indeed slicing and dicing when we got home, on a board laid across the arms of her wheelchair. The two of them worked well together. As usual, I stayed out of the way, my culinary prowess being rarely in demand.

After dinner, Leo put on his coat and beckoned to me to follow. We went across to the barn. He switched on the light and nodded at the Cadillac. "How did she handle?"

"Pretty well. I was surprised."

"Yeah, I've updated her a little. The purists wouldn't like it, but then they never drive the goddamned things either. You want to borrow her until you get another one?"

"No, Leo. I wouldn't want to take the risk. I don't seem to be leading the most sedate of lives right now."

"So I hear. What are you going to do about a car?"

"I don't know. I can bum rides until I find another one."

"Pretty weak, Joey. You can't borrow mine 'cause you'll smack it up, but you can destroy someone else's—and possibly its driver—with no problem. Did I get that right?"

"You're a pain in the ass."

"Right. Here are the keys." He slapped them into my hand.

"Remember, one scratch, one smudge, one single bird dropping, and we never speak again, okay?"

"Okay."

He covered the Corvair and revealed the green T-bird, the most garish of his collection. "You heading out?"

"Uh-huh. Heavy date." He got in behind the wheel.

"The gas station owner?"

He furrowed his brow, visibly pained. "Oh no, not in this. Tonight's very high-class. I've found a Dartmouth prof. She's a Roman civilization nut."

The engine started up with a mellow, deep-throated roar. He grinned with pleasure. "See you later."

I turned off the lights after he'd left and walked back to the house. It was a full moon, and the snow around me exuded an eerie pale-blue glow.

Mother was back at her station, the TV off, the radio burbling in the background. The single lamp on one of the tables made her white hair shine, setting her apart from the surroundings as if she were floating in the dark.

I sat in an overstuffed armchair across the room from her. "How was your afternoon?"

"You ought to know. He just lent me the Cadillac."

"He's a nice boy. A little strange, but I'm glad I have him. When you two were little, I never would have dreamed things would turn out like this."

"You two really get along, don't you?"

"He does all the work. I'm just a cranky old lady. I sometimes wish he would go out on his own so I could die peacefully, but that doesn't seem to be the way it will happen."

"You worried your dying will knock the pins out from under him?"

"Good Lord, no. I'm much more selfish than that. I would just like to get it over with, and that's hard with him around—he's so irrepressible."

I smiled. "Is it that bad?"

"No. I suppose not." She reached for something beside her and pulled out a large book. "It's just that when everything else you've known is dying around you, you sort of feel left out. When I heard of your accident, I had Leo get this out. It's your album."

Over the years, she had built up separate photo albums for Leo and me. Typically, the only signs of her and my father were fleeting appearances in the background of some of our pictures. I got up and laid the book open on the table under the light.

Whatever pains we might recall from endless photo sessions, grinning for some relative until our teeth began to dry, there is something magical, years later, about the result. I saw myself in those pages, from babyhood on, looking ahead; not to what I now was, but to what I was to be and yet had never become. It was like looking at pictures of the twin brother I'd lost to history. He had my face, he shared my memories, but he'd ended up somewhere else in this world.

Frank began appearing in the photographs, at first peripherally and out of focus. I found one taken at town fair. I'm about nine or ten, holding a kitten we later named Heather, and in the background is Frank, a skinny blond in overalls talking to a girl, one foot maturely planted on a tree stump—the older teenager, soon to go off to war— not that any of us knew it then.

He steps forward thereafter, coming into focus at my side, laughing, painting the house, working with my father, grooming a horse. Suddenly, in his World War II uniform, he retreats, looking again like the boy at the fair, gathering his courage in front of him so he can believe what he sees.

Then comes the crucible—the years immediately after, when, giving up on my father as a guidepost to the future, I narrowed in on Frank, the returning veteran. He'd blazed through the protective bubble created by my parents, returning wiser and more bold. When my turn came to pose in front of the Army camera, it was Frank's steps I was following, even more than my own desires.

There are lots of shots of Korea in that album; everyone seemed to have a camera. They were mostly taken during R & R, or at rest spots far from the action. Some were taken in the field but only when nothing was happening. They don't show the wounded men we all saw later during Vietnam; they don't show burning huts or huddling civilians or helicopters bearing body bags. They just show erstwhile kids, looking the same as when they left—dirtier maybe, thinner certainly—but lacking something fundamental, as if only the photographer had noticed they were no longer tied to their pasts.

I began to weep then, flipping through those pages. Nothing terribly emotional, of course—I couldn't let go that much. But the tears still fell, no less real. I missed Frank, and missing him made me cry. I guess we don't really cry for the dead, but for the people they leave behind—ourselves.

Somehow, our lives had branched apart. He had married and had kids. I had married and she had died. He'd become a cop and had made captain. I'd become a cop and would become captain over his dead body. And yet he'd gone into that river without a struggle, already conceding death before knowing when it would come. And I had not—and would not. Perhaps in exchange for having lost the standard human goals of life, I felt imbued with a sense of survival, as if I were standing by the side of a road, watching everyone else walk by.

17

The first person I met when I drove into the Municipal Building's parking lot was Stan Katz. He was standing by the steps, his hands shoved deep into his pockets, a frozen camera around his neck, a cloud of vapor in front of his face. I wondered how many days he'd been waiting.

I had hoped to park quickly and make a run for the side door, but Leo's taste in automobiles precluded that—Stan saw the car before he realized I was driving it. Like a well-trained factotum, his hand was on the door handle as soon as I cut the engine.

"Is it true you've been named acting captain of Support Services?"

"Nice to see you too, Stan."

"What exactly were the causes of Frank Murphy's death? Rumors are floating around that there might have been foul play."

"Did you talk with the Mass State Police?"

"Of course."

"Well, they're the guys with the answers. As far as I know, it was an accident." I gently shoved him out of the way so I could get out.

"The state police mentioned finding a cooler in the back of your car marked Human Remains. Any comment on that?"

"No."

He stared at me for a second in silence. "What's the cover-up, Joe? What are you guys hiding?"

"Nothing, Stan. We're digging. You know how that works."

"I'm not sure I do this time. We've never had a cop murdered before."

I stopped midway up the steps. "Where'd you get that? Did I say a cop had been murdered?"

"Word's out it's a possibility."

"Word's out Adolf Hitler lives in Paraguay. Do you believe that?"

I opened the side door that led straight into the police department, bypassing the central hall. He called out to me one last time.

"You know, Gunther, if you could hear what I hear, you'd be suspicious as hell. Bodies are piling up out there and you people aren't coming clean. You know that stinks."

I had to sympathize with his frustration. We were treading a fine line. I stopped by Max's cubicle to sign in and to pick up last week's pile. To my surprise she got up and gave me a hug. "Welcome back."

I kissed her on the cheek. "Thanks, Max. Nice to be back."

"The chief's waiting for you in his office, by the way. The State's Attorney is with him."

I put the paperwork she'd handed me into my box in the patrol room. I had met with Brandt the night before, as soon as I'd gotten back from Thetford, to tell him what Frank and I had found out in Connecticut. I'd also asked him to set up a meeting with James Dunn.

They were both smoking as I entered Brandt's office—the chief his pipe, Dunn a cigarette. The place looked like a fog bank had rolled in off the ocean.

Brandt stood up and shook my hand. "How are you feeling?"

"Fine." I nodded to Dunn, a far frostier fellow. He smiled slightly and nodded back. "Tony's been telling me about your latest activities. I'm a little disappointed you waited this long to bring me in."

"I'm sorry about that. Until we met with Dr. Kees, we didn't really have anything to go on. The whole thing might have died with his findings."

"The Kimberly Harris aspect of it might have died, but the maniac in the mask is still on the loose. It would have been nice to know they were related. This last week the press has been after me every single day. It's been relentless."

"Again, I apologize. But we don't have anything on Ski Mask either. I don't really see why they were after you anyway. You don't have anything to do with this yet."

He stubbed his cigarette out as if he wished the ashtray were my eye. "I happen to know that. They don't give a damn. The point is, you people have put the Harris case under a cloud. That, perhaps, is your prerogative, but I damn well expect to be let in on it."

Brandt shifted in his chair and cleared his throat. "I think that's a legitimate beef. If Joe hadn't been in a coma the better part of a week, I think things would have been handled with a little more grace. So, better later than never. Here we are at last; I've told you what we know. What do you think?"

Dunn lit up another one. My eyes were beginning to water. "I think we should bring in the state police. This should have been theirs from the start." He paused, but neither of us responded. "Look, our two offices work pretty well together, but let's face it, this is out of your league. We have a murder once or twice every ten years; half the men on your staff have never even seen a corpse. Let's just pack it in now and hand the thing over."

I kept a neutral voice. "We haven't been able to do anything because we didn't have anything to go on. The state police would have been in the same bind. Now we can start moving."

"On what? A paper chase after some prescription? From what I was told, you still don't have much. Have you even thought about who this guy might be?"

"Sure we have, but we don't have much to go on yet. We checked Davis out—background, friends, family, all that. As far as all this recent shit is concerned, he looks clean. Ski Mask may be Kimberly Harris's brother or lover or the father of her fetus or maybe a sister who's undergone a sex-change operation. We're digging. We're not pinning it all on finding a prescription."

"Sounds to me like you're shoveling smoke. I mean, you've got nothing."

"We don't have as much as we had to jail the wrong man, that's true enough."

Dunn tore the cigarette from his lips. "Wait a damned second. You haven't one shred of evidence that Davis isn't exactly where he belongs. You've let some homicidal basket case dictate everything from the very start. From what I hear, even your old friend Murphy thought you were way off base on this one."

"You haven't the slightest idea what Murphy was thinking."

"I think," Brandt interrupted, "we ought to give Joe a few days to see what he can come up with. After all, we have now ruled out everything except the connection between the Phillips killing and the Harris case. We're no longer chasing every stray possibility; we're building a case now."

"Give me a break, Tony. We're looking at a man with a white cane here—he's hardly Sherlock Holmes."

Brandt held up his hand. "Granted. Let's look at it another way. Right now, Murphy's death has been ruled an accident—by a state police force, no less—and Ski Mask is laying low. And the press hasn't made the connection to the Davis jury yet. The selectmen and the town manager are jumping up and down, but they concede it's still mostly a PR problem. They're caught between the news boys and the public. If we bring in outside help, all that's going to blow sky-high."

"Municipal politics are not my concern."

"Maybe not. But if the state police do come in, the fact that the Harris case is officially under investigation will come out. You might have to face some embarrassing questions, for which none of us have the answers—yet."

Dunn crossed his arms and glared out the window. "I stand by my actions in the Harris case."

Neither Brandt nor I said a word. In the long silence that settled among us, we could hear the boiler in the basement fire up and the radiators begin to rattle and ping.

Dunn finally let out a long puff of breath, as if he'd been holding it all this time. "Well, it isn't really my decision to make. It's still police business at this point. If you want to hold on to it a while longer, be my guests." He got up and put his cigarettes and lighter into his pockets. "Do try to let me know what the hell is going on, though, will you?"

Brandt nodded. "Absolutely. Thanks for coming by."

I waited until he closed the door behind him. "Stan tells me I've been made acting captain."

Brandt shook his head. "God, I'm starting to think we ought to hire him as a messenger boy. Yes, you have been." He paused, feeling for a reaction. "Is that all right?"

I got up. "Yeah."

He let it be. "So, what's your first tack?"

"To get reorganized. I want to check on what came in last week. Let me see what's what and I'll get back to you. From the way it looks now, though, we're going to end up putting a lot of people on this. If anything else breaks loose, we won't have a choice about bringing the state police in."

Among the pile Max had given me was a letter from Beverly Hillstrom confirming the survival of the samples, the official accident report from the Mass State Police, and a message that Floyd Rubin had called.

He was tending to a customer when I walked in, so I loitered by the magazine rack and waited. He saw me and came straight over, leaving the woman at the counter, money still in her hand.

"Lieutenant Gunther, I heard about the accident. I'm so terribly sorry about the other man."

"Thanks. Why don't you finish up with her so we can talk."

"Certainly."

He returned to the counter and nervously set to work. His demeanor was totally unlike when we'd first met—I'd expected a far more hostile reception. Now, he seemed more scared than anything else.

He showed the woman to the door and locked it behind her, pulling down a shade marked "Closed." I started to tell him not to bother but then kept quiet. Maybe it was best we were left alone.

"Did you find those time sheets you mentioned?"

He nodded quickly. "Oh yes. Very soon after we talked. You said you'd be going out of town for a few days, so I held on to them, and then I heard about your accident. I became very frightened."

"Why?"

He rubbed his forehead. "I don't really know. When we talked, I was left with an ominous feeling, and then the newspaper started reporting on all those incidents, trying to tie them all together to a masked man. And then you almost died, and the other man did. I couldn't help but feel that your looking into Kimberly's death was somehow connected to it all. I began to feel very nervous, as if I was in the middle of something, but I didn't know what."

"You are."

He leaned against the counter. "Oh, my Lord."

"You didn't tell me everything that went on between you and Kimberly, did you?"

His eyes closed tightly and he shook his head. "Yes, I did. I may have down played my affection for her, but that's all."

"You did love her?"

"Yes, I suppose. I know that's stupid—it's like a boy falling in love with his teacher. It's not real—it wasn't real. I know she felt no similar feelings for me. In fact, she laughed when I told her. Not cruelly, mind you—I mean, I had to laugh with her. She just saw how silly it was, which I couldn't see until she showed me. That's why she left and why I didn't keep in touch. I was too humiliated to tell you all that. You can see why, surely."

"Don't worry about it." I patted him on the shoulder. He looked so utterly humiliated I didn't have the heart to ask him flat out if they'd actually made love. Odds are they had, which explained his embarrassment cutting so deep. "I am going to ask you for a favor, though, and chances are it's going to make you twice as uneasy."

"What is it?"

"A blood test. There is absolutely no suspicion of your being involved in this case in any way whatsoever, understand? But I'm asking everyone who had any kind of involvement with Kimberly for the same thing, just so the totally innocent people don't clutter up the picture." I was overstating the case, of course. For all I knew, this man was a closet psychopath. I doubted it though.

Still, he looked shocked.

"You can refuse, of course. This is a request only," I added quickly.

His voice was subdued. "No, I quite understand. Of course I'll do it. It's as if this whole nightmare was happening all over again, isn't it? I'm beginning to feel her loss again, long after I thought I'd put it behind me. I feel like such an idiot." He shoved his glasses up on his forehead and rubbed his eyes with his fingertips.

"Why don't you give me those time sheets and I'll get out of your hair."

"Of course, of course." He shuffled off to the back of the store and returned with a shoe box. "Here they are. I put tabs on all the three-day weekends I gave her."

"Thank you. That was very thoughtful. I'll send a man around later to drive you to the hospital for the blood test. What time do you close?"

"Seven. But I can close earlier."

"Seven's fine, and don't worry—really."

I was almost out the door before he called me back, "I forgot to tell you: I remembered a friend she had when she was here. You had asked me earlier."

"Yes. Who was it?"

"Her name was Susan Lucey. I hired her just for the Christmas season that year. She didn't really work out and I never saw her again, but I remember that she and Kimberly used to leave together after closing quite often, as if they were going to do something together in the evening—a movie or something. She's the only one I could remember. I put her address in the box too."

18

Susan Lucey's address on Prospect Street was located on a plateau driven into the Y formed by Canal and Vernon Streets—right where John Woll had been mugged—and held tightly in position by St. Michael's Cemetery, which cut, higher still, across its back. Previously the eighteenth-century neighborhood of a thriving middle class, it had been left behind at some point, high on its exclusive perch, to watch the rest of the city grow prosperous without it. Its homes—the multi-storied gingerbreads and Greek revivals so prevalent in New England—were now weather-beaten and worn, cut up into ramshackle apartments overlooking debris-strewn streets and scruffy yards. It was not a dangerous area, really—although it had its moments—but it was about as forlorn as Brattleboro could offer.

Number 43B was on the second floor of a building half faded red, half bare and graying wood, with a set of stairs attached to its side by pragmatic afterthought. There was no particular reason why Susan Lucey should be home in the middle of the day, but after checking the phone book and finding the address was still hers, the omen was too good to pass up.

I cautiously climbed the unshoveled, icy steps, the banister wobbling under my right hand. The wind whipped at my pant legs and froze my ears. I knocked on the door.

I waited a minute in total silence and knocked again, just for the hell of it. I heard a bang from somewhere inside. Footsteps crossed the floor and the door opened a crack, revealing a young woman's round, unhealthy-looking face framed by heavy, dull brown hair.

"What do you want?" The voice was flat and hostile.

"Miss Lucey?"

"Who are you?"

"My name's Gunther. I'm with the police."

"You got a warrant?"

"Do I need one?"

"Fuck you, Mac."

"No, wait." I put my hand against the closing door. "I wouldn't want a warrant. I just want to talk to you about Kimberly Harris."

"She's dead."

"Let me make you a deal. Whatever you've got in there, whether it's dope or gambling or who knows what, I'm not interested, okay? I just want to talk."

"This is ancient history."

"I don't think so—not any more."

She didn't answer, but she didn't close the door, either.

"Did you read about the killing in the newspaper?"

"Yeah. What's Kimberly got to do with that?"

"Maybe you can help me find out."

She sucked on her lower lip and thought a moment. The back of my neck was starting to freeze. "No bust for anything you find in here—right?"

"Not unless it's a dead body."

She snorted. "It might as well be. Come on in." She opened the door and I stepped into a dark cave of hot, rancid, pungent air. She walked across the room and kicked the far door open, a solid naked leg protruding from her stained bathrobe. "Party's over. It's the cops."

There was a muttered oath from beyond and the sound of clothes being put on in a hurry. The outline of a man appeared in the doorway. He quickly turned his face away. "What is this?"

"I just want to talk with the lady."

Lucey grabbed him by the arm. "That's twenty bucks."

He glanced over his shoulder at me; I could hear his brain working. "Pay the lady, or I might ask for some ID."

He reached into his pocket. "Christ, it was hardly worth it."

"Mutual, I'm sure." She plucked the twenty from his fingers and shoved it into her pocket.

He walked sideways through the room, keeping his face away from me, tripping over a pile of dirty clothes on the floor as he went. I grabbed his elbow and steadied him. He jerked away and stormed out with a bang.

"All these guys. Pretend they're hotshots. Who cares what they look like?" She settled into a disemboweled armchair, tucking her legs under her. As an afterthought, having made sure I'd had a view, she tucked her robe around her more tightly. "Thanks for the support."

I moved a smeared paper plate from a wooden chair and sat. "Don't mention it." My eyes had become accustomed to the dark and I glanced around. The place looked like a cyclone had hit it; from the smell, it had been a long time ago.

"So, how do you connect me to Kimberly?"

"Charlie's Pharmacy."

"Oh, that old fruit."

"How well did you know Kimberly?"

She smiled her best Scarlett O'Hara, complete with tilted head. "Why do you ask?"

I sighed. "How much time did that twenty buy?"

"Usually, as long as it takes. That guy was into overtime. But this might be dangerous—isn't that what you said?"

"Not if we move quickly. If we can't, everyone I come in contact with might be hurt."

She let her head fall back and stretched her neck. "Compromise time, huh? Okay, twenty'll be fine." She wiggled her fingers.

I pulled out my wallet, got up, and laid the bills in her hand. At this rate, she was making a lot more than I did.

"I knew her well enough. We did stuff together."

"What kind of stuff?"

"Dinner, movies...We did a few doubles."

"What do you mean?"

She laughed. "Not double features. Boy, you haven't been around much. Two on one—you know. Guys pay a lot for that; makes them feel masculine. The joke is, we do it mostly for us. Closet lesbians, I guess." She laughed again. "I hadn't thought of that before."

She reached into her pocket and pulled out a cellophane bag. She pushed some of its contents into a small pipe and lit up. "Want some?"

"No. Thanks. Was she experienced at that kind of thing?"

"Tricking? No, but she was good at it. That's one of the reasons we broke up; she got too good. I mean, she really got into it. With me, it gets to be a job after a while, if I'm at it for too long. But with her, the more she did, the more she wanted, and she'd give it away too—to total strangers. I don't suppose partnerships last too long in this business anyway. Ours was no different."

"How long did you work together?"

"Not too long. A couple of months, maybe."

"Starting around Christmas?"

"Yeah. How did you know that?"

147

"Charlie again."

"Oh." She took a deep drag and held her breath.

"What was Kimberly like?"

She paused before letting the smoke out in a long hiss. "She was a hot little number. Touch her anywhere and she turned on. I got the feeling sex for her was like water for a man in the desert. And kinky, too. She didn't care. I mean, there are things I won't do, you know? But not her. She'd try anything."

"Did she talk about her past? Where she came from, things like that?"

"Nope. Not a word. I asked her a couple of times. You know, like I once said she must have spent her life in a convent to come on the way she did, but she never picked up on it and I let it be. You learn not to ask too much."

"I bet. Still, there are usually slips of the tongue, references to the past. Everybody talks about themselves at least a little."

Lucey took another hit, and I waited for the process to be over. "Not Kimberly. She said she had nothing to look back on—everything good lay ahead."

"Unhappy childhood?"

"Hey, I told you: I don't know."

"So what prompted the comment about not looking back?"

"Oh, that was weird. We'd taken on this real strange one—an older guy. He was real skinny, didn't talk much, never smiled. We did a number on him, a pretty good one, too, because we were both feeling good, but he just lay there. I mean, he wasn't limp—he worked okay—but he didn't get involved. None of the usual routine, you know? No sweat and wrestle. I said to Kimberly afterwards that he could have gotten as big a kick from his hand, instead of paying for us. I think I called him a cold fish, and that's when she said something like, 'Just like my old man.' And then a little later she said what I told you."

"Aside from her prowess in bed, what was she like? I mean her personality. Did she laugh a lot? Was she serious? Did she seem well educated?"

Lucey drew on the pipe again and then stretched, bending as far backwards as she could. Her robe parted slightly, revealing a thin line of naked skin from her throat to her lap. She didn't bother covering up. "She was a little schizo, if you ask me. She could be a lot of fun—a real turn-on—and then she could be real cold and calculating. She could work people, especially old men, or older men, at least. That's

148

what we did most of, in fact, when we doubled. She wasn't interested in younger guys much, unless they were super young, like teenagers. It was like she had to have some power over them, you know? Men our age didn't interest her much. I thought that was too bad. I like an occasional roll in the hay with someone who knows what he's doing and won't have a heart attack doing it. But Kimberly had some kind of thing going. I'd watch her sometimes when we were right in the middle of the action, and sometimes—not always—she'd be looking at the guy's face with, I don't know, a real calculating expression. And when he finally shot his wad, she always looked pleased with herself. And superior, too, as if somehow she'd put one over on the guy. Maybe that's why we broke up. I never thought about it before."

"What do you mean?"

"Well, it was kind of unnatural, you know? I mean, God knows I don't get turned on every time I get laid, but I enjoy it most of the time. If the guy's not too weird, it feels good, right? But I don't think what I thought felt good was what Kimberly thought felt good—she was into something else. It was like I couldn't figure out what was turning her on, the sex or the power trip. Does that make sense?"

"Yeah. It must have been a little unsettling."

"That's it. It was hot and cold mixed together. I mean, she was the best I've ever been with, but...unsettling—that's the word."

She took a final drag from her pipe and then cleaned it out onto the floor.

"You mentioned she said everything good lay ahead. What were her plans?"

"Money. She wanted lots of money. Nothing new there, I suppose, except with her it wasn't just wishful thinking. I mean, I want money too, but I know I'll never get it—takes too much effort. But she was going for it."

"How?"

She shrugged. "Sex, I guess. She didn't have anything else that I could see."

"Prostitution ?"

"In this town? Give me a break." She opened her robe wide with a laugh. "I may not be much, but I'm about the best you're going to get around here."

I smiled, embarrassed. "Was she zeroing in on anything specific that you know of?"

She got up and crossed over to the kitchenette in the corner. "You want some coffee?"

"No, thanks."

She found a dirty cup in the sink, spooned in some instant coffee from an open jar on the counter, and filled it with hot water from the tap. I was glad I had passed. She returned to her chair. "Something was cooking. She had that look in her eye—you know, the calculating one I told you about—but she wasn't about to tell me."

"Did you keep in touch after you split up?"

"No. I saw her around some, but she wasn't in the business anymore. She was looking good, though; nice clothes and all. I just figured she'd hit her target."

"What did you think when she was killed?"

She shrugged. "What's to think? It was too bad, but somehow it didn't surprise me. I mean, I wasn't looking for it to happen, but it didn't surprise me when it did. She didn't strike me as the safest driver on the road, if you get what I mean."

"Do you think the black guy did it?"

"Hey, who knows? She was a secret. I figured her death was too."

"Going back a little, what was her relationship to Floyd Rubin?"

She laughed and shook her head. "That was pathetic. She played him like a violin. I don't know why she bothered—the little faggot—but she got him around her little finger. That's what I mean, see? An old guy, right at death's door, and she did a total power thing on him. Typical."

"Did she have sex with him?"

"I don't know. We didn't—that's for sure. I wouldn't have done him for a hundred bucks."

"Why not?"

"Self-righteous little creep, that's why. The day I set eyes on him, I knew he thought I was beneath him. The only reason he hired me was because Kimberly liked me—she had a quick eye. But as soon as the Christmas rush was over, he dropped me like a rock."

"But you don't know if Kimberly and he had a thing going?"

She shook her head. "It wouldn't surprise me, except that he's such a tight little asshole—he'd probably think it was immoral."

I looked at the dusty, debris-covered floor for a moment, trying to think of anything else I might ask. "Where do you think she was from?"

"Not far from here. I mean, she didn't have a weird accent or anything. I don't think she was a Vermonter, though. She came across like a flatlander, but she seemed to know her way around."

"I don't suppose she ever alluded to a home state or town or anything."

Susan Lucey shook her head.

I got up and buttoned my coat. "Well, I guess that's it. If you think of anything else, you know where to find me."

She hadn't moved from her chair. "I do have something else."

My hand was already on the doorknob. "What?"

"Did you get your twenty bucks worth?"

"I did all right."

"Well, then I guess that's it."

I sighed. This kind of money was hard to get back from petty cash. "How much is your tidbit worth?"

"Why get complicated? Another twenty'll do."

"You do all right for yourself, don't you?"

"Some days. I can throw in a little extra if you'd like. A good-will gesture." She passed one hand across her breast and down to her stomach. I had to admit she wasn't bad looking, in a round, compact kind of way. It was her environment that gave me the willies.

"I'll settle for the information." I fished out another couple of tens and handed them over. "Not that I'm not flattered."

She took the money and smiled. "Kimberly Harris wasn't her real name."

"What was it?"

"I don't know. She just told me once that she'd chosen Kimberly because it sounded classy—a name men would like."

"Was Harris invented too?"

"I don't know."

"That's it?"

"Yup. That's more than you knew before, isn't it?"

I shook my head in defeat. "You're very good at this." Again, I reached for the door.

This time she rose and crossed over to me. "You said everyone you came in contact with could be hurt. Where's that put me?"

"I hope it doesn't put you anywhere. As far as I know, I'm the only one who knows about you, except Rubin. But I may have been followed here."

"Now you tell me. Who's out there?"

"We don't know, but if anyone else asks you about all this, don't play games, okay? There's no profit to be made from this man—or men."

"What am I supposed to do in the meantime? Wait until some creep kicks in my door?"

"You could go somewhere else. Stay with a friend or relative for a while."

"What about police protection?"

I shook my head. "That's movie stuff. I can have a patrol car swing by every once in a while, or even have a cop check your door, but we don't have the staff for full protection. I doubt you'll need it anyway. Just be careful."

"That's a real comfort. I should have hit you for ten times this, you asshole." She held up the money I'd given her.

I opened the door, and she gathered the robe around her throat against the gush of cold air. Her face was hard. "I better not get shafted for this. I played straight with you. Shit, I even offered you a freebie."

"I appreciate that. You'll be all right."

"Says you."

As I inched my way down the rickety steps, her last words rattled around in my mind. I hadn't overlooked the fact that Frank's death was a direct result of my hanging on to this case. The addition of Susan Lucey to the list was not something I wanted to see.

19

I sat at my desk, the long-awaited case file open before me. It was thicker than most, not surprising considering the subject, and it had the usual ragtag appearance of its peers—official reports, photographs, torn notepad pages, copies of letters, scribbled-on napkins, and whatnot—but it was missing the tone that should have been there. After a few years' practice, these case files took on the feel of music manuscripts. Beneath the hodgepodge of mismatched paperwork, there was a rhythm of progression; beyond the banality of a beginning, a middle, and an end, there was the tempo of building enthusiasm, of increasing light being cast into dark corners.

It might have been all I'd gone through prior to this day, or the fact that my mind was already clouded with suspicions about the contents of this file, but I knew for a fact that something was wrong here.

Perhaps it was the lack of unanswered questions. Normally, especially on the odd scraps of paper, officers would scribble "what ifs" to their colleagues—questions designed to force them off their scent for a moment's reflection, like a dog sniffing the air as well as the trail. Frank had done this with me when he'd proposed that Jamie Phillips might have been the victim of life insurance fraud. In any case where you didn't find the burglar climbing out of the window with a bag full of silverware, this was standard practice—except here.

Here, everyone had marched in lockstep. The suspect had been caught, his rights had been read to him, evidence had been gathered, people had been interrogated, a case had been built according to the rules. But no fundamental questions had been asked—at least none that I could see. Kimberly's bank records, her extraordinarily skimpy background, her curious lifestyle—or lack of one—all passed without challenge in the shadow cast by the evidence against Bill Davis. That— the superficial blood tests, the broken lamp, the scratch marks, the drugs, the rope used to tie her down, and all the rest—was the case.

Nothing, from what I could read, was allowed to disturb that. Not even the most obvious question of all: why had the crime occurred?

I got up and crossed the hall to Willy Kunkle's office. The door was open. He was sitting behind his desk muttering into the phone, his face twisted with frustration and anger. He saw me before I could duck away.

"I didn't mean to interrupt."

He covered the phone with his hand. "What do you want?"

"I need to talk about the Harris case. I'll be in my office. No rush."

I went back to my cubbyhole and waited. If Kimberly's case file could be compared to a manuscript, then Kunkle was its editor. He had taken all the bits and pieces and put them in order; he had made sure all the forms were filled out, the procedures followed, the details attended to. He was neither the author nor the publisher, and therefore was not solely responsible for its contents. But more than anyone, he knew the workings of the whole.

Unfortunately, he was a head case. A Vietnam vet with an impeccable record, he had started, like most of us, from the bottom. Always high-strung and introspective, he had nonetheless channeled a furious energy into his work, spending hours of overtime on cases, regardless of their merit, and had wound up being regarded as an all-around grind. Despite this and coupled with a fifty-grit personality, there was no denying his capabilities. He became one of the youngest corporals ever to make Support Services. He also married, and the dual achievement made us hope his rough edges might round off.

But that didn't happen. Inside his pressure-cooker mind boiled a thwarted ambition. He had left the Army because of slow promotions, and when Murphy elevated me to lieutenant a few years back, all but locking up the succession to captain, Kunkle began to unravel. His disappointment either led to or was heightened by his disintegrating marriage, a fact made all too obvious when a patrol car was called to his home by neighbors complaining of a domestic dispute. His eye-blackened wife didn't file charges, but the story made the rounds.

We watched him, as cops will, with both sympathy and wariness. The bonds on a police force are stronger than elsewhere, allowing for an extraordinary amount of friction. But even in a department like ours, with minor exposure to truly dangerous elements, cops have to gauge the colleagues who might be asked to save their lives. So Willy Kunkle rode a seesaw in the eyes of his peers, and while most of us—

most of the time—wanted him to settle on the right side of things, we all wished like hell he'd stop his teetering. He'd been at it for years.

He finally appeared at my doorway and stood there, his hands in his pockets. "You're really going to blow it up, aren't you?"

"I've got to look into it. It's not my choice any more."

"You realize I'll probably get sued by that bastard Davis as soon as he gets a whiff of this."

"If anyone gets sued, it'll most likely be the town."

"That's a big comfort. My ass'll be the first thing out the door."

"You've got to admit something strange is going on."

"I don't have to admit a damned thing. I don't happen to know what the hell is going on. People have been tiptoeing around here for weeks, and I haven't been told word one."

"You weren't alone. Brandt didn't know about most of it till just a while ago. Believe it or not, Murphy and I were trying to keep a lid on it to the end. If the shit hits the fan, we're all going to be in the way."

"So the lid is off?"

"It will be, yes."

He looked at me with withering contempt. "Thanks a lot."

"Don't feel so sorry for yourself. Frank Murphy is dead because of all this, as are a few other people."

"What, because he drove off the road?"

"No. Because we were forced off by a truck—deliberately."

He knit his brow. "Why?"

"Because we were asking some questions that weren't asked from the very start."

"Like what?"

"Like who was Kimberly Harris really? Like wasn't some of the evidence against Davis unbelievably overwhelming? Like what was behind the mysterious payments that started showing up in Harris's checking account? Like why wasn't the apartment manager exposed as a Peeping Tom?"

"Bullshit."

"Fact, Willy—by his own admission. His nose greased her window night after night. Every time she jacked off, he was an appreciative audience. You should have heard his reviews. In fact, they ought to be part of this file."

"I knew it. You *are* going to string me up."

I slapped the desktop with my hand. "God damn it, why won't you get your face out of the mirror? I could give a shit about stringing you up. I need a little cooperation here. Help me get the job done and may-be we can all avoid getting sued. Don't you get it?"

"I get it. I just don't happen to believe it."

I took a deep breath and held up my hands. "All right—whatever. If that's what you want to believe, that's fine with me. Will you at least go over the file with me so we can maybe find what we missed the first time?"

"When?"

"Now."

His eyes dropped and he passed his hand across his mouth. "I was going to take some personal time."

I thought a moment. It might not be the worse thing to cut him a little slack, as a peace offering. "How much?"

"Just a couple of hours at the most. I got some trouble at home."

"Go to it. We'll do this later."

He didn't burst into a smile and give me a hug, but his tone softened a shade. "Thanks."

"No sweat. By the way, do you keep your old note pads?"

Gone was the soft tone. "Why?"

"I was thinking maybe we could compare them to this"—I put my hand on the file—"help freshen your memory."

He shook his head scornfully. "You must think I just fell off the truck. I'll go over that lousy file with you—that's part of my job. But there's no way in hell you're ever going to see that note pad. That's private."

"You can read from it. I won't even touch it."

"Give me a break. Maybe we'll all be standing in the way when the fan gets turned on, but I'd sure as hell be a convenient scapegoat. Bet-ter me than the saintly departed Murphy, right?"

"What's that mean?"

"What do you think it means? Christ, he was captain—nothing hap-pened without him knowing about it. My name's on that file because I was first on the scene, but the whole thing was his baby. You better believe it—including the bullshit."

He walked away, leaving me nailed to my chair. It was like hearing the one clear note in a jumble of sound. Kunkle had to be right. The cause of Murphy's hedging at the start of all this wasn't simple pre-re-tirement jitters. I remembered the night he'd driven me home from the morgue. "I did everything I could to speed things up," he'd said. I'd taken that as an apology for his having been such a jerk until then, but it had been more. He'd been edging toward an admission he'd never directly made.

I grabbed my coat and headed for the car. The implication cut beyond Murphy's integrity. It also made a joke of my loyalty. I'd made assumptions and from them had drawn conclusions that were possibly criminally wrong. I had never entertained the remotest possibility that Frank's behavior went beyond the fumbling of a boozy old cop counting his last days. The realization that he may have consciously allowed the wrong man to go to jail spread through my chest like ice water.

Martha Murphy was still in Massachusetts with her daughter, although she was due back that evening. I found the spare key wedged behind the mailbox.

I knew the house as I knew my own. They had lived here for over twenty years, and never had a week gone by that I hadn't come to visit at least once, and usually more. I had helped move furniture, select drapes, repair the plumbing. When they'd gone on their rare vacations, I'd watered the plants and brought in the mail.

I walked straight to the roll-top desk Frank had referred to as his office, parked in a corner of the living room, and started going through the large lower drawers. I found a thick packet of small black note pads, bound by a rubber band, arranged in chronological order. It was my good fortune that for all his flaws as a human being, Frank had been a very neat cop.

For the next two hours, I dug through the pads like an archaeologist looking for bone fragments. It was not easy work. The purpose of these things was to merely stimulate what was already in the mind of the writer. Sometimes codes were used, or abbreviations bordering on shorthand. Cases were referred to indiscriminately, one on top of the other. An FBI file number, standing in total isolation, might hover over a reminder to pick up some pickles at the store.

But they did go page by page, each page representing a progression through time, so once I'd located the book whose dates bracketed the Harris case, at least I had some sense—however vague—of forward movement.

I didn't find much in quantity. People don't write notes to themselves on how to subvert their own integrity. But I did find what I'd hoped I wouldn't. It was a reminder, presumably written too late in the day for immediate action: "Stop KH print code."

That was as far as I went. I rebundled the pads and put them back in the drawer. I sat for a while by the large north window, the one with the view of the Connecticut River valley.

I can't really say I was upset. Frank was dead, after all, and despite Kunkle's nasty jab, I never had considered him a saint. His gradual winding down through the years had been visible to all. In fact, the best description of his life was probably found in my own mirror. We all get old and slow down. And most of us get fat, become complacent, maybe drink a little too much, and tend to let things go towards the end. Obstacles to this easy, introverted, downhill slide either get put off or are muffled in routine. Sometimes—as in this case—they are even physically removed. It's not so much an act of corruption, it's just something to make life more convenient.

When Kimberly Harris's fingerprints had been taken, they were translated into a transmittable code. Routinely, such codes are sent to the FBI's Identification Bureau for filing and an immediate comparison check. It's not as accurate as comparing the actual prints—something which can be done later—but it's a workable and fast beginning. The FBI has the prints of virtually every individual who's ever been booked at a police station, along with those of a lot of other people as well. More often than not, when we send a print code to Washington in a felony case, we get some kind of readout. Murphy's note implied that Kimberly's code had never been sent.

I didn't make any ominous connections here. I knew the man—obviously not as well as I'd thought—but well enough to know that all he'd done in his own mind was to keep things streamlined and simple. If you don't ask the questions, you won't hear the answers you dread. On the face of it, Frank had an open-and-shut case, and everyone else agreed with him. But he was a good, if tired cop. He knew it was all too pat, he knew "Kimberly Harris" didn't have enough historical baggage. He knew that if he asked too many questions, the last yard he had to go until retirement would suddenly vanish into a big, black fog.

I drove back to the office and called Danvers at the FBI—the same man who had responded so quickly to our inquiry on Ski Mask's electronic bug.

"So this time it's a phone call, huh? Things must be heating up."

"Maybe. Frank Murphy's been killed. It's listed as an accident for now, but I have my doubts."

"Damn. I'm sorry."

"I was wondering if you could do me a favor. It might tie in to that bug you're so interested in."

"Oh?"

"It's a fingerprint code."

"That's all?"

"Yeah. But it's very high priority."

"Sure."

I pulled the code out of the case file and read it slowly over the phone. "By the way, you wouldn't have something on that bug that might do us some good, would you? Something you might not have felt entirely free to share?"

There was a slight pause. "No. We're as curious about it as you are."

I didn't believe that for a second. I thanked him and hung up.

I spent the next several hours writing the report of my life, bringing everything up to date from the last two weeks. I synopsized the Harris case as I'd found it in the file, revealed what I thought were its flaws and omissions, and crediting Ski Mask as the catalyst for the reinvestigation, detailed my progress so far. I left out any hypotheses on why Frank was killed and merely let it stand as an accident. I also didn't entirely finish the report. I expected Danvers to get back to me before the day was out and hoped I could add something tangible from what he had to say.

Late in the afternoon, the windows dark and the day staff just departed, I knocked on the chief's open door. He was sitting at his desk, a cold pipe in his mouth, writing.

He leaned back in his chair, smiling, and gestured me to sit. "Been doing your homework?"

"Yup."

"So what's our course of action?"

"Kimberly Harris's employer gave me her time sheets. Throughout her year with him, she took a series of three-day weekends off, I think to do some serious gold digging. I spent an hour today with a part-time hooker friend of hers who told me she wasn't all that surprised Kimberly ended up the way she did. Also, her real name wasn't Kimberly, and it may not have been Harris. I'm having Danvers check that out right now; I'm just hoping she had a record somewhere."

Brandt removed the pipe and scowled. "Wasn't that done a long time ago?"

"Apparently not. Frank never transmitted the print codes."

He stared at me.

"I ought to warn you right off that even if we pull this thing out of the fire, even if we find that we have the right guy in the jug, we're in for a lot of heat. The ball was dropped several times, and I doubt that fact will pass unnoticed."

"What are we talking about exactly?"

"Exactly? Time will tell. But generally, I think we're looking at a whole bunch of people moving too fast for their own good."

"Like Murphy?"

"Like Murphy, like Kunkle, like Dunn, like me and you, for that matter. Frank wanted a clean getaway into retirement; I suspect Kunkle wanted a fast and quick promotion, or at least a little recognition; Dunn liked the tidiness of the initial evidence and made a pointed effort not to dig any deeper; and the rest of us played along, pleased as punch we weren't hitting any snag. Only Ski Mask wasn't satisfied."

"Do we know why he wasn't yet?"

"No, but I think either Kimberly or Davis will tell us, and my money's on her. What I'd like to do is to isolate those long weekends and then compare them with local airline, car rental and travel agencies to see if we can come up with a match. I'm sure it'll only give up phony names, if that, but I'm hoping for at least a pattern. I also want to get the DEA to run a list on all prednisone prescriptions issued in this area during the two-month period just prior to Kimberly's death."

"That'll take forever."

"Do you have any contacts with them? Mine are all regional men. It would take them just as long."

He shook his head. "There's too much coming and going over there. The FBI's like IBM. DEA's more like a game show—lots of turnover. I can circulate it around, though. One of the other guys might have a contact."

"Okay. If we come up empty by tomorrow afternoon, I'll just put it through normal channels. We'll also need a pile of evidentiary warrants. If I get you a list of all the agencies I want canvassed and the specific dates of those long weekends, could you do that tonight?"

He checked his watch. "I don't see why not. It'll be easier getting a judge at night than during the day, and as far as I know, everyone's in town. How soon can you get it to me?"

"An hour, maybe an hour and a half?"

He nodded. "What about the Davis angle?"

"I think it's a long shot, but it's still possible Ski Mask's motivation is merely to get Davis off the hook. Now that the Harris case can see the light of day again, I want to assign someone full-time to look into Davis's past. He was in the Army; that bug I found in my place was military ordnance. There may be a connection."

"Sounds better than a long shot."

"I don't think so. This is more complicated than that. Ski Mask has got something bigger on his mind and so have the people who killed Frank. My nose tells me Davis was in the wrong place at the wrong time, and that was near Kimberly Harris—or whatever her name was."

"Okay . You get me the list; I'll get the warrants."

I noticed a light on in Kunkle's office. I knocked and stuck my head in. He was sitting at his desk with his hands flat on the tabletop, as if in a trance. He looked up at me, startled. "What?"

"Just wondered if you came back."

"Bed check?"

"No. We were supposed to meet."

"I forgot."

"It doesn't matter. Are you all right?"

"What's that supposed to mean?"

"Pure and simple concern. Not that you'd consider me a candidate, but there are people you can talk to if you're feeling all boxed up inside."

He gave me a sour smile. "Write me off as a wacko."

I shook my head. "Willy, I already think you're a wacko. I'm just worried you're going to end up killing yourself—or someone else."

"Thanks. Same to you." I closed the door and went back to my office.

I had almost finished my list for Brandt when the phone rang. It was Danvers.

"Her real name—or at least the one we've got for her—is Pamela Stark. She was arrested in Boston for soliciting." He gave me the file reference number. "Does that do anything for you?"

"It opens a whole new can of worms."

"Sorry."

"No, I'm grateful. Right now, a can of worms is exactly what I need. By the way, do you know anybody over at DEA—preferably in records?"

"Why?"

"I think the guy who killed Pamela Stark sported a drug-induced hunchback."

There was a stunned silence at the other end. I heard him chuckle. "I thought Murphy was bad. You'll do anything for a favor, won't you?"

"It's true."

"I'm sure it is. You couldn't pull that one out of your hat. As it turns out, I'm pretty good friends with one of the old-timers in that department. But I want something in return."

"What?"

"When this whole thing is over, send me a copy of the final report, will you? It's got all the makings of a classic."

I said I would and gave him the information I wanted checked by the DEA. I had just hung up the phone when it rang.

"Hi, Joe." Gail's voice sounded cautiously neutral.

"Hi."

"Long time no see."

"Yeah, it feels that way."

"You want to come over?"

"It'll probably be late, if at all."

"What's up?"

"Martha's back in town. I thought I might go over for a visit."

"That's nice. I think she'd like that. She really missed you at the ceremony. The offer still stands, though—it doesn't matter what time. The door'll be unlocked."

"Sounds good."

"I was wondering," she added after a pause. "Well, I guess it's kind of stupid . . ."

"Go ahead."

"How were things at your mother's?"

"All right. Cleared my head a little."

"About us?"

I looked at the phone in surprise. "Us? No. I guess I mostly sorted out losing Frank. That kind of stuff."

"Oh. Of course."

"What about us?"

"Nothing. Things have been a little weird lately, you have to admit." Her laugh was like a misplaced punctuation mark. "You almost died twice that I know of. Did anyone shoot at you today?"

"Not so far."

She sighed. "I missed not seeing you when you got back."

"Oh yeah. Sorry. I wanted to bring Tony up to date."

"I thought you were going to call me to bring you back." Her tone had a false heartiness to it, as if she were just clearing up some procedural details.

"Leo lent me one of his cars."

"That was nice. Which one?"

"Cadillac."

"Good Lord...I've missed you, Joe."

"I'll try to get over tonight. I just don't know how things'll go."

"Well, I didn't mean just for that. It would be nice, but I mean… Well, with all this stuff going on, I've been kind of worried, you know? I'd really hate to lose you."

"I think you're safe there."

"Sure…"

I could feel her struggling on the other end. I knew it wouldn't take much from me to help her out, but I kept silent. "Well, I'll let you go. I know you must be busy. Give Martha my best."

The line went dead, and I carefully replaced the receiver in its cradle. So much for that.

Aside from Frank and Ellen, Gail was the one person for whom I'd developed a love. Being with her, sometimes just watching her from a distance, crumpled something up inside me. Now she was the only one left.

I stared at the phone, knowing that calling her back and seeing her tonight would be a hell of lot more important than holding Martha's hand. It would be the breach in the pretty picket fence we'd constructed between us, the fence that allowed us to do everything but permanently share the same backyard. A large part of me ached to do just that—to simply admit what I so often felt—and that was especially true right now, with Frank's death clinging to my shoulders.

And that was the catch—the excuse. I was too vulnerable right now, like other times when I'd shied away from trusting myself, and Gail, to make more than we had of our separate lives.

I pushed the phone to the corner of the desk and returned to my list of names.

Martha silently gathered me into a hug once she saw who was at the door. We stood there for quite a while, between the warmth of the house and the cold outdoors, before I finally felt I could risk letting go. The television was on in the den—Frank's old lair.

She offered me milk and cookies and we sat together on the couch watching one idiot show after another. She fell asleep at last, her head on my shoulder. I stretched her out, covered her with my jacket, and watched the tube until the station went to static. I never did get to Gail's.

163

20

A woman was severely beaten in her apartment last night, apparently by the same man in a ski mask who has been responsible for a recent rash of crimes in Brattleboro. Starting with the shotgun killing of James Phillips by Thelma Reitz on January 3, this mysterious masked man, whom police have yet to identify, has been involved in a series of assaults, thefts, and possibly one other death—that of police Captain Frank Murphy on January 10—now officially ruled a traffic accident.

With this latest assault, however, a possible motive has been found for the unknown assailant's previous actions. Susan Lucey, last night's victim and a "part-time" prostitute, told this reporter that the man police have labeled Ski Mask forced his way into her apartment and demanded to know what she had told police earlier in the day about the death of Kimberly Harris, found murdered at the Huntington Arms apartment complex on September 15, 1983. Harris and Lucey reportedly worked together as prostitutes for a brief period several months prior to Harris's death.

The Harris case, the most sensational in Brattleboro's history, ended with the conviction of William Davis, who at the time of his arrest was the janitor of the Huntington Arms complex. Davis, a black Vietnam veteran originally from Baltimore, claimed throughout the trial that he had been framed and was innocent of all charges.

It seems the police might now be in agreement. Lt. Joseph Gunther, acting head of the Police Department's Support Services, has been rumored for weeks to be investigating the old case. Indeed, it was Lt. Gunther who visited Susan Lucey yesterday before she was assaulted and who questioned her on her relationship with the late Miss Harris.

I stopped reading half way through and put the paper down. "Exciting stuff."

Tom Wilson, the town manager, glowered at me. "Did you read it all?"

"I got the gist of it."

"I want you to read it all. If I end up doing something you'll live to regret, I want you to know why."

I nodded and looked at the other people in the room—Brandt, Dunn, Patrol Captain Billy Manierre, and town counsel Robert Denby.

They sat like boys outside the principal's office. I went back to reading. Katz had dug up much of what there was to dig, especially on the prostitute angle. Surprisingly, he still missed the connection between Ski Mask's early victims and the Harris jury members, as irrelevant as that was now. He also didn't bring out a lot of what we were currently holding—all the forensic stuff, Harris's time cards, her bank records, or even the fact that her name wasn't Harris. All that just revealed how good he was at combining peripheral knowledge with some jazzy writing. Still, he knew more than we had officially released, and I couldn't deny that the news of Susan Lucey's beating came as a double shock.

I put the paper down a second time.

"Finished?" Wilson asked.

"Yup."

"Just to give you the benefit of the doubt, is it true you saw Lucey and talked to her about Harris?"

"Yes. This is the first I heard of her being beaten up. I'd like to talk to her."

"Talk to me first, assuming that isn't monumentally inconvenient."

"To be fair," Brandt interrupted, "Joe would have had no reason to talk to you until now in any case. He reports to me. I report to you."

"In theory, you mean."

"I've kept you up to date."

Wilson's face reddened and he grabbed the paper out of my lap. "Then why the hell is most of this new to me? I had no idea Harris was a hooker." He was tense, but under control.

"Most of it isn't new. I've kept you apprised of the major elements in this case. The prostitute angle is less than a day old. You know a lot more than Katz does, and you'll know even more before the end of the day. These are political and PR problems. They had to surface sooner or later."

"I'd say they were legal ones," Denby softly said.

Wilson glanced at Denby and nodded. "He's right. We could be taken to the cleaners on this thing. I'll give a shit about the politics when I'm up to my ass in lawsuits. How the hell did Katz make the Kimberly Harris connection?"

We all looked at each other. I finally stated the obvious. "He says it was through Lucey."

Wilson shook his head in exasperation. "I know that, for Christ's sake. I meant, how did he find her?"

There was silence in the room. "I don't know."

"Maybe we should ask him." Denby said.

"What would he get out of a conversation like that?" asked Dunn. Brandt started fiddling with his pipe. "We could give him something—trade a little. Up to now, he's been baying at our walls, trying to get in. If we let him in, he might at least tone things down a notch. The closer we get to cracking this thing, the more harm stories like that will do us. He might even be of some help if we approach him right."

"That'll be the day."

Wilson held up his hand. "Fine; whatever. If you want to try playing footsie, it's okay with me. I just want to know what's coming next. I'm tired of being blindsided. The selectmen put me on the griddle every time we get together—and that's been a lot lately—and I don't have anything to tell them."

"That was per agreement. You were willing to take the hot seat," Brandt reminded him.

"What was agreed was that we should let as few people know what Gunther was doing as possible, until he was sure we couldn't get out of this thing." He shook the paper again. "Wouldn't you say that time has come? In fact, wouldn't you admit we missed the boat a little on this one? I'd have been a whole lot happier if the selectmen had read this with the dubious comfort of advance knowledge. As it was, the damn paper wasn't even distributed before my phone started ringing off the wall."

Brandt finally stopped fiddling and lit up his pipe. "We have no way of knowing when Ski Mask is going to pop up."

Wilson shook his head. "You miss the point. As it reads now, the police department has been reinvestigating the Harris case for weeks, piling up data, stepping over a growing number of corpses, opening us up to Christ-knows-how-many potential lawsuits, and the board hasn't been let in on any of it. I mean, Jesus, I gather Dunn here was given inside information. He's not even a town official."

"Amen," muttered Dunn.

Wilson glared at him. "Tony, I was willing to play dumb with the board on the premise I'd be the first to know of any developments. You've probably gotten my ass fired, you know that?"

Brandt took the pipe out of his mouth and shut his eyes for a moment. Ten long seconds drifted by before he spoke. "All right. Let me talk to them. Until Joe and Frank went to Connecticut, we weren't even sure Harris shouldn't be left just where she was. A lot has happened since then; some of it, like Joe's meeting with Susan Lucey, is so new we haven't been able to digest it yet." He pointed at the paper with his pipe. "That's the real damage here. Katz blew the whistle before the players were ready to start. I do have one major misgiving, though, and it's the same one I've had from the beginning. If I have to give everything I've got to the board, I doubt any of us will have to wait for the next paper before the word's all over town."

"Could that be any worse than the way things are now?" Wilson asked.

Brandt nodded. "Yes. We still have a lot Katz doesn't know. If it gets out before we've been able to put it to use, all sorts of things might go wrong, some of which we might never even hear about."

"For example."

I interrupted here. "For example, we pretty much know Ski Mask got this whole thing started because he wanted the investigation reopened; what we don't know is why. We've also got a pretty good idea that he's not the only player in this game—there may be others whose motives are even murkier. Now if we just dump all we know on the table without playing with it first—at least for a while—we run the risk that Ski Mask or the other guys will recognize something we don't and will proceed on their own, in private. It seems obvious right now that Ski Mask at least needs us to do his homework. If we don't maintain that role, and allow him to dispense with us, we'll either be left with the strong suspicion that we have the wrong man in jail, but with no way to prove it, or we might have a growing stack of bodies for which we'll have no explanation. Either way, we'll look like a traffic cop who's being totally ignored by the traffic. If you're worried about lawsuits, that's when I'd advise running for cover."

Wilson passed his hand across his eyes. "God. We're not geared for this. Okay, Tony, I'll call a special session for this afternoon or tonight—as soon as possible. You tell them what you want. But pretend it's all you've got, will you? I mean, it's not inconceivable that some of them might try to sue you for withholding vital information if they found out about it. Right, Bob?"

Denby nodded. "Or you for conspiring with him."

I tossed Denby a salute. "Thank you, Robert."

"He asked."

Wilson stood up. "All right, all right. Let's just do it and hope it doesn't all blow up in our faces. Let me know how the meeting with

Katz goes. It would be a big help if we got him to cool his jets a bit."

He got to the door and stopped before opening it. "Needless to say, gentlemen, this conversation is not to be repeated, right?" He stuck his finger in Brandt's direction. "And Tony, never again—my playing dumb for you is over."

Brandt, Manierre and I stayed behind.

"You certainly were chatty," I said to Manierre.

He smiled. He was a large, gentle, grandfatherly sort, always immaculate in uniform, looking like the stereotype of the friendly cop from the 1950s, which he was. "Oh, I'm just a goldfish around you sharks."

"Impressive, were we?"

"I was thrilled. It reminded me of Military Intelligence."

Brandt tilted his chair back against the wall. "I wanted Billy to know what was going on."

"Let me know when you find out."

"I also got all those warrants and thought Billy's men might be of some help. I told him what they were all about."

"Can you spare anyone or do we pull in the state police?"

"How many are you putting onto it?"

"Everybody."

"How about three from the morning shift and two each from the other two?"

"Great. What's the story on Susan Lucey, by the way? Did she ever call us, or did she go straight to the newspaper?"

"She called for you, but no one knew where you were. She wouldn't talk to anyone else and wouldn't say what was wrong. I don't know how she got together with Katz. Where were you, anyway?"

"With Martha Murphy. I forgot to call in. Where's Lucey now?"

"She's at home. We tracked her down after we read about the attack, but she refused to talk. There wasn't much more we could do."

"How badly did he beat her?"

"I've seen worse. It wasn't the beating, really. I think he scared the living daylights out of her."

Brandt handed me the warrants. "Why don't you guys set all this up? Use the interrogation room if you need space." We both rose. As I put my hand on the doorknob, he added, "Don't wander away without checking back. I'm going to try to set up a meet with Katz and his boss as soon as possible."

Manierre and I gathered our troops. Excluding ourselves, we had six men. Between us, we had to request and search through the files of four travel agents, eight car-rental agencies, one airline, two taxi services, two bus companies, and one railroad. Each man took one warrant and headed out the door. Mine was for the Good Times Travel Agency. First, however, I went to my office to use the phone.

My first call was to the hospital to check on the blood sample Floyd Rubin had left there the day before. He was a type O, the same as Bill Davis, which ruled him out as the fetus's father. Technically, it also meant he could be the semen depositor, pending an analysis by Kees, but I felt on safe ground ruling that out. It was a character judgment, but I was sure Floyd Rubin didn't have it in him to kill this particular woman.

The second call was to Don Hebard at the Boston Police Department. He had been on our force about ten years ago but had found it too tame and uninteresting. Since his move to the city, he'd had his share of complaints, but never those two. I arranged to meet with him around 11 P.M. at Boston's police headquarters downtown, after the usual chaos in their records department had subsided to a murmur.

The intercom buzzed a minute after I'd hung up. It was Brandt.

"I've got Katz and Bellstrom in my office. You want to come over?"

"Christ. That was fast."

"We're a hot item."

I crossed to the south side of the building and joined them. Katz was standing nervously by the window, as if waiting for an accident. His boss was sitting with his legs stretched out in front of him. Dick Bellstrom had been editor of the *Reformer* for over fifteen years. He was a rumpled moderate Democrat with good common sense, and he had a finger on just about every pulse in town. He also had a closet sense of global outrage that would pop out on occasion on the editorial page. Despite his laid-back looks, he was not a man asleep at the wheel.

I nodded to both of them and took a chair.

Brandt opened. "It will be no surprise to either of you that I was hoping we could talk a little about Kimberly Harris. First off, I'd like to congratulate Stan on his article this morning. It was very flashy and mostly accurate. It also caused a bomb to go off at the town manager's office."

Bellstrom chuckled. "Is he rallying the troops for a little damage control?"

"I'll let him tell you what he's doing. I don't consider the article damaging. I do have my concerns, though."

"I bet," Katz said.

"Before I go on, I'd like you both to consider this conversation—at least for the moment—completely off the record." Katz looked at Bellstrom, who just nodded, still smiling. "It is true we've reopened the Harris case. Certain discrepancies were discovered by Joe here that were missed the first time around. So far, nothing indicates that Bill Davis didn't commit the murder, but some things have raised the possibility that he may not have been the only suspect."

"Are you saying if you keep pushing at that possibility, you might come up with a different killer?"

"Maybe."

"I can see why Wilson's getting sweaty palms."

"Well, he's a politician. Sweaty palms are his business."

"Still, they might cost you your job."

Brandt nodded. "Mine and a lot of other people's. But that's the luck of the draw. If, in fact, we didn't do our homework the first time on this, maybe a few heads ought to roll. The point is, we've come to a very dicey crossroads in this investigation, and I thought it might be a good idea for the four of us to get together and maybe come to some sort of understanding."

"In other words, butt out of your business," Katz said.

Bellstrom laughed and reached out to pat him gently on the arm. "Down, boy, down."

Brandt resumed. "There was a lot missing from this morning's story, a lot that would give it more coherence and that might also reduce some of the hysteria. People are starting to see this Ski Mask as a marauding cutthroat, randomly knocking people off. In fact, he's being very methodical and has but one goal in mind. Now, I would love to share as much as we've got on him with you in the hope of setting the public's mind more at ease."

"In exchange for what?"

"In exchange for some advance warning on your future articles."

Katz jammed his hands into his pockets, but kept quiet. "You want to read the articles first?"

"Well, if not read them, at least hear about what's going into them. This isn't too ominous, by the way. It amounts to merely hearing both sides of a debate before publication—pretty standard practice."

"When we choose it to be. There are a couple of problems I can see, the most practical of which is finding one of you guys in the middle of the night before we go to press. This morning's story didn't have much lead time, and I wouldn't have been able to waste more of it chasing after you."

"I understand. That's an unusual circumstance."

"There is one more important point. If we tell you what we've got before we publish, that opens the door to a lot of similar interference. People could legitimately lay claim to the same right we give you. Every board meeting, every feature article, every sports report would be open to the same scrutiny. We'd never be able to get to the printers."

Brandt pulled his prop out of his pocket and started fiddling. "I understand. It's hardly a new argument, nor is mine for that matter. In fact, under normal circumstances, I wouldn't even have this conversation. In our cases, it's an I-do-my-job-you-do-yours kind of world—it has to be that way. But, and please pardon the cliché, this is somewhat of a special case. We may have put the wrong man in jail. We have to either find enough to get him off the hook, or nail someone else in his stead. If we don't do one or the other, he stays where he is. The legal process put him in; it'll have to get him out. But it can only do so with our help. If you folks find something and publicize it before we can nail it down, it might blow his chances at getting out. I don't want to censor anything you might get; at the most, I might ask for a little time before you publish it."

"I don't like it." Katz muttered. He turned away from the window at last and faced us. "I mean, it sounds swell and bighearted—you guys working overtime in order to clear an innocent man. But it doesn't have to be true. I'm not calling you liars, but look at what you're facing. There are two alternatives: you reaffirm Davis's guilt and get rapped on the knuckles for having been slightly sloppy; or you discover he's totally innocent, and you all get fired and sued within an inch of your lives. You'd like us to believe you're hell-bent on suicide. I'm a little skeptical."

"It is true," Bellstrom added, "that by clearing everything through you first, we jeopardize the integrity of the facts as we find them. You could conceivably influence us to color things just enough to change their meaning. Look, Stan may not like to admit it, but we both know you folks are okay. We've worked well together over the years. But the fact remains that we're lambs and tigers—I'll resist saying who's which—but we're natural enemies. We may spend most of our lives in perfect harmony, but that doesn't mean that one morning Mother Nature won't suddenly remind us of who's who, and then it's best-friend-for-breakfast time."

Brandt sighed. It wasn't noon yet, and I could feel him staring ahead at a long, long day of similar conversations. "So. No deal."

Bellstrom gave him his most sympathetic smile. I'll grant him that—he had the perfect personality for this kind of discussion. "I'm afraid not, Tony, at least not formally. Let's leave it that we'll play it by ear. On the assumption that our hearts are all in the right place, that ought to be enough."

Brandt gave him a weary look. "I'm sure Davis would agree."

Bellstrom stood to leave and wagged his finger. "Cheap shot, Tony."

Brandt nodded and stood also. "I know. Sorry. Look, the earlier offer still stands. I have to huddle with the board soon, but afterward I'd like to let Stan in on some of the detail stuff. There's no point letting people think Ski Mask is more of a menace than he is, and what we've got won't jeopardize what Joe's looking into right now."

"All right. Thanks. Is that okay with you, Stan?"

"Sure, as long as I don't have to promise I'll publish any of it."

Brandt shook his head. "Christ, what a hard-ass. I think you'll consider it news, even coming from me."

"That reminds me, Stan." I asked. "How did you link up with Susan Lucey?"

Stan smiled and shook his head.

"Come on, Stan, give him that much." Bellstrom nudged his arm.

"It's not like you're revealing a source."

Katz was obviously torn between keeping a secret and revealing his cleverness. He finally gave in. "I followed you. After you left her place, I had a chat with her myself. You made a big impression on her and she wasn't very giving, although I sure as hell was—she's very expensive. Anyway, I didn't learn much, but I left her my number and told her to call me—that I'd make it worth her while.

"So she calls me in the middle of the night. She's been beaten up; you're nowhere to be found; she feels totally betrayed. She said she asked for protection and you ignored her. All of a sudden, she wasn't so keen on you, so she spilled her guts. That's about it. You ought to be nicer to your snitches."

He was right.

21

"Who is it?" she asked from behind the door. "Joe Gunther. The cop who talked to you yesterday."

"Go fuck yourself."

"I came to see how you were."

"Lousy, thanks to you."

"I've got a peace offering."

The door was almost ripped off its hinges. Her face, its left side badly bruised, was red with fury. "A peace offering? What the hell do you think this is? A lover's spat? Your first visit gets me beaten up, this one'll probably get me killed, and you have a peace offering? You're a real head case, you know that?"

Her hand was half lifted to strike me, so I filled it with what I was holding. It was an automatic coffee maker. It looked more extravagant than it was; the whole thing had set me back about fifty dollars. That was certainly less than meeting me had cost her.

She stared at it with her mouth open. A gust of wind blew past me and hit her in the face. She grabbed my coat, pulled me inside and slammed the door. "Don't get any ideas. I just don't want to catch pneumonia." Still, she kept the coffee maker. "What the hell made you choose this?"

"I noticed you didn't have one."

She peered at it closely. "You think this cheap piece of crap is going to get you off the hook?"

I didn't answer.

She gave me a long baleful look. "The bastard hurt me—bad. I asked you for protection."

"I know. I'm sorry."

"That doesn't do me a hell of lot of good, does it? I'm not going to get much business looking like a smashed grapefruit, am I?"

I was probably reaching, but I thought some of the heat had gone out of her.

"No."

"So what gives you the balls to drop by with presents, huh?"

"Nothing. That's it. I just wanted to see if you were okay. I paid your hospital bill."

She shook her head and crossed the room to put the machine on the kitchen counter. "Bully for you. You really are a bastard, you know that? I ought to shove this thing down your throat."

"I won't stop you."

She leaned against the counter and crossed her arms. She was wearing blue jeans and a sweat shirt of dubious cleanliness. "Where the hell were you, anyway? I thought you cops were supposed to keep in touch with each other."

"A partner of mine got killed a week ago. His widow got back home from her daughter's last night, so I went over to keep her company. I thought she might be lonely, her first night back in her own house. I forgot to leave word where I was."

She didn't say anything for a few moments, and when she did, her voice had finally softened. "Was that the guy who died in the car crash?"

"Yeah."

"Gunther…You were the one with him, weren't you? The one who ended up in the hospital."

"That's right."

She flared up again briefly. "Why the hell didn't you tell me that the first time? I might have known what to expect."

It flashed through my mind that if I told her someone else had killed Frank, she'd probably throw me through the window. I pretended Ski Mask was the one and only. "I never thought of it. I did warn you, but to be honest, I didn't think you'd ever set eyes on him. What he did to you was totally out of character."

"Out of character? What do you know about his character? Katz says the man's a fucking nut case, and I can swear to it."

"Katz only knows half of what we know, and we don't know much. But everything Ski Mask has done has been thought out beforehand, with no visible emotion."

"My God, he's killed people. How emotional do you want him to get? And he sure as hell wasn't cool, calm and collected when I met him."

174

I couldn't argue with that. Considering my prowess to date, any psychological evaluations by me were rightly suspect. "I screwed up. I am sorry."

She waved her hand at me angrily. "Sorry, sorry. All right, so you're sorry. I'm sorry I ever set eyes on you, so that makes two of us." She crossed over to her armchair and sat. "I'll live." She reached under the chair for her stash and began filling her tiny pipe. She lit up. "Want a pull?"

I shook my head. "Are you going to be all right?"

She held her smoke for a couple of seconds and exhaled. "You tell me."

"What did he want?"

She snorted. "Same thing you did. So I told him what he wanted to know—I mean, shit, it was no big secret, right?"

"No."

"I did what you told me to do, right?"

"Right."

There was a lull. She smoked some more, stared at the floor, ran her fingers through her hair. When she spoke again, the anger was missing. "He wasn't just after information. He had something else going, you know? When I told him about some of what Kimberly and I had done together, he kind of flipped out. That's when the beating started. I mean, I knew I had blown it. I shouldn't have told him as much as I did. Then he wanted to know everything. I had to tell him positions, whether we'd made it together without a guy in the middle, whether she ever took it up the ass, all kinds of stuff. I mean, he scared the shit out of me. I'm not going to forget him for a long, long time."

As she talked, her voice as tough as usual, the light from a gap in the curtains caught the tears running down her cheek. "He had real pale eyes, not really blue or anything. They were weird—colorless—and cold. I mean, I knew sure as hell I wasn't going to live, that he was going to kill me and that it was going to hurt. And he did hurt me bad. Not the face stuff—I'm used to a few punches—but there was other stuff, things he enjoyed. The more it hurt, the more he liked it... Fucking creep."

She raised her eyes to me, openly crying now, the toughness suddenly gone. She looked like a kid in dirty clothes, her body shaking helplessly. "If you ever catch him, could you blow his balls off for me?"

I knelt and put my arms around her. The embrace was prompted by more than mere sympathy. Through her suffering, Susan Lucey had just illuminated one of the murkier corners of the case. Ski Mask's reaction to the information she had given him went a long way to connecting him emotionally to Kimberly Harris rather than to Bill Davis. While I still didn't know specifically what Ski Mask was after, I now felt pretty sure it wasn't solely to get Davis out of jail. Susan Lucey had paid a large price to get me that information. I was definitely in her debt.

After a short while, she stopped sobbing and pulled back a little. Her hands were clasped in her lap. Her face was flushed and bruised and wet with tears. "Fuck, I probably would have met someone like him sooner or later. I probably will again. It's the turf."

She hesitated a moment and then gave me the best—and longest—kiss I'd ever had in my life. It left me misty eyed and breathless. "Thanks for the coffee maker, you creep." She said it without a smile.

Despite the wide scope of our search for Kimberly Harris's activities during her three-day weekends, none of us really believed we'd hit pay dirt searching train, bus or cut-rate car-rental files, so all of us that morning had taken either travel agencies or the airline. The airline was going to take longer, of course. Its records were not held locally, and we sent one man across New Hampshire to hunt them down. But in principle, for once we were on the right track.

At the end of a long afternoon plowing through box after box of computer printouts, we found two travel firms that clicked. One of them had handled tickets for a Miss Julie Johnson on seventy percent of the right dates, and another had ticketed a Mr. L. Armstrong for the same dates and destinations.

I found Brandt in his office at about six in the evening. He was sitting in virtual darkness—only his desk lamp on—with his feet on the table and his chair tilted back. His eyes were closed and he was smoking.

"Rough day, huh?"

"Long, yeah."

"How did the board go?"

"On and on. I gave them more than they had and less than they wanted. They let me know, in their words, that my 'future hangs in the balance.' Utter crap, of course; they're confusing my job with my life. Typical asshole pomposity."

Unusual words for a usually unflappable man. I was hoping his condemnation wasn't universal—one of those assholes was a woman for whom I had a particular fondness.

"Did they all come down that hard?"

He sighed. "No, not all." Then he chuckled. "Your own Miss Zigman was her normal levelheaded self, but she was wise enough to lay low in the storm. What have you got?"

"Julie Johnson and Louis Armstrong had a penchant for flying the same airplanes to the same places, at least according to two separate travel agencies."

"Louis Armstrong?"

"The irreverence of torrid love, I guess. They certainly had an eye for glamour: Vegas, Lake Tahoe, Miami, San Francisco—all the hot spots. We interviewed the agents who booked most of the tickets. It was all done in cash, and it sounds like Kimberly did the arranging for both of them, although she was apparently in disguise—dark glasses, hair hidden, stuff like that. Just enough hocus-pocus to make her impossible to forget. I guess that makes the guy a well-heeled married local, or at least one with access to funds. From what Susan Lucey told me about Kimberly's taste in men, I would also assume he's—as they say—mature in years. Either that or a shy-but-precocious fifteen-year-old." Or, I thought, even Ski Mask himself.

"Good." He still hadn't opened his eyes or moved. "Now what?"

"Now I go to Boston. I have a date tonight with a friend at the police department."

"In search of Pam Stark?"

"Yup."

"Happy trails. Don't get mugged."

I called Gail before I left and congratulated her on surviving the afternoon. She said Brandt had displayed the stoicism of Saint Sebastian and had fared about as well. I apologized for not showing up last night and told her not to expect me tonight either. I had a feeling that what I would find in Boston would keep me out of town for a while. Her reaction was matter-of-fact, with no hint of the emotion she'd shown the day before. The seesaw was back in balance, thanks to me, and for that, idiotically, I was now sorry.

To me, driving to Boston at night is slipping toward the heart of a gigantic landlocked amoeba, whose thin and ragged outer fringe extends far beyond its inner core. From narrow, unlit New Hampshire farm roads, lights gradually begin to cluster along the sides of the highway. Occasional houses become occasional towns; the towns begin to link first tenuously with filling stations and a restaurant here or there, then with modest "miracle miles"—commercial stretches of small retailers, low-rent discount stores, and fading supermarkets.

Finally, still well over an hour from the city, suburbia takes over in an endless chain of lights and malls and parking plazas and increasingly maddened traffic. By the rules known only to these particular urbanites, behavior behind the wheel metamorphoses into animal cunning. Speed limits are ignored, traffic lights are useless; drivers maneuver for room and advantage, speeding and braking, flowing from one side of the road to the other in a ceaseless attempt to get ahead of the other guy. I entered Boston, as always, like a leaf in a torrent, my only thoughts turning on ways to avoid the rocks.

I finally beached myself downtown, not far from the city's government center, and entered the Boston Police Department's main building on Stuart Street. I found Don Hebard as promised, loitering outside the records division, a plastic coffee mug in hand.

"Welcome to Beantown."

"You people actually call it that?"

"Sure, sometimes. Especially to tourists." He led me through a set of double doors and signed in. "How was the traffic?"

"Probably what you'd call normal."

"Go on red, stop on green?"

"Yeah. Why don't they do that in New York or anywhere else I've been?"

He continued down a hallway and ushered me into a large room jammed with floor-to-ceiling shelf units stuffed with cardboard boxes. There was a counter near the door with a computer monitor on it. "Ever been to Rome or Athens or Cairo?"

I shook my head.

"Well I have—once each. I was on one of those Mediterranean whirlwind tours—real waste of money. It's my theory that when all of us came over to this great American melting pot, some of us opted to stay in Boston. Now the reason we did that was some cosmic genetic glitch we share with people who ended up in Rome and Athens and Cairo. It's that gene that makes us all drive the same way."

I nodded in silence. The less I said the better. I'd forgotten Hebard never took comments about the traffic or the weather as mere icebreakers. To him they were subjects of real merit, comparable to religion and sports.

"What's the name?"

"Stark, Pamela."

He entered it on the computer and watched a spume of green letters wash across the screen. "Shit."

"What?"

He pointed to a series of numbers. "That means it hasn't been put in the data banks yet." He waved at the room beyond the counter. "All that is going on computer, along with everything that comes in now, but we haven't quite finished. I'm afraid your girl is buried in the stacks."

He copied the reference number from the screen and led me behind the counter. We walked up and down looming, claustrophobic corridors, checking numbers, until he came to a halt and dropped to his knees. I joined him on the floor.

"I never find these things at waist level, you know? It's started to make me wonder."

I helped him pull the box off the bottom shelf. "You didn't drop by the Cairo Police Department, did you?"

He looked serious and pursed his lips. I took the box from him and stood up, flipping it open. "What's the last number?"

He rose slowly and gave it to me. I pulled out the appropriate folder and handed the box back. "You got some place I could read this?"

He led me to a table against the far wall and left to get some more coffee, still lost in thought. Hebard was no longer a street cop; he was in administration. It gave him lots of time to wonder about things.

Pamela Stark's file consisted of some mug shots, a fingerprint card, and a badly typed arrest report, along with all the paperwork attending an overnight stay in the Boston jail.

I compared the picture I had of Kimberly Harris—taken the morning she was found with a belt around her neck—to the shot of a young and sulky Pamela Stark. It was a match. It made me feel odd, seeing her alive for the first time. I'd looked at the other picture so often it had become her real portrait, rather than the face of a muscleless corpse.

I stared at the mug shot for a long time. She wasn't beautiful in the advertisement sense—no chiseled cheekbones or aristocratic brow. She had the look of an aging teenager whose choices now would deter-mine her appearance. She could either carry her cheerleader softness into gentle maturity, or lose it to bitterness, hardship, and the grind of a hopeless life. From the little I knew of her, she'd opted for the former by dancing near the latter, obviously a shortcut that hadn't worked out.

According to the report, she'd been busted virtually off the bus while selling her favors to an undercover cop. She claimed she'd been in the city less than twenty-four hours, had no pimp, no family or friends in the area, no lawyer, little money, and no remorse. It was the arresting officer's opinion that this would not be the last time she and the police would do business. She gave her home address as 24 Stone Creek Road, Westport, Connecticut. She also gave her age as nineteen.

Hebard saw me writing down the address. "You know to take that with a grain of salt, I guess."

"How big a grain?"

He looked at the arresting officer's report. "She hardly sounds like the virgin-from-Peoria type; stupid maybe, but not impressed by authority. I'd say you could eat the whole salt-shaker. She was above the age of consent and pleaded guilty; there was no reason for us to check the address—or the name, for that matter. Still, you never know."

He reached over my shoulder and picked up the photo. "Pretty girl. Very pretty, in fact."

"Before and after." I handed him the picture I'd been carrying around.

He looked at them both. "Kind of gives you a queer feeling, doesn't it?"

"Yeah."

22

I woke up in the middle of the night with a start. Gail's arm, thrown across my chest, tensed instantly.

"What is it?" Her voice was a hard, urgent whisper.

I reached over and touched her cheek. "I'm sorry. It's nothing. I just thought of something."

She lifted her head and looked around, her face half covered with a cascade of hair. "God, you scared the hell out of me."

"No, it's all right. Go back to sleep." I noticed the glowing red numbers of the digital clock beyond her; it was 2:43 A.M. She lowered her head back to the pillow.

I hadn't really been asleep, at least not in a deep sleep. In fact, I'd only returned from Boston a half hour ago. I'd taken Gail at her word, albeit twenty-four hours later, and had slipped into her bed as quietly as possible, waking her just enough to say, "Hi."

She moved closer, wrapping one leg around my own, a glutton for snuggles. "What woke you up?" Her voice had regained a sleepy fuzziness.

"Bill Davis said all along that the drugs we found at his place were planted there, something we never paid much attention to. But if he was telling the truth, then that means someone else bought them beforehand, probably the same guy who killed Kimberly—I mean, Pam Stark."

"Who's Pam Stark?"

The interruption surprised me, as if everyone should know what I knew. "That's Kimberly's real name; at least I think it is. It's the name she used when she was busted for soliciting in Boston four years ago."

Her eyes became more focused. "Hey, that's right. You're supposed to be in Boston now. What're you doing here?"

"I thought I was going to go from there to wherever was listed on the arrest sheet, but the address was a phony, at least according to directory assistance, so I came back home. But that's not important—"

"Right—now you're sniffing after heroin. Isn't that a little hopeless?"

"Not if we apply the same wishful thinking we're using in the prednisone search. If we do that, it gives us a hunchback buying drugs in a back alley—something a local pusher is liable to remember for quite some time."

"Find the pusher and you find the buyer?"

"If we're lucky. If nothing else, the pusher might remember the hump, in which case we know for sure the guy we're after definitely had a long-term prescription, which would help cut down the search a lot. It also wouldn't hurt as a piece of backup evidence."

I smiled at the ceiling. The machinery was finally beginning to turn in our favor—or at least it wasn't turning against us. We had the off chance of pinning a physical deformity to someone who'd had close ties to Kimberly—possibly along with a prescription naming that someone—we'd matched her with a man during her three-day weekends, and we'd given her a new name, possibly a real one. It was all pretty iffy, but it was developing. We were already combing the area looking for Ski Mask, we'd soon be asking the Connecticut local cops to locate any and all families named Stark, and my bright idea about tracing the drug sale—as unrealistic as it might seem—was making me beam. Things were happening. I felt like a man who was slowly slogging his way to the firmer ground at the edge of the swamp.

Gail kissed the inside of my ear. That always sent shivers down my spine. "My hero. You're so smart." She slid her thigh up between my legs. "I'm all awake now."

"I can tell."

Her hand slipped down across my stomach and she giggled. "You're all awake too."

I stopped by Maxine's window early the next morning and picked up the daily report. Brandt had entered everything I'd dug up to date.

"You've certainly been busy."

"Not having to write your own reports helps." She rolled her eyes. "Friends in high places. He wants to see you, by the way."

"Did he ever go home?"

"He was here when I came in."

I thanked her and went back to Brandt's office. He looked the same as always—no stubble on the chin or bags under the eyes. The man seemed immune to the common signs of wear and tear. "Thanks for this." I waved the report. "How was Boston?"

I laid a copy of Pam Stark's arrest sheet on his desk and settled in a chair. "I think the address is bogus; I don't know about the name." He read it over quickly. "Pam Stark, huh?"

"Yeah. I looked at a map of Connecticut this morning. Assuming she didn't tell a bald-faced lie, she might have picked the name of a town near hers, which would make it Norwalk or Bridgeport or Wilton, something like that. We could query the local cops on it, and if we come up dry, we could try the state police."

Brandt nodded. "Sounds good to me. I'll get on it."

I stood to go and he leaned back in his chair to look up at me. "I thought you'd like to know that John Woll did a little investigating on his own yesterday."

"Oh?"

"He thought our mysterious friend might have bought his ski mask in a local store, so he went to every outlet he could think of and asked about recent purchases—this was during his time off."

"And?"

"And nothing; he came up dry. But I thought you'd like to know."

I smiled and shook my head, remembering Murphy's wrath at the man. "Poor bastard; he's going to be living that one down for years."

"What're your plans, by the way?"

"Mend fences with Willy Kunkle."

I stopped by Maxine's window again on my way to my cubbyhole office. "Has Willy come in yet?"

"Nope."

"Give me a buzz when he does, will you?" I had mixed feelings about dealing with Kunkle. He was so totally irascible I was half-inclined to let him self-destruct in private. But he was still a functioning cop and had once been a good one. He had also become my direct responsibility, now that I was acting captain, and in all conscience I couldn't let him slide without at least offering a hand. My timing, though, was utterly self-serving. Kunkle, more than any-one on the force, was wired to Brattleboro's small but intense narcotics trade.

The phone buzzed before I even sat down. "He's hot on your heels."

I stuck my head out into the hallway and caught him as he entered. "After you've read Brandt's summary, could I see you for a minute?"

"What about?" His voice was neutral, which for him was probably a good sign.

"I'll tell you when you're finished; it's related."

He was in my doorway three minutes later, a sour look on his face. "Is this where I get my walking papers? Or do we go the 'you've-been-under-a-lot-of-strain-lately-why-not-take-some-time-off' route?"

"No. We do the 'why-don't-you-put-your-butt-in-that-chair-and-can-the-crap' bit. Is that acceptable?" He didn't answer, but he sat.

"I need your help on this thing, but I want to make something clear first. We all know you're in some sort of personal bind. So far it hasn't gotten in the way of you doing your job, although you seem hell-bent on that happening. Maybe you want out and you don't know how to do it—beats me. So I'm asking you—pure and simple, no strings attached—do you want to be a cop or not? Because if you do I've got some business I want help with."

"What?"

"Answer the question, and think about it first."

He thought, but not the way I wanted. "What are you after? What's the game?"

"The game is I'm trying to get to the other side of your paranoia. I want to know if you, William Kunkle, want to be a cop. Yes or no."

"And if I say yes, then I've got to go see a shrink, right?"

I shook my head and sighed. "I think you need a shrink in any case, but if you say yes, then I've got business on my mind." I pointed at the summary in his hand. "Relating to that."

"All right. Yes."

"Thank God. Now promise you'll try something for me, will you? Let's just work together on this thing. I won't ask what's bugging you, and you stop assuming everything I say has a double meaning. Deal?"

"You're really making me into a nut case."

"The way I feel now, I'm the one headed for the rubber room." I took a deep breath. "Look, Willy, I think maybe we all let you down a little here. Cops have more stress than any professionals I know. It's as common as the flu. We ought to help each other out more because of that, but maybe the macho thing gets in the way; I don't know. In any case, it's easier for cops to let a fellow cop slide, pretending he's just eccentric, than to offer him help. And on the flip side, it's normal for that cop to think he can deal with it himself—that if he asks for help, or shows he needs it, everyone'll think he's a weenie. So everyone loses. I think that's what's happening to you and I also think it stinks. For what it's worth, I'd like to apologize for not having done something earlier."

"And what are you going to do now?"

"Nothing you don't want me to. I'd like to bring you into the Stark thing because I just thought of a drug angle and that's where you're hot. But I'd also like you to know that I'm approaching this as if it were a whole new case. The fuck-ups that landed Bill Davis in jail are past history, and we've all got to answer for them—you probably least of all, because you were lowest on the totem pole. If any heads roll, they'll start at the top, among Brandt and Dunn and the board and Tom Wilson, and they'll even dig up Frank Murphy and wave him around before they get to me and you, so I wouldn't worry... You want to do business?"

"Yeah."

As usual, it didn't make him break into song, but this time—for the first time—I actually sensed I might have penetrated. I ran him through everything then, in chronological order, from the Jamie Phillips killing to my flash in the night a few hours ago; I also included Frank's cover-up, an admission I could tell he appreciated. He sat and listened, looking carefully at the contents of the file I was building, item by item, without saying a word.

"So," I ended up. "Who's the local gossip in the trenches?"

"Ted Haffner. He's not the gossip; he's not even in the business much any more, but a couple of years ago, he was the number-one heroin man in town."

"What happened?"

Kunkle gave a little smile. "These people aren't much for job security. He got interested in other things, mainly sampling his wares."

"Is he friendly?"

"He's not a snitch, if that's what you mean. He'll take some work."

"Well, let's do it."

Kunkle remained seated, his face regaining that familiar cloud. "So who shakes him down?"

I stood and showed him both palms. "Hey, Willy, he's your baby. I'm just riding shotgun."

Still Kunkle stayed where he was, reading the summary. "So Stan followed you to Susan Lucey's and supposedly Christ-knows-who tailed you from Connecticut. Have you been watching your back lately?"

I still hadn't told anyone about the private detective from Burlington. "I didn't see much point."

"Why not? It sounds like an easy way to pick up bad guys, maybe even Ski Mask."

"So what do we do? Get one of our own to tail us, and hope he picks up the competition?"

"It's an idea. We might get lucky. If nothing else, it might dissuade people from following you around and lousing up the case."

It seemed silly as hell to me. I don't know why—pride maybe—but I wasn't going to antagonize Kunkle now that he'd agreed to help out. I picked up the phone and arranged to have an unmarked car follow us from a distance.

Ted Haffner lived in a trailer park on the outskirts of West Brattleboro—the last cluster of urban dwellers before Route 9 began its gradual climb into the Green Mountains. In fact, it was so much on the fringe it was hard to tell whether the homes or the trees were gaining the upper hand in taking over the real estate. My personal bet was on the trees. Mostly evergreens, they stood tall and dark, their bristling skirts massive and ancient in the flat, gray light. The trailers, by contrast, sandwiched between the icy crusts on their roofs and the rough turmoil of ground-up, dirty snow around them, looked like the remnants of a civilization long on the ropes.

We bumped along a winding track, weaving between snow covered sofas, rusting cars and assortments of trash and cordwood. No one was visible, although several of the battered, dark-windowed homes leaked thin strings of gray smoke from their oily metal chimneys.

"I see the drug trade stood Mr. Haffner in good stead."

Kunkle was at the wheel, trying to save his car's suspension from as much abuse as possible. "Like I said, as a businessman, his mind tended to wander." He stopped before an oblong metal shack, modest even by these standards, a mobile home whose only movement was toward disintegration. "This is it."

We climbed out and walked unsteadily across the frozen debris scattered outside the small aluminum front door. Kunkle pounded on the wall. "This is purely a formality. He never does answer."

He grabbed the doorknob and pulled. As the door swung back, I noticed a faint, wispy cloud billow out like a belch. Kunkle put his foot on the high threshold and heaved himself inside. I followed him, my nostrils flaring at the overheated stench. Before my eyes adjusted, I thought the place was totally blacked out, but a faint glow slowly grew at the far end, where Kunkle was already talking with someone.

"Hey, Ted. How're you doin'?"

There was a mutter in response. I groped down the length of the trailer, leaving the decayed and littered kitchen/living area where we'd entered, squeezing through a tiny hallway with a stinking bathroom on one side and ending up in a heavily curtained bedroom. Kunkle was sitting on the edge of a bunk, looking at a long-haired, bearded man propped in the corner against a pile of blankets and dirty pillows. To say Ted Haffner appeared unwell is an understatement—I'd seen pictures of Egyptian mummies that looked healthier. Curiously, his eyes were clear and normal looking, as if the body and the mind were totally separate entities, the one dying, the other trapped within.

I could distinguish the slurred muttering now. "This is private property. Scram."

"Don't be hostile, Ted. This may be worth your while."

"How much is my while worth?" I thought that was a good question, given his appearance.

"Twenty bucks."

"Fuck off."

"All right. I'll ask the question, and you put a price tag on it."

"Five thousand for the time of day."

"What's your problem?"

"I don't like you."

"Hell, my wife doesn't like me; she still takes my money."

"She's greedy and stupid then."

"So I guess that makes you just plain stupid, right?"

"Why don't you get out of here? You're trespassing." Haffner made an attempt to get up, but it was half-hearted and unsuccessful. He lay back, breathing heavily.

Kunkle placed his hand on the man's bony chest. "You don't look too good. You got something around I can get you?"

"Yeah, shoot me up."

"Food, Ted, food. When was the last time you ate something?"

"Fuck off."

"You can't afford it, can you? I got a history question for you; it's not a snitch job. You tell me about old times, I lay a fifty on you and you get a square meal, or a trip to outer space. What's the harm?"

Haffner looked at us sullenly, weighing the offer. "What's the question?"

"About three years back, when you were top dog, a buy was made—a one-bag deal that ended up in the room of the black guy who iced the chick at the Huntington Arms. You remember that?"

"Sure I remember."

"But the black guy didn't make the buy, did he?"

Haffner gave us a big smile. "You said history. This sounds more like current events."

Almost simultaneously, I heard the floor creak behind me and felt a cold draft on my neck. I turned to see a tall man wearing a black jump-suit and ski mask pointing a gun at my head. He had made the distance from the front door to the back bedroom in an instant. "Hi, Joe."

Kunkle jerked around, his hand moving to his belt.

"Don't do it."

Kunkle saw the gun, now jammed in my throat.

"What the hell's goin' on?" Haffner again tried to sit up.

"Shut up." Ski Mask moved into the room and looked around. I was having a hard time breathing with my windpipe half closed off. He motioned to Kunkle. "Hand over the gun."

Kunkle handed it over. Ski Mask slipped it into his jumpsuit pock-et and added mine to it. He then told Kunkle to slip his handcuffs through the handle of the closet door farthest from Haffner's bunk and to lock himself in. He attached me to the other end. Finally, he patted us down, took the key to the handcuffs, and sat where Kunkle had been.

He put his own gun away and smiled at Haffner. "So, what were they asking you?"

"Who the fuck are you?"

Ski Mask turned toward us. "What's his name?"

Kunkle looked at me in amazement. "Is that him?"

I might have laughed if I hadn't felt such an enormous sensation of menace in this man. Ski Mask was like a panther who had stalked his prey for days on end, calming his growing hunger with thoughts of the inevitable feast. The tone in his voice indicated that mere thinking was no longer doing the job, that some action was required, at what-ever cost to all concerned. I was scared to hell for everyone in that hot and fetid room.

I felt all this because he was obviously taking a calculated chance. The two questions he had asked—Haffner's name and the topic of our conversation—indicated just how much he was gambling that this one half-dead man might give him a crucial advantage. In fact, if we were lucky, he'd gambled too high; I was thinking of the tail Kunkle had insisted upon.

"His name's Ted Haffner, but he's got nothing to tell you. He's a dead end."

"Maybe that's because you don't know how to ask the right ques-tions." He reached into his breast pocket and pulled out a long, black, cylindrical object. It clicked sharply in his hand, and a thin, tapered blade sprang into view, glinting in the half-light. "Or maybe your methods are ineffective."

Haffner started to squirm on his bed. "Who the hell are you, man?"

"I'm here to collect all the answers you weren't going to give these gentlemen."

"What do I get out of it?" Haffner's voice didn't carry much conviction.

"Nothing."

"We were looking for a drug dealer. The one who sold Bill Davis his junk," I interrupted.

"Why?"

"Why not? It might give us something. It was a long shot."

"Not a hot lead, huh?"

"Not with him. He was our first stop of the day."

Ski Mask turned his back to me. "That right, Ted?"

"Yeah. I know nothin' about nothin'."

I heard Ski Mask chuckle. He grabbed one of Haffner's hands and placed the point of his knife at the hollow of his arm, on the inside of the elbow. "Have you ever carved a chicken, Ted?"

Haffner's eyes were huge and white against his grimy face. "Sure."

"You know how you've got to get your knife right into the joint to cut off the drumstick?"

Haffner didn't answer.

"It's a good thing the bird's dead, because that little maneuver hurts like hell." He applied a little pressure. Haffner let out a small noise and a single drop of blood appeared at the knife's point.

"Jesus, man. What do you want?"

"I want the simple truth. What were they asking you?"

I spoke up again. "What I told you was the truth. You're going over the edge." My hope in the backup car was fading fast.

He didn't even look at me. He just pushed the knife a little harder. Haffner whimpered. Ski Mask's voice was absolutely flat. "Joe, every time you interrupt, I'll stick him a little harder." He shifted his weight slightly. "Now, what were they asking you?"

"They wanted to know who bought the junk that ended up at that nigger's place."

"And what did you tell them?"

"Nothing. I don't know."

"I've done this before, Ted. The pain is like nothing you've ever known."

189

"I swear to God; I really do. I got no reason to lie to you. I don't know who bought the stuff. It wasn't someone anybody knew. It was a one-shot deal. No one ever saw the guy again—honest."

"Then who sold it?"

Haffner's face was shining with sweat. It was dripping off his chin. His breath began to come in quick gasps. "Oh, Christ, what was his name?"

Ski Mask's arm moved ever so slightly.

"No, no, stop, please. Wait—I remember. It was Hill. Lew Hill. Lewis Hill."

"Where does he live?"

"Now? I don't know. I swear I don't know. People move around a lot down there."

"Where? Where did he live, last you knew?"

"Near the old organ warehouse, on Birge."

"What's the address?"

"Jesus, the address. I don't know. Who knows addresses? It's a big place, near the turn-off to the bridge. They call it the Misery Hilton. People know it around there; just ask. I'm sorry, I don't know the number." He was weeping now; the sweat and saliva sprayed from his lips as he spoke. His entire body was trembling.

Ski Mask let him go and withdrew the knife. Haffner suddenly closed his eyes hard. His mouth opened and closed a couple of times, and then everything ceased. A final breath of air escaped from between his lips, causing a line of bubbles to drip down his chin.

Ski Mask placed a finger alongside the carotid artery, paused for a moment, and then stood up. He carefully replaced the knife in his pocket. "Heart attack, I would guess."

Kunkle and I watched in stunned silence as he left. We heard him walk to the front door and slam it behind him. Then all was quiet, and we watched the sweat dry on Haffner's face.

23

Kunkle and I were uncoupled a full hour and a half later by two very sheepish plainclothes patrolmen who had been cooling their heels at the entrance of the trailer park, watching for a man who had apparently come and gone at his leisure. Kunkle's fury was such that it rendered him speechless, a fact for which I, and certainly the other two, were extremely grateful.

All personnel—every patrolman and detective—were sent out to find Hill before Ski Mask did, and I later felt that if there was a God, he displayed his mercy by allowing Kunkle to come up the winner. Hill was located two hours later in the back room of Login's Cafe, bracing himself for the day ahead with a half bottle of scotch. As it turned out, he needed all the numbing he could get—he was already the worse for wear by the time Kunkle dragged him through our doors.

I raised my eyebrows at the spreading blue and red bruise on the dazed man's cheekbone.

"He resisted," Kunkle muttered and shook Hill by the collar as if to show the fight was still undecided.

It seemed to me Kunkle's grip was the only thing keeping Hill on his feet. He rolled his eyes and whined, "Resisted, hell. I didn't even know who the son of a bitch was. I ought to sue somebody."

I walked with both of them downstairs to the holding cells. "Consider yourself lucky to be alive. The reason you're here is because somebody is out to kill you."

Hill twisted around to stare at me. "Who?"

"You remember Ted Haffner?"

"Haffner? Give me a break. He can't even get out of bed."

"I won't argue with that. He died two hours ago, right after he put the finger on you."

"What the hell did I do?"

Kunkle shoved him into a cell and slammed the door shut. The metallic crash reverberated off the concrete walls. Kunkle hit the switch of a flood lamp for the closed-circuit surveillance camera aimed at the cell. Hill shrank under the effect. His voice was little more than a murmur. "What are you guys talking about?"

"We'll be back."

We returned upstairs. I asked Kunkle to start filling out the report on this morning, and then I called Dunn's office to request the immediate presence of one of his people. I finally went into Brandt's office.

He was on the phone, listening. He motioned to me to sit. After a couple of minutes, he said, "Thanks. I'll get back to you," and hung up. He tilted back in his chair and put his hands behind his head.

"We've got Hill downstairs."

"Has he said anything?"

"I haven't asked. I thought you and someone from Dunn's office might like to listen in. Kunkle smacked him around a little—claimed resistance."

Brandt shook his head slightly. "What was your assessment of Ski Mask this morning?"

"Mid-forties, athletic, very precise and under control, cold as ice. He's a fast-moving son of a bitch, I'll give him that, and I would guess he has a military background, or at least that kind of training. And," I added, "he doesn't have an accent."

Brandt gave me an odd look. "Did he kill that man?"

"No. He didn't help him along any. He certainly abused him—tortured him might be better—but Haffner died just a tad before his natural time, maybe a full half hour, the way he looked when we found him."

There was a knock on the door and an assistant state's attorney named Powers stuck his head in. "You rang, Sahib?"

Brandt stood up. "Let's find out what Mr. Hill has to say." On the way down, I told Maxine to get Kunkle. I didn't want his nose any further out of joint. It took him thirty seconds to join us in the basement.

Hill was leaning with his forearms through the bars of his cell full of renewed self-confidence. "What's this bullshit about some guy trying to ice me?"

"He hasn't tried yet. When he does, he'll probably succeed. He seems very good in that department."

"Who is he?"

"We don't know. We're calling him Ski Mask for now."

"Hey, I've been reading about him. What would he want with me?"

"Three years ago you sold some smack in a one-shot deal that ended up in the apartment of the black guy we nailed for Kimberly Harris's murder. Do you remember that?"

Hill's eyes rested warily on me. "I remember the murder."

I pointed to Powers. "He represents the state's attorney and is here to assure you total immunity for anything that might be said today, right?"

Powers dutifully nodded.

"So, you're not under arrest, and we don't want you for the deal or for anything else. We're only after information. If you want a lawyer for some reason, be my guest, but understand that the only reason you're in here is for your health. If you want to leave, you may leave."

He smiled and looked at the bars before him. I gestured to Kunkle to turn the lock. "Satisfied?"

He pushed the door open but then settled on the cell bunk with his legs crossed and his hands behind his head, feeling cocky. "What makes you think I had anything to do with that deal? It's not like you can trace a serial number."

"You were Haffner's dying words. And you people have your trademarks—word gets around."

He thought for a minute. "What's this Ski Mask after?"

"We don't know for sure," I said. "We thought he might be a buddy of Davis's—the black guy in jail—but he's obviously connected to the girl who was killed, possibly the father of her unborn child. Whatever he is, he's a nasty son of a bitch. He tortured Haffner."

"To death?"

"He's dead all right." I saw no reason to belittle the impression.

Hill dropped his feet to the floor and rose to a sitting position. "It was a long time ago."

Brandt smiled. "Haffner remembered—with a little help. You tell us what we want to know, and we'll be able to spare you the same kind of help. If not, you're on your own."

"I'm on my own anyway. You guys obviously weren't too useful to Ted. I'll take my own chances."

I turned off the floodlight. "It's a free country, as they say. What about the deal?"

Hill rose and walked out of the cell. "I sold the stuff. I don't know who to, though. He kept his face covered and whispered a lot—pretty corny."

193

"Was there anything else about him? Young, old, tall, short—stuff like that?"

"Hard to tell, you know? It was at night, just for a couple of minutes, and he was wearing a shitload of clothes. He must have been sweating like a pig." There was something in his eyes—a great sense of enjoyment. He knew what we were after.

I tried to indulge him. "Do we have to ask for your theory on why he was wearing so many clothes?"

His pleasure burst forth. He grinned broadly. "Could have been the hunchback."

Kunkle muttered, "You asshole."

I held up my hand. "You sure it was a hump? It might have been a disguise."

"No, no. I'm sure. I mean, this guy freaked me out. He was so weird, you know? I couldn't resist it. After we did the deal and he started to leave, I slapped him on the back, real friendly, just to check it out. He wasn't too pleased, but it was a real hump, all right. I felt it." He shook his head and chuckled. "That one really made the rounds."

He started for the stairs.

"You leaving?"

"Yup."

"You may not live through the day."

He smiled again, but this time I sensed little pleasure. "Yeah, well, the story of my life. Stay out of trouble, guys."

We listened to his footsteps. When he reached the top, I turned to Kunkle. "Follow him. As soon as he settles down, call in and we'll send reinforcements. If we're lucky, we'll keep him alive and grab Ski Mask at the same time."

Kunkle left. Powers took the hint and followed suit after I thanked him for coming over. Brandt pulled out his pipe and began filling it. "You think Ski Mask'll bite?"

"I'm hoping for anything; he's under more pressure now. Maybe the best we can shoot for is just to keep them apart. The longer Ski Mask doesn't know about the hump, the better."

"You think this guy is still running around looking like Quasimodo?"

"Hell, I don't know. Why don't you call Danvers back and tell him to contact his DEA connection. It looks like we can rule out the short-term, low-dosage prednisone prescriptions—maybe that'll speed things up a bit." I hesitated before resuming. What I was about to say represented a major hurdle I wasn't sure Brandt would be willing to take.

"I also think it's time to bring in the state police." He busied himself lighting the pipe and setting up a smoke screen that totally obliterated his face. I'd never thought of pipes being that strategically handy.

When the smog cleared, I saw him nod his head impassively. "How do you want to use them?"

"Mostly to back up Kunkle. We could use them other places too, though."

"Like where?"

"Like putting more pressure on Ski Mask. So far, we've been combing the motels and increasing patrols and talking to damn near everybody over the age of six, but he's still been able to sit and watch, and to pop up at will. Kunkle suggested putting tails on some of us, trying to either catch him or dissuade him. It didn't work this morning, but it was a good idea. Also, if the DEA comes through with a huge list, we'll have that paper trail to track. The backlog of our normal work is starting to strain every desk in the department. We just need more help, period—for everything."

Brandt nodded again. "All right, I'll see what I can do. I might start with the sheriff's department, though."

"All right. Sheriff's men for the noncombat stuff and state troopers to help cover Lew Hill."

He took the pipe from his mouth and looked at me. "He really has you worked up, doesn't he?"

"You didn't see him with Haffner. This bastard's a real number—a man who loves his work."

Brandt nodded a third time. "I'll make some phone calls."

He led the way upstairs. At the top, looking his usual bird-dog best, was Stan Katz.

"Conspiring in the basement?"

"Be nice, Stanley. We might be nice back."

Brandt shot me a questioning look.

"Oh?" said Katz.

"Yeah. Give me a few minutes and I'll let you know."

"What about the dope dealer being killed in his trailer this morning? Is is true you and Kunkle were witnesses?"

"It was a heart attack, Stan, and just hold your horses. I'll be right back."

I escorted Brandt to his office and shut the door behind me. He parked on the edge of his desk. "As the man said: 'Oh?'"

"I was thinking we could do worse than invite him to the stakeout.

We've really got nothing to lose—or at least not much. If we pull it off, we've given him a scoop and made a few points; if we totally screw up, he'll find out about it anyhow and only make it tougher on us for having been excluded. He might even show us doing our job instead of standing around with our thumbs up our asses."

Brandt shifted to sit properly at his desk and reached for the phone. "I somehow doubt that, but feel free."

I crossed over to Maxine's cubicle to see if Kunkle had called in yet. He hadn't. I then told Katz to hold on for a couple of more minutes and gathered DeFlorio and Tyler into my office and told them about the tail on Lew Hill.

"Ski Mask is like nothing we've ever seen. We've got to think of him as a terrorist or something—a cold and careful killer. Don't underestimate him and don't make assumptions based on what you've learned over the years. This is a new ball game, all right? And keep in constant touch with each other, visually if possible."

"What about additional backup in case we need it?" DeFlorio asked.

"I'm arranging for undercover state police, but I want you two ready to move as soon as Kunkle calls in. And I want Katz to go with you."

They both looked at me slack-jawed. I held up my hand. "He'll write about this anyway, so let's humor him for once. But keep him out of harm's way, okay? And don't get too chatty—just let him know what's up."

Katz was waiting patiently by Maxine's cubicle. "So, were you and Kunkle caught with your pants down or what?"

"Don't be rude, Stanley, we're giving you a break. You can go on a stakeout for Ski Mask as long as you keep out of the way, capish?"

"In return for what?"

"Don't be such a cynic."

At nine o'clock that night, Brandt dug under the paperwork we'd spread all over his desk and answered the phone. For hours we'd been sorting through the accumulated shreds of the case, uncertain whether we were looking for something new or just nervously killing time. He listened for a moment and silently handed the receiver to me. It was Kunkle. "You better get down here. We got problems." He sounded even more dismal than usual.

The Misery Hilton was actually a large, five-story, bunker-like apartment building on Birge Street. Butternut-colored by day, in the freezing dark it looked more like a cubic black hole, blotting out the stars with its mass. The only sign that it wasn't as inert as the ground beneath it was a perpetual foul odor of human decay. Whenever calls for the police came from here, the men responding made sure they wore boots—preferably washable ones.

There was an ambulance parked outside when I got there, along with a group of unemployed-looking plainclothes state police. I knew before entering that Ski Mask had somehow found his man.

Kunkle was waiting for me on the third-floor landing. He was leaning against the wall, so turned in on himself he barely noticed I was there. I stepped past him into the room beyond.

The bare bulb hanging from the ceiling made the whole scene look like an Edward Hopper nightmare. There were no soft angles, no single place where the eye could rest without offense. The walls were stained, peeling, cracked, and punctured. The toilet in the adjoining cubicle had overflowed so many times that concentric stains spread across the floor like geologic footprints. The single window had long since ceased to hold glass and was badly boarded up with splintered plywood. There was a three-legged armchair oozing stuffing in one corner, a scarred and mangled chest of drawers next to it, and a bare mattress on the floor along the opposite wall. On the mattress—tied down like a specimen on a lab table—lay Lew Hill. His dry eyes were wide open and his teeth bared against a pain long gone.

There wasn't much blood, just a few small holes where Ski Mask's thin stiletto had done its work. I went back outside to the landing. Kunkle hadn't moved.

"Any theories?"

"I fucked up."

"How do you figure that?"

He looked at me incredulously.

"No, I mean it. So far, one way or the other, he's whacked Phillips and now Hill—and he sure as hell helped Haffner along. He's run circles around us from the start, and the only times any of us have even set eyes on the guy was when I was gassed and when you and I were cuffed together. You might as well take the blame for all of it. It would sure as hell make the rest of us feel better, knowing it was all your fault."

"Fuck off."

"Don't beat yourself up. You're a member of the club. Go home to bed; I'll see you tomorrow morning."

He didn't move. I went back downstairs and found the head of the

197

state police detail. Stan Katz was standing slightly behind him. "So how did he get in?"

"The question should be: 'How did he get out?' He was in all along, as near as we can figure. Of course, we were brought in late. It wasn't our setup."

"Are you complaining?"

He looked at me quietly for a moment. "Are you?"

"No."

"Me neither. Kunkle laid it out okay. We were watching for comers, not goers. From what I can figure, your guy went straight from this morning's killing to Hill's apartment and camped out all day there. I still don't know how he got out, but this place has a lot of traffic."

I asked him to send me a copy of his report the next day and returned to my car. I started the engine and kicked on the heater, but I didn't drive off. Instead I sat there, much like Kunkle leaning against his wall, and gave in to a feeling of total hopelessness.

Katz opened the passenger door and slid in. "Some mess, huh?" His voice was pleasantly muted and unaggressive. I looked over at him. He was just staring out the window at the "Hilton." His face changed from white to red and back again in the flashing lights from the ambulance and patrol cars.

"Did you go up?"

He nodded. "What the hell is going on? What does Lew Hill have to do with Ski Mask or Kimberly Harris or Murphy's death?" The question was almost philosophical in tone.

I shook my head. "Don't know, Stan. Sometimes I think we've almost got it, other times I'm afraid we'll miss the boat entirely on this one. It's a bitch. And," I added, "none of that's a quote."

"That's okay."

He was silent a while more, and then he opened the door and swung his legs out. "I hope you get him. Good night."

I did too, but I wasn't sure how realistic that was. All our progress had been toward finding Pam Stark's killer, and in that area I felt pretty good. Things were falling into place; there was a momentum building that usually boded well. We might well succeed, maybe even soon, but somehow that didn't seem to matter. In the end, I was convinced Ski Mask would do what he had set out to do—whatever that was— just as he had from the start. Maybe Bill Davis would end up free as a result, but I couldn't stop thinking that if Ski Mask had a hand in it, that process would be perverted and corrupted, a variation on the one that had jailed him in the first place.

24

Tony Brandt came out of his office with a large smile and met me as I entered from the side door off the parking lot. "Danvers called. The DEA report is on its way, but he gave me the top three contenders on the phone." He handed me a sheet of note pad paper. "We also found out how Ski Mask got out. He had a rope strung between Hill's building and the garage next door. Hand over hand and out he went, probably right over our heads."

"Christ." I looked at the names. "Are these doctors or patients?"

"The first names are doctors, the names after them are patients. By the way, Katz's article on last night was a monument to restraint. Maybe you're breaking through."

I waved the list. "You want to wait for the full DEA report before deciding what to do about this?"

Brandt allowed an uncharacteristic grin. "Hell, no. In fact, I'd like to interview one of these guys myself." He reached into his pocket. "Three *duces tecums.*"

A *duces tecum* is a writ or subpoena ordering the person served to hand over specified materials. Unless every *i* is dotted and every *t* crossed, they are the legal equivalent of skating on thin ice, especially if you're trying to breach the physician/patient privilege.

Brandt read my thoughts. "They're as tight as they can be. The patients are identified by name, as are the exact medical records we're after. Even the dates are in there. If it's specificity they're after, I couldn't get any better."

He kept one subpoena for himself and handed the other two to me. I laughed and shook my head. "Busy as a beaver aren't you? Can I bring Kunkle in for the third one?"

"You two courting or something? I didn't think he was your type."

"He's not. Any objections?"

Brandt tilted his head slightly. "He wouldn't be my first choice as an interviewer." He paused for a moment and finally made an odd movement with his upper lip. "All right. I don't suppose he'll start slapping doctors around."

There was an awkward pause. "Are you getting close to letting him go?" I asked.

"Yes, I am."

"Does last night have anything to do with that?"

"It didn't help his career any."

"Would you have thought to check out Hill's room before he got there?"

He looked at me warily. "That's not really the issue, is it?"

"None of us are overly trained—not for this stuff."

Brandt took a deep breath and passed his hand across his mouth. "What's on your mind, Joe?"

"I just want to know if you're going to let him see this case through to the end."

He smiled, just barely. "I can't afford the loss of manpower just now."

"Thanks. Did you arrange with the sheriff to set up tails for us?"

"They're waiting in the parking lot. I'll tell them who to follow."

"Thanks. See you later." I crossed the hallway to Support Services. Kunkle was laboring over his typewriter. I knocked on the open door. "Report?"

He looked up at me, his expression as sour as ever. "It's not my resignation, if that's what you were hoping."

"Well, whatever it is, I've got something else for you to do." I put the subpoenas on his desk. "DEA just gave us three doctors who might have treated the guy with the hump. Brandt took Goldbaum; which one do you want?"

He glanced at the papers and leaned back in his chair. "Why me?"

"Why not?"

"You're doing me a favor, right? Keeping me involved, showing what a good leader of men you are?"

I hesitated. There was always the option of crowning him with his typewriter. Instead I answered, "Yes."

He stared at me for a long minute and then glanced again at the subpoenas. "I'll take Morris."

That left Duquesne—he had only one patient we were interested in. I headed out back to one of the unmarked cars. The lower the profile, the better.

Dr. Duquesne worked on the top floor of the Professional Building adjacent to the hospital. It was a brick structure, cheaply made and minimally maintained, with a screeching front door, threadbare carpeting and the general look of a motel on the downward slide. There were already two people in his small, paneled waiting room, despite the early hour. I went to the nurse's window and showed her my badge.

"Is he available?"

"You'll have to make an appointment."

"I'm not here for treatment. This is official."

"Will it take long?"

I closed my eyes for a moment. "I don't know."

She looked unsure. "I've only seen this happen on TV. Am I supposed to interrupt him now and tell him you're here?"

"Is he with a patient?"

"Yes."

"Is he almost finished or just starting?"

"He's almost finished."

"Then I'll wait here, and you can tell him about me between patients. How's that sound?"

She gave me a radiant smile. "That's wonderful. That's what I'll do. Won't you have a seat?"

I had a seat. It was shaped for a body other than mine. After five minutes of staring at the paneling, the two pictures of ducks on the wall, the coffee table laden with ancient magazines, and my two far more ancient co-waiters, I was rewarded by the appearance of a small boy and his mother and a tall, white-haired man in a lab coat. The man crooked his finger at me and faded back to the interior hallway. I went after him.

"What can I do for you?" His tone was meticulously neutral.

"I need to ask you about a prescription you wrote three years ago for a patient named Steven Cioffi."

"I'm not sure I can tell you that."

I gave him the *duces tecum*, which he read slowly and carefully. "He's a murder suspect," I added when he'd finished.

Duquesne pursed his lips and looked at the floor. "Maybe I ought to call my lawyer."

"You can. It'll probably mean tying all this up long enough for Cioffi to get away, assuming he's our man. If he's not the one we're after, he'll never know about it."

Duquesne hesitated a little longer, tapping the subpoena against his thumbnail. Finally, he cracked open the door to the receptionist's office. "Lisa, get me the file on Steven Cioffi."

His office was small and compulsively neat, which I suppose is a good sign in a specialist. I sat in one chair; he sat in the other. His desk lay between us like a dock.

"So, who is this man suspected of killing?"

"Kimberly Harris."

His neutral eyebrows rose. "I take it the wrong man is in jail?"

"Not necessarily. It gets a little complicated. Several people may have been involved. Did Cioffi have Cushing's at that time?"

"Oh, yes. I was treating him for acute asthma. The Cushing's episode lasted only a few weeks, and then we brought it and the asthma under control."

"Is he still your patient?"

"As far as I know. I don't see him very often now that he's on regular doses."

"Still prednisone?"

"Yes, but in lesser quantities. That heavy dosage was only to bring him back from the brink. How did you know he had Cushing's, by the way? The hump?"

"Initially it was a semen sample found on the victim. The hump was identified later. Do you happen to be friends with this Steven Cioffi?"

The doctor smiled thinly. "I'm not friends with many of my patients. If I were, Mr. Cioffi would not be among them."

I sensed that had been a factor in Duquesne's decision to cooperate. The nurse appeared at the door with the file. The doctor took it from her and nodded her away.

"Not one of your favorite people?"

He opened the file and began leafing through it slowly. "No. He's not a nasty man, mind you; he's just totally lacking in…I don't know what you'd call it…Charm, maybe."

"Charm?"

"Well, you know. He's not particularly bright or well spoken. He seems dull and single-minded. He has absolutely no sense of humor or curiosity. He's just kind of blah…You know the type?"

Looking at Duquesne, I decided to duck the subject of type. "Does he have the makings of a killer, in your personal view?"

"We all do. It is interesting that you think he may have been involved in a murder just as the Cushing's was manifesting itself, however."

"Why?"

"Well, it gives him an extra edge in that department. Heavy doses of prednisone can make one moody, depressed, sometimes even delirious."

"And you think that may have happened with Cioffi?"

"He was more prone to it than others I've treated—it may be some reflection of sociological background. Of course, that isn't my field."

"What's a man capable of when he has Cushing's? I mean, is he as strong as usual? Can he run around the block?"

"Under normal conditions, I'd say no. His inclination is to rest. There is some muscular weakness associated with the syndrome. In Cioffi's case it was not debilitating. If his adrenaline were pumping high enough, he'd have normal strength. However, I don't see him running around the block, as you say, under normal conditions. He's kind of a tubby, flabby man."

"How is he now?"

"Fine—for the moment. The asthma is under control. His looks are back to normal."

"What's 'for the moment' mean?"

"He's developed aseptic necrosis in the right hip—it's a degeneration of the femoral head. Prednisone does that sometimes."

"So he limps?"

"Now he limps. He uses a cane. Later, in two or three years, he'll be in a wheelchair."

"Jesus. Isn't that a high price to pay for asthma?"

"It's a trade-off. His asthma wasn't just a little wheezing. It was about to kill him."

"But he can get around now."

"Oh, yes. He could even run around your proverbial block, again if he were adequately stimulated. Of course, it wouldn't improve his hip any."

"Do you have an address on him?"

Duquesne closed the folder and passed it across his desk to me. "I suppose most of this is yours now anyway. You'll find everything you need—or at least everything I know—in there."

"How about blood samples? Do you have any of those?"

"Several. I take them and urine samples periodically for monitoring purposes."

"Do you have any that date back to when he had Cushing's?"

"Yes. They're at the hospital—in the deep freeze."

"If you could call the hospital as soon as I leave and tell them to release those samples to us, I'd greatly appreciate it."

He frowned. "Am I obligated to do that?"

I opened his warrant and showed him the paragraph that dealt with the specific and dated materials in question.

He sighed and muttered, "All right."

I thanked him and stood up. "There is something else I ought to tell you, doctor. We aren't the only ones looking for Cioffi."

Duquesne just stared at me.

"Have you been aware of what the newspaper's been calling 'the man in the mask,' or Ski Mask?"

"Certainly. I'd have to live in a cocoon not to."

"Well, he's the other one interested in Cioffi, although he only knows him as a mysterious hunchback right now."

"Why tell me?"

"He's a very motivated, dangerous man. He's also very resourceful. If he does happen to discover your connection to all this, he'll come knocking at your door, one way or the other. It's happened before."

Duquesne was very still. When he spoke, the neutrality had tilted toward the hostile. "Then you've just exposed me to a certain amount of danger, is that right? As you did with that prostitute?"

"Not necessarily. If he does contact you, just tell him everything he wants to know. That should be the end of it."

"Are you going to give me some protection in the meantime?"

"He may not even get in touch."

"If that were true, you wouldn't have brought it up."

"Giving you protection might cause more harm than good. If Ski Mask senses an obstacle, he's usually pretty good at removing it."

"That sounds more like your area than mine, Lieutenant. Perhaps I can be more persuasive: let's say that if any harm does come to me while I'm unprotected, my lawsuit against your department will stand a far greater chance of success."

He smiled. I smiled. I showed myself out. It occurred to me that for all her street smarts, Susan Lucey could learn a thing or two from an operator like that.

It turned out Dr. Duquesne wasn't the only one not living in a cocoon. Town Manager Tom Wilson was waiting for me in the hallway back at the Municipal Building.

"Give me an update, Gunther."

"I'd prefer to let Chief Brandt do that."

"I don't care what you prefer. Tell me what's going on—right now."

"We're digging, and it's getting easier and easier. We should have something before long."

Wilson stabbed my chest with his finger. "Don't give me that crap. You guys are not the CIA. You work for me and the board, and you are accountable for everything you do. Early on, I let you play coy because we were all trying to duck the publicity. That, in case you haven't read today's newspaper, or heard the radio, or seen Channel 31, is no longer a consideration."

"I know. We're famous."

"Don't be cute. I've been fencing with the press from Rutland and Keene for a couple of days already. Now I've had calls from the wire services and two of the three networks. A Boston TV station has a news crew due here this afternoon, for Christ's sake. We've got to do better than 'We're digging and it's getting easier.' They'll eat us alive. Even worse, they'll start digging on their own. I can't believe you want that."

"All right, but I'm still not going to say anything without Brandt. He should be back any second." I crossed over to Maxine's window. "Any word from Tony?"

"He's heading back. He just called in."

I turned to Wilson. "Why don't you wait in his office? I'll be right there."

He grumbled, but he went. I took a left into the squad room and poked my head into Billy Manierre's office. "I need someone to run a blood sample to a forensic pathologist in West Haven, Connecticut. Can you help me out?"

"Whose blood?"

"I'm pretty sure it's the same guy who sexually molested Pam Stark or Kimberly Harris or whatever you want to call her."

"Yeah, I can get someone. Give me names and addresses."

I quickly scrawled out what he wanted on a sheet of paper and then made a fast track to my office—still clutching Duquesne's file—to draw up requests for two search warrants: one for Cioffi's office, one for his home. I was halfway through when my phone buzzed.

"Joe?" It was Brandt. "What are you doing right now?"

"Preparing warrants for a guy named Steven Cioffi. He's the guy with the hump."

"All right. Go to it. Don't bother to come powwow with Wilson and me. We'll sort that out. It'll probably mean some kind of press conference later today, so don't skip town."

"Right." I hung up and finished typing, praying I would find a judge available across the street at the courthouse.

I did—in the men's room. He wasn't terrifically pleased about it—probably something about his dignity—but he signed on the dotted line against the tile wall. I returned to Brandt's office and brought him up to date.

When I finished, he stood up, pocketed his pipe and smiled. "Well, maybe this press conference won't be such a bad idea after all."

25

Cioffi worked at Leatherton, Inc., a manufacturer of industrial parts whose name I'd always thought was better suited to a luggage-making firm. In fact, this one modest factory was one of several subsidiaries of Thomas Leatherton & Company of Toronto, Canada, which was their version of Westinghouse—a big deal, in other words.

The building reflected the stature. Covering half an industrial park recently built south of town near the interstate, it was the region's latest statement in modern architecture, which may not have been saying much. Still, it was an eye-catcher, made of dark glass and earth-toned brick, and it did exude a sense of capitalist power and well-being.

We arrived in two squad cards. Kunkle and I were in one, Capullo and Woll in the other. I had the two patrolmen cover the front and back entrances, just in case our fat and flabby erstwhile hunchback decided to limp off into the sunset.

As it turned out, he'd already done so. From the receptionist downstairs to his secretary on the top floor, we got the same message: "I'm afraid Mr. Cioffi's not in right now."

His secretary was an attractive young bottle-blonde with too much eye shadow. I pointed to the closed door behind her. "Is that his?"

She looked at it doubtfully. "Yes, it is."

I laid the court order on her desk and walked around her to the door.

"Stop. I mean, hold on a second. What is this?" She held up the warrant.

Kunkle answered for me in modulated officialese. "That's a court order allowing us to enter this office and remove specific documents related to the case we have building against Mr. Cioffi."

Her eyes widened. "Against Mr. Cioffi? What for?"

"Read the warrant."

She looked from us to the paper in her hand. "I think maybe I should get somebody."

"That's fine. We'll be in here." I opened the door and went inside. What we entered was the archetypal coveted corner office. Two walls of windows, a rug soft enough to swallow our shoes, a mahogany desk, a leather sofa and two armchairs custom-made for an English men's club. Lining the other two walls was a built-in bookcase stuffed with stereo equipment, fancy artifacts, and elegantly placed collections of leather-bound books. It did not fit the mental image I'd painted of Cioffi from his doctor's description.

Kunkle looked around and whistled. "Jesus, if I worked here, I'd never go home."

I pulled the walkie-talkie from my belt and called Dispatch. "Tell Brandt to secure Cioffi's residence. He's not at his office. If Brandt wants the court order covering the house, I've got it."

"Ten-four."

I took down several of Cioffi's fancy books and opened them. None showed any signs of overuse. In fact, the same could have been said for the entire office.

I went over to the desk. Except for the usual executive knickknacks, it was bare. I pulled at the drawer directly in front of the chair; it was unlocked. Inside, I found a book marked "Appointments." I checked today's date. Nothing was scheduled.

"May I help you?"

The voice belonged to a thin, wispy-haired man, soon to be bald, probably in his midthirties. He was dressed in a dark pinstripe suit that fit him very well. Cioffi's secretary hovered behind him.

Kunkle took an instant dislike to him. Maybe it was the suit. "I doubt it. Who are you?"

"My name's Arthur Pelegrino. I'm the head of Public Relations." Kunkle obviously was not in a handshaking mood and I was too far away. Pelegrino seemed ill at ease forgoing the formality; his hands fidgeted in front of his belt buckle. "Could you tell me what this is all about?"

I took pity on the man, crossed over, and shook his hand. "I'm Lieutenant Gunther. We have a warrant for certain documents in this room. I would also like to ask some questions of Mr. Cioffi's secretary, if I may."

Pelegrino smiled nervously and stepped aside, exposing the secretary fully.

"Alone would be best, actually."

The PR man bit his upper lip and nodded. "I think I better get someone from the legal department." He squeezed by the secretary and disappeared.

"What's your name?" I asked her.

"Mona."

"You originally from the area?"

"Dummerston."

"Been working here long?"

"A couple of years. I got the job straight out of college. I went to UVM."

"Did Cioffi hire you, or did you just end up working for him?"

"I was assigned to him."

"Do you like him?"

"He's okay, I guess."

"How would you characterize him?"

"What?"

"Is he friendly or abrupt, supportive or uncaring, easy going or tense, things like that."

"Gee, I've never thought about that. I don't really have much to do with him, really."

"Does he work you hard?"

Her face lit up at that. "Gosh no. My boyfriend says I have the cushiest job in the world. I guess he's right. I mostly just sit out there. I used to read a little, but they said it didn't look good."

"What exactly does Cioffi do?"

"He's Vice-President of Industrial Relations."

Kunkle broke in. "What the hell does that mean?"

She smiled and shrugged. "I'm not really sure. He travels a lot. I think it has something to do with conventions."

"He goes to a lot of conventions?"

"I think so."

"Don't you make the travel arrangements for him?"

"No. He does all that. I answer the phone and write letters sometimes. I don't see him a whole lot."

There was some noise from outside, and Pelegrino reappeared with a short, fat man, also bald and also dressed in a dark suit. They looked like a cartoon together. Pelegrino introduced his companion as Mr. Kleeman, who, from his self-inflated manner, was obviously from the legal department.

Kleeman was not a hand-shaker. He grabbed the warrant from Mona and read it from front to back. He finally folded the warrant and put it in his pocket. "Have you gone through anything yet?"

"No," I lied.

"Good. I will keep you company throughout your search and will inform you if you stray from the guidelines of this order."

Kunkle sneered at him and walked over to the desk and began opening drawers.

We ended up with very little—his appointment books for the past several years, some specifically dated correspondence, mostly letters setting up meetings with people at various conventions, and we obtained a copy of his employment record at Leatherton. That was about it. Neither Kleeman nor Pelegrino knew much about Cioffi, despite the fact that technically, "industrial relations" came under the general public relations umbrella.

What we found at his home—another lavish spread straight out of *House Beautiful*—didn't add much to the picture. He had obviously taken off. Most of his socks, shorts, shirts, etc. were missing, and we could find few personal possessions of any sort, although we did come across several conspicuously empty drawers. But there were no address books, photo albums, diaries, account books, or anything else listed in the warrant. The place looked like a high-priced hotel room after maid service. Our disappointment was palpable.

So was Tom Wilson's. "I thought you said you had this thing wrapped up."

"He flew the coop. It's a temporary setback. Once we analyze all we've collected—or all we will collect—we'll be able to track him. It just isn't as convenient as we were hoping."

Brandt stopped talking and emptied his pipe into his ashtray. There were just the three of us in Brandt's office: Brandt, Wilson and me. I was trying to act invisible.

"I suppose you realize that at this point, there is no way this department is going to walk away unscathed. Heads will have to roll."

Brandt raised his eyebrows. "Oh?"

Wilson scowled at him. "Give me a break. The mutterings from the board were bad enough; now even the *Reformer* has joined in. Bellstrom's editorial this morning questioned just about everything you people have done to date, the biggest item being your refusal to bring in extra help until it was too late."

"I remember that topic coming up pretty early on. I recall all sorts of people not wanting to attract undue attention. Isn't that the way you remember it, Tom?"

"A lot has happened between then and now. You can't deny you and your crew have been a little bull-headed about this thing."

"What—aside from spreading the blame a little thinner—would have changed had we brought in the troops?"

"The point is you didn't." Brandt shrugged. "We'll get the guy."

"That may not be enough."

Brandt changed the subject—sort of. "What about the press conference ?"

"What about it? It's still on."

"Are you going to roll heads then?"

Wilson slapped the arm of his chair and stood up. He crossed over to the window and looked out at the frozen parking lot. "Christ, I hate this. No, I'm not going to roll heads. We're standing together, at least in public. You just tell them what you've got and handle questions—as agreed this morning."

Brandt looked over at me. "What you got cooking so far?"

"A team is going over everything we grabbed at the office and home; I've got a blood sample being looked at by Kees in West Haven; I'm getting a warrant for all his phone records, from both office and home; we've lifted his fingerprints and are having them coded; and I'm having duplicates made of the photos we found in his medical file—Dr. Duquesne was a very thorough fellow. We've also located his dentist and are having copies made of his X-rays and charts. By the time we finish, we should have as complete a description of him as we could want. Once we spread the word—as discreetly as possible—we should be able to nail him. If nothing else, his medical problems will get him; he needs a steady supply of prednisone, and according to Duquesne, he won't even be able to walk in a couple of years."

Wilson flapped his arms. "A couple of years? Hallelujah. That ought to satisfy everybody. What's this mystery man's name, anyway?"

Brandt and I looked at each other.

Wilson immediately flared. "Hold on a goddamn minute. You're going to sit on his name? After what I've done for you bastards?"

Brandt laid a hand on his shoulder. "The name's Steven Cioffi. He's a VP at Leatherton, but we don't want that out yet. That's why we hesitated."

Wilson shook off the hand, but he was calmer. "Christ. We finally get something and you don't want to release it. What the hell is the problem?"

His narrow focus was beginning to irritate. "We only found out who this guy was a few hours ago. We got to figure out what we're holding before we start bragging."

"There is another reason," Brandt added. "The way Ski Mask is stepping out front, we're fearful of giving him anything he might take advantage of. If he gets to Cioffi ahead of us and kills him for some reason, then we—and Davis—might be stuck high and dry."

The phone rang and Brandt picked it up. He listened for a while, took some notes, thanked the caller, and turned back to us with a big smile. "Hey, just like in the movies. You wanted something to tell the press? Looks like we just located Pam Stark's home address." He waved the slip of notepaper in his hand. "She had given a phony to the Boston cops, but it turns out she was from Connecticut—Danbury—or at least she was born there, daughter of Henry and Eleanor Stark. They tracked her through vital records. Then—I'll give these guys high marks—because they couldn't find a current address, they checked the state tax records just for kicks, and sure enough, Henry and Eleanor still own some Connecticut land, and the bill is sent to Voorheesville, New York. That's just next to Albany."

Wilson merely shook his head and kept staring out the window. "Pam Stark's address." He finally muttered, "Three years too late. Christ."

After a while he turned to face us. "What good is Pam Stark's address?"

I answered that. "She's the keystone to this whole thing. Judging from what he did to Susan Lucey, Ski Mask is obviously linked to Pam in some strong emotional way. And now we know Cioffi is definitely connected to her. If we can talk to her parents, they might help us bust this thing wide open. This is exactly what wasn't done the first time around and what landed us in this mess."

Brandt handed me the note he'd made with the New York address. "Look, Tom, Joe can follow this up right now. It'll take him a couple of hours to drive there; we're assessing everything we've collected so far. This will just add to the hopper, maybe in a big way. We'll know before the day's up."

Wilson mulled it over. "All right, fine." Then, after a pause, "Are you two absolutely positive you've got the right man in Cioffi? Or are we opening ourselves up to yet another lawsuit by some clown who may be just on vacation?"

Brandt and I looked at each other. This was not a question either one of us relished, but it was probably better that Wilson brought it up before the cameras started rolling.

Brandt cleared his throat. "What we have in Steven Cioffi is a man who in all probability was involved in the Pamela Stark killing."

Wilson stared at him, his eyes widening. "That's it? 'In all probability'? I'm supposed to stand next to you in front of a bunch of reporters and that's what you're going to say?"

"If they ask me that question—and without mentioning his name."

Wilson's face reddened. "And how the fuck do you think that's going to go down? They'll eat us alive."

"That's all I can really tell them right now. We've got a circumstantial case. Had we located Cioffi, it might have been different, but right now, that's it. Given more time to dig through what we've got, I'll probably have more, like Joe said."

Wilson seemed to have stopped breathing. He glared at both of us for a long moment after Brandt stopped speaking, and then he stormed out of the room, slamming the door behind him.

Brandt smiled at me. "I think the press conference is off."

26

Voorheesville, which I reached by heading due west on Route 9 through Bennington and Troy, was the epitome of the bedroom community. I'm sure it had a town center, or at least a cluster of tasteful buildings passing for one, but from what I could see, it consisted of mile after mile of undulating, well-kept interweaving blacktop, hemmed in by tamed trees and regularly placed, half-seen tidy houses. Some of these were pretty grand—English Tudor near-misses and combination Federalist-Southern plantations with swimming pools out front, but for the most part they were white, wooden, neat, and reclusive. They clung to the centers of their two-acre lots, surrounded by enough shrubs and trees to shield them from all but a glimpse of their neighbors' roofs.

I stopped at a filling station among an odd and incongruous collection of fake-Georgian commercial buildings and got directions to the address Brandt had given me. It was located in what must have been the low-rent district. The trees were not as tall, the lawns not as large, the shrubs not as fat, and the houses, with a couple of garish exceptions, were downright self-effacing. Along a spur marked Dead End, cluttered with split-levels on half-acre lots, I found a mailbox marked Stark.

I pulled into the driveway and parked in front of a one-car garage. Above the door, its six-foot wingspan painted in peeling gold, was a wooden bald eagle. To the right of the garage, parallel to the driveway, was a one-and-a-half story white clapboard house as lacking in distinctive features as the one-dimensional boxes in children's drawings. I walked up the shoveled path to the front door and knocked.

The door swung back two feet, revealing a short, thin, white-haired woman who instantly struck me as the cleanest, neatest person I'd ever met. There was not a wrinkle or a fold out of place. Her dimly flowered housedress and cardigan sweater looked as if they were on a hanger; her brown laced-up shoes were spotless and scuff-free; her face and hands pale pink and practically shimmering; every hair was rigidly in place.

"Yes?" Her voice was barely above a whisper.

"Mrs. Stark?"

"That's right."

I pulled out my badge, something I rarely did at home. "My name is Lieutenant Gunther. I work for the police department in Brattleboro, Vermont. I called you a few hours ago?"

She nodded, just barely.

"I have no jurisdiction down here, so you're under no obligation to talk with me, but I was wondering if I could ask you a few questions about your daughter, Pamela."

Her eyes, which had been focused somewhere over my shoulder, dropped to my shoes. In that one gesture, I sensed some vital part of her anatomy giving way. She said, just audibly, "Of course," and, turning from the door, vanished into the gloom of the hallway beyond.

I hesitated—the door was still barely open—before I followed her inside. From what I could see of it as my eyes adjusted to the dark, the hall was empty. I walked its ten-foot length and looked to both sides. To the left was another hallway leading presumably to some bedrooms; to the right was a totally green living room. Mrs. Stark was sitting on the edge of a straight-backed chair, her immaculate hands in her smooth lap, looking at the green shag carpeting. She seemed so lost in her thoughts, I wasn't sure she remembered I was there.

The room was dark, the only light a green seepage through thick drapes drawn across a large patio window. Hanging on the walls, along with the occasional half-visible picture, were several military swords—some cavalry, some oriental—four glass-faced display frames filled with medals and insignia, and two oil paintings, both depicting modern battle scenes, one featuring World War II–vintage tanks, the other Vietnam-era helicopters. Above the dark green mantle at the far end of the room was another eagle, surrounded by gold stars. The rest of the room looked more normal—no army cots or pup tents—but I did notice that most of the furnishings were equipped with sanitary fail-safe devices: antimacassars on the backs of armchairs, a doily under every lamp, glass cups under the table legs, small rugs on the carpeting in front of each chair. The entire room was as neat and antiseptic and green as a freshly filled fish tank. The only sound I could hear was a clock ticking somewhere.

I walked over to the sofa and sat gingerly, conscious of squashing its pillows' perfect plumpness. "Mrs. Stark, when did you last see your daughter?"

She looked up at me slowly. "Three-four years ago."

"And where was that?"

"Here. She was living at home. She and the Colonel had a fight, only this time she left—forever."

"The Colonel?"

"My husband."

"And where is he?"

"Gone. I don't know." She went back to staring at the floor.

I looked around the room again. Of all the scenes I'd played in my head prior to coming here, this was not one of them.

"Did he go shopping or something?"

"No. He left."

"When?"

"A couple of months ago."

I wanted to return to her daughter, but something tugged at me to keep this line going. "Why did he leave?"

"To find her."

"Did he?"

"I don't know. He found something." One hand rose slowly and barely touched her forehead with its fingertips before resettling next to its peer. It was like the kiss from a solicitous bird. "She is dead, isn't she?"

"Yes, I'm afraid so."

She let out the softest of sighs. "And now he's dead too."

"Your husband?" She nodded again.

"Not that I know of." I reached into my pocket and pulled out the photograph of the late Kimberly Harris. "Mrs. Stark, I hate to do this, but I have to ask. Is this a picture of your daughter?"

I crossed the room and laid the picture in her lap, face up. She didn't touch it, she didn't even react, but she did look.

"Yes," she said simply, her voice unchanged. It was an utterance from someone drained of any emotional reserves. She was like a well of tears long run dry.

"If your daughter left home several years ago, why did your husband wait so long to go after her?"

Another sigh escaped her, a sound so gentle in this quiet green room I could almost see it. "They say fathers and daughters are supposed to have a special bond, don't they?"

216

"I've heard that."

"Colonel Stark and Pam had that once, when she was a little girl. They seemed able to talk to each other without saying a word. It troubled me, because of what he did for a living. I was afraid that one day something would happen to him, that he would be gone forever, and she would be destroyed."

"What did he do for a living?"

She looked surprised. "He was a soldier."

It was my turn to nod.

She didn't say anything for a moment. I was afraid my interruption might have broken her concentration, but she went on. "Perhaps that's what should have happened. She would have loved him if he'd died. Instead, they grew older, and began to fight."

"About what?"

"Nothing. Everything. Private things. She was no longer a little girl. And she grew up to be a young woman. I think that surprised him. He wanted everything to be the same. Of course, it wasn't." The hand fluttered up again and settled down. "It's a little confusing. I don't know. Maybe he loved her too much—not like a real father and daughter."

A sour taste came to my mouth. I remembered Susan Lucey saying something that had struck that same chord. "What do you mean, exactly?"

She shook her head slightly and shrugged.

"The Colonel was more than just a soldier, wasn't he?"

"Oh, yes. Very special, very secret. He would just go off."

I thought of the bug I'd found in my apartment. Very special. "So they had one last big fight and she left?"

"That's right."

"Then what happened?"

"Nothing."

"I mean, how did your husband react after her departure?"

"He didn't."

"What did he do?"

"He left on assignment for two years."

"And when he came back?"

"He was different."

"How so?"

"He talked about her all the time. He thought she'd be here when he returned. He couldn't believe it—that she had really left. He thought I was lying when I told him I hadn't heard from her since that day."

"The day of the fight?"

"Yes."

"What was that fight about?"

She looked at a spot on the wall about a foot above my head. "They fought a lot."

I took a shot in the dark. "About her behavior...like with men, maybe?"

"Yes." There was a pause. "Boys her age...the Colonel was a jealous man."

The odd taste returned to my mouth. "So what happened after he discovered she'd been gone all that time and wasn't coming back?"

"He was convinced she was dead—that that's the only reason she hadn't come back to him. Some man must have killed her." She emphasized the word "man."

"He started looking for her, calling police departments, checking the newspapers in the library, going on trips. Finally, he left for good."

"About two months ago."

"That's right."

"Do you know where he was headed?"

"No."

"Did he mention Boston or Brattleboro or Vermont?"

"He didn't mention anything."

"The day he left, did you know he was going for good, or did you think he was just off on another of his little outings?"

"I felt he was going on duty."

"How's that?"

"When he'd get his orders to go somewhere I couldn't be told about, he'd call that 'going on duty.' I always knew when that was about to happen because he changed. That's what it was like."

"And he's never gotten in touch?"

"No. But I didn't expect him to. He didn't do that."

"You mean send letters or call home?"

"That's right."

"How about when Pam was little?"

"He did then. He'd call her sometimes, but only when she was little."

"You mentioned he'd go places you weren't supposed to know about. Was he in Intelligence?"

"Yes. Maybe."

"You don't know?"

"Not really."

"Is he still on active duty?"

"I don't know."

"Do you know who to call in the government about something like this? A superior officer or something? What was it, by the way? The U.S. Army?"

"We started in the Army, but I'm not sure anymore; it stopped being normal a long time ago. I don't know who to call."

"Has anyone called you about him?"

"No."

I closed my eyes for a second. This was one weird couple. "I don't mean to pry, Mrs. Stark, but I think your husband is in big trouble, and I need to know everything I can about him. I get the feeling he was a little unusual—that is, that he may have had unusual habits. Is there anything you can tell me about him that might help me to find him?"

She frowned and leaned forward in her chair, picking something invisible off the rug and putting it into her cardigan pocket. Then she rose and walked over to the glowing green curtain. I expected her to throw it open and let in the sunlight, but she just stood there, her nose almost touching the fabric. Her hands reached out to either side and her fingers played gently on the folds of the curtain, making it ripple like murky sea water.

Her words, when they came, were slow and carefully chosen. "Our marriage was not a conventional one, Lieutenant. We shared very little. I did as I was told and he supported me. If it hadn't been for Pamela, we might still be together. Having a daughter was very complicated—I don't know why. Maybe we all got too close." She shook her head and repeated. "I don't know."

I decided not to press it. "Did your husband have an office or a den I could look at?"

She didn't move. "Yes. It's upstairs to the right."

I got up and left the room. I'd noticed the staircase when I'd come in. The office was a small room tucked under the eaves, half its ceiling sliced away by the slant of the roof. But it was white and brightly lit by two unshaded windows—a positive relief from the funereal gloom downstairs.

Again the walls were like those of a military museum, covered with odds and ends: bayonets, several old rifles, more medals, a couple of helmets, photographs of groups of men in uniform, either in the field or all spruced up as if for graduation. I looked for a face common to all the pictures, figuring that would be Stark, but I couldn't do it. The hats or helmets and uniforms—not to mention the obvious passage of years—made them all look pretty much alike. I did notice, though, that the uniforms weren't just American. One shot showed what was definitely a French group, and at least two others had an anonymous Latin American look to them. Our boy apparently got around.

The room was dominated by a large antique desk. I sat behind it and went through its drawers. Its contents were conspicuously neutral. A filing cabinet against one wall was empty except for one .45-caliber Colt semi-automatic pistol. I copied its serial number and left it there.

I looked around a little longer with no results and returned to the living room. Mrs. Stark was sitting again in her chair, just as before.

"Was your husband carrying a lot when he left the last time?"

"No. Just his duffel bag, as usual."

"What about the contents of his filing cabinet?"

"He came for those later."

"When?"

"I don't know. He must have waited until I was out of the house. He did that sometimes."

"You mean sneak into his own house?"

"Yes."

I passed on that one.

"Would you have a photograph of him and your daughter?"

"Yes." She got up and pulled a framed picture out of a drawer beneath the coffee table. It showed the three of them in front of this house, in the summer. They all wore shorts and T-shirts, but each looked pulled in from a different part of the world. Mrs. Stark, old and demure in Bermudas and a sedate polo shirt; the Colonel, hard-eyed, crew-cut, tall and lithe, dressed in Marine-style gym clothes; and Pam, her face cold and remote, turned away from the camera, wearing very brief running shorts and a shirt that revealed her bare midriff. None of them touched one another, none of them smiled, and only Stark stared straight into the lens with the pale blue eyes that had so frightened Susan Lucey—and which I had seen for the first time when Ski Mask pulled me out onto the landing of my apartment.

"What was Pamela like, as a daughter?"

"Angry, like her father."

"She ever get into trouble?"

"Trouble ?"

"Yeah, like at school. You know, the usual things nowadays—drugs, sex, stuff like that."

She looked straight at me for a long moment. It was the first time she'd made direct eye contact. "That was very controversial."

I waited for more, but that was it. This woman's laundry was not for public airing—especially this laundry, I thought. I held up the photograph. "Can I borrow this? I'll send it back as soon as I have copies made."

"Yes. It doesn't matter."

I pulled a business card out of my wallet and handed it to her. "I'll get out of your hair. Thanks for your help. Do call me if he gets in touch, will you?"

She took the card without looking at it.

I walked toward the entrance hall with the picture in my hand. She stayed where she was. I hesitated at the door. "Mrs. Stark, is there anything you would like to know about your daughter's death? You can ask me if you'd like—it's all right."

She stood there in the middle of the room, arms slack by her sides, again looking into some nebulous middle distance, as abandoned and as lonely as the only living bird in a desolate forest. "No."

I let myself out.

"Danvers."

"This is Joe Gunther in Brattleboro."

"How'd you make out on that DEA stuff?"

"Hit the jackpot. We haven't nabbed the guy yet, but we know who he is—Steven Cioffi, in case you're interested. Many thanks."

"Sure. What's on your mind? I don't guess you called to kiss me on both cheeks?"

"No, there is something else."

"Just so nothing's left unsaid here, you do realize I've helped you out so far as a favor, right?"

"But you are interested in that bug."

"To an extent, true."

"And you're not going to tell me why."

"True again."

"So much for altruism. Here's something for nothing then: Colonel Henry Stark. He's the one in the ski mask, the owner of the bug, and the father of Kimberly Harris, a.k.a. Pamela Stark. I have a feeling he's been around in various service branches, but the Army might be the best place to start. Maybe the CIA too."

"Lovely." He didn't sound pleased.

"Of course, we'd be more than happy to request an interminable file search through normal channels for our own humble selves, and hope to get it before we're all dead of old age, but I'm hoping your curiosity matches ours and that you can cut a few corners."

"I'll be back in touch."

I put down the receiver and smiled at Brandt. "He'll do it."

Brandt had propped the photograph of the Stark family on his desk. "Hardly *Father Knows Best*, is it?"

"No, but it's a great shot for our purposes. What do you think about distributing an eight-by-ten blowup of his face all over town—and letting Katz have it, too?"

"What if Danvers says he's a superspook or something and we're supposed to keep our mouths shut?"

"If the damage is already done, then that's too bad. We're only a bunch of hicks, after all—no sense of global priorities."

Brandt rubbed the side of his nose and smiled. "I'll call J.P. tonight and have it ready for tomorrow morning's edition." He picked up the picture and looked at it again. "You know, we're sticking our necks out a little. We still don't have proof Ski Mask and Stark are one and the same—legally, that is."

I shrugged. "So don't put Stark's name on it. He's probably going under Smith or Brown or Jones anyway—everyone else is. The worst that can happen is that Colonel Stark will return from some illicit affair in Guatemala, where he's been subverting the natives for the last two months, and sue us for everything we own."

"Yes, I suppose. That's comforting, at least."

The following morning, Brandt met me in the hallway with a copy of the *Reformer*. "Sneak preview; that's an early run of today's edition."

I opened it up and saw Stark staring at me again. ski mask revealed, say police was the awkward headline; the caption under the picture asked, "Have you seen this man?" and gave our telephone number. It also identified Stark by name. "I see you decided to go whole hog."

"The name? Yeah, I figured, what the hell, when you're nine-tenths in, you might as well take the bath."

"That make Wilson happy?"

"Hard to tell. I think he's on a general hate binge. I've got more, though."

I had to smile at the light in his eyes. "Oh?"

"I got a call from Danvers at the crack of dawn. He said he couldn't send us anything on Stark officially—apparently the man's classi-fied— but he did give me a rough outline, which is all we really need."

"And?"

"It's even better—or worse—than you suspected. Stark's a su-per-spook of sorts—CIA, maybe, although Danvers won't say; it might be Military Intelligence. Anyhow, he's done covert work in Korea, Latin America, Africa, Beirut, you name it. He was in Special Forces during Vietnam and worked a lot behind the lines. Apparently, he's a real hands-on guy—not an administrator. I also got the feeling that behind all the patriotic crap about someone having to do a dirty job in a dirty world, the guy is regarded as a bit of a maniac—not just a stone-cold killer, but a quote-unquote real strange guy to boot, what-ever that means. He's so good, though, that he has 'the longest leash in covert operations.' Those are Danvers's words again."

Brandt took back the paper and folded it under his arm. "I would guess with all this mess that the leash is about to get yanked—hard."

27

The press conference did take place, later that morning, but only Wilson was there to answer questions. He didn't reveal Cioffi's identity but only that the police department had zeroed in on one particular suspect—who had apparently already fled—and that hopes were high for "a rapid resolution of the case."

When asked about Bill Davis, he said that while the case against him wasn't as "structured" as it had been originally, it still didn't exclude him from "the realm of guilt." No evidence had surfaced that didn't "fit the scenario that Davis had possibly worked with the man now being sought."

About Henry Stark, Wilson revealed nothing from Danvers's report. He conceded that the colonel's rash actions had caused a reopening of the case, but he was not to be construed as some avenging angel, as one New Hampshire reporter implied. He was a dangerous killer, and he would be "tracked down and brought to justice." A series of redundant questions concerning the progress of this tracking met with: "The situation is increasingly under control."

He took an unusually nasty beating from the reporters, none of whom was remotely satisfied with his comments, and I must admit I grudgingly tipped my hat to him for maintaining his cool, if not his control over the English language. That calm demeanor was reserved for reporters only, however; the rest of us gave him wide berth when he walked fuming back into the building.

Not that many of us were there to get in his way. Even with the added help from the state police and the Windham County Sheriff's Department, we were stretched so thin we had meter maids out directing traffic—a breach of rules we were bound to hear about at some later date.

The rest of us were either tucked away in offices, scrutinizing every scrap of Cioffi's belongings, or out on the road asking questions about his background. At the rate we were going, his anonymity wasn't going to last for long.

Steven Cioffi, we slowly gathered, had been employed at Leatherton for twenty years. He'd begun as a young clerk at their previous factory near Bellows Falls, working out of the accounting office. According to the office people we interviewed, all in the company of the rotund Mr. Kleeman "from legal," his personality through those years remained as Dr. Duquesne had described it—dull, humorless, and utterly without charm. An early orphan, he had been raised by his stern maternal grandparents until they were both killed in a car crash when he was sixteen. His only sibling was an older sister, still living in Bellows Falls, with whom he had little contact and who, on the afternoon we talked to her, showed no interest in him whatsoever.

He graduated from high school, living off a small sum of money he'd inherited from his grandparents, and then embarked on an unremarkable round of local odd jobs until he landed the position at Leatherton, which had just moved to town and was hiring people from the area.

He worked hard, if without visible inspiration, and his efforts were traditionally rewarded. With the relentless energy of a growing weed, he infiltrated up through the ranks of the accounting department, suddenly leaping to his present unrelated position three years ago. Curiously, none of the people we interviewed could explain the career jump, nor could they remember a single outstanding feature about the man.

So what he did as vice-president of "industrial relations" remained an enigma. It had something to do with conventions, as his secretary had vaguely pointed out. It also involved keeping in touch with—and keeping friendly with—the various unions working for the Leatherton network of factories. But primarily, as one disenchanted observer remarked, Cioffi was a case of deadheading; he had worked his way into a crack in the corporate wall, closer to the top than to the bottom, and had effectively disappeared. It was this man's opinion that the wall was full of such cracks and that all of them were stuffed with Cioffis.

One interesting but unprovable comment surfaced late in the day linking Cioffi's financial well-being to his ties with the unions. The allegation was that Leatherton's peaceful relationship with its work force was maintained by something more tangible than corporate harmony. What that meant precisely was never explained and would demand more than a scant few hours of research.

What was gnawing at me by the end of the day, however, wasn't the possibility of under-the-table payments between management and labor—with Cioffi and God knew who else skimming off the top—but rather, where that money was stashed. The only bank accounts we could find in Cioffi's name were negligible—enough to keep his bills paid, but in no way reflective of his obviously expensive tastes.

Willy Kunkle, on temporary bright-eyed leave from his manic depression, gave me the answer at ten o'clock that night. He poked his head around my door and gave me a grin I'd never before seen, "I think I found the loot."

"Where?"

He waved a thick sheaf of papers. "Phone records, going back over the past four years. Most of it's crap, but there's one number that pops up as regular as rain."

He came in and laid the papers on my desk. On sheet after sheet, sometimes in clumps, sometimes singly, but never separated by more than a week, was the same New York City number.

"Who's it belong to?"

"Timothy Cramer. He's a stockbroker."

I smiled. "Bingo."

I was on the first flight to New York the following morning, traveling under an assumed name. I'd had Kunkle tail me all the way to the Keene airport to make sure I wasn't followed. If Timothy Cramer did in fact have Cioffi's money, I was convinced it would lead me to the man himself. Considering Cioffi's lack of personal attachments—hobbies, interests, or people—money seemed the only lead left, and judging from the number of calls he'd placed to Cramer, it was obviously a big one.

I found Cramer in an enormous, brightly lit room on the fifteenth floor of the headquarters of a large, well-known brokerage house. He sat in one of a long line of cheek-by-jowl cubicles, each equipped with a metal desk, two chairs, and a computer. It reminded me of someone's pessimistic vision of the future.

He was an affable man, still in his twenties, and very much impressed by the sight of a badge. I explained to him it was utterly worthless in New York and that he was under no obligation to speak with me.

"No, no," he said, getting up and leading me to another row of glassed-in conference cubicles lining the wall. "This is a nice break. Unconventional, too, which is saying a lot for this place."

He opened the door and ushered me in. The silence after the glass door had closed was eerie, as if all the activity within our sight had suddenly had its sound unplugged.

We sat in opposing padded plastic chairs, like contestants in a game show.

"So, what can I do for you?"

"I gather you handle the account of a man named Steven Cioffi."

"That's right."

"Would you be able to tell me how much it comes to?"

"I could but I can't, if you know what I mean."

"Sure. Could you tell me at least if it's big or small?"

He gave me a lopsided smile. "Those are relative terms, especially around here, but I could say that I personally don't consider it small."

"And is it still in place? Has he liquidated yet?"

He looked at me curiously, his face suddenly still. "No, I've still got it. Why do you ask?"

"He's wanted for murder." I watched for his reaction, hoping I could tell if his surprise was genuine or not.

His mouth fell open. "Holy shit."

I believed him. "He knows we're after him. He's already cleared out of town, taking everything with him, but I was hoping things had been a little slower at this end. Has he asked you to liquidate?"

"Yes, about a week or so ago. In fact, I was getting ready to mail him a check for a large chunk of it."

"Where to?"

"A post office box somewhere in New Hampshire. I'd have to look at my notes to tell you where exactly. It didn't mean anything to me. Who did he kill?" He suddenly looked embarrassed. "Is that all right to ask?"

"Sure. About three years ago, we think he was involved in the rape and strangulation of a young woman. Have you ever met him?"

"Never set eyes on him. He just called up—about three years ago, now that you mention it—and started doing business. I didn't have anything to do with it, really. He calls—he called—his own shots; I just carried them out."

"Did he do well?"

"Extremely well. He really does his homework."

"How did he strike you as a personality?"

Cramer held up his thumb and index finger and formed a circle. "Zip. He didn't strike me as anything. At first, I tried being friendly, you know? Maybe a light comment or two? But there was nothing coming back. I felt like I was pitching pennies into an empty well, so I stopped. It was all business."

"And a lot of business, according to his phone records."

"You bet. He calls me more than any of my other clients, giving me orders and asking for research."

"Did he send you a lot of money to invest?"

"Oh, yes, regular installments would come every month. That's not unusual, though. Lots of people take a set sum out of their monthly paycheck or whatever and put it on the Street."

"When did he contact you last?"

"Just a couple of days ago. He asked if I had the money yet and I said, 'Almost,' and then he gave me the post office box number."

"Could I have that?"

For the first time his face clouded. He looked doubtful. "That would probably get me fired. Is there any way you could get a warrant?"

"Yes, but it'll take time, and I'm not sure we have it. So far, he thinks he's covered his trail; if he senses something's wrong, we may lose him."

"Is there any way you could just keep me out of it?"

"Sure. It's just an address. I could have gotten it from any confidential source, as they say. Of course, if and when we catch him, the State's Attorney might want to ask you about Cioffi's dealings with you, but that'll all be through proper channels. This conversation will never come up."

He quickly nodded once—a man used to making fast decisions. "Okay. Follow me."

The name of the town in New Hampshire was Gorham, a small pinprick on the map just north of Mount Washington, high in the middle of the state. The name Cioffi had told Cramer to use on all correspondence was John Stanley.

I arranged to have Cramer send an overnight letter in twenty-four hours to Cioffi stating that he would Express Mail the first check in two days. With any luck, that would give us three days to infiltrate the Gorham area without attracting attention and to be in place when Cioffi came to collect his loot.

On the surface, it looked pretty straightforward. But as I sat on the tiny lurching seat of the puddle-jumper flying me back to Keene, I couldn't shake the feeling that I'd hooked something unusual swimming in murky waters. Whether I could reel it in—or it would pull me overboard—was something I wouldn't know until it actually happened.

I had gone from having too few pieces of this puzzle to having an excess. How did shady union dealings, a sudden promotion, Cioffi's lucrative interest in the stock market, and Pam Stark's jump in income and subsequent death all coincide? And the fact that Cioffi graduated from the accounting department—had Cioffi discovered something scaly in the numbers? Did it have anything to do with unions? Who would decide a promotion like that, and how did they tie in? And was Pam more than a simple gold digger? And what about the fact that the fetus within her belonged to neither Davis nor Cioffi? Despite the scant attention it attracted, I couldn't shake the feeling that the pregnancy was more than a biological penalty being paid by a modern promiscuous girl.

There were other things nagging. Why the elaborate frame, assuming Davis was indeed framed? Why not a simple bullet in the head—clean, efficient, unsensational?

And finally, what about Stark? Was he simply a neurotic father run amok? Or did his intelligence background have something to do with all this? Who were the people he'd warned me about—the people who'd killed Frank? And what had become of them? Since Frank's death, things in that quarter had been totally still—lurking like some wild animal waiting for the kill.

But Stark consumed my thoughts most, as he had done from the start. This was his play we were acting out; he was the director. I was utterly convinced that from his precarious relationship with his daughter, he'd created a cause as big or bigger than anything he'd ever undertaken.

I looked out the window at the darkening black-and-white landscape below—shadowed fields and stark forestland, the flat pale disks of frozen ponds, an occasional house, its lights just beginning to glimmer. I floated between two realities: one serene and unreachable, being swallowed up by the night, the other violent and calculating, lurking just beyond my comprehension.

28

I got back to the office around six that evening. It was already dark, and moonless. The radio cautioned about heavy snow in the near future; how far in the future was uncertain. Very helpful. By the sounds that greeted me as I pushed through the Municipal Building's double doors, I wouldn't have guessed quitting time had come and gone an hour ago. The place was as jammed as it was in preparation for George Bush's little pre-election pep rally in the eighties.

I sought out Brandt in his cloudy office, leaving the door half-open to allow some minimal circulation.

He looked up at my knock. "Close the door. What'd you find?"

"You might think I'm losing my marbles, but I'd like to tell you that outside in the parking lot, if you don't mind."

Brandt glanced around and smiled. He got up and put on his overcoat, and we both went into the dark, cold night.

He stopped when we were about equidistant from everything but cars. "We did have the place swept, you know—never found a thing."

"Humor me—he's screwed us enough times. I don't want to underestimate him now."

"All right. What have you got?"

"Cioffi will be waiting for his money, addressed to John Stanley, at a post office box in Gorham, New Hampshire, in three days."

Brandt positively grinned. "Hot damn."

I gave him the details, which he absorbed with little nods and grunts, his shoulders hunched and his hands jammed deep in his pockets. I also filled him in on the peculiar swirl of coincidences that had so changed Cioffi's life three years ago.

Brandt continued nodding. "Yeah. Complicated fella all of a sudden, isn't he? By the way, your friend Kees called in his report on those blood samples you had delivered."

"So soon?"

"He said it saves time when he knows what to look for."

"Is Cioffi our man?"

"To a T. The semen was definitely his. Can we go back inside now?"

I ushered him toward the building. The place and the date of Cioffi's planned reappearance were the only two pieces of information I deemed crucially confidential. Considering the growing number of people tied up in this investigation, everything else was fast becoming common knowledge.

I settled into Brandt's guest chair after taking off my coat and rubbed my eyes with my palms. Kees's report on the semen was the first and only rock solid evidence we'd gathered despite all the dust we'd kicked up. In legal parlance, it placed Cioffi at the scene of the crime, but I'd been mulling this one over so long now, legal parlance was no longer enough. "I wonder what the hell happened in that room?"

Brandt sat and put his feet on his desk. He twitched his chin up in half a nod. "I know what you mean. Things are so tangled now, I wouldn't be surprised if the man's semen did get delivered without him." He paused and pursed his lips, "I almost hate to tell you this, considering, but your little duckling Kunkle has come up with something that isn't going to help much."

I raised my eyebrows, but he merely answered by picking up his phone and asking Kunkle to join us. There was a knock on the door in less than a minute. Kunkle entered carrying a thick file.

"How was your trip?" The civility stunned me. I wouldn't have been more surprised if he'd kissed me.

"Good. If everything works, we'll have Cioffi in the bag pretty soon. Tony says you've found a monkey wrench."

Kunkle laid the file on the desk before me. "Yeah. I think I have. We all figured Cioffi's convention schedule was a perfect cover for all those trips 'Louis Armstrong' took with Pam Stark, right?"

"Yeah."

He bent over and flipped open the file. "Well, I ran a comparison check between his appointment calendars and the passenger manifests we got from the travel agents on Stark and her boyfriend. They don't coincide."

"But he filled in the appointment calendar, right?"

"Yeah. That's what I thought—he was covering his tail. So I got a warrant for the tickets he bought—from a different travel agent, by the way—and matched them to his books. They fit."

"So Louis Armstrong is not Cioffi."

Kunkle shook his head. "Not according to the records. I've started the paperwork to track whether he was actually seen at those conventions, but I have a feeling they were legit."

He was quiet. I looked at Brandt, who gave me that little smile. I sighed. "So we've got Davis, who might have been framed, Cioffi with the semen, which might have been planted, and Louis Armstrong, who might be the father. We also have the remote possibility that all three are innocent of her murder and that a fourth guy did it, or that all three were in her room that night and did her in together."

"And on and on," Brandt muttered.

I shrugged. "Well, what the hell. Let's go with what we've got."

Brandt dropped his feet off his desk. "Suits me. There is one other item, though. The good colonel located Dr. Duquesne and squeezed him about Cioffi."

Something sagged inside me. "How?"

"He called up and said he'd grabbed Duquesne, Jr., and would cut his heart out or something if the doc didn't spill the beans. It was all done by phone and apparently the kid never was grabbed—he was at school all along. Duquesne was pretty bent out of shape and threatened to sue. In any case, we better assume Stark isn't far behind us, as usual."

I shook my head. "How the hell does he do that?"

Brandt reached into his trash can and tossed me that morning's paper. "We live in an information society. Katz found Duquesne and interviewed him. All Stark had to do was read the paper."

"What do you mean, 'Katz found Duquesne'?"

"Dunno."

I stared at the front page article without reading it. Katz wasn't the only one who amazed me; Duquesne's stupidity was pretty awesome too—I guessed the urge to talk to a real live member of the press was more than he could resist, even considering the risks. That was one lawsuit that wouldn't keep me up at night.

I put the newspaper back in the trash. "You know, if we hope to lay a net around Cioffi without attracting attention, we're going to have to put a stop to this."

"Any suggestions?"

"We could try what they did on D-Day: involve the reporters in exchange for exclusives after the fact."

"Those were different times, Joe. Pre–Woodward and Bernstein."

"I think Katz is too big an asshole to trust." Kunkle's voice startled me. I'd forgotten he was still in the room.

"I won't argue with that part, but he does a hell of a job." Kunkle's eyes widened. "A hell of a job? That son of a bitch tries to screw us every time we bend over."

"That's because we're on the receiving end. You got to admit, if he weren't so good, we wouldn't hate him so much."

Brandt lit his pipe and blew out some smoke. "I think the imagery is getting disgusting."

I held up a hand. "All right, but wait. This is a legitimate point; he usually does get his facts straight, right? What about the stakeout story at the Misery Hilton. That was fair."

Brandt shrugged. "Granted."

"So maybe it's our fault, and that's what pisses us off. It's not like we're dealing with some jackass from the *National Enquirer* who just invents what he can't get."

"Joe, no one's arguing the man's abilities. It's his personality—and the times. He's a very ambitious guy, and that gets rewarded. You don't get recognition in his world for being friendly with the authorities."

"And I still say he's an asshole," Kunkle muttered.

I stood up. "Well, let's find out. You and I'll go talk with him."

Kunkle made a sour face. "Why me?"

"Because you have nothing better to do."

"Oh, give me a break—"

"And you might learn something about human nature." I turned to Brandt. "Call the paper and tell them we're coming, will you? See if you can line up Katz and Bellstrom both."

"Good luck."

I led the way back to the parking lot. Kunkle was still clutching his file. "I don't need a goddamned nanny, you know. If I want to find out about human nature, I'll do it on my own."

I stopped halfway out the double doors, the cold air reaching at my throat through the gap. I buttoned my coat. "Fine. Let me put it another way. You are the biggest head case I have on this investigation, so I want you to know every detail of my conversation with Katz and his boss so you won't fly off the handle later if and when you see Katz hanging around. Is that more acceptable?"

He nodded, which I took as a good sign. Nothing like a series of murders to snap one out of a depression.

We found Bellstrom and Katz in the editor's office, ready and waiting. Bellstrom was his usual laid-back, affable self. Katz was back to being Katz. "Getting Brandt to work as your secretary? That's hardball for a mere acting captain."

"Asshole," Kunkle muttered one more time.

"Hello to you, too, Stanley," I added.

Bellstrom had made a steeple of his fingers and was tapping it gently against his lower lip. "Since it's getting on toward dinner time, maybe we ought to get started." He then smiled apologetically. "My wife just called. Her sister's in town, and if I'm not home for dinner, she suggested I spend the night at a motel."

"The life of a press lord?" He shrugged.

"All right. We've had some of this conversation before and didn't get anywhere, so I'm offering a new approach."

"To what?" Katz asked.

"To mutual back scratching. Unless I guess wrong, you've got every reporter, every stringer, and probably every janitor in your building out covering this Colonel Stark thing. That includes working your police moles overtime and wearing out shoes. How did you find Duquesne, by the way?"

Katz looked at Bellstrom, whose expression didn't change. Katz then smiled. "That was hard work. I heard one stray comment about prescriptions—nothing specific—and based on that, I had everyone who could handle a phone call every doctor in town and ask why the cops had dropped by recently. Duquesne bit. He said something like, 'That's confidential,' and I knew I had my man. I showed up and his ego did the rest."

I turned to Bellstrom. "Is this the biggest story this paper has ever covered?"

"It's a big story," he agreed with a poker face.

"Pulitzer big, maybe?"

"Conceivably. It's nice to dream."

"Well, I wish you well. Unfortunately, some of that eagerness could have gotten Duquesne's kid killed if Stark had played it another way."

"Break my heart," Katz grumbled. Kunkle shoved his hands into his pockets. Bellstrom looked uncomfortable.

"It was just an illustration. We're getting very close to opening the front door to this whole mess, but like I said at our last get-together, if Stark gets there before us, we'll probably never find out what's inside. He'll throw in a hand grenade. That puts us in a quandary, since you guys are reporting every move we make. So I have what Tony Brandt seems to think is a fairly quaint proposition."

"Which is?"

"I will involve you in every phase of our operation from now on for the next three days in exchange for exclusive coverage, if you give us

234

some room to arrange our plans discreetly—kind of like they did at D-Day."

Katz shook his head. "Three days—you that close?" I ignored him. Kunkle didn't, but he kept quiet.

Bellstrom closed his eyes for a moment. "Times have changed a bit since then."

"Seems like it worked pretty well at the stake-out. You'd be in on everything—every meeting, every planning session, everything. It would be your choice to go where you wanted."

Bellstrom shook his head. "We have arrangements of our own with other news agencies—wire services and the TV people, not to mention other papers of our own chain. It's kind of like a pool."

"Kind of, but not officially, right? You're not contractually required to reveal each detail of a story as you uncover it, are you?"

"No, of course not."

"If you go along with this, the whole thing's yours. If you don't, we'll just throw it to the dogs and let them sort it out. I might add, by the way, that we intend to really clamp down for the next few days. The normal flow of communication in the department will stop. All information will be on a need-to-know basis. We're going to bend over backwards to keep everything we can from the press."

"Then why this conversation?" Bellstrom asked.

I noticed Katz was looking thoughtful rather than combative. That, I hoped, was a plus for our side. "Because we've got higher priorities than keeping you in the dark. Besides, this way, if we do screw up and let something out of the bag, it won't necessarily hit the front page next day. I'd like to be able to concentrate on wrapping this up with you, not in spite of you. For that matter, if you want to get sentimental, this might be the only chance for Bill Davis to be declared an innocent man. Surely it's worth three days of insider work to be able to crow about that later."

There was a long silence. Bellstrom's eyes wandered over to the window that separated his office from the now deserted newsroom. "You could mislead us more easily from the inside; use us to your advantage."

"That's a risk. But it's a risk all the time anyway."

"I can handle that," Katz muttered.

I fought down a smile. I could feel the Pulitzer bug chewing at Katz's mind.

Bellstrom looked at him, mild surprise on his face. "You like this?"

"I don't see any problems with it. It's only three days. A trade-off sounds good. Like he said, it worked last time."

Bellstrom checked his watch. "The principle stinks, if you ask me. I've said it before—I don't like sleeping with tigers; it's not natural and it's not healthy. I'm not even sure it's ethical."

"But it might make for a hell of a story," Katz added.

The phone rang. Bellstrom picked it up, listened for a moment, said "I'm on my way," hung up, and got to his feet. "I've got to go. . . All right. I think it stinks, but I won't fight it. But," and he stuck his finger at Kunkle and me, "if there's any show of something screwy, we're out of it." He looked hard at Katz. "Stan, I know you want more out of life than this paper. But if you sell me out on this, if you give them more than just silence during these next three days, your ass is grass. Is that understood?"

Katz nodded. Bellstrom looked at us all as if we'd just emerged from a swamp, and walked out of the office to lock horns with his sister-in-law.

I turned to the other two. "Well. Now that everybody's happy, I suggest some shut-eye. It might be the last we'll get for quite some time. We'll reconvene at headquarters at 6:00 A.M."

Gail's driveway had been plowed and sanded, for which I was extremely grateful. Where my old car had usually given up halfway up the hill, I doubted Leo's could have climbed ten feet. I walked up to her sliding glass door and knocked.

I was a little surprised she hadn't beaten me there, standing look-out to see how I fared on the slope. I slid open the door and called out her name. She answered from the kitchen.

I closed the door behind me and hung up my coat. I heard her walk into the room.

"Hi, Joe."

The terror in her voice made me whirl around. She was standing in the kitchen door, wide-eyed and pale. Behind her, holding a gun, was Henry Stark. "Yeah. Hi, Joe."

For a split second, I was frozen still, my heart hammering. Pictures flashed in my mind—of Jamie Phillips, Wendy Stiller, Ted Haffner, Lew Hill, and all the others this man had mentally or physically maimed. And now Gail. I fought back an explosive surge of absolute rage—something so violent, I had to reach back to Korea to remember its predecessor.

Stark smiled and pushed her gently toward the living room sofa. "Strong, silent type, huh? Why don't you follow your girlfriend after depositing your gun gently on the floor? I hate the way they throw guns around in the movies." He shook his head, "Dangerous."

I did as I was told, thinking he sounded a lot like a movie himself. Gail and I sat side by side on the sofa.

"That's right. Lean way back. Put your feet up on the table and keep your hands folded in your laps." He sat comfortably in an armchair opposite. He was dressed neatly in the dark blue jumpsuit and paratrooper boots I'd seen him in earlier. His face looked just as it did in his photo, except in person he positively oozed graceful menace. I had seen that once before, in a *National Geographic*, looking at a straight-on close-up of a panther in the wild. Even the pale, inert eyes looked the same.

"I felt I ought to introduce myself personally, since you now know who I am. I also wanted to thank you for having done such a good job, albeit with some prodding. I have the definite feeling we won't be at this too much longer. We're getting very close, don't you agree?"

I was so roiled up inside I was having a hard time breathing, much less coming up with pleasantries to exchange with a psychopath. In the abstract, I'd had the leisure to deal with this man's actions, to think about them one by one. Sitting here facing him, I just wanted him to go away. It was as if all he'd done—to his wife and daughter, to almost everyone I'd had to deal with for weeks—was suffocating me.

"If you hadn't been such a screwup as a father, none of this would have happened."

He tightened his mouth slightly, but that was all. "Aren't we judgmental."

"Your daughter was an accident waiting to happen. If you want to find out who really raped and strangled her, look in the mirror."

He remained outwardly impassive, but he also stayed silent. I felt Gail's eyes boring holes into the side of my head. She was evidently unhappy with my approach.

But I'll grant Stark this much: he had more self-control than I. After a long sixty-second count, he resumed in the same tone as before. "If you were actually trained by someone to talk like that to a man holding a gun on you, I suggest you report back that the method needs revision."

I heard Gail let out her breath softly. Stark rearranged himself in the chair, stretching his legs in the process. It seemed to relax him a bit. He smiled again. "Whether you admire me as a father or not, we're stuck together on this thing, so we might as well get it over with quickly."

"You've got to be out of your mind if you think I'm going to cooperate with you. I fully intend to stop you long before I nail whoever it was who killed your daughter."

"Utter crap and you know it. The only case you have is the one we're on together. You're no closer to catching me than you were the night Thelma Reitz turned Phillips into Alpo, which, by the way, wasn't my fault."

"Wasn't your fault? Who the hell's fault was it then?"

"I had no idea she had a shotgun in the house. Not that I really minded—the results were satisfactory."

"Phillips was the only guy who tried to stop this whole mess."

"Oh, come, come. His actions are what count. The jury was unanimous—he just tried to get the best of both worlds. Pure hypocrisy."

I knew I wasn't doing this right—that I should be conversational and supportive, trying to get as much out of him as I could. But I was both angry—at him and at myself—and nervous. With everybody poised to move on Gorham in the next few hours, I was now chatting with the one man I wanted kept in the dark. I felt everything I knew was printed across my forehead. "Why the hell didn't you come to us in the first place and ask us to reopen the case?"

That brought a chuckle. "Would it have worked?"

"Maybe. I don't know. Stranger things have happened. You never gave it a thought, did you?"

He waved his hand. "Water over the dam."

Another blast of anger made me struggle to get up and lunge at him. He placed his pistol barrel against my forehead so fast I barely saw him move. "Sit back." He pushed lightly with the gun, and I fell back against the pillows. Gail instinctively reached for my hand. Stark didn't stop her.

"Who killed Frank?"

He looked at me for a long moment and then smiled and rose. "That's enough for now. I merely dropped by to say hi. Perhaps we'll meet again later."

"When we do, you'll be in jail."

He slowly raised his pistol to where it was pointing at my right eye. "I want you to understand something here, Joe. You are not in control. You are my stalking horse. I put you in place and you've done your job. In a short while, the quarry will be exposed and you'll be expendable."

His arm moved slightly to where the gun was pointed at Gail's head. "But in the meantime, you had better remember: you people live at my discretion. That includes Miss Zigman, your mother, Leo, Martha Murphy, and all the other people you'd better place above your moral outrage. Because if you don't, I'll have to remind you how responsible you are for their safety."

The arm went down and he smiled again. "I'll let you two get cozy. I know you haven't seen each other in a while." He walked to the door and picked up my gun. "I'll leave this on the hood of your car. Good night."

And he was gone.

Gail twisted around, put both her arms around me and held on tight. I kissed her ear and rubbed her back. "It's okay. It's okay."

She didn't answer, but her grip tightened.

We didn't talk for a good half hour, which was probably just as well. We ended up instead lying on the couch, with her head on my chest, silently running it all through in our minds, again and again. Finally she sighed deeply, and asked, "What are you going to do?"

"Gut reaction? I'd like to start by getting everyone out of harm's way."

She looked up at me. "What do you mean?"

"Protecting all the people he mentioned—you, Mother, Leo—all of them."

"How?"

"I don't know. Police protection maybe. I could get Martha to return to her daughter's. I could get the state police to watch over Thetford."

"You can't do that, Joe; you know it. Shy of putting us all into a tanker and pushing it out to sea, there's no way of protecting us. If he really wants to, he'll find us. Besides, he could put you in the same position by threatening a total stranger. It doesn't need to be one of us."

The point was inarguable, but seeing him point that gun at Gail's head had shaken my priorities. What, after all, did I really care about Bill Davis? He was a moral abstraction, a victim of circumstance. It was idiotic that I risk the lives of everyone who mattered to me for some principle no one had liked from the start.

"You've just got to keep going the way you have been, Joe. From what he said, the worst thing you could do is to change course. It would force him to set you straight again."

"And setting me straight means I lead him to his daughter's killer so he can execute him and fade back into the woodwork."

239

"You've already pulled him more into the open—he's no longer the anonymous Ski Mask. Maybe he'll trip up; maybe you can make him trip up. Just because he says he's in control doesn't mean it's true. Your harping on him and his daughter showed that. I didn't appreciate that one bit, by the way. You'd have a short life as a psychiatrist—he was right about that."

That made me smile.

She propped herself up by putting her elbows on my chest and looking me straight in the face. "Joe, you're a decent, honest man. You can't do anything other than what you've been doing. I know Stark can carry out his threat, but it's not what he wants. His focus is on finding who killed his daughter, and that's where yours has to be too. It's the only way the two of you will ever be on close to an equal footing."

I rubbed my eyes with the palms of my hands. "Christ, I don't know. I wish I were ticketing cars right now." She leaned forward and kissed my chin. "Let's go to bed."

29

The procedure for camping on another town's front step until the bad guy rides in involves more than notifying the local sheriff, much to Hollywood's chagrin. Nowadays, the hierarchy of the "need-to-know" extends right up to the governor's office of each state involved. Luckily, it's quicker than it sounds, although the three days I'd allowed us was still cutting it fine. Due to the notoriety of the case, I wasn't too worried about hitting snags; nobody wanted this thing to get stalled because of them. But I was worried about leaving Gorham uncovered until all the paperwork was in. So, bending the rules a bit, I gave three of my men official time off and told them to spend their vacations in beautiful Gorham, New Hampshire, where the post office was renowned as one of the world's true scenic wonders. I forgot to let Katz in on this.

My biggest headache, as I saw it, was keeping Colonel Stark out of the picture. He had prematurely moved into the open when he'd questioned Haffner and killed Lew Hill. It was a mistake he wouldn't repeat. I was absolutely sure that when I saw him again, it would be for the last play of the game. I only hoped that when that happened, we would already have Cioffi under wraps.

For the next two days, we escorted the paperwork through the process like a kitten through a kennel—very quietly. James Dunn agreed to handle all his office's details personally, including the typing. A judge was found in the middle of the night to sign on the dotted line. Kunkle drove the papers up to Montpelier and hand-delivered them to the governor's man responsible for state warrants. He then drove over to Concord, New Hampshire, and made the connection with their people.

In the meantime, I organized the troops, picking my men, coordinating with the New Hampshire State Police—who would actually make the bust—and poring over maps of Gorham to determine the best plan of attack. I did all this in parking lots, other people's cars and secretly rented motel rooms—all places I was sure Stark couldn't have bugged beforehand. Through it all, Katz was the perfect gentleman, which was just as well. Including him in all the cloak-and-dagger stuff made most of the people I dealt with think I had totally lost my mind.

The solution to Stark's following us to Gorham and to Cioffi—brilliant, I thought—was to fly everyone there by helicopter, leaving Stark to watch us vanish into the sky. When I stepped outside the Municipal Building after almost forty-eight hours of nonstop preparations, I knew that part of the plan was shot. It was snowing—heavily.

Kunkle appeared out of the gloom, his head and shoulders speckled white.

"What are you doing here?"

"The chopper pilot said the flight's off. I guess we drive."

That's not what I wanted to hear. "What's the forecast?"

"This shit for thirty-six to seventy-two hours. It'll get worse before it gets better. Travel advisories are already out."

"Damn."

Kunkle hesitated a moment. "I've got Katz in the car, along with the equipment."

"Equipment" was a euphemism for rifles, shotguns, and bullet-proof vests. I appreciated his forethought.

"I guess we go, then."

He led the way across the parking lot to his car. Katz was sitting in the back.

"Hello, Stan."

"Hi, Joe. Not quite the weather you were hoping for, is it?"

I slid onto the front seat and Kunkle started the car. "Not exactly."

We already had three of our men in Gorham, which had miffed the New Hampshire State Police—they felt we were doubting their prowess—so I'd restricted the second wave to just the three of us. I hadn't told our new allies who Katz was.

That was a detail he hadn't overlooked. He knew that once we crossed into New Hampshire, my deal with him had no value. If the state police over there didn't want him around, that was it. My silence had made him friendlier than I'd known possible—a definite plus. It was going to be a long drive, and I was grateful my two normally over-bearing companions had lightened their personalities.

Still, the trip was tense. Looking out the windshield was like staring at an interminable swarm of fireflies on the attack, careening at the car and veering away at the last instant. The sudden appearance of other cars was the only startling reminder that we were still on the road. The memories of my last trip with Frank were real enough to be scary. I kept looking over my shoulder to check for headlights, but except for when we came to the occasional town, there was nothing.

"Did you check the car for bugs?"

"A couple of times. It's not my car anyway. I borrowed it at the last second from a friend, just to be sure."

I looked at Kunkle's profile in the glow from the instrument panel. It made me think of that nursery rhyme about what's-her-name: "When she was good, she was very, very good..."

It took us all night to reach Gorham, a trip that normally lasted three hours. By the time we rolled to a stop in the parking lot of the Swiss Alpine Lodge, daylight was struggling to penetrate the cotton candy around us.

The three men I'd sent on ahead had booked two adjoining rooms on the ground floor. It was Ron Klesczewski who answered my knock. He was wearing his undershorts and a T-shirt and was still only semi-conscious. That changed when he looked past me.

"Holy shit. It's snowing." He stuck his head out and looked up—a gesture that has never made much sense to me. "Jesus. It's a goddamn blizzard."

He focused on Katz. "My God. What the hell is he doing here?"

I planted my hand against his chest and pushed him back into the room so we could enter. "Hello to you too. Do you always wake up in such a state of amazement?"

He blinked a couple of times. "No. Well, I mean...I didn't expect it; or him. It is unusual, you got to admit."

"Katz is observing. Don't tell the state police who he is or there'll be hell to pay. Where's DeFlorio?"

"Here." The voice was muffled by the pile of blankets on the far bed. "Morning, Dennis. Rise and shine."

A hand emerged from the pile and groped for a watch on the night table. Both disappeared and were followed by a groan. "Jesus. Too early."

The connecting door to the other room opened, and J.P. Tyler stepped in, shaved, showered, and fully clothed. "Hi, Joe; Willy." He nodded at Katz without comment or visible surprise. From his appearance, it might have been the middle of the day.

I pulled open the curtains, without great effect, and switched on the overhead light. "I take it you're aware of that." I pointed at the snow-storm.

"Yeah. Last radio report had it at almost two feet. Worst in years, they say."

"Has anyone been in touch with the locals yet?" I knew the answer for DeFlorio and Klesczewski, but I thought I'd be polite. Among his peers at least, Tyler never failed to assume unofficial command.

"I talked to them after I heard the weather. They've been in touch with the Postal Service. Things will be delayed, but they'll still come through. As far as the state police are concerned, the operation is on without changes."

"They still headquartered at the school?" He nodded. There was a large school building in the middle of Gorham, several blocks southeast of the post office. The assumption was that a small cluster of cars wouldn't seem out of place there, even in this mess. Tyler added, "By the way, they managed to get a man inside the post office, posing as a mail sorter."

"Has anyone seen Cioffi?" I asked.

"Nope."

De Florio had by this time emerged from his blankets and was sitting with his back against the wall. "Are we sure we're ever going to see him?"

"Yes. I called his broker yesterday. The deal's still on. There was a bit of a problem with Express Mail because of the post office box delivery address. Cioffi is anxious to be there when they make the delivery, so we'll probably see him loitering around the post office."

"He'll be a snowman unless he loiters inside." I checked my watch. "I'm going over to the school. I want to get the lay of the land. You guys meet me there as soon as you can."

"You can't see the lay of the land."

Kunkle, Katz, and I trudged back out to the car. We slithered from the parking lot to the road in the gloomy half-light, Kunkle fighting to keep us from the ditch. The motel was on the north end of Gorham, a small, flat town tucked between the parallel curves of the Androscoggin River and the railroad tracks. There was one central street, predictably named Main, which served as a brief convergence for Route 2, running east to west, and Route 16, which cut from north to south.

We crawled down the deserted street, our eyes searching the white turmoil outside for the post office. We found it in the middle of town, on the right, situated like the hub of a three-spoke wheel amid Charlie's

Restaurant on one side, a small laundromat-supermarket complex on the other, and an abandoned greasy spoon across the street.

Katz spoke up for the first time in hours. "Well, that answers where he'll probably be loitering."

"I wonder if the state police have a plant in the supermarket, too," Kunkle muttered.

The school was several short blocks farther down the street, set back in the middle of its own lot of land. It was a typical Victorian monstrosity, not unlike the Municipal Building back home. I noticed two Sno-Cats parked by the side, blending in with some town sand trucks and graders. If the weather kept up, they'd be the only way to get around. I hoped someone knew where the keys were.

We piled out of the car and stumbled up the broad steps toward the school's large double doors. They swung back before we reached them and revealed a Marine Corps poster come alive—mean of eye, hard of belly, complete with a crew cut perched on a six-foot-four frame. I had to look twice to confirm he wasn't in uniform.

He was Captain Kevin McNaughton of the New Hampshire State Police—the man with whom I had coordinated the fun and games ahead.

He looked icily at Kunkle and Katz. "More? That wasn't what we discussed."

I shook his hand and stepped in past him. "I know, but this is it. We won't get in your way."

"How can you help it? You've got almost as many men as I have now."

I sincerely hoped that wasn't true. "Just consider us troops. Put us where you want us."

He closed the door behind us and ushered us into a side office. "You'd think we were after John Dillinger."

I took my coat off and laid it across the low counter that split the room down the middle. Two plainclothes troopers were sitting at the back drinking coffee. "It's not getting Cioffi that worries me. It's Stark getting him, like I told you in Brattleboro."

McNaughton shook his head and all but sneered, "The mysterious masked avenger. He must really be something if you think he's going to pop up today."

"He's a dedicated man." I moved to a large table covered with a map of the region. "Any change of plans with the weather?"

McNaughton sauntered over. "If anything, I'd cut back, but I suppose I have to put your men somewhere."

I looked at the map and thought again of what I might have missed. Since we didn't know where Cioffi was hiding, we'd planned for four two-car roadblocks—two for Route 2, two for Route 16—to swing into place only after he was identified at the post office; we had to be sure he wouldn't see us on his way in. McNaughton had one man in the post office—an extra we hadn't counted on—plus one in the laundromat and one in the restaurant flanking the post office. It was good coverage but thin, which is why I'd brought so many of my own people. I was going to double what he had wherever I could.

"Do we have access to the greasy spoon?" I pointed at the small rectangle across Main Street from the post office.

"We can get it. I have the fire chief on call. Does it matter?"

"You don't have anyone in there now?"

"No."

"It can't hurt. In fact, that's where you and I could hang out—and him." I nodded at Katz. "If that's all right," I added.

McNaughton sighed and nodded at one of his men. "Call DuBois and ask him for the keys." He looked down at the map. "So, you want each of your guys to ride shotgun on the roadblocks?"

"All but one. I'd like Kunkle here in a non-block car, just in case."

McNaughton shrugged. "They been told who's boss?"

"Yes." I looked at my watch. "The post office opens in a half hour. We better get in position."

The captain sighed and shook his head, but he reached for his jacket. For reasons I couldn't figure, he'd insisted on downplaying all this from the start, as if the whole thing were a major inconvenience, best handled by a meter-maid unit.

The front door opened and Klesczewski, DeFlorio, and Tyler appeared in a gust of snow. The first two still looked half-asleep. I told them which roadblocks they were to share and sent them back out the door along with McNaughton's troopers.

We pulled up to the greasy spoon five minutes later, just as the fire chief, looking like a great bundled tree trunk, was unlocking the front door. Kunkle left the motor running.

"Where are you going to position?" I asked him as Katz and McNaughton slid out of the car with one of the equipment bags.

Kunkle shook his head at the weather. "With this shit, I could park on the sidewalk and he wouldn't see me." He paused and looked around, more out of habit than for anything he might see. "I guess my best bet is to park in front of the supermarket. The snow'll cover me fast enough."

I opened my door. "Don't forget to clear your tailpipe every once in a while."

He gave me a withering look and remained silent. I didn't care. More than one cop had inhaled too much monoxide during a winter stakeout.

I got out and thanked DuBois and entered the abandoned building. It was a standard diner—counter along one wall, booths and front door along the other. The windows were mostly boarded up, with a gap here and there. McNaughton and Katz were already settling at a booth next to one of the gaps. I slid in beside Katz and peered past him out the window.

Across the street, as in some half-developed photograph, I could just make out the vague pale outline of the one-story brick post office. To the left, even less visible, was the supermarket and laundromat; to the right was Charlie's Restaurant.

McNaughton pulled out his radio. "Frequency check. All units report in."

One by one, the men responded with their call names and the formal, "in position." Kunkle merely muttered, "P-Five."

McNaughton put the radio down and stretched his legs out. "That one's a little different."

"Kunkle? He's all right."

"Looks like a time bomb to me. We had a guy like that once. Stopped a motorist one day and asked the usual. The driver got ornery so our guy beat the shit out of him. Just snapped."

Katz muttered. "Sounds like a good lawsuit."

"Would have been, but we got lucky. The driver had some weed on him so we said we'd leave him alone if he'd do likewise, but it was the end of our boy. We got rid of him."

I moved to a stool so I could lean against the counter and look straight out the cracked window. The diner was as cold and dark as a refrigerator. "Kunkle's just a little tense."

"So was the Boston Strangler."

McNaughton unzipped the long equipment bag and exposed its contents: three Winchester pumps, ammunition, and three bulletproof vests. I leaned over, picked up one of the shotguns and loaded it. "I thought you said this guy's almost in a wheelchair."

"I keep telling you, Stark's my concern, not Cioffi."

The state trooper handled the second Winchester but didn't load it. "I think you're a little paranoid about that guy. I mean, I know he's

247

caused you guys a lot of grief, but he's not Arnold Schwarzenegger."

"You don't know him. He as cold-blooded as a nightmare, and I'm laying bets he's already here."

McNaughton didn't answer, but after a couple of minutes he non-chalantly loaded the gun. Katz left the third one alone.

That was it for conversation. For the next hours we sat and stared at the snow falling. It never varied in intensity. Untouched by any wind, it crossed our sight from top to bottom like a ragged white sheet on rollers. I began to feel I was seeing the same flakes go by. Every quarter hour, McNaughton conducted a radio check.

At about ten o'clock, sounding like an incongruous angry bee, a snowmobile bounced to a stop by the post office's front door. The bundled figure on its back slowly detached itself from the saddle and awkwardly stood in the deep snow. He paused for a moment, looking around, and then bent over the snowmobile, working at something on its far side. When he straightened again, he held a long, thin object in his hand, hard to distinguish through the flurries. "What the hell's that?" McNaughton muttered.

The figure planted the object in the snow, leaned on it, and took his first step toward the post office.

"It's a cane," I said.

30

McNaughton picked up his radio, his nonchalance suddenly gone "All units from P-One. Heads up. Suspect's entering post office."

"I hope he is," I muttered.

"Is what? Isn't that Cioffi? You said he had a cane."

"He does, supposedly. So do lots of other people. Do all your guys have those mugs I handed out?"

The furrow between his eyes deepened. "Of course."

"Can your inside man make a match without getting himself in trouble?"

McNaughton didn't answer. He jabbed the transmit button. "P-Six, this is P-One. Match the suspect with the mug shot, and let me know when you're clear."

We waited for several minutes before the radio hissed at us. "P-One from P-Six. Hard to say. Lots of facial hair and it's the wrong color."

"What about height and weight?"

"That fits."

"What's he doing now?"

"He asked if the Express Mail had come in yet. He's just standing around."

"Okay. Let me know when he moves."

McNaughton put the radio down and was silent. It was the first time I'd seen him hesitate. I let him stew in it.

He finally gave me a sidelong glance. "You want to grab him?"

"Nope."

"Why not?" His tone was neutral.

"Well, if you want to get complicated, until he signs for the envelope, we have no proof he's our man. I don't want to run the risk of spooking Cioffi."

"That's a little academic, isn't it? Whoever he is, if we let him get on that snowmobile, we'll lose him."

249

I let a slow count of five pass by before I said, "We sure will."

The fact that McNaughton had not anticipated a snowmobile hung in the room like a fat, fourth person. Despite that, I gave him high marks for composure. Of course, maybe he just didn't give a damn, but I doubted that. More likely, the man's ego had just been rushed into surgery and he was surviving on a stiff upper lip. Of course, I wasn't in much better shape—the snowmobile had caught me by surprise too—but I wasn't about to give him that comfort. Besides, I was counting on having enough time to grab Cioffi between when he received the package and when he headed for parts unknown.

McNaughton picked up the radio again. "All blocking units, this is P-One. Watch the roads but don't close 'em up. And don't show yourselves. Report all traffic."

A voice came back. "P-One, this is P-Three. There is no traffic. These roads are closed to anything normal."

I pulled out my own walkie-talkie and raised my eyebrows at McNaughton. He nodded. "You there, Willy?"

"Where the hell else am I going to be?"

"You got the snowmobile in sight?"

"Yeah."

"See if you can put it on the sick list."

His voice lightened. "You got it."

All three of us moved closer to the window.

"Do you have access to those Sno-Cats at the school?" I asked McNaughton.

He pleasantly surprised me. "I had 'em put there." He followed that by picking up the radio again. "Base, this is P-One. Roll one of those Sno-Cats in our direction. Take it easy, though. No rush."

In a couple of minutes, Kunkle's blurry dark shape appeared slowly from the left, picking its way carefully through the soft, clinging snow. He crossed over into the post office's parking lot and approached the snowmobile as if he was making for the door.

The radio made us jump. "All units from P-Six. Suspect's going outside."

We watched in utter stillness. Kunkle stopped dead in his tracks and then altered his course slightly away from the snowmobile. At the same time, the man with the cane came out of the post office. Kunkle raised his hand in greeting. The other man nodded in response as they passed. Kunkle entered the building and disappeared.

McNaughton muttered, "Jesus."

The man glanced at his vehicle and then looked around. He hunched his shoulders and began to cross over toward the restaurant.

"What the hell's he doing? The place is closed."

"He doesn't know that."

McNaughton said "Jesus" again and hit the button. "All units from P-One. Suspect's proceeding to the restaurant."

We saw him struggle through the snow to the front door and pull at it without success. He hesitated, and then suddenly cupped his hands against the glass to better see inside. There was a pause, and he backed away and began stumbling as fast as he could toward the post office.

"This is P-Eight. We're blown. We're blown."

"P-One to all units. Everyone out. He's heading for the snow-mobile." McNaughton shouted into the radio.

I ran for the door, Katz hard on my heels. McNaughton was still yelling. "Close the roadblocks. Get that Sno-Cat here now."

I stumbled outside in time to see Kunkle burst out of the post office and point his revolver at the man with the beard. His shout of "*Stop. Police.*" was answered by the sharp crack of a rifle. Kunkle collapsed against the wall. A moment later, Cioffi reached the snowmobile and filled the air with its scream. I saw dark shapes running from both restaurant and laundromat as the snowmobile lurched forward, ran over Kunkle's extended leg and slithered toward the street. There were a couple of shotgun blasts before the target vanished into the blizzard, heading toward the school.

McNaughton appeared at the door. "Suspect's headed southeast. Whoever's on the Sno-Cat, heads up for a bright red snowmobile.

There's an officer down; call for backup and an ambulance."

I pointed across the street. "Take Kunkle's car."

McNaughton broke into a clumsy run. I headed for the post office and got to Kunkle just as his car fishtailed into the street. The radio in my hand was alive with voices.

"This is P-Nine. He cut around me. He's still on Main."

"P-Nine from P-One. Turn around and wait for me. I'm almost there. Get the second Sno-Cat in pursuit."

"Ten-four."

Kunkle sat in the snow, his back against the wall, his face as white as the world around him. The only bright color anywhere was a crimson half circle of blood spattered on the wall above us and a tomato-sized stain high on his left arm. His eyes were wide open and dreamy.

He blinked and tried to focus on my face. "Go get the son of a bitch."

251

"That's being taken care of. Where're you hit?" He shook his head. "I don't know. Shoulder, I think—arm some-where. Not much pain; not any, really."

I didn't touch anything, but from the look of things the shoulder had been shattered.

"It wasn't him," he added after a sigh.

"Who shot you?"

"Yeah. It came from the right."

A man appeared at my side, breathing hard. He had a small detached earphone dangling over his collar.

"You with McNaughton?"

"Yeah. Corporal Wilcox."

"You got a car?" I stuck out my hand.

He nodded. "Jeep. Out back. Keys are in it."

I made Kunkle focus on me. "You're in good hands. I'll let you know."

I got the Jeep sliding down Main before I radioed in. "This is P-Two. What's happening?"

"P-Two from P-One. Good news, bad news. The eastern roadblock worked, but he doubled back and is heading south. That gave us a little time. Can you get to the school?"

"I'm almost there."

"Catch a ride on the second Sno-Cat and head south on Route 16."

"Any sign of Stark?"

"Fuck Stark. What's with Stark?"

"Who do you think shot Kunkle?" I dropped the radio in my lap and put both hands on the wheel. I had no idea why I was still on the road. I couldn't see a goddamned thing, and my foot was flat on the accelerator. After a pause, I heard McNaughton's one word response: "Shit."

I caught the dim flicker of a yellow flasher ahead and slowed down in time to avoid crashing into the Sno-Cat. One trooper was at the controls. I baled out of the Jeep and climbed up next to him.

"How's your guy?"

"Shoulder wound—bad."

The engine noise climbed to a howl, and we lumbered quickly down the street to the Route 16 turnoff.

"This is P-Three. Suspect is in sight." That was the roadblock just over one mile ahead. There was a full minute of silence before the radio crackled again. "This is P-Three. Suspect doubled back. We cannot pursue effectively."

"I got him." It was McNaughton's voice.

Another fifteen-second pause followed. "P-One to all units. Suspect's off the main road. He's headed west up a logging road. We're in pursuit."

My driver picked up speed now that we were clear of town. The engine between us let off a deafening high-pitched wail. The blurred treads by the side of the cab sent up a flurry of snow which mixed with the blizzard. The only half-clear view was straight ahead.

I suddenly saw where McNaughton's tracks took a violent cut to the right. We slammed into a crablike skid and followed suit, bursting through a gap in the trees and going straight up a steep, narrow trail cut in the woods, barely wide enough for the Sno-Cat.

"Where can he go from here?" I shouted over the noise of the engine.

"Anywhere if he can really drive that thing, but it's rough going. And with all this shit, we might find him wrapped around a tree."

"Is there any other way onto this mountain?"

He hesitated. "You mean Stark?"

"Yeah."

"Sure, if he's got a skimobile too. But I don't see how he'd know where to go without following some tracks."

I listened to the radio chatter as we crawled up the steep hill. A wall of trees pressed in from both sides, simultaneously cutting down on the light and the falling snow.

McNaughton's voice was rearranging his troops, ordering more backups, positioning vehicles at roads that meant nothing to me. For a man who had laid too loose a net and let the fish escape, he was remarkably calm and organized under pressure. I, on the other hand, was neither. Not only did I share the blame for this fiasco, but I couldn't shake the feeling of Stark's breath hot on my neck.

"Where does this lead?" I shouted to the driver.

"Dunno. We're northeast of Mount Washington. There's not a hell of a lot around here. Field and forest is all I know."

I radioed McNaughton. "P-One from P-Two. Can you position some men where this trail hits Route 16? We might get Stark."

There was no argument. I heard him give the orders.

"I think we're in better shape than we thought," the driver suddenly shouted.

"Why?"

"If he was a real hot dog on that machine of his, he wouldn't be sticking to this road—he'd be in the woods."

I looked at his profile and saw him smile—the happy hunter.

I was less thrilled. As I saw it, I was lurching across the countryside like some Keystone Kop with a mysterious cripple out front and a slippery homicidal maniac on my tail—maybe. The fact that Cioffi was not the Evel Knievel of the snowmobile set was of little comfort.

The radio crackled and announced that Klesczewski and a trooper had been dropped off at the trees at the foot of the mountain road. More men were "continuing pursuit."

I looked out the side window at the slow parade of passing trees. Hotshot or no, I couldn't imagine that a man on a snowmobile couldn't outdistance a Sno-Cat as if it were standing still.

"Jesus." The driver threw the controls and sent us into a grinding, sliding halt. Off to the right was the first Cat, lying on its side, wedged between two trees. McNaughton and one of his men were climbing out of the cab.

I opened my door and McNaughton got in beside me and yelled at the driver. "Get around that and head down the slope to the right. The son of a bitch cut off the road."

He jabbed his radio key. "All units. P-One and P-Two are now on same vehicle."

We moved forward a couple of yards. A skimobile's thin imprint sliced between the trees bordering the road and vanished down the steep, treeless slope beyond. The driver continued on until he came to a similar gap wide enough for us. He turned the Cat and paused at the edge.

"Go, man, go." McNaughton was half-crouching by the door next to me, his eyes glued ahead.

The Cat lurched up and over the bank and plunged with a sickening shudder straight down the slope. Despite the seat belt, I slammed both my hands against the dashboard to keep my teeth from being buried in my kneecaps. McNaughton ended up pressing against the windshield. The Cat's engine noise climbed to a scream, the gearbox began a high-pitched whine, and the snow burst from the thrashing caterpillar treads like foam from a tempest-tossed ocean. There was no room for any more sound, but as I glanced at McNaughton's face, I could see he was shouting into the mike.

The roller-coaster dive lasted for what seemed like an hour—probably two minutes. At its bottom, we found a half-buried wooden fence, and caught between two of its broken rails was the red snowmobile. Our driver killed the engine and wiped his face with his glove.

The sudden quiet impressed us all. Without a word, we opened our doors and swung out onto the treads. Dimly, high above, we could hear the other Cat laboring up the mountain road. The smashed snowmobile was alone.

"I guess he couldn't stop in time," McNaughton said quietly. He spoke into the radio, bringing everybody up to date.

In the meantime, his trooper reached back into the cab and brought out three pairs of snowshoes and handed a couple to us across the roof. We all sat down on the treads to put them on.

Far below, to the right, came a series of shots, first two sharp and high-pitched, as from two stones rapped together, followed by the mechanical rattle of a machine gun.

"Holy shit," McNaughton murmured. We looked at each other and waited. Several minutes passed during which we heard the other Cat pause at the top of the slope.

The radio crackled. "Officer down. We need help. This is P...Shit, I don't know. Move it." It was Klesczewski's voice.

"P-Four from P-Seven. We're on our way." I recognized Tyler. I reached inside the cab and unhooked the transmitter. "P-Four from P-Two. What happened?"

"A second snowmobile blasted through us. He caught Reynolds right in the chest. It looked like a Mac 10. I don't think he's going to make it."

"Are you okay?"

"Yeah. I'm real sorry, Lieutenant."

"What about the shooter?"

"We got off two shots, but it was like fighting a hail storm. He's on your tail now."

"Okay. Hang tight."

I heard the other Sno-Cat start up again and cautiously edge its way over the lip of the mountain. "Why not leave them there as a rear guard?"

McNaughton shook his head. "They're too thin—better we team up."

I finished attaching my snowshoes and hopped off the Cat. There is a fraternity among cops despite the bickering and class distinctions.

The saying goes that if a cop is in a jam, he can count on any other cop to at least try to pull him out of it. So I felt sorry for McNaughton. I was also mad as hell it had taken one of his men's lives to catch his full attention.

They also say that when you're maddest, it's usually because you screwed up. Whoever "they" are, they're right. I, more than anyone, knew how determined Stark was. And yet I'd allowed most of this to happen.

I was standing over the red wreckage of the snowmobile when the second Cat clattered to a halt. Stan Katz appeared at my side in a couple of minutes, carrying my shotgun. I hadn't realized until then that I'd run off without it.

"Thanks, Stan."

"Don't mention it."

I jerked my thumb back at the second Sno-Cat. "How'd you manage to hitch a ride?"

He smiled thinly. "They still think I'm a cop."

"You may have to do more than pretend, the way things are going. We'll need every gun loaded."

He nodded. "So I heard."

A momentary silence passed. We could hear the others talking behind us—that and the sound of ammunition being loaded.

"This thing's a real mess, isn't it?" he finally added. His voice was quiet, even comforting.

"It's not our finest hour; I'll give you that."

"A failure to communicate, as the saying goes?"

"Let's just say they fucked up; I fucked up; we all fucked up."

Katz smiled again. "You'll never be a MacArthur with lines like that."

McNaughton stepped into our stillness. "Any tracks?"

I nodded to a crooked line of oblong holes that trailed away from the broken machine. McNaughton swung his snowshoed feet deftly over the fence. "All right, gentlemen. Captain Gunther and I will form the middle. I want a line with ten foot intervals off to either side."

"What about Stark?" I asked, it seemed for the hundredth time.

"If we get Cioffi, we've got a bait for Stark."

It made sense, as everything had before it—only my trust in sense had gone out the window. I was also troubled that with the arrival of the second Cat, there were only six of us.

"I think we should wait for more people," I said.

"I don't." McNaughton's voice was flat. "I don't want to lose the bastard now."

We spread out, shotguns in hand, like gentlemen at a country shoot, and started off across the snowfield. To both sides of me, I could just perceive the ghostly outlines of my neighbors but no further. I relied on them to be keen to what lay ahead; my own concentration was given to what lurked behind.

We walked for forty minutes in total silence, the only sound being the muffled shuffling of the snowshoes and the occasional squawk from the radios. Even so equipped, it was slow going. Unless you do it regularly, snowshoeing is exhausting work, and in groups speed is reduced to the slowest member. Still, it is easier and swifter than plunging along without them, and I had to admire our prey for his stamina.

But stamina has its limits, especially if your hip is grinding away at the socket, reducing the bone to dust. We found our man eventually, peacefully sitting in the snow, staring at his lap.

McNaughton stepped up to him, the muzzle of his shotgun three feet from his head. "Are you Steven Cioffi?"

Cioffi looked up and smiled slightly. He had the appearance of a man in mid-daydream.

"Answer."

"Yes." His voice had a feminine softness to it.

"I have a warrant for your arrest."

As the New Hampshire men lifted Cioffi to his feet and searched him, finding nothing unusual, McNaughton read him his rights. When he was through, there was a curious lull, a palpable disappointment that the hunt had ended with such a murmur.

McNaughton radioed in to find out if the backup troops were anywhere near. They were not. The weather had bogged everything down, and they were waiting for additional Sno-Cats.

"Well, I guess we slog home." I looked around. "Is that wise?"

McNaughton gave me an exasperated glare. "Wise? What the fuck is wise? Our tracks are half-covered already. If we sit it out here, we won't be able to find our way back, and the backup won't be able to find us. We might protect this clown, but we'll all freeze to death in the process. We got to get back. We can hole up in the Cat if you want."

I rubbed my eyes. Once again it made sense. I felt like I was attending a wake for which the corpse hadn't quite arrived. I looked over my four companions. "Does anyone have a vest?"

One of the troopers opened his coat to reveal the bulletproof vest underneath. I cocked an eyebrow at McNaughton. "Give it to him." McNaughton pointed at Cioffi.

The transfer took place. Then McNaughton clustered us around the prisoner as tightly as our snowshoes would allow. "All right. Let's get the hell out of here."

Cioffi raised his hand like a boy in a schoolroom. The New Hampshire cop glared at him. "I can no longer walk."

"The hip?" I asked.

He smiled faintly and nodded. "I'm afraid I've done it some real damage."

We rigged a small litter from a couple of shotguns and an extra pair of snowshoes someone had brought along for Cioffi. It was too short to lie on, and sitting astride proved too painful, so Cioffi sat as on a park bench, with both feet dangling off one side. It was a precarious rig, by nature unbalanced, but it was the best we could think of. I walked along one side, holding Cioffi's hand to keep him from toppling off like a rag doll. Katz was on the other side and McNaughton and one trooper held the point ahead of the stretcher bearers. It was the best we could do to shield Cioffi from any line of fire.

31

Some five minutes into our silent return trip, Cioffi gave my hand a gentle squeeze. "I feel a little silly, holding hands."

"You'd feel even sillier lying on your back with your legs in the air."

He let out a small chuckle and nodded. "I suppose you're right." He sighed and tilted his face up, letting the snowflakes collect on his eyelids, as we all used to do as children. It was a gentle gesture, and grotesquely out of kilter with the image we had formed of him. But then, he'd done nothing but debunk that image from the moment we had found him.

In itself, that didn't surprise me. Violent criminals often reflect startlingly peaceful exteriors. But this man had been made part of a larger and bloodier whole over the past month. The road leading to him had been veiled in pain and deceit and littered with the bodies of friends and strangers alike. Had Helen of Troy been revealed as a fat and pimply teenager with an addiction for chocolate éclairs, the irony would have been no greater.

Perhaps it was because of this absurdity—that the pursuit had utterly overshadowed the prize—that I couldn't suppress a shared wistfulness with this man, made all the more real by the intertwining of our hands. Somehow, sitting there like a child at the park, he had become less the cause of all this mayhem and more its ultimate victim. The toss by him of the very first stone was ending in an avalanche that would sweep the mountain from beneath him.

"Did you kill her?"

He opened his eyes and blinked at me. The question obviously startled him, as if the correct answer might somehow get him off the hook even now. But then he looked around and let out a little sigh. "Is that man really after me? To kill me?"

"You murdered his daughter."

He nodded dreamily. "I guess I saw it as self-defense," he said softly.

I noticed McNaughton turn to say something—no doubt some tough cop wisecrack that would make Cioffi clam up—but he didn't, and after a moment's hesitation he turned back to watch where he was going.

Cioffi shook his head and smiled gently. "It was such a long time ago."

I waited for more, the self-cleansing confession, but he lapsed into silence and studied our joined hands, bobbing chest-high before him. I noticed his false beard was beginning to peel away at the temple. I let a few minutes elapse, but nothing happened. Normally, I might have left it at that—a tentative beginning on which later conversation could be based. But the self-defense line was irresistible. Of all the possibilities that occurred to me while I had stared at the photos of Pam Stark's bound and strangled body, that one had never even flickered.

"How was it self-defense?"

"To keep Teicher in line."

There was a small pop from behind me, as from a champagne cork sprung from far, far away. Simultaneously, a red dot appeared in the middle of Cioffi's forehead. He raised his free, mittened hand to it in astonishment and silently toppled backward off his stretcher, landing at Katz's feet.

"*Down*," McNaughton shouted. "*Everybody down.*"

Both stretcher-bearers dropped like stones, grappling for their side-arms. McNaughton let off two booming rounds from his shotgun. Only Katz and I remained standing, staring at each other as if frozen in time. His left arm and leg were splattered with red and there was a small pink lump of something stuck to his cheek. He looked down the length of his body to his boot, where most of Cioffi's head rested sleepily. The face, aside from the hole, looked normal enough, but from a point behind his ear, the skull's contour lost its definition. It looked soft, deflated, and it pumped blood onto Katz's snowy boot with a rapidly decreasing rhythm.

"I said get *down*, you stupid bastards."

I looked at McNaughton, spread-eagled and half-buried, and then I glanced over my shoulder. The mesmerizing, shimmering wall of falling white snow was as impenetrable as ever. I took a couple of steps into it and sensed, more than saw, a small white rectangle detach itself from its surroundings. It was a sheet, propped up by two stakes, looking like one half of a dissected pup tent. I looked over its top at the trampled snow behind it. "He's gone."

I heard some swearing behind me as McNaughton and his two troopers regained their footing and composure. I also heard Katz throwing up.

McNaughton shuffled up next to me, his face red with fury.

"What the fuck is this?"

"It's a blind."

"I know what the fuck it is. Oh, Jesus. What a fucking mess. How the hell?"

I pointed at two thin parallel tracks in the snow. "Cross-country skis. He used them to follow our footprints and then waited. Chances were pretty good we'd retrace our steps."

I left him to curse some more and to radio in the results of our little hike. Katz was kneeling in the snow beyond the body, retching. He'd pulled his foot out of his boot and had left both boot and snowshoe where Cioffi had pinned them. I slipped them from under the head and tried to wipe them off a little with my mittened hand, mostly just smearing them with pink snow. I crouched by Katz's leg, separated the boot from the snowshoe, and began to put it on him.

He pulled away. "Don't."

"Your foot'll freeze."

I reached out and straightened his leg, loosened the laces, and put the boot back on. Katz was as submissive as a child.

"What happened?"

"We were ambushed. He stalked us on skis, set up shop behind a white sheet, and blew our friend away with something like a twenty-two, I'd guess."

"Come on. A twenty-two?"

I finished lacing the boot and stood up. "Explosive shell." I leaned over him, and flicked the small lump of brain from his cheek. He stared at it and gagged again. Then he rubbed his face with snow.

In the distance, I could hear the low growl of a Sno-Cat engine. McNaughton was standing over Cioffi's body.

"The troops?" I asked him.

"Yeah. Too little, too late."

"Join the club."

32

Gail found me fast asleep on a hallway bench outside Kunkle's hospital room. I dreamed of her before I saw her, interspersing her face with dim snow-shrouded images of shouting policemen, Eskimos with crossbows, and peaceful half-heads haloed in pink blood.

She brought me back with a few gentle strokes across my forehead. "You want to go to bed?" She smiled.

"Aren't we in bed?" I blinked hard several times and rubbed my eyes. I leaned forward, propping my elbows on my knees, and looked at the floor. It was speckled linoleum, with bright stripes running down the middle.

Gail rubbed my back; the sensation was muted by my coat. "What time is it?"

"Almost midnight. How's Kunkle?"

"Depressed—that's normal for him. I'll give him good cause this time, though. Doctor says he might lose the arm. He'll sure as hell never play basketball again."

"What happened out there, anyway?

I rubbed my eyes again. "The roof fell in. It all came apart. Pretty fitting end to this whole stupid mess."

She stood up and pulled me to my feet. "Come on home."

It had stopped snowing sometime that afternoon, the storm dissipating with the suddenness of its arrival. The sun had glared from low on the horizon on a snow-thickened landscape of gentle curves and dips. The Sno-Cats had crawled in various directions across this smooth and sparkling world, inanely following Stark's dim ski tracks, carrying Cioffi and the dead trooper back to the highway or just wandering back and forth across Mount Washington's broad foot, their growls rendered tinny and ineffectual by the unimpressed white mountains staring down at them.

Gorham had become a town besieged as state troopers, sheriff's men and even the town constable marched about in contrasting uniforms, notebooks in hand, radios squawking. Patrol cars, ambulances, snow plows, a coroner's station wagon all sported blue, red, and yellow flashing lights with a competitive energy wasted on the local population, none of whom was in the way. In contrast to the chaos that had led up to it, this flurry of post-shooting investigations had all the earmarks of textbook efficiency. McNaughton, I and everyone else had been interviewed again and again by the representatives of those offices who now had to pick up our broken pieces. The veiled skeptical glances and toneless questions had done little to bolster what was left of our pride.

The day had concluded with several hours of isometric exercise on a jump seat in the back of the lurching ambulance carrying Kunkle home to Brattleboro. By the time I slumped onto the front seat of Gail's car, I had been awake and tense for roughly thirty-four hours.

And yet, now that I was back in the lap of normalcy, heading toward bed with nothing but warm and soothing comfort attending, my mind began to stir from its torpor. I ran it all through, from the discovery of "Kimberly's" twisted nude body to the snow-dusted corpse of her murderer, and all I could see were unanswered possibilities. The only light left, the only potential oasis in this desert, floated in Cioffi's last words.

"Does the name Teicher ring any bells?"

"John Teicher?"

"Maybe. Who is he?"

"Head of Leatherton, Inc. I met him a few times when he was coaxing a building permit out of the board for that industrial park—not that it was any great feat. We were pushovers. Why?"

I didn't answer at first. I was basking in the oasis. This piece of chit-chat had handed me the source of Cioffi's wealth, the probable reason for Pam Stark's death, and, I thought, the father of her fetus. The sensation that washed over me was not unlike pure bliss. For the first time, I was convinced all the puzzle pieces were on the table—and I had just caught a glimpse of the box top.

"Why, Joe? What's Teicher got to do with this?"

"I don't know. His name just came up. Drive me by the office."

She stared at me in amazement. "Joe, it's the middle of the night."

"I need to talk to Tony."

"You can barely talk to anyone. Can't it wait?"

"No. Please."

She shook her head and turned the car around.

"You're not going to be able to get a warrant just because Cioffi mentioned his name. You know that." Tony was sitting on the edge of a cot he'd set up in his office. He was wearing his pants and an undershirt.

I nodded.

"You also know that if you waltz through his door and piss him off, he's liable to stir things up a little—like reporting you to Tom Wilson or the board."

I nodded again.

He stood up and put his shirt on. "You look like hell."

"Thanks. Can I do it?"

"You're asking permission?"

"I want backup—lots of it."

"You really think this is it?"

"Yes."

Brandt gave me a half smile. "We're in such hot water now, I don't see where a little extra can do any harm. I've already been given thirty days vacation without pay, so you might do me some good for once."

"They suspended you?"

"Yes and no. They won't identify it, but I'm out of here next week for a month. That'll give 'em time to decide whether to make it permanent or not. If you come up with something, I might be invited back." He gave me an odd smile, and added, "Of course, that's a two-edged sword for you. They plan to have you stand in for me while I'm out. That might grow on you."

"Bullshit."

He continued smiling. "Thanks. Well, I'm off to the hospital, for what little good it'll do. Let's reconvene here at 8:00 A.M. I'll set everything up." He put on his jacket and patted me on the shoulder. "I'm sorry about the screwup, Joe. Try to get some sleep."

33

"Want any?" Billy Manierre offered me a cup of coffee.

"No thanks." I checked my watch. It was 8:15. "How are we set?"

"I've got three patrol cars, two men each, one van with a driver, and all the special gear I could find. What are we doing anyway? Taking a fort?"

"I just want to talk to a man—forcefully." Aside from Brandt, no one knew what I had planned.

"I guess."

We set out in single file toward the Leatherton, Inc. headquarters, driving along the back roads as much as possible. I'd collected seven hours of the deepest sleep I could recall. Now I sat in the passenger seat of Tyler's unmarked car, squinting against the glare off the early sun-bleached snow, wondering for the first time if I was right. I wondered if my desperation to save at least one piece from the chess board was clouding my judgment, or worse still, whether I was leaving open yet another hole for Stark to gain the advantage.

Leatherton had been open since eight o'clock, but I'd wanted every-one to get settled before making my play. I'd also wanted to make sure that Teicher would be there. His secretary had assured me he would when I'd anonymously phoned twenty minutes before.

We drove up, lights flashing, and clustered around the two entrances—the van, Tyler's car, and one patrol car out front, the rest covering the back. I led my four men, armed with Winchester pumps, through the lobby, past the startled receptionist and up the stairs to the top floor. There I showed my badge to the woman at the first desk I saw and demanded to see Teicher. She looked at the badge, at the guns, at her phone and then silently pointed down the hallway. We marched off like a bunch of commandos in search of a battlefield, and I threw open the double doors at the end of the hall.

We fanned out into a large, square, dark-paneled office that looked as if it had been helicoptered in from some New York corporate penthouse. It made Cioffi's digs look humble by comparison. Whatever other philosophies fueled Leatherton's machine, one of them was obviously to pamper the executives. In this case, the executive was a middle-sized man, both in girth and height, with a swept-back shock of dazzling white hair and a wide-open mouth. He was standing next to a ping-pong-table-sized desk, holding a folder in his hand.

I pointed to Tyler. "Watch the door." Tyler made a nice snappy move with his shotgun and put his shoulder against the doorjamb, looking fully prepared to die for the cause.

I crossed over to the man, whose mouth was beginning to close, while at the same time ordering one of the patrolmen to close the curtains. "Are you John Teicher?"

"Yes. What's going on?"

I grabbed his elbow and propelled him to the corner of the room away from the window. I noticed the patrolman looking through the curtains. "See anything?"

"No, sir. All clear."

Teicher was now standing with his back against the wall. "What's this all about?"

I ignored him and pulled my radio from its pouch. "Red Two, this is Red One. Do you read?"

I had to admire the response. Billy Manierre was enjoying himself. "Roger, Red One. That's affirmative. The perimeter's secure. No sign of hostiles. I've opened a field patch to headquarters." Total baloney, of course—we were all on the same frequency.

"Roger. Red One out." I pocketed the radio. "Mr. Teicher. We have strong reason to believe your life is in danger. Are you aware of the man the newspapers have identified as the Masked Avenger—Colonel Henry Stark?"

He blinked several times and wet his lips. "I've read something about it, yes."

"Well, we believe he has made the connection between you and his daughter's murderer, Mr. Cioffi. He has vowed to kill everyone even remotely involved in her death, and you are very high on that list."

I was crowding him, and he started to step away but bumped into the wall. His eyes were flitting around the room, as if looking for a place to rest. "I'm not sure I understand."

"Come on, Mr. Teicher. Cioffi and I talked before he was shot through the head with an explosive bullet. Your name, shall we say,

266

came up rather prominently. Now, if you want to play dumb, that's your prerogative, but I doubt you'll live to see the end of the week. This man's very good."

Now was the break point. This had all been pretty hokey, but I was hoping he had been spending the last few weeks watching the waters slowly rise around him. Unless he was made of stern stuff indeed, he had to be feeling pretty isolated by now.

It worked. His head suddenly slumped to his chest, and he rubbed his forehead with his hand. "Christ. What a nightmare."

"Then, just for the record, you admit to knowing that Cioffi killed Pam Stark and to covering up that fact?"

"Yes, of course."

"I'll have to place you under arrest."

He nodded dumbly, and I read him his rights. After he'd acknowledged them, I steered him to the sofa lining the wall to his right. "You want to talk about it now, or wait for a lawyer?"

He sat down heavily and laid his head back so that he was staring at the ceiling. "How much do you know?"

I thought hard for a second, deciding how far I should stick my neck out. "I know you'd been having an affair with Pam Stark at the time of her death and that she was pregnant with your child. I also know that Cioffi put the squeeze on you for a promotion and a steady payoff. What I don't know is how you tie in to her murder."

He stared at me anxiously. "I had nothing to do with that. I was in love with her. I was going to divorce my wife and marry her." He looked away, his face creased with sorrow, his voice suddenly low. "I guess in that sense I did have a hand in her murder."

"How so?"

"Cioffi had been blackmailing me with the affair. Somehow he'd found out about us. It was odd, actually. It wasn't like anything you see in the movies. He was very polite about it, and not very greedy. In a funny kind of way, I liked him then. He was the one person I could talk to about Kimberly—I mean Pam Stark. He would listen and sympathize and sometimes even give me advice. Kimberly could be pretty demanding and she was a lot..." He groped for the word. "...Younger than I was; I mean in her tastes, if you get my meaning."

"Sexually," I muttered.

"Yes. Her needs were considerable. Anyway, things changed all at once, it seemed. Cioffi became quite ill—I think it was his asthma—and began taking massive doses of medicine. It changed him completely, physically and emotionally. He was like a temperamental time bomb. He became very suspicious of me and insecure about his position. I noticed he began to follow me around after work. He also began visiting Kimberly—Pam—and making friends with her. That upset me a bit. And then, right in the middle of it all, she became pregnant."

"Did you think Cioffi might have been the father?"

He looked at me wide-eyed. "Oh, Lord, no. She thought he was a joke; she would never have done that with him—at least not then. No, she loved me, I think; or that's what she said. In retrospect, I think I wanted to see more than there was. But anyhow, she wanted to get married and have the child."

He sighed and shifted his weight. "At first, I couldn't see it. I do love my wife, too, you see. And we have children. But Kimberly was like something I'd never dreamed could be mine. I couldn't imagine giving her up, even though I subconsciously knew she'd probably tire of me before long. So I told her I'd do it. That's what made Cioffi kill her. That's how I'm responsible."

"He saved the golden egg by killing the goose."

He gave me an odd look, which I suppose I deserved. "I guess so. He was really quite unbalanced. It was like being with a schizophrenic, listening to him describe every detail. He demanded that I know it all—every move."

"He framed Bill Davis."

"The black man? Yes. Knocked him out with her lamp and dragged him into the room, scratched Kimberly's dead fingernails across his face, left incriminating evidence all over. He was like a madman; completely demented. He said he wanted the scene to look as gruesome as possible so that no one would ever forget. But it was more personal than that. I realized he'd harbored a real hatred of me all that time, despite his amiability—he hated me for my money, my relationship with Kimberly, even my health. He told me time and again how he was going to end up in a wheelchair and that I was going to pay for that. He told me he did things to Kimberly, and that she'd done things to him, that were guaranteed to get at me. He was totally unbalanced."

"What do you mean, 'he did things to Kimberly'?"

He rubbed his forehead again. "They were sexual in nature. When he first came to see her that night, I guess he threatened her or something. He said she made love to him—orally, that is. He claimed it was her choice, but I don't believe it. Then he killed her, tied her down, arranged the scene, and finally he masturbated on her—just before he left. I couldn't believe what I was hearing. He was watching me like a hawk as he was telling me all this, looking for my reaction. I felt I was with a monster."

He was slumped over in his seat by now, his hands clasped behind his neck, as if warding off an avalanche. He raised his head and sought my eyes with his. Tears were on his cheeks. "I was terrified. Terrified of him, of what he'd done, of what it would mean if it came out. I didn't know what to do."

"So you did nothing."

"No. Not even after he was off the drug and was normal again and tried to make amends."

"Make amends?"

"Well, that's what it seemed like. He became friendly again, dropping by here after hours, telling me about his stock market coups. But I remained scared of him forever after. It was like waiting for Mr. Hyde to reappear; instead, it was Colonel Stark who appeared." He paused and wiped his eyes.

"What happened when it started coming out—when Stark did his little number and the newspapers grabbed hold of it?"

He gave an enormous sigh. He seemed utterly exhausted. "We were like two men in a sinking lifeboat; totally different from one another but bound together, you know? We spent more time together these last few weeks than we had since Kimberly's death. I never would have imagined any of this happening to me—not in a million years... I'm glad it's over."

"You may not feel that way when all this comes out."

"I don't have much choice, do I?"

"Not any more." Unlike, I thought, ten minutes ago.

34

I groped for the phone with my eyes still closed, hoping the call would be brief enough that I could handle it without fully waking up.

"Gunther?" It was James Dunn. I opened my eyes. "What?"

"What the hell are you doing? You sound half asleep."

"I am. Tony sent me home. Said I was a hazard to operations." I looked at my watch. It was seven o'clock at night.

"Sorry. Thought you'd want' to know the judge kicked Teicher loose at the arraignment."

"What?" I sat straight up.

"Released on his own recognizance."

"But what about protecting him from Stark?"

"Stark has made no threat against him, real or implied, as the saying goes."

"But he's a witness, goddamn it."

"To what? All the principals are dead."

"How about Bill Davis?"

"He's being processed out anyway, and as quietly as possible I might add. That's a hint, by the way, in case you decide to rub noses with Katz again."

"Where's Teicher now?"

"I think he went home."

I hung up and dialed Brandt. "You hear about Teicher?"

"Yeah. I didn't want to wake you up."

"Dunn did the honors. What are we going to do about it?"

There was a pause. "Not much we can do."

"Stark's going to kill him."

"Why? Teicher was going to marry the girl. That's hardly a killing offense, even if it didn't work out."

"Stark doesn't know that; he just knows Teicher knocked her up—that's a capital crime in his book. Jesus, Tony, what the hell have you been doing all this time? Paying me lip service? Why did you let me do all that razzle-dazzle with the shotguns at Teicher's office?"

"You told me that was to squeeze him for a confession."

"Well, it was, but all I did was soup it up a little. The threat is real, believe me."

There was a momentary silence at the other end. "What makes you so sure?"

I couldn't believe I had to replow this field. The frustration made me blurt out: "Because by approaching Teicher like a platoon of Marines, we've all but challenged Stark to knock him off. I thought you understood that."

Brandt's voice went totally flat. "It wasn't clear. Why did you go home without laying it out?"

"I thought Teicher would be locked up for a while. The arraignment wasn't supposed to be until tomorrow. Look, I don't know what I thought. Maybe I got cold feet, setting Teicher up as bait."

"You sure choose your moments to be coy." I let a petulant flash of anger cover my guilt. "I told you he was in danger. I told Dunn that, too. What the hell did you guys think? That I'd suddenly gone soft in the head? Hasn't Stark proved he's nutty enough for something like that? Teicher's all we have left, for God's sake."

"All right, all right, let's drop it. You challenged him to a duel and Teicher's the prize. We better get him back under cover. I'll send a patrol out to his house now to sit on him until you get there."

I fumbled with my clothes in a blind fury. Once I'd set the ball in motion, I should have covered it like a blanket. There was no excuse for slacking off at the last moment. I'd been complacent and stupid and scared to play by Stark's rules to the end. As I slammed the door behind me, I inanely swore it wouldn't happen again.

As it turned out, I was lucky. I found Teicher intact at his home, a patrol car parked out front. But he was obviously not a happy man.

"What do you want?" A superior emphasis was placed on the "you."

"I just heard you were out of custody. I came to arrange security."

He gave me a sour expression. "From what my lawyer tells me, you're the one I should need security against."

"What did he tell you?"

"That you lured me into confessing; it was blatant entrapment, and it'll get thrown out of court. He said if I'd kept my mouth shut, my wife would still be with me and I'd still have a job."

I was surprised at the speed of his demise. "You travel with a fast crowd."

"Fuck you, too."

"None of that abrogates your responsibility to Bill Davis."

"Don't give me that." He turned his back and walked into the house. I followed him. "The only novelty of a man like that being in jail is that he's innocent of this particular crime."

I liked him better when he was a bowl of jelly. "I don't really care if your case is thrown out of court. My job now is keeping you alive."

He stopped and faced me. "That's another thing my lawyer pointed out. Why the hell would Stark want me dead? He got his revenge."

I felt like the boy who'd cried "Wolf" once too often. "That's not how he thinks. He's killed or beaten up every person who had anything to do with Pam Stark, including most of the jurors who sent Bill Davis up the river. I watched him torture a man with a knife just for a little information. Do you really think he's going to ignore some snotty rich adulterer who knocked up his daughter? Not hardly."

He didn't answer, but I could tell he was mulling it over. He turned on his heel and continued down the hallway until we both reached a small study at the back of the house. There he sat on an overstuffed leather armchair—something I've always coveted—and crossed his legs with an elegant flourish. I noticed he was wearing tassled loafers—something I've always thought was for the birds.

"So what do you propose?" I realized for the first time he had the same lilt to his voice I'd heard in 1930s movies.

"To put you under wraps for a while until we can get a fix on Stark."

"As bait?"

"You're bait right now."

"He's dessert."

The voice made us both whirl around, I with my gun in my hand. Stark was standing in a side doorway, a short, nasty-looking pistol-grip crossbow in his hand. It was pointing directly at Teicher's chest. Humiliation and anger thunderclapped inside me—the son of a bitch had beaten me to the end.

I motioned my gun at him. "Put it down. You can't win this—not with that thing."

Teicher was squirming in his chair. "Who is this man?"

Stark smiled and clicked his heels. "Colonel Henry A. Stark, United States Army, probably retired by now." The crossbow never wavered.

Teicher merely swallowed.

"Come on, Stark, this is stupid. If you move a muscle, I'll fire. And you only have one arrow."

"It's called a bolt and it's intended for that man's chest. This didn't happen accidentally, Joe."

"What didn't?"

"This situation. I've been waiting for you. And this"—he nodded at the weapon in his hand—"is for your benefit. It is palpable proof that I have but one shot. Not, of course, that I don't have other weapons on me—ones I can reach and use in just under one second—but that's my gift to you. You have one second to kill me after I dispatch Mr. Tassle Loafers here; after that, I kill you."

I stared at him in stunned silence. From the start, this man had dictated my actions with the simpleminded brutality of the weapon in his hand. He had mocked the complexities that had plagued every actor in this drama, from Jamie Phillips's struggles as a juror to his own daughter's battle with the ghosts screaming inside her head. He had made his decisions without contemplation, without pros and cons, but merely with a goal in mind. As a bullet seeks its target, so he had sought this final meeting. It was as foreign to my way of thinking as could be, and, I realized now, he had mysteriously known that almost from the beginning. I had been his perfect implement.

That was hard to swallow. I lowered my gun as I might have upon discovering I'd been aiming at my own shadow. "You've got to be out of your mind. Cops are on the way right now; that's why I'm here, and the people out front. It's suicidal, for Christ's sake. What's the point?"

"Put the gun back up, Joe. And I wouldn't count on the two out front." He waited for me to comply. I did, suddenly aware that regardless of how I saw things, Stark was going to force them to work his way. It was no time for me to weigh the various aspects of the situation. I either became like him or I was going to die.

"Good." He gave an approving nod and quickly glanced at his watch. "We have a few minutes yet. You asked me a question the other night that I promised to answer at a later date. I doubt we'll get much later than this."

"About Frank?" I was amazed at his performance. Once the arrow— or bolt—was sent into the middle of Teicher's chest, Stark was going to briefly expose himself to whatever fate might dole out. There was a strong likelihood he had but a few minutes left to live. And yet he was calm, polite, even considerate. I no longer had any doubts that I was dealing with a nut. It scared the hell out of me; it also made me think that the wisest thing to do right now was to shoot him in cold blood. But I didn't.

He almost beamed with self-satisfaction. "Frank's death was an auto accident, plain and simple."

"Bullshit."

"Didn't anyone tell you how you were found? With your head held out of the water by your seat belt? That didn't just happen. I was tailing you two when you went over. You knew that because you joked about it—remember Frank saying he'd drive in that muck just to find out if I was a flatlander?"

I nodded.

"Joke was on you guys. I heard the accident over the bug I planted. I found the hole in the guard rail, checked you both out, propped your head, and called the cops on the roadside phone. Frank was dead when I got to you, Joe. It was an accident, just like the state troopers said."

"I don't believe it."

This time he laughed outright. "You're a credit to my imagination. Surely you've noticed that the bad guys I warned you about have mysteriously disappeared."

I didn't answer. The anger at having been manipulated to that extent—and at that emotional level—was strangling me. I dropped my eyes to the gun in my hand, so long ago the symbol of a young cop's belief that he could thwart the evils of the world through its use. I hated that remembrance and had worked hard to bury it.

"I made them up. I was the one who gassed your apartment. I thought the extra pressure might help. Do you remember the torn scotch tape you found across your door—the one that made you crawl all over your apartment sweating bullets?"

"Yes."

"I did that. Too good to resist; I couldn't believe you'd set yourself up so well. And the bug in the phone? Remember that?"

I let him talk. In the back of my mind, I was hoping he might screw up, even in the last minute of the last hour; that he might somehow expose a small gap through which I or someone else might quickly fit and thus let me off the hook.

"When you picked that phone up and a strange voice said your name and then broke the connection, that started you wondering, didn't it?"

"Yes."

"So you looked at the phone and realized that it had been placed wrong end around on the cradle. You wondered why, you opened the phone, and out fell the bug. It was a dud, by the way. I never owned the other half of it—the receiving end—but it did its job anyway. All for building up pressure."

"And Frank's death wasn't a part of that?"

"Pure serendipity. How was I going to guarantee having an eighteen-wheeler in the right place at the right time in the middle of a snowstorm? And why would I? You guys were hot on the track of Cioffi and this miserable bastard." He nodded at Teicher, who looked like he was trying to disappear into his overstuffed seat cushion. "I wasn't about to get in your way, despite your best efforts."

He paused for a moment. "You almost got me on the way to Gorham, though. Your pal Kunkle switched cars at the last minute; I'd planted a radio in his. Still, it worked out."

I thought of Kunkle's shattered arm. "How? We didn't see any cars."

"I followed you with my lights off. I latched onto your taillights and hoped to hell you wouldn't lead me straight into a ditch. I'll credit you that much—that was one time in my life I thought I might lose the game...almost lost control."

"Like when you beat up Susan Lucey?"

His face lost its almost meditative look. "You're a lousy conversationalist, you know that? Besides, it's a little late to be probing the dark recesses of my soul." He looked at his watch again. "In fact, I'd say time's up."

The crossbow moved slightly in his hand.

I too knew time was up. Now—finally—I was in a position to stop him before he did any more damage. Still I hesitated. "You killed the man who murdered your daughter. What does this guy matter? He was going to marry her, for Christ's sake."

Stark half smiled, "Jesus—what a thought. No, I like things the way they are. I kill him, you kill me—maybe. That's neat and tidy; and if you're not fast enough, I live to play a different kind of game for a while."

"I will shoot."

"As soon as you published my identity, I was dead anyway—I have 'friends' in high places."

"I could shoot you now, save Teicher, and ruin it for you."

He smiled. "I don't think so."

So that was that. No gray areas. Just yes or no. The years I'd spent struggling for alternate choices were useless to me now. I was back to where I'd started as a rookie cop, back to when my thinking shared the same narrow ledge as Stark's. My gun felt huge and awkward—a bloody steel monument to stupidity. I barely felt its recoil when I fired.

The arrow flew as my bullet hit him high in the chest and I heard Teicher scream from the chair. Stark slammed against the door frame and momentarily stood there, motionless, his eyes locked onto mine; then they closed, his body relaxed, and he slid to the floor.

Keeping my gun on him, I knelt by his side and felt for a pulse. There was none. I could hear noises outside: slamming car doors, the sound of broken glass. I walked over to Teicher, who was now whimpering. The arrow had gone through his right thigh and had pinned him to the chair.

"My God. It hurts, it hurts. Jesus, it hurts." I laid my hand on his shoulder. My brain was almost totally numb. "Be grateful. It's a sign you're alive."

He stopped for a second and looked at me.

"Sorry. I'll get some help for you."

I left him to let the others in, but I paused at the hallway door and looked at Stark again, curled up like a sleeping child on the floor. Fate or divine guidance or whatever had put my bullet in his heart. He had the contented look of a man who'd lived a clean and simple life and who'd left with his affairs fully in order, with no doubts and no regrets.

I envied him all of that.

Did you enjoy this book?
For more, go to

ArcherMayor.com